She loved him with every ounce of energy in her body, yet she had known from the beginning that he was going away. Perhaps she had just been a fool, but there was nothing else she could have done. She had felt that it was fate that had brought them together and she still did. *Of course* he would come back to her.

Meanwhile, she had to soldier on, pretending at home that he had never existed, and waiting for his letters. How was she ever going to get through the next two years? If she could be sure that he felt the same way about her, she could just about bear it. She had given him all she had to give – her heart and her body, yet he had never even said that he loved her.

'Oh, Dad,' she sobbed. 'I've lost you, and I've lost the only other man I'll ever love.'

Patricia Beale was born and brought up in Portsmouth, with the exception of periods during the war when she was evacuated. She and her husband first lived in Cornwall, and returned there when they retired. *Queen of the May* was inspired loosely by her own family stories.

# Queen · of the May ·

PATRICIA BEALE

Mandarin

A Mandarin Paperback

QUEEN OF THE MAY

First published in Great Britain 1995
by William Heinemann Ltd
and Mandarin Paperbacks
imprints of Reed Consumer Books Ltd
Michelin House, 81 Fulham Road, London SW3 6RB
and Auckland, Melbourne, Singapore and Toronto



A CIP catalogue record for this title
is available from the British Library
ISBN 0 7493 1851 1

Printed and bound in Great Britain
by Cox & Wyman Ltd, Reading, Berkshire

For my family, past and present,
and for the brave men who served
in the 'little ships'
of the coastal forces.

My special thanks to my aunt, Peggy Chandler,
for giving me details about life in these times;
and to my very good friend, novelist Jane Pollard,
from whom I have learned so much about the
business of writing.

# · One ·

Queenie May Ellis was just scooping up a penn'orth of chips when some sixth sense made her look up – straight into the sailor's eyes. Her heart galloped and a prickle ran down her spine.

It was him! The one she had been waiting for. She knew it as surely as she knew that today was the sixth of May, 1935 – the Silver Jubilee of old King George and Queen Mary.

'Queenie!' Pearl nudged her with her elbow, and she realised that she was standing there staring at him and the chips were dropping off the scoop. She flashed him a smile enhanced with Tangee 'Flame', and glancing up at him from under her lashes, gave him the benefit of the Marlene Dietrich look that she'd been practising in the mirror.

Her violet-blue eyes and long lashes didn't seem to be having the effect on him that they had on local boys. He stood there, unsmiling, looking as unobtainable as . . . as Edward, the Prince of Wales.

'Salt and vinegar, Frank?' she asked a regular customer before wrapping his fish and chips with trembling fingers, all the while conscious of the stranger's gaze.

*What was he thinking?*

He waited, silent, among the group of noisy, joking sailors, most of whom she knew because they came in once or twice a week. Being near Portsmouth Harbour, the Navy provided a lot of their customers.

'Queenie, Queenie, "give us your answer do",' sang

'Gracie' Fields, the fat one. Some of the others joined in. '"We're half crazy, all for the love of you."'

She gave them a flirtatious smile – for the benefit of the newcomer – but she had two more customers to serve before she could give the sailors her full attention.

'Are the next lot of chips, ready, Fred?' she asked, scooping up the last of the batch. 'And we're goin' to need some fish brought through, Pearl,' she told the other girl assistant, anxious to get her out of the way in case the newcomer liked blondes.

'Get it yerself!' Pearl answered indignantly. 'What did yer last one die of?'

'And send Jimmy out with some more chips, Pearl,' added Fred – proprietor of 'Freddie's Famous Fish And Chips', where only the purest dripping was used. Pearl went with a flounce.

Queenie, with racing pulse, targeted her quarry with another inviting smile, but he merely looked solemnly back. She didn't usually have this sort of trouble. How was she going to get through to him?

'Won't be a minute, Gents,' Fred told his customers, scooping up a sieve full of sizzling fingers of potato, and pinching one. 'Nearly ready. Worth waiting for. They'll be piping hot.'

Jimmy, Queenie's eleven year-old brother, appeared with a white enamel pail of chipped potatoes and a sullen expression on his face, having been press-ganged into service on this hectic night when he'd rather have been joining in the Jubilee shindigs with his mates. But Ma had insisted – she needed the money.

'Jimmy and Josh was given lovely Jubilee mugs at school,' Queenie said enthusiastically, but her brother sent her a disgusted look.

Fred tipped the next batch of raw chips into the bubbling fat to the accompaniment of a loud sizzling and a great puff of steam, and Queenie wiped the sweat off her forehead with the back of her hand. Whew, it was hot for

May! She was sure she wasn't looking her best. She winked at Doggo, the big, hearty sailor.

'It's your lovely girls we come in here to see, you know, Fred.' Doggo grinned. 'We don't come for the grub, good as it is.'

Her eyes sparkling, Queenie tossed back her head, wishing it was not done up like a suet pudding in the white net turban that Fred insisted upon for hygiene. Yes, that was it. If her long black hair, her crowning glory, was on view, she was sure he would look more impressed.

'Who's your friend, Doggo?' she asked boldly.

'This is Stonewall, Queenie May. And don't let his touch-me-not expression fool you. He's a devil with the women.'

'Ooh!' she exclaimed, giving Stonewall the eye again and straining her young bosom against her white overall. It was a funny sort of name, but then he wasn't ordinary. 'I love devils.'

Stonewall's nicely-shaped mouth merely twitched and he raised an eyebrow, not bothering to deny Doggo's remark. Was it true then? If so, it made him all the more exciting.

What was it about him that set him apart from his companions? Queenie wondered. Was it that curious silence and aloofness while the others were all chatty and joking? Because apart from that he was not remarkable, being not much above average height, and slimly built. Yet there was a natural superiority in the way he held himself, as though he were destined for higher things. Sort of special.

His eyes were quite dark – grey or brown – difficult to tell what colour in the artificial light, but his intense gaze made Queenie all fluttery inside.

'Don't you never smile, Stonewall?' she asked saucily. 'It don't cost nothin', you know.'

'When there's something worth smiling about, I do,' he

answered crushingly in a surprisingly cultured voice, and the sparkle went out of her eyes.

'Don't take no notice, Queenie. That's his technique,' explained Doggo confidentially, leaning over the counter. 'Very clever. Women come from miles around, just to try and cheer him up.'

'Oh, yes? Bet I could cheer him up!' she challenged with a grin.

But from the rim of his cap, set low on his brow and bearing the tally HMS *Vernon*, to the deep cleft in his chin, there was no response, not the vestige of an answering smile. Just a sardonic gleam in his eye.

Queenie, who, with a casual sultry glance, could have members of the opposite sex panting after favours which she never bestowed, was puzzled and intrigued. Stonewall was a challenge – and that was something she could never resist.

Bravely – fearing another rebuff – she asked, her head to one side and a hand on her hip, 'Ain't you going to ask me for a date, then? Most sailors do.'

He stared at her speculatively.

'Go on! You *never* go out with matelots, Queenie,' exlaimed Brum, from Birmingham.

'Only 'cos the ones I fancy are married,' she flirted. 'You ain't married, I hope, Stonewall?'

A quirked eyebrow was his reply.

'*He's* not stupid,' grumbled Gracie, in the process of rolling a cigarette.

'I love sailors,' she continued, her arch look encompassing every member of her navy-suited audience. 'Must be their starched collars and bell-bottoms. My Dad, *and* his Dad, were in the Navy. And so're two of my uncles. I was born here in Pompey, and my Dad used to say that I had sea-water in me veins, not blood.'

'Chatter-box!' Fred shook his head with an affectionate grin as he scooped up sizzling chips in a sieve, shook them, and tipped them into a section of the cabinet.

Pearl came from the back room carrying a tray of floured fish.

'How's our precious Pearl tonight?' asked Brum.

The girl gave a simpering giggle.

'A right little gem, that's what you are, Pearl.'

'You're not so bad, yourself, Brum.'

'I pay you two to *serve* the customers, not flirt with them,' grumbled Fred, his mock severity hiding his pleasure, well aware that his pretty girls were an asset to his trade, particularly his naval trade.

Pearl suddenly noticed Stonewall and gave him an appreciative, wide-eyed smile.

'He's mine,' warned Queenie out of the corner of her mouth, and elbowing Pearl aside, she asked, 'What's it to be, Stonewall?'

'Cod and a penn'orth of chips, please, Queenie.' Ooh, he sounded ever so posh.

'Cod and chips all round, my loves,' repeated Doggo, leaning his arms on the glass cabinet that housed crisp, brown-gold nuggets of fish, saveloys and pies. 'A couple of pickled onions for Gracie, 'cos no girl's going to kiss *him* tonight, or any other night, very likely. And a double helping of chips for me – I've got to keep me strength up – going home to the wife on Saturday! Spot of leave before the off.'

'Where you off to then, Doggo?' asked Queenie, depositing an over-generous double serving of golden chips and a piece of fish onto the white wrapping paper for her favourite sailor. Or he had been until . . . she stole a quick glance at the newcomer.

'The Mediterranean and the sunshine. Just the ticket.' Doggo blew on a hot chip before he put it in his mouth, then executed a crisp salute while clasping his newspaper bundle to his chest with the other hand. 'Straight after His Majesty has reviewed his Fleet off Spithead.'

'All right for some,' grumbled Fred, swishing the floured fillets around in a bowl of batter before lowering them by their tails into the bubbling dripping. 'Being in the Navy's as good as a holiday, if you ask me.'

'Now, now,' protested Doggo. 'Don't forget how our lads protected "this Hallowed Isle" in 1914.'

'That's right, Doggo, you tell 'im.' Queenie flashed an indignant look at Fred. 'My Dad did 'is bit for King and country.'

'Seriously,' went on Doggo with his mouth full, his face earnest for once. 'This is no pleasure trip. All this unrest in Europe. A lot of the Mediterranean ports, particularly Malta, are very vulnerable . . .'

'D'you think we'll get involved again?' asked Fred with a worried frown.

'The Germans have thrown out the Versailles Treaty and re-introduced compulsory military service,' Stonewall added in his cultured voice, leaving Queenie blinking. 'And if that's not cause for concern, I don't know what is.'

Doggo shrugged. 'All I know is, we've got a job to do, shipmates. More than that we ain't allowed to say!'

'With you boys out there, we *know* we'll be safe,' said Queenie. There couldn't be another war, could there? It didn't bear thinking about.

Picking out the largest piece of fish in the cabinet, she plonked it on top of a scoop of chips, and enclosing the feast in a piece of folded newspaper, handed it over the top to Stonewall with a smile that would have launched a thousand ships.

'Thanks.'

'Are you off too, Stonewall?' she asked anxiously, hoping that she was not to be denied the opportunity for conquest.

'Not just yet.'

'He's just arrived from Portland.' Brum, receiving his supper from Pearl, supplied the information that the stranger seemed reluctant to part with.

''Spect we'll see you again, then?' Her eyes and lips beckoned an invitation.

'If these chips are as good as they look, you might.' He sprinkled them liberally with salt and vinegar.

And with that, Queenie had to be content, because he spoke not another word as she and Pearl served the others and gave them all their change. 'Good luck, Doggo,' she called as they were leaving. 'I'll miss you.'

The big sailor winked and grinned back at her. 'I'll miss you too, girls. 'Bye, Fred.'

''Night, Stonewall,' Queenie called wistfully. He nodded in their direction.

'That new one was a bit of all right,' said Pearl appreciatively as the sailors walked past the window.

'Hands off!' Queenie hissed, her eyes sparking.

'You know what they say about sailors – "a wife in every port."' Fred nodded sagely as he served another customer.

'Yeah, but they're lot more exciting than most of the blokes round 'ere.' With her turbanned head wagging from side to side, Queenie broke into the song, 'All the nice girls love a sailor,' making the remaining customer laugh.

'You just watch it, my girl.'

She winked at her employer. 'Give me a sailor any day. And they don't come much better than my Dad. Coo, the stories he used to tell . . .' And Queenie was off, regaling them with one of her father's stories until the next customer came in.

Walking home that night, arm-in-arm with Jimmy, both too tired to talk, Queenie let her mind dwell happily on Stonewall and the prospect of hooking him. In spite of his coolness she knew he'd be back. She believed in fate. She knew that he was meant for her the moment she saw him – all she needed was the opportunity to convince him.

She had always assumed, without giving it much thought, that one day she would be a sailor's wife. It was simply a question of waiting for The Right One.

She had made a vow to herself when she was pinching coal off a lorry at the age of eight – when the family's welfare was at its lowest ebb – that one day *she* would get away. She knew from films and magazines that there was a better life out there, and she was determined to find it. Her Dad had told her he wanted her to do well for herself and that she was to grab any luck that came her way. 'You've got talent, my girl. You use it.'

She didn't know what talent he referred to, but she recognised Stonewall as an opportunity she could not afford to let slip through her fingers. Besides being the most attractive man she had ever met – after her Dad, it went without saying – she felt certain he was the one who could help her escape from Ma and a life of drudgery.

Queenie and Jimmy gave sighs of relief as they let themselves into the old terraced house in Baker Street.

'Whew, I'm knackered,' Jimmy complained.

'You wait till you 'ave to get out and earn your own living,' his sister told him cheerfully, 'then you'll know what knackered means.' She raised her voice as she went along the narrow hall to the kitchen. 'We're home, Ma. Dying for a nice cuppa.'

Stonewall came back a few evenings later – on his own.

Queenie's heart lurched as he came into the shop. She had been waiting impatiently and thinking about him constantly since their last meeting. She had even hung around the Vernon gates one night, hoping to see him, and been accosted by more than one tipsy sailor with an indecent proposal.

In her bed at night, she imagined their first date, their first kiss. She walked up the aisle towards a smiling Stonewall in a filmy white dress.

Then suddenly he was there in front of her – a total stranger. Unsmiling.

It was nearly closing time and there were only three pieces of fish left in the cabinet. Queenie let Pearl serve him and watched with thudding heart, feigning indifference while she wiped the white tiles clean. The direct attack had not succeeded last time. Perhaps an aloof air, to match his own, would prick his interest.

He was so good-looking!

He took no notice of Queenie, or of Pearl's fluttering eyelashes as she served him; paying his money and sprinkling condiments on the fish and chips with a brief 'Thanks'.

But his eyes locked with Queenie's as he pocketed his change and her breath was suspended. He winked – and was suddenly approachable.

Queenie gave a delighted smile. 'Goodnight, sailor,' she said.

His 'G'night' embraced them all – but he had winked at *her*. Oh, yes, he'd be back!

Outside the shop, on the corner of Queen and St James Streets, the girls parted and turned homewards. Pearl towards Victoria Park and Queenie, still a-tremble from Stonewall's acknowledgement, towards the harbour. Each carried a parcel of the remaining fish and chips under her arm, as they were always allowed to take home any that were left over, a source of pleasure to Queenie's brothers.

It was a clouded night, the street lamps making little havens of radiance in the dark, deserted street. And in the pools of light, Queenie could see the bunting from the earlier Jubilee street party, strung from post to post and across the road. Muted light hazed from behind drawn curtains, though one family had left theirs open and were sitting around a table playing cards. Queenie paused for a moment to enjoy the scene.

Suddenly a figure materialised out of the shadows across the road, causing her to start in alarm. Then she saw it was a sailor. But not just any sailor.

# · *Two* ·

Stonewall walked across the road to her. She stopped and stared up at him. 'We seem to be going in the same direction. Walk you home?' he asked.

She nodded, dumb with surprise. He had waited for her! He fell into step beside her and though she was bursting with triumphant pleasure, she felt unusually shy.

He cleared his throat. 'Dark evening for May.'

'May's my lucky month,' she replied, failing to think of anything witty or interesting to say.

'Why's that?'

'Everything good happens to me in May. I was born on the first of the month and my Dad said I was his little Queen of the May.'

'Hence the name.'

Hence! He *was* posh! She nodded her head, glancing up to see him watching her in the lamplight which made his face mysterious and exciting. His eyes, deep in their shadowed sockets, were those of a stranger now.

'You've just had a birthday then. Seventeen? Eighteen?'

'Yes . . . my eighteenth,' she lied. He would drop her like a hot potato if he knew she was only just sixteen. How old was he? she wondered. He seemed very mature.

'What else has happened to you in May?'

'Last year I was May Queen for the Portsea Carnival. I was up on this big float with three attendants. We was all dressed in white with garlands of flowers round our heads and we looked gorgeous – though I says so who shouldn't.'

'I can imagine.' There was amusement in his voice.

'The year before that I won *thirty bob* on a sweep-stake. We didn't half have a knees up. My Dad's birthday is . . . was in May. You'd have liked my Dad – everyone did. *He* was in the Navy. In submarines. He went to Russia in his submarine in the war.'

'He was a brave man, then. I'd hate to be stuck down below in a sub. It can be bad enough tossing around on top of the "Oggin".'

'He was ever so brave. Coo, the stories he used to tell us! D'you know, the Tsar of Russia sent for Commander Laurence – to thank the British Navy for saving Riga, and he said they'd probably saved Russia, too. What d'you think of that? And they all got medals – the Russian medal of St George.'

He nodded down at her. 'You're right to be proud of him. Was he killed in the war?'

'No. But he was invalided out of the Navy afterwards and they never even give 'im a pension,' she said bitterly. 'And he died young. Six years ago, when I was t – twelve.' She just pulled herself up before letting the cat out of the bag by saying ten. 'He was only forty-one. Did you know – ' she knew she was gabbling a bit because she was so nervous ' – that they had to destroy their own submarines to stop the Germans getting them after they signed a treaty with the Russians?'

'Yes, I have read about that, now you mention it.'

'My Dad said they cried when they sent them to the bottom. Those horrible tin cans 'ad become home from home, he said. He 'ad to come back on a troop ship and he used to tell me this story – ' She broke off.

The story she was thinking of had meant a lot to her even after she realised it wasn't true, but Stonewall would only think it silly. And she was talking too much. She was going to put her foot in it, if she wasn't careful.

She thrust her newspaper packet at him. 'Would you like some more fish and chips? We always take the left-overs home. Sometimes there's quite a lot and then my brothers don't have to fight over it. But there's only one portion tonight.'

'No, thanks. What I've just had was more than enough. I'd already had supper earlier.'

'Then why . . .?' She looked up with a glad smile, feeling she might burst with pleasure.

'Came to see *you*, didn't I?' Then quickly changing the subject as if he regretted this admission. 'How many brothers have you got?'

He was *really* nice, Queenie decided, and he seemed to be genuinely interested in her. She usually turned down Kent Street but now she led him the longer route via St George's Square because she wanted tonight to go on for ever. 'I got five brothers. They're not all at home now, though. Billy's in the Army. He's married to Vera – a right bloody cow, she is. Oops! Pardon my French.'

Stonewall chuckled.

Then there's our Eddy. He works down the dockyard and lives at home. He's got a club foot, so he's a bit shy. John is a marine and he can't do no wrong in Ma's eyes. He's got 'imself engaged to a nice girl called Phyllis. Then comes me, the only girl and bleedin' skivvy to the rest! And after me, Jimmy, and Josh who's only nine. He was named after my Dad – Joshua. Joshua Ellis,' she finished proudly.

'Quite a family.'

'I'm rabbiting on, aren't I? I always do when I'm nervous.'

'What are you nervous about?' Again the amusement in his voice.

'Oh I don't mean frightened. It's just that . . . I don't know nothing about you, do I?'

'There's not much to tell. My father's a commercial traveller for Radio Rentals. My younger brother is training to be a chef. I've signed up for twelve years, to see something of the world before I settle down to something mundane.'

What on earth did *mundane* mean? She wasn't going to ask him – reveal her ignorance. She'd never had anything to do with a man like him before. She'd have to watch her language a bit, or she might put him off.

It's a good life,' he was saying. 'I like being part of a team with no real responsibilities. And in August, *I'm* off to the Med.'

'Lucky you!' Coo, she'd have to work fast to get him hooked. 'I've never been *anywhere* unless you count across to the Isle of Wight, and twice to London to visit my Dad's parents. That's where 'e was born.'

They had reached St George's Square, an expanse of grass studded round the edge with trees, with narrow streets of old terraced houses radiating from it. Queenie stopped outside the lighted portals of the church where her parents had married in 1908, where she and her brothers had been christened and where the family came every Sunday morning.

Her Dad's funeral service had taken place in St George's. Billy had married Vera here and no doubt this was the church that she would be married in. To Stonewall? She gave him an excited glance.

Strange how this old brick building – 'The Shipwrights' Church' – seemed to be the hub of their lives and yet they were not really a religious family. Like the majority, they went through the motions and kept the Christian traditions with an unquestioning acceptance. They would have felt lost without them.

'That's where I live. You go down Butcher Street into Baker Street. I've lived in number twelve since I were born.' Queenie pointed across the road, desperately reluctant to let him go yet even more reluctant to let him walk her to the door.

Ma had sharp ears and if they stood talking under her window she would lean out and shout at her to come in, like she did when Queenie was going out with Tommy Williams. That was embarrassing enough – but if she was caught with a sailor they would really get an earful. Not that Ma had anything against sailors, of course, but she knew what they were like and would reckon Queenie was far too young.

'A stone's throw from Vernon,' commented Stonewall, looking across the main road to the high wall of the naval base, the huge gateway to which was just through the railway arch. He stood looking at her uncertainly, as if he was not quite sure what he wanted to do about her.

Queenie cast about for something to say – to keep him there. 'I said May was my lucky month, din't I? Must be, 'cos now I've met you.'

'Oh – yes.' He cleared his throat, shuffled his feet.

'There's ever such a good film on at The Palace,' she continued desperately. 'Errol Flynn in *Captain Blood*.' There was a pause. 'Don't you like Olivia de Haviland?'

He shrugged. 'She's got nice eyes.'

'Has she?' She gazed at him, willing him to say what he said next.

'So are yours. Very expressive. And lovely hair.' He reached out, picked up a strand and let it fan out before falling back into place. His light touch tingled through her hair and she shivered.

'Cold?'

She shook her head and flirted a smile up at him. 'You're not bad, yourself.'

They stared at each other for a giddy moment. Queenie wished they could stay like this for ever – caught in the bubble of light from the church lamp. Then she realised that she wanted much more than that because Stonewall's gaze was stirring delicious sensations deep inside her, the like of which she'd never felt before.

'Want to go, then?' he asked at last, apparently making up his mind. 'What night are you free?'

'The shop's closed on Mondays,' she answered breathlessly. Could she wait that long?

'Meet me here at six? Will that give us time to get to The Palace? I don't know my way around Portsmouth yet.'

'Yes, but not *here*. Someone might see us and tell Ma. She wouldn't half give me a belting – I mean . . . it takes her a while to get used to things. Know what I mean? I could meet you at Vernon gates.'

He hesitated. 'No. Look, let's keep this between ourselves, shall we? You don't want your mother to find out and I don't like the fellows knowing my private business.'

'Oh. A bit of private business am I?' she asked pertly. 'I've been called some things in me time! So I've got to pretend I don't know you when you come into the shop with your mates, have I?'

'Well, I think it's best to be discreet . . . for the moment. Don't you?'

Queenie actually wanted to shout it out loud, but she politely agreed. 'Walk along to The Hard then. I'll meet you at the railway pier at six. We can get the tram from there.'

'Fine. You'll be all right now?'

'Yes, thanks. I'm not afraid of the dark. I walk home every night by meself.'

'Shouldn't think much frightens *you*, Queenie May. Cheerio, then.' He turned and walked away from her with squared shoulders, brisk steps and not one backward glance. He hadn't really *smiled* at her once, but oh, he was The One! Queenie watched him out of sight, hugging herself with joy.

She didn't know how she would get round Ma on this, but she was determined that she was going to do it. Even if she did get a beating. Like that time she went mudlarking at The Hard when she was about nine.

Well, the boys had dared her and she couldn't resist a dare.

She squirmed as she remembered how she had taken her shoes off and squelched into that evil-smelling black mud, loathing the ooze of it up between her toes, and dreading what her feet might encounter. Crabs. Worms. Rusty tins. Glass?

Bravely smearing herself all over, she had joined the boys in calling up to the train and ferry passengers who were passing along the pier. 'Throw us a penny, Guv', or 'Spare a copper, Lady'.

The on-lookers, leaning over the railings, were certainly intrigued and obliging, laughing and shouting at the children, encouraging them to splosh around and throw the foul stuff at one another.

'You're one of the gang, now,' Joe Sutton, the gang-leader, congratulated Queenie when they emerged like some species of slimy marine-life from the harbour. He shared out the takings. 'We'll do it again next Thursday. That's the day the bobbies don't seem to come round.'

'I won't be around next Thursday when my Ma cops this lot. She's goin' to kill me!' she quipped before walking the short distance home in real fear. Her only hope was that Ma would see the funny side of it or appreciate the bounty she had collected.

She had crept up the alley and let herself into the back yard. Perhaps she could sneak into the scullery and get some of it off with cold water, so that she would not look quite so bad.

As bad luck would have it, Beatrice Ellis, small and round, was in the yard hanging out washing. She turned with a row of pegs between her teeth as the gate opened, and seeing the horrible apparition that oozed in, spat out the pegs with an almighty shriek.

'It's all right – it's only me, Ma.'

The scream turned to one of absolute fury. Queenie was ordered to stripp off her clothes and get into the scullery.

'I've got lots of money, Ma,' she cried. The mud-caked coins were scattered all over the concrete as she was dragged into the little back room by her foul-smelling hair and thrust into the remaining soapy water in the copper, through which several batches of clothes had already passed.

Queenie screamed. 'It's too hot, Ma!'

'Too bad! I'll *kill* you if you ever go near that mud and those disgusting kids again. God help me, so I will!' Beatie shrieked, scrubbing and damn-near drowning her, before plucking her out of the hot water and dunking her for a cold rinse in the tin bath.

Queenie screamed again and received a clout round the ear.

Beatie Ellis, after a lifetime of doling out summary punishment to erring brothers and sisters and her own offspring, delivered a hefty swipe for so small a woman.

'Ain't you going to put me through the mangle?' Queenie demanded with shrill indignation. 'Might as well finish the job proper!' Which earned her another clout.

'Don't back-chat me, you cheeky little sod! These clothes are ruined and I can't get it out of yer hair. Just you remember – and *you* take note – ' she swung round to her two younger sons who were peeping round the door ' – if I catch any of you mudlarking again, I'll 'ave the skin off your back.'

'You already have,' wailed Queenie. 'I look just like a bloody lobster.' And received her third clip round the ear.

'I don't know what your father's goin' to say when he hears about it, poor man.'

Queenie couldn't bear the thought of her misdemeanour being recounted to her Dad when he came in grey-faced and exhausted after working on the roads or a building site. Not for proper wages, either, but for Public Assistance Welfare tickets which could only be exchanged for food. 'Ow, don't tell him, Ma – please. I promise I'll be ever so good.'

'He'd be *ashamed* of you! The Ellis family may be hard-up but we've got our pride. We'll never stoop that low.'

That really made Queenie cry. 'I'm ever so sorry, Ma. Don't tell him. Please! I don't want to make him more ill.'

To her surprise her mother started to weep, lifting the corner of her mud-smeared apron to wipe her eyes. Her silver-streaked, black hair had come loose from its bun and now straggled round her hot cheeks. 'I work my fingers to the bone for this family – never 'ave a moment's rest. But it's always "Dad this" and "Dad that". You never give *me* a minute's thought, do you?'

Queenie, feeling completely nonplussed by this unusual show of weakness in her mother, attempted to put an arm around her shoulder, but was shrugged off.

'Clear this mess up and bale out the copper,' Beatie ordered sharply, stomping off to the kitchen. Queenie looked after her with a mixture of resentment and perplexity. She could never get close to her mother and it hurt. Everything was for the boys as far as Ma was concerned. *She* didn't count at all – except as a slave!

But Beatie earned her daughter's gratitude on this occasion by not mentioning the episode to her husband. What happened to her ill-gotten loot Queenie never discovered, and had the good sense not to ask.

No, Queenie didn't want to get on the wrong side of her mother, but *nothing* was going to stop her going out with Stonewall.

# · *Three* ·

Would he come?

Queenie had been on tenterhooks for days but now she waited nervously at Portsea Hard, dressed in a blue cotton dress, with bare legs and white, high-heeled sandals and carrying a white cardigan over her arm. Her dark hair, loosely waved and curled under at shoulder level was being stirred by a gentle sea-breeze. Would she recognise Stonewall? She had not yet seen him in daylight. Apart from his serious expression and intense eyes, her picture of him was hazy.

Still, she imagined sitting intimately beside him in the back row of the flicks, or perhaps they would take one of the double seats at the side. The thought of him putting an arm around her and pressing his thigh against hers was delicious. Would he kiss her? She had never been *properly* kissed by a man.

Tommy Williams had tried it on at the pictures *and* put his hand on her breasts, but his fumbling inexperience had irritated her.

There was that time last year when Uncle Bert had pushed her up against the wall in the darkness of the hall, rubbing himself against her and slobbering a horrid wet kiss on her lips.

'Living in the same house as you is driving me mad,' he panted hotly against her neck.

'Don't be filthy!' she hissed, pushing him away and wiping her mouth with the back of her hand. 'If you can't stand living in the same house, you better get your own place – stop sponging off Ma. And if you *ever* touch me again, I'll tell her.' She knew that would cool him down, quicker than a bucket of cold water.

He had moved in when he married Ma's younger sister, Ethel, soon after Dad died. To help with the rent, they had said, but it just made extra work for her and Ma. Ethel went out to work and sat around doing nothing when she got in as if that was her right, but Ma would never hear a word against her. And Bert drank too much. One night he had come in, pissed as a newt, and peed in the potty in the baby's high chair in the kitchen rather than go down the yard to the lav. He was crude.

Soon after the episode in the hall, he had miraculously found a flat and they moved out. Ma missed the money until Queenie got the job at the fish and chip shop, but life was a bit easier. Bert and Ethel still came every Sunday for tea of course, with Ma's two brothers and whichever members of their families were at home. But Uncle Bert kept his distance and she rather enjoyed the power she had over him. She only had to threaten to tell and . . . she reckoned she could have got anything out of him she wanted, but he wasn't worth her attention.

Where was Stonewall? Biting her lower lip, Queenie looked anxiously back up the road towards HMS *Vernon*, but she knew she had come early.

A couple of sailors strolled by from the direction of the dockyard. 'Waiting for *me*, are you sweetheart?' one of them grinned at her.

'Depends what you got to offer,' she replied saucily.

'Enough to keep any girl happy.' He swaggered towards her.

'I'm waiting for my boyfriend, actually,' she replied quickly, wishing that she didn't always feel compelled to joke back. Stonewall might be annoyed if he came along and saw her talking to other men.

'Come on, Lefty. You can't win 'em all.'

They moved off just in time. Stonewall was approaching

with his brisk walk. Her heartbeat quickened. How could the same uniform look so ordinary on those others, but so distinguished on him? There was an all-togetherness about him, a freshness, and he held himself well.

'Hello, Queen of the May,' his expression serious. 'Flirting again, I see.'

She grinned. 'I can't help it, can I, if men like me.'

They examined each other. She saw that in the daylight his eyes were hazel. Green, flecked with gold and brown. Thick dark brows. A long, strong nose. Good skin. His neck was smooth and tanned above the white summer vest. He was *lovely*.

'I'd forgotten how pretty you are,' he said. 'That bluebell colour matches your eyes.'

Queenie was astonished to feel herself blushing. She'd been called things like 'gorgeous' and 'smashing' and a 'nice bit of homework', but had never had such a sweet compliment before. Watching her, he actually *smiled*, the corners of his eyes crinkling attractively.

'You should smile more,' she told him, 'it makes you look ever so nice. We get the number 13 tram over the road. There's one due any minute now.'

'Right.' He placed his fingers lightly under her elbow, causing a little tingle to run up her arm, and looking both way at the kerb, he led her across the road. He wasn't like the boys she knew.

'Upstairs,' he said when they mounted the platform of the red and cream tram.

Queenie's breath came fast as he swung into the seat beside her and she felt the warmth of his body along her arm and thigh. His eyes roved over her face appreciatively at close quarters and she smiled up at him. 'You could be Margaret Lockwood's sister.'

'I've been told that before,' she answered, pleased.

He leaned against her more heavily as he fumbled in his far pocket, pulling out a pouch of tobacco which also contained a packet of Rizla cigarette papers. Queenie watched his long fingers shred the tobacco, stretch it along the middle of the paper, roll it and carry it to his lips to lick the edge.

'My Dad could do that with one hand.'

'He was a real matelot.'

'Don't I get one, then?'

He raised an eyebrow. 'I wouldn't usually expect a lady to smoke a tickler, but I haven't got a packet of decent ones on me. Have it if you like.' He handed it over.

She breathed deeply as he flicked his lighter flame under the crude cigarette – and choked on the smoke, spluttering and coughing, with tears starting from her eyes.

'Navy shag is pretty strong,' he said, passing her a clean handkerchief.

Queenie was furious with herself. She was supposed to be eighteen, a woman of the world, and here she was, wiping her mascara off onto his clean hanky. 'Sorry.' She handed back the handkerchief.

'Shall I have that?' he asked, and taking the cigarette with two crescents of her lipstick adorning it, he placed it between his own lips, inhaled and blew a smoke ring. Sophisticated. 'All right, now?' he asked, glancing sideways at her.

'Yes, thanks. Silly of me. I don't really smoke. I can't afford to spend *my* hard-earned money on fags,' she said by way of explanation.

'Sailors have disgusting habits.'

'I've heard!'

'You don't believe all you hear, do you?' His sideways glance was intimate, thrilling.

'As far as sailors go, I do.' She gave him an arch look.

'I can see I shall have to redeem our reputation. Can't have you believing that all "Tars" are tarred with the same brush.'

'Redeem your reputation!' she mocked. 'Blimey. You *are* posh. For a sailor *you* seem very respectable, but then

I've been told – ' she glanced up at him from under her lashes ' – you shouldn't believe everything you see.'

The conductor rattled his ticket machine at Stonewall's shoulder. 'Two twopenny returns to Guildhall Square, please,' she told the conductor and her escort fumbled in his pocket again for some change.

The tram was now passing the end of her street, rattling along on the rails, and she turned her face away from the window, not wanting to be seen. She was supposed to be out with Pearl.

'Where're you from?' she asked.

'Derby, originally. My grandfather is a tailor – a "Gentlemen's Outfitter" he calls it. Got a big shop up there. My father used to work with him before the war, but packed it in when he was demobbed. There was some sort of row. My parents live in Portchester now.'

'Oh. That's not far.'

'No, I've been posted to Portland or away on commissions, so I haven't got to know Portsmouth. You can be my guide . . . if you like.'

'I'll show you round.' She flirted her eyes at him. 'Bet you could show *me* a thing or two, too.'

He quirked an eyebrow. 'I get the feeling you know it all already, Queenie May.'

She poked the tip of her tongue at him between her lips, meaning only to be cheeky, but from the sultry way his eyes held hers, she realised she might have given him the wrong impression. Something she did far too often.

'D'you swim?' she asked quickly.

'It's more than my life's worth not to – I might fall overboard one night when I've had too much to drink.'

'We'll go swimming at Sally Port one day, then. And we'll go up Portsdown Hill. You can see the whole town spread out below, and Portchester Castle, and the whole of the harbour and right out to sea, to the Isle of Wight. Oops! This is where we get off.'

They leapt up and clattered down the stairs, Stonewall

jumping off and offering his hand as she alighted. He was a real gentleman and no mistake.

'Very impressive,' he remarked of the Guildhall, a great square building near the central railway station, with a dome, Grecian pillars and stone lions guarding the steps.

'It looks old-fashioned don't it, but it was built about fifty years ago.' She led him across the road in the direction of The Palace, where Stonewall bought seats in the circle and invited her to choose some sweets. She felt very special as she preceded him up the stairs. Looking back at him over her shoulder, she grinned. 'I could get used to this sort of treatment, you know.'

He did not lead her to the back row or the double seats at the side, and she wasn't sure whether she was disappointed that he was not going to take the opportunity to cuddle her, or whether she was pleased that he was showing her respect. She decided on the latter; it was quite a novelty.

They were only just in time. The organist came to the end of his recital with a flourish and disappeared into the bowels of the building with his Mighty Wurlitzer. The audience clapped, shouted and stamped their feet in appreciation.

'I adore the flicks,' sighed Queenie. She loved the feeling of anticipation, of shared pleasure – complete strangers laughing and crying side by side. She loved the plumes of smoke rising from cigarettes, the crackle of sweet and crisp packets. You could lose yourself in the dark; become Greta Garbo or Loretta Young up there on the screen, with Clark Gable or Cary Grant drooling over you. Or Errol Flynn. Ooh!

Occasionally some dirty old bloke would push his leg up against yours and try it on, but you only had to grind your heel into his foot and he soon moved. Taking off his cap, Stonewall laid it on the upturned seat beside him and ran his fingers through a glorious mop of wavy brown hair. Queenie's breath caught in her throat. Lor, but he was handsome. Who needed Cary Grant!

She leant against him, laying her hand on his sleeve. 'I wanted to be an usherette at one time – then I could have watched the films over and over. Heaven. But Ma put her foot down. Said she she didn't want my head filled with bleedin' rubbish. But where's the harm?' She smiled at Stonewall. 'I saw *Lorna Doone* in January. It was ever so romantic. Tiny little Victoria Hopper and this great big chap. I didn't half fancy him. And then there was this "baddy", Carver Doone – I fancied him an' all – but he got sucked down in a bog. Horrible it was, but he deserved it – '

Stonewall nodded. 'I read the book when I was a child.'

Queenie digested this information with a frown on her face. She didn't read books, only the women's magazines that Fred's wife passed on to her when she'd finished with them. 'Ejucated, that's what you are.'

The lights dimmed and the curtains swung back to reveal the screen. Queenie shuffled in her seat a little until her knee was lightly, seemingly accidentally, touching her escort's thigh. The thrill of that small point of contact was out of all proportion. She grinned to herself. Now she understood why old men did it.

The first item was an old Charlie Chaplin film. Her companion's easy laughter was a surprise to Queenie because he always looked so serious, and stealing glances at him, she noticed how much younger he looked when his face was relaxed in laughter. He dipped his long fingers into her box of Liquorice Allsorts when she offered them and even that seemed intimate.

In the interval she went 'to powder her nose' and Stonewall bought her an ice-cream when she returned, preferring a cigarette himself. The lights dimmed for a Mickey Mouse cartoon and *Movietone News* before the main feature. The news was all about the Jubilee celebrations and the Thanksgiving Service in St Paul's cathedral. 'Don't Queen Mary look lovely with that jewelled collar. I adore the Royal Family,' she murmured to Stonewall. There was an item about an Anglo-German Naval Agreement, which she didn't understand, but her companion's 'Huh!' beside her, told her that he was not impressed.

'I adore Errol,' she told her companion as the title appeared on the screen. 'He's my ideal man. Or he was – 'till I met you.' She nudged his arm with her elbow and grinned at him, thinking that there was a resemblance with that cleft in his chin.

Stonewall winked at her.

In spite of her exciting companion, Queenie soon became totally engrossed in the story of the young surgeon who, wrongly condemned for helping rebels, escaped and became a pirate in the Caribbean. She'd love to go to a beautiful part of the world like that, with sunshine all the time, and white beaches and surf.

Coo! Fancy being Olivia de Havilland and having that handsome bloke swashbuckling all over the place for you with his sword. Thrilling. She was biting her nails with the excitement of it all, and shedding a few tears in the tender moments, quite unaware that Stonewall was watching her until he passed her his handkerchief again to mop them up.

She gave him a shaky smile in the dim light and he reached over and took her hand in his warm, dry grasp. Queenie's heart tripped at the contact, as if from an overload of electricity, and she was so aware of the current flowing from his fingers into her that she almost lost track of the rest of the story.

'Enjoy it?' he asked as the lights went up, his shoulder against hers, and a whiff of tobacco on his breath. His warm, hazel eyes smiled into hers at close quarters. Ooh, if only he'd kiss her, she wished, looking at his nice, curvy mouth.

'It was lovely!' she breathed, smoothing the navy serge of his sleeve with her fingertips.

They stood for the National Anthem, Stonewall jamming his cap on his head and standing rigidly to attention, while beside him Queenie swelled with pride. She slipped her arm through his, feeling the thrill of ownership as they went down the stairs with the chattering crowd.

'Who needs Olivia de Havilland?' he asked, giving her arm a squeeze.

He took her to Verrechia's near the railway station and Victoria Park. It was an ice-cream parlour with marble-topped tables in little cubicles divided by glass partitions. 'This is a real treat,' Queenie smiled as she ordered a cup of tea and a doughnut and looked around at the mirrors and wall-lamps that gave the place a sparkly effect. 'Perhaps Fred should go in for a bit of this stuff – give his place a bit of class.'

'What did Fred's classy assistant do on her day off?' asked Stonewall, setting down his cup.

She blinked in surprise. 'You mean me? That's a laugh. Day off! That's a laugh too. Monday's me busiest day.'

'For what?'

'Chores! I do most of the housework in the mornings before goin' to Fred's at eleven, 'cos Ma goes to work at five o'clock. But on Monday's I've got special things to do.'

He was frowning. 'Your mother goes to work at five – *in the morning*?'

She nodded. 'She goes over on the ferry to the naval hospital at Haslar – works in the laundry. And she goes out cleanin' in the evening.'

'Good God!'

'Don't your mother work, then?'

He shook his head and Queenie realised with a jolt that he was shocked and that he probably had no idea how poor the Ellises were.

'You don't know the half of it,' she told him, liking a bit

of drama. 'Ma sometimes has to pawn her wedding-ring to pay the rates. Or her crystal – she's ever so proud of those cut-glass vases and bowl her mother left her.'

'That's awful.'

'It's nothin' unusual where *I* live.' She giggled. 'You'd pop yer bleedin' kids if "uncle" would take them.'

'Like I was saying – on Mondays I 'ave to black-lead the Larbert Range, do the front door-step with Cardinal Red, though why it can't just be scrubbed like any other bloody door-step – ' She was ticking off her list of duties on her fingers. 'The front room 'as to be done out – the family make a sodding mess of it on Sundays. The curtain bands have to be Brassoed. Mum loves those, 'cos Billy made them for 'er when 'e was apprenticed and they keep the curtains away from the bleedin' aspidistra in the winder.'

He laughed. Pleased to be entertaining him, she went on, her eyes sparkling. 'Prize aspidistra that – Ma sells the shoots. Well, every penny helps, don't it? Then I have to wash and polish the lino – it has to be clean enough to eat off to please *my* Mum. But it don't matter how clean you keep those old houses, you can't get rid of the 'roaches.'

'Cockroaches?' He grimaced. 'You're having me on.'

She shook her head. 'And bed-bugs every spring. Look.' She held out her arm so that he could see the inflamed spots on the tender skin of her inner-arm and the pale mauve blotches of previous bites. He looked appalled. She grinned. 'Know the best way to catch bed-bugs?' He shook his head. 'With a damp bar of soap – they stick to it.'

He nodded solemnly, but his eyes were glinting with amusement. 'I'll remember that.'

'Then I 'ave to fill the boiler and light the fire under it, after Jimmy's broken up the orange-boxes we get down the NAAFI. Then I get the boys off to school, feed the chickens, *and* the bleedin' rabbits because Josh won't get out of bed in time to do it. He don't tear up the newspaper for the lav, neither, like 'e's told. But he *never* gets a thick ear. Then I take the bottom sheets off the beds, mince the

Sunday left-overs for the faggots.' She'd ticked off both hands and started over again. 'That's twelve things – '

'I get the picture,' he interrupted. 'Poor little Queenie.'

'And if I'm sittin' down lookin' through a magazine when Ma comes in at lunchtime, there's hell to pay. "Git off your lazy backside and do so-and-so",' she mimicked. '"Do *I* ever git time to sit down? Do *I* ever have a day off?"'

Stonewall chuckled.

'Anyway, I've got it all worked out now. I 'ave a sit down in the middle of the morning, so I'm still workin' like stink when she comes in. That keeps 'er happy. Sorry, I talk too much, don't I?'

'Life isn't a barrel of fun for you, is it?' he said sympathetically.

She shook her head. 'That why I want . . .'

'What do you want, Queenie?' he asked softly.

She shrugged. *Careful. Don't scare him off!* 'Oh, something . . . better. What d'you like to do in your time off – when you're not out chasing the girls or boozing?'

'Well, those are my favourite pastimes, of course. But apart from that, I like to sketch and read.'

'Sketch? Drawring you mean? You must be ever so clever. My Dad liked to read. Always had 'is nose in a newspaper or a Zane Grey.'

'Cowboys are not quite my cup of tea. No. At the moment I'm reading Darwin's *Theory Of the Origin Of Species*.' he said with a sly grin, watching for her reaction.

Her eyes widened. 'Ya what?'

'Evolution.' She frowned. He laughed. 'Do you believe in Adam and Eve and the Garden of Eden?'

She turned her mouth down at the corners and shrugged. ''Course. It's what the Bible says, ain't it?'

'Darwin doesn't. He says we're all descended from primates – '

'*What* mates?'

'Primates. The monkey family.'

'Speak for yourself, mate. *I* don't come from no bleedin' monkey family.'

They both laughed. 'No – you're far too pretty,' he told her with an appreciative look that brought a glow to her cheeks.

'Don't you believe in the Bible and God, and that?'

'No. I'm an atheist.'

'A what! But ain't it wicked not to? I mean . . . I believe in Hell, don't you?'

'I don't think so. I think you make your own hell – on earth. Ideas change, you know, Queenie. If they didn't we would never have progressed past the ape stage.'

'Coo! You're too clever for me.' Some of the light went out of her eyes as she reflected on the gulf between them. 'Ejucated – that's what you are.'

He shrugged. 'My grandfather paid for my brother and me to go to a good school.'

''Spect you think I'm pig ignorant?' she asked with a bitter note in her voice. *How could he think anything else? How could he bear to sit and listen to the rubbish she talked?* 'I better get back. Ma will be wonderin' where I am.' She stood up, pushing her way clumsily out of the cubicle, leaving him to settle the bill.

# · *Four* ·

'I haven't upset you, have I?' He caught her up and took her arm as they walked to the tram stop. She had not said a word for a full five minutes.

'No. It's just . . . I been thinking. We're too different.'

'That's what makes it interesting, isn't it? Don't worry about it. I'm not going to. Come on now. Where shall we go next Monday?'

She looked up at him with a glad smile. 'You really want to see me again?'

'Why shouldn't I, Queen of the May? I like you. You're beautiful, amusing, and – gutsy.'

'Oh, charming!' she laughed.

They boarded the tram and sat hand-in-hand on the short journey back, her fingers palely interlaced with his dark ones.

'Can you get time off during the day?' she asked, happy that all was not lost. 'We could go swimming next Monday.' Then she could show him something *she* was good at.

'I'll see if I can swing it. I'll come into the shop one evening and let you know.'

'Oh, it's all above board now, is it?' she exclaimed, pleased.

'Ah, well . . . We'll keep it to ourselves for a bit longer, shall we?'

She *had* to keep it from Ma, but why did *he* need to keep their meetings secret? Was he married? Or engaged? Or just ashamed to be seen with her? She tried to laugh.

'You won't get court-martialled for going out with me, you know. I'm respectable, I am.'

He grinned, a sensuous expression in his eyes that made her feel hot all over. 'What a pity,' he murmured.

She tore her eyes away. *So that was it.* She knew now what he was after. Or she had a hazy sort of idea of what it was, being pig-ignorant where sex was concerned. *That* was a dirty word in her house.

She was a right fool. What else did she have to offer a man like him, anyway? 'What sort of girl d'you think I am, then?' she asked in a truculent voice to disguise her bitter disappointment. 'As if I didn't know.'

He put his arm around her. It was what she had been wanting him to do all evening, and it felt wonderful. Or it would have done if her heart was not as heavy as lead. She leaned against him.

'Come on, Queenie, don't be like that. I don't know what you want from me . . .'

*Love. Marriage. Security. A better life.*

' . . . but I just want a bit of fun with no strings attached. Some company in my time off for the next few weeks.'

'Oh, is that all!' she said with false gaiety. '*I* was beginning to think you was after me body.'

He brought his mouth close to her ear. 'Well, I wouldn't say no to that . . .' he murmured, his breath stirring her hair and causing her to shiver. 'But we'd better get to know each other a bit better first, don't you think?'

*He did want to get to know her better.* But he also wanted . . . It was all so confusing. Well, she would have to play it his way, but she was jolly well going to *make* him want her – for more than just her body. Though if it took that . . .

She turned her face up to his with a smile, and he bent his head and brushed her lips with his own.

'So, getting back to next Monday. I'll come into the shop and if I say 'hello' to Pearl, you'll know it's on. Shall we meet in Gun Wharf Road just up from Vernon gates?

Where the road curves round.' She nodded. 'Ten o'clock too early?'

'No. I'll get up early – when Ma goes – and do my chores. I was puttin' it on a bit – she won't mind me goin' for a swim as long as I've got everything done.'

He left her at the church. With mixed emotions, she watched him go with that brisk walk of his, wanting to call him back. Kiss him goodnight. Take him home to show her Ma. She was elated but at the same time afraid that she would not be able to keep him.

She walked slowly down Butcher Street, past The Eagle Pub on the corner with the NAAFI warehouse opposite. These streets of tall, drab, terraced buildings had been her playground as a child; sitting on the doorsteps with the girls, or playing hopscotch and skipping games. Kicking balls around and playing 'chase' with the boys. Taking off their shoes and paddling when the high spring tides overflowed the harbour and flooded the nearby streets.

There was always something to do, something exciting to watch. A fight outside a pub at closing time, a street squabble between neighbours, kids up to mischief. She loved it, yet she yearned for something better.

She passed the Boys' Rotary Club, Brown's the Newsagent, Russell's Dairy and Valerio's General Grocery store. Ma liked shopping at Valerio's because all the women gathered here for a good gossip, and the Italian shopkeeper didn't mind giving 'tick' when his customers ran out of money. On pay day, Ma would always buy them a hap'orth of Custard Tips – gorgeous they were.

Past Ayling's Café, where Queenie occasionally and wickedly, squandered a ha'penny on a fizzy Vantas drink. Raspberry was her favourite. The coal yard was opposite, where all the kids used to go with old prams or home-made go-carts to buy a penn'orth of coal or coke.

Then came Mrs Russell's Twopenny Supper Shop, where you could get delicious faggots and peas, or a pie. Jones, the cobbler had a good business – it wasn't often the inhabitants of these streets could afford new shoes.

A lodging house – 'doss house' they used to call it. Some very rough types lived there. There was an Irish family once and Tess, the drunken mother, used to be carried home regularly by her sons – singing at the top of her voice and surprisingly sweet notes coming out of her toothless mouth. Once they had her by the arms and legs and the kids could see she had no knickers on. They didn't half giggle.

The Mitre Pub. Whatever else they lacked round here, it wasn't pubs. Then a little lane leading to the abattoir. Billy used to earn a few coppers down there before he joined the Army, but Eddy wouldn't go near the place. Lots of kids used to hang around the yard and watch the animals go in and listen to their crazed bellows, but Queenie thought it gruesome. And Cole's, the Butcher, was on the corner.

Saturday lunchtime was quite a little ritual for the women of the streets bordering St George's Square. Anyone not familiar with it would think it some quaint old Portsea custom, seeing the groups of women standing around chatting with shopping bags on their arms. Until the emergence of 'Uncle Cole', the butcher, to cross the road to The Mitre would herald a mad dash to the shop.

Then his nephew and the other assistant would share out special bags of 'sixpenny fries' to the customers buying their weekend joints. In it would be some sausages, chops, odd bits of steak, liver and kidney. Always good value. It was all a game, as 'Uncle' would always return halfway through the fevered transactions and pretend to scold his assistants for giving away his profits. When they could afford it, the Ellis family had a sixpenny piece of beef, pork and lamb for the weekend in addition to the 'fries'. Any left-overs would go into the faggots.

Queenie crossed the road to Baker Street. Always a lovely smell of warm bread as you passed William's, the bakery on the corner. Where Ma did her evening cleaning job and was often given a stale loaf or left-over cakes. The Ellis family got by, one way and another.

Queenie thought about her Dad.

She was sure he would have approved of Stonewall. He would have told her what to do. Even after all these years she missed her Dad something awful. A tear rolled down her cheek as she remembered him as she had last seen him.

Wetting the middle finger of each hand with the tip of her tongue, Queenie had gently smoothed out her father's unruly eyebrows as she was in the habit of doing. But this would be the last time she would be able to perform this loving gesture – because tomorrow he was to be buried.

She let her fingers trail gently over the cold, death-sharpened planes of his face, the hollows deeply shadowed in the flickering candle-light. Stroked the thinned greying hair that had once been as black and shiny as her own, the lids closed forever on the clear violet-blue eyes that she had inherited; the large blunt nose, fortunately modified in her; the well-shaped mouth now drawn tight over teeth that in his youth, like hers, had been white and even.

'Oh, Dad, what will I do without you? Nobody loves me like you do,' she whispered brokenly, her eyes filling with tears as her fingertips lingered on the folded hands which had so often held her and comforted her. Now the strong, square fingers were cold and appeared to be made of wrinkled yellow wax.

The tears overflowed and washed her cheeks and dripped into the coffin. Where did they all come from? She'd cried bucketsful in the days that he had lain here in their little-used front room, with the curtains drawn all over the house in mourning.

Even though she had long been aware that he was ill and having those frightening fits, writhing on the ground and foaming at the mouth, it had still been a terrible shock when they brought him home almost unconscious from Eastern Road. He had collapsed with a bad fit, and because he had been unable to work on road-building that day, he hadn't even received the 'tickets' that Portsmouth Borough Council paid disabled men with – to exchange only for food, not tobacco and booze.

The doctor had been called, even though the half-crown fee would mean hardship for the rest of the week, but there was nothing he could do for her darling Dad.

Ma had come out of their bedroom early the next morning in her flannel nightgown, with her black plait of hair hanging over one breast, and found Queenie huddled on the landing.

'Queen. Go and get Daisy and Lil.' Her face was white and set. Queenie had known then, but not wanted to believe.

Old Daisy, their neighbour, and her bossy daughter, Lil, who was completely subdued for once, bustled up and down the stairs with bowls of water and towels. What were they doing?

The family congregated in the kitchen. 'Your father's dead,' Beatie, stony-faced, told four of her six children. 'We've had a difficult life, God knows, since he was invalided out of the Navy, but it's going to be even harder from now on and you're all goin' to have to pull your weight.'

The two little boys, who were only five and three, did not understand what was going on. Eddy looked white and shocked, and Queenie felt that her chest would burst open with the pain of it.

Then Lil came down, laid her hand on Ma's shoulder, and said, 'Poor Josh is decent now, Beatie.'

'Thanks, Lil. I'm ever so grateful – couldn't have done it meself. And thank God the burial premiums are paid up. At least poor Josh won't have to be buried on the Parish – he couldn't bear the thought of that. The insurance won't run to a headstone, though. But 'e won't worry about that.'

Queenie now understood what the extra, ill-afforded, sixpence was for, paid along with other insurance to the man from the Co-op who called each week.

They all trooped up the stairs to the front bedroom. Queenie's heart was knocking against her ribs.

Dad lay, looking surprisingly small, under a white sheet, and there were pennies on his eye-lids. To keep them shut, she supposed. He didn't seem like her Dad any more. She was all clenched up inside but she couldn't cry till much later, but Jimmy cried and Eddy stood twisting his hands together. Little Josh just looked frightened.

Then the men came and took Dad away and brought him back in a coffin. And Billy had come home from the Army and John from that boarding school at Ipswich that the Navy paid for. And they all had to war black arm bands.

She stayed with Dad that last night, watching over him, reluctant to say goodbye. Sniffing wetly, she lifted her nightdress, dabbed at her cheeks and eyes with the hem, becoming aware as she did so of a muffled rhythmic sound coming from the room above. Her brow wrinkled in disbelief. Her mother was sobbing!

That cold, hard woman – who seldom had a loving word for any of them, least of all her poor, sick husband, and had been like a block of granite since his death – was actually crying.

'Let her cry!' she whispered vehemently to the corpse. 'She never loved you like I do.' She stroked his head. 'And Dad, even though I used to like that story you told me that you smuggled me home from Russia on that troop ship, and it made feel sort-of . . . special, I'm glad it wasn't true. 'Cos if I *was* the daughter of a Russian count or sumfink, what got murdered in the Revolution, I wouldn't be *your* daughter, would I?'

She huddled, shivering, on the chair beside the coffin.

Her belly was hurting and she crossed her arms over her middle, pressing against the pain. Her 'monthlies' must be coming on again. Bloody nuisance.

She'd been terrified when she'd found blood in her knickers a few months earlier – thought she was dying and ran shrieking to her mother in the kitchen. Then Ma, red-faced with embarrassment explained, 'It's something women 'ave to put up with every month. If you din't have it, you wouldn't be able to have babies when you grow up.'

'I don't want babies if it means I have to go through this every month,' she wailed, not understanding at all and rocking backwards and forwards with pain.

'Don't be soft,' her mother said, 'you'll get used to it. I'll make you a hot water bottle and you can go to bed.' Ma fixed her up with rags and safety pins and put her to bed with a hot drink.

Later Dad came up and cuddled her and stroked her hair. 'Ma told me what's happened, and you're not to be frightened. You're a little woman now, my Queen of the May. It's something to be proud of.'

'It hurts, Daddy,' she had cried like a baby.

'It's a bit painful, eh? But like Ma says, you'll get used to it. I suppose men think they're lucky, but they're missing out on something wonderful, 'cos only women can have babies. Remember our little Hannah and how much we loved her?' And they cried together over Queenie's baby sister that had died before she was a year old.

Oh, Dad! How tender he was. Queenie, stomach clenched against the pain of womanhood, folded her arms along the rim of his coffin and rested her forehead upon them.

The next thing she knew, her mother was shaking her by the shoulder and she shrieked in fright, waking so violently in the room dim with morning light filtering through the curtains, the candles burnt out, and her Dad lying there, grey and dead.

'It's all right, Queen, it's only me. *You been here all night?*' Beatie looked shocked and her eyes were red-rimmed. Queenie nodded and her mother pulled Queenie's head against her round stomach – over which was stretched her *best* apron today – and stroked her hair.

Queenie wiped tears of remembrance from her cheeks as she pulled on the string that raised up the door catch to number twelve. The doors of Baker Street were never bolted till last thing at night – no one round here had anything worth stealing.

Queenie gave a shuddering sigh. That morning – the morning of her father's funeral had been the last time her mother had held her close like that.

# · Five ·

At a quarter to ten the following Monday morning, Queenie thankfully shut the front door behind her.

As she was wearing her costume under her skirt and blouse, she carried a string bag containing her underwear wrapped in a towel, a pouch with mirror, lipstick and comb, and a parcel of egg sandwiches.

She had left a note saying she had left at *twelve* to go swimming with Pearl. Ma would never believe she had jumped out of bed when she heard the door close at five, in order to get her chores done in time.

She bought two cakes from the baker and was up the road from the Vernon gates in good time. It was a glorious blue and gold day, very warm for the time of year.

Coming round the bend towards her, Stonewall really gave her a surprise. He looked a different person in casual attire of slacks and open-necked checked shirt, his wavy hair unfettered, and carrying a small duffel bag slung over one shoulder.

He gave her the raised left-eyebrow treatment. 'You're a sight for sore eyes!'

'So are you.' Her eyes were alight with pleasure. 'I don't know if I like you better as a sailor or a civvy – you're gorgeous both ways.'

'You shouldn't say things like that to men, you know.' His face was serious but his eyes twinkled. 'They might take advantage.'

'You wouldn't. I trust *you*. We'll walk round to Sally

Port – it isn't far, and we can pick up a couple of bottles of lemonade on the way – I've got sandwiches.'

'You've thought of everything. I got off after parade – got to be back by five, though.'

Seven glorious hours. At his side and very aware of him, Queenie led him along Gun Wharf Road, following the high wall round the naval base. She listened with fascination to his cultured voice as he told her about his life at HMS *Vernon*.

They stopped off to look at commercial and fishing boats in busy Camber Dock. She pointed out the roof and dome of the church in the High Street which had become the Cathedral nine years earlier, when Portsmouth was elevated to a city. In White Hart Road Stonewall bought lemonade and apples.

'Here we are.' Thrilling at the contact, Queenie pulled him by the hand across Broad Street and through the open archway of the old wall that was part of a fort that had been built as a defence against Napoleon. Through the arch was a wooden platform with railings and a few steps down to the pebble beach.

'I been coming here ever since I can remember,' she told him, running her fingers lovingly over the wooden balustrade worn smooth by countless hands. 'I start swimming in April, whatever the weather.' She led the way along the platform, glimpsing through the slats, the ochre, cream and white pebbles below.

They spread their towels and sat down. 'We got it all to ourselves,' Queenie observed, pleased. The little beach was open to the narrow strip of sea that was the entrance to Portsmouth Harbour, and virtually enclosed on three sides by the stone walls and the fort, with a round tower to the right of them which would be surrounded by water when the tide was high. 'That's HMS *Dolphin* and Haslar Naval Hospital across there.' They looked across to the brick buildings of the naval base. 'Hope my Ma isn't looking over here at me.' She giggled and waved.

'She wouldn't really mind, would she?' he asked lazily, lying back with his arms crossed behind his head and his eyes closed.

'She'd 'ave your guts fer garters – she thinks I'm out with Pearl.'

'You don't think she'd approve of me?'

'D'yer think your mother would approve of *me*?' she asked mischievously.

He sat up quickly, looking sideways at her, a frown on his forehead. 'Look, Queenie . . .' he floundered.

She had her answer. Her mouth tightened. 'Not good enough for your fam'ly, am I?'

'It isn't that. It's just . . . well, we hardly know each other, do we?' He reached out and touched her nose with the end of his finger.

She shook her head and looked away, not wanting him to see her pain. She stared out of the harbour entrance at the round Napoleonic forts that guarded the Solent, the stretch of water between Portsmouth and the Isle of Wight. Sun sparkled on the living water like diamonds. It wasn't far to the Island, but the gulf between her and Stonewall was too wide. She was hoping for the impossible, wasn't she? 'I know – I'm just working-class.'

He started throwing pebbles into the water. 'I don't believe in all that stuff. We're moving towards a classless society anyway, according to Karl Marx. Once the workers of the world have overthrown the Capitalists – '

'There you go again – talking about things I don't understand,' she said sulkily.

'I'm not denying that we have different backgrounds. But that doesn't stop us being friends, does it?'

She shrugged. ''Spose not.' *But she wanted so much more than friendship.*

'Come on, Queen of the May. Don't spoil this lovely day.' He grinned infectiously.

Well, she'd never get anywhere being sulky, would she? 'Come on, then,' she cried. 'Last one in's a sissy.' Stripping off her blouse and skirt, and kicking off her shoes, she ran down to the water's edge. The sea washed cool over her feet. 'It's lovely,' she called, turning to see Stonewall hobbling painfully over the pebbles.

'You must have wooden soles,' he grumbled.

'We Ellises are tough,' she laughed at his delicacy, while allowing her eyes to roam over him with pleasure. She was thrilled to see he was wearing shorts instead of the full bathing costumes most men still wore. He wasn't particularly muscular, but looked wiry and strong. He had nicely shaped, somewhat hairy legs, a smattering of dark hair on his chest, and was slightly tanned as if he did some of his duties without a vest or shirt on. He didn't look as if he had just crawled out from under a stone like a lot of men did.

Queenie turned and swooped with the grace of a dolphin into the clear water, swimming a few strong strokes before surfacing. 'Lovely,' she called, exhilarated, shaking her long wet hair back. 'Come on!'

He was gingerly testing the temperature of the water with his toes. 'It's bloody cold.'

'Sissy!' she laughed, her good humour restored. 'If you don't come straight in, I'll come and splash you.'

'You dare!' he warned.

Well, she could never resist a dare, could she? She'd broken an arm when she was small because someone dared her to dive off Sally Port Stairs. Giggling, she moved into the shallows, jumped up and splashed him furiously.

Bellowing, he ran into the water and she swam away, laughing. 'You're for it,' he shouted, striking out after her. He was a good swimmer, but she was better. He tired first and they paddled around for a few minutes before gravitating towards one another, treading water. 'Little devil. You're a damned good swimmer, though.'

She basked in his admiration. 'You have to be careful here when the tide's going out. It whooshes out of the entrance something awful. But it's coming in now, so we're all right.'

He swam up to her, his hair darkened and slicked down with water. A couple of feet apart, they smiled into each other's eyes. His lashes were spiked with drops of sea-water, and his eyes were luminous green in its reflection. He grinned and she saw that his teeth were good. He looked no more than a boy now and she wanted to kiss him so badly. 'You're not as old as I thought you was,' she said.

'Nearly twenty-one.'

'Ooh! You'll soon have the key of the door then – freedom!'

'I've had that for a long time. One of the reasons I joined the Navy. No one tells me what to do, any more.'

'Men have all the luck.'

They stood now in their depth. 'You look all funny,' she laughed, and they both looked down through the water at his body, distorted and shimmering greenish-white like the belly of a fish, and at her own limbs, foreshortened in the pale green brine and lit with shafts of sunlight.

She whirled her arms in the water, making bubbles under the surface. 'It looks like lemonade, don't it?' She suddenly shrieked as a small crab scuttled over her foot. Then an Isle of Wight ferry went past, its paddle-wheels swishing through the water, and they were gently tossed to and fro in its wake.

Back on the beach, they rubbed themselves down, towelled their hair, and stretched out on their damp towels. Wriggling to make comfortable hollows, Stonewall grumbled, 'I prefer sand, I must say.'

'Then we'll go to the Island one day – it's lovely sand over there. But don't you like the smell of the pebbles? All sort of washed and clean.'

'Mmm.' Folding his arms behind his head, he quoted some poem about going down to the sea again, and a tall ship and a star to steer it by.

'Wish I was ejucated,' Queenie observed. 'The only pome I know is about three old ladies locked in the lavatory. Bet you could be an officer if you wanted.'

'Well, I don't. I don't intend to be fettered by responsibilities – '

She spluttered. 'Fettered by responsibilities,' she mimicked in a la-di-da voice.

He grinned. 'I want to be free. Like those clouds up there. Just look at that azure sky. Actually, I want to be an artist one day. When I've done my time, I'd like to go to Art School.'

'Coo, that sounds ever so . . . romantic. An artist. Why d'you join up then?'

He sighed. 'Maternal pressure to do something "worthwhile".'

'Can't you speak sodding English!'

'What? Oh. I mean my mother didn't want me to be an artist. I don't know what she *does* want. But she's probably right. It's difficult to make a living as a painter unless one is exceptional – and to be honest, I know I am not.'

'Modesty! P'rhaps you'd like to paint *my* portrait?' she invited archly.

He looked sideways at her. 'Yes, I'd like to.' He sat up and pulled his duffel bag towards him and to Queenie's surprise, he pulled out a little sketch book and a box. Opening the box, he took out a pencil. 'Sit up, then. Let's see if I can draw you.'

'Arf a mo'!' Queenie, excited at the prospect of his full attention, sat up and got her comb out of her zippered pouch. 'Let me do me hair first.' She dragged it through her wet and tangled locks until her hair fell to her shoulders, shredded into fine strands by its teeth. 'There. How do you want me?' She wriggled round to face him, curling her legs under her.

'I'd better not answer that,' he grinned, his eyes skittering over her body.

'Cheeky!'

'That's all right. I can only fit your head and shoulders in anyway.' He gazed at her before committing a few strokes to paper. 'Queenie May, the Mona Lisa's got nothing on you.'

'Moaner who?'

'Never mind. Sit still.'

She sat smiling at him as he glanced from her face to his sketch book and back again, his face serious, absorbed in his drawing. His hair was all over the place and a lock of it fell over his forehead. As Queenie watched him, a tremulous and hopeful joy blossomed in her heart again. She wanted him so much that her desire must surely communicate itself to him. She would do *anything* to get him.

At last he handed the sketch to her.

'It's ever so good,' she breathed, not knowing whether it was or not, but impressed by the likeness, the bold lines and contrasting areas of fine shading. 'You're really clever, you are.'

'It's a bit stiff,' he said, studying it criticially.

Queenie sat smiling at his work. In her opinion it was perfect. She looked up as she felt his eyes upon her; not as they were when he was drawing her, but as a man looks at a woman, slowly and all-encompassingly.

His gaze lingered on her breasts and she wished they were more voluptuous. Judging by the women in her family, she was sure they would be when she matured, but she couldn't tell him that when he thought she was eighteen. So she just looked at him softly, blushing, and forced herself not to cross her arms over them.

'Queen of the May, you are rather beautiful,' he murmured at last, his eyes dark and slumbrous, and she smiled artlessly in pure delight. Surely she was getting through to him. Then, frowning slightly, he looked away, breaking the spell with 'Where are those sandwiches? I'm famished.'

'Men!' she grumbled. *What* was wrong now?

They gobbled up the sandwiches and swigged lemonade

out of the bottles, saving some for later. She rubbed an apple on her damp costume till it shone, and offered it to him. He moved closer leaning on one arm. 'Are you trying to tempt me, woman, like Eve in the garden of Eden?'

This was more like it. She grinned. 'But you don't believe in the Bible.'

'Well, there are times when it suits me to refer to it. More romantic – '

'Than monkeys?'

'Definitely. And today you look just like Eve must have done when she offered the fruit of the Tree of Knowledge to Adam and – '

'Give over – have a bite. I'm afraid I've forgotten me snake.'

She put the red apple to his lips and he took a bite. Examining his teeth marks in the white flesh, with the tender pink stain just beneath the skin, she overlapped the toothsome wound, taking a bite herself. The juice ran down over her bottom lip as her eyes sparkled up at him. He groaned, and his expression stilled her laughter, captured her breath.

Stonewall lowered his head and delicately licked the juice from her rounded chin, the tip of his tongue trailing upwards to tease her lip. The eroticism of his action sent a shaft of sweet pleasure to the core of her body and she trembled. Keeping her lips parted, she closed her eyes. His mouth came down on hers, moving with gentle pressure and she responded with ardour.

His hand cupped her breast and she shivered.

'You're sweet,' he murmured. 'Apple and salt on a lovely girl's lips. Quite a heady combination.'

Queenie snorted. 'Quite a heady combination,' she teased, laughter in her eyes. 'Does that mean it was nice?'

'Nice,' he agreed.

They went on sharing bites of apple, kisses and giggles, until it was finished, eating it right down to the stalk. 'Phh.' As Queenie spat out some pips she noticed a group of children watching them and smirking. Spoiling it. 'Enjoy the peepshow?' she called crossly, even though she would have done the same thing herself not so long ago.

'Let's go for a walk down to the Point,' she suggested. 'We can have another swim on the way back.' They pulled their clothes on over their still-damp costumes and she lent Stonewall her comb, delighting in the way he swept back his straightened hair with it, then pushed it forward in one or two places to encourage the natural wave back.

'Vanity,' she chided. 'Want the mirror?'

The children poked their tongues out at Queenie as she passed, and she returned the compliment over her shoulder, careful that Stonewall did not witness her childish behaviour.

Once through the gate, they wandered down Broad Street and cut down an alley to the Round Tower. Across the harbour, they could see the submarine base at Gosport. 'My Dad was stationed at HMS *Dolphin*, off and on.'

'Thought a lot of your dad, didn't you?' Stonewall asked, tucking a strand of almost dry hair behind her ear in a tender gesture.

'He was a wonderful man. My mother never . . .' she bit her lip. 'He was ever so kind and I was his favourite, being the only girl. He used to tell us wonderful stories.' Her eyes filled with tears. 'It's sad that the people we love most have to die so soon.'

Stonewall tilted her chin with his long fingers and touched her lips with his. Queenie threw her arms around his neck. 'And now I love you!'

'I hope that's not a bad omen,' he joked, but she felt his withdrawal from her before he removed her arms gently. *Oh, she was a fool to say that.*

'Seriously, Queenie, I like you a lot, but I don't want you to get too fond of me. I'm going away for two years soon, and when I return I'll expect to see you married with a couple of kids. I think you're a sweet girl and good fun.

But I'm not the marrying kind. I thought we could have a bit of fun together for a few weeks. That's all.'

Queenie's long eyelashes, unadorned with mascara today as she was swimming, swept down. 'Of course,' she said lightly, though her heart was clenched in her breast, 'that's all I want, too.'

They walked hand-in-hand down Broad Street, Queenie trying to be cheerful and not to dwell on what he had just said. Give her half a chance and she bet she could change his mind for him.

They watched the car-ferry leave Point for Gosport on clanking chains, and Stonewall pointed out and named some naval ships they could see in the dockyard, past the pier. They had a cup of tea in a café, then swam again in deep water at Point, from the little beach next to the old weather-boarded Quebec House built out into the sea.

Now that a few kisses had been exchanged, and he had set limits to their relationship which appeared to be acceptable to her, they allowed themselves further intimacies. She splashed him in order to be grabbed in retaliation and his hands circled her waist and fondled her hips. She was so glad that he did not duck her, as most boys would have done, to prove their masculinity. Winding her arms around his neck, her legs about his thighs, she nibbled his ears. And thrilled to his kisses.

They walked hand-in-hand back to Vernon for five o'clock because he was on duty that evening.

'I'll say goodbye now and go on ahead of you,' he told her, curiously stiff now as they approached the gates, in case they should be observed by any naval personnel. 'I've enjoyed the day very much. I'll come in for some chish and fips one night and see you home.'

Queenie nodded, her throat constricted with disappointment as she watched him go, as usual without a backward glance. How *could* he be so casual after the wonderful day they had spent together? Didn't he feel like she did?

Excited by their kisses, wanting more, knowing that they were meant for each other. *She loved him.*

But there, she tried to console herself, men were a bit shy talking about their feelings, weren't they? In spite of his warning that he was only after a good time, she was sure he loved her too. He just needed time. Every man wanted to get married in the end, didn't they?

Stonewall whistled 'It was just one of those things', as he walked jauntily back to the Ratings' Barracks in Warrior Block. The sun, the relaxation, the sexual excitement and the fun of Queenie's company gave him a feeling of well-being and virility.

She was quite a girl. Spirited, beautiful and boy! did she know how to use her eyes to stir a fellow up! Good for a bit of fun. He'd been hopelessly attracted to her from the night he first saw her in Fred's Famous Fish and Chip Shop. Her saucy look – full of life and promise, and the way her face lit up when she talked about her father. Pity about the Pompey accent.

He knew that she fancied herself in love with him, but girls fell in and out love all the time, didn't they? It was the centre of their universe. He just hoped she would not become too clinging. She had said she trusted *him*, but he had given her fair warning. It was up to her now.

He did a little jump in the air, clicking his heels together. He really liked Queenie. To be honest, he much preferred her type to the Cynthias and Beryls of this world that his mother was always trying to pair him off with, well-brought up young ladies who looked as though butter wouldn't melt in their mouths.

With girls like Queenie, and Sylvie, the little waitress he had gone out with when he was at Portland, you knew where you were. They were straightforward, said what they meant. You didn't have to pussy-foot around. Well, he certainly didn't have to with Sylvie. She came up trumps and furthered his sexual education for him.

And now, Queenie May. Well, Queenie may – or Queenie may not! But he rather thought she would.

# · *Six* ·

Portsdown Hill basked lazily under a cobalt sky on Stonewall's last day in Portsmouth before his posting to join Battleship *Barham* in Plymouth.

Queenie and he strolled hand-in-hand through dry grass studded with daisies, dandelions and lilac-coloured scabious. Here a clump of bristling musk thistles with crimson flowers, and there clusters of yellow lady's bedstraw. A warm breeze swept up the hill, stirring the long grasses and their hair, and carrying summer smells to their nostrils. Stonewall's shirtsleeves were rolled up, his top buttons undone and he carried the picnic basket in his other hand with his sports jacket threaded through the handle. Swinging her white handbag to and fro, Queenie was wearing the blue dress he liked so much.

'I shouldn't think the Med could be much warmer than this,' she remarked.

'Probably not. But at least, out there, you know it's going to last. It may be pouring with rain here next week.' The sun illuminated his eyes to a brighter green and glinted off his teeth as he smiled at her.

'You're really excited, aren't you, you lucky old sod?'

He laughed. 'It'll be more fun doing something useful out there than waiting around in Blighty for a war to break out.'

'Even though I'm here?' she asked lightly, but her heart was heavy with the certainty that even if he was given the choice he would choose to go. 'That's men for you,' she went on before he could offer a less than sincere comment.

'But – you don't really think there's going to be a war, do you?'

'Sooner or later, I'm afraid. Europe is in turmoil, isn't it? Fascism, Communism, Republicanism, Nationalism – this trouble brewing up in Spain.'

'But we're just a little island – we can keep out of it, can't we?'

He stopped and put an arm around her shoulders and she placed hers around his waist and snuggled up against him. She could feel the warmth of his flesh through the cotton, smell his shaving soap, see the pores in his skin. Pressing her lips against the base of his throat, she felt a pulse beating. She wanted to melt into him, become part of him.

Resting his chin on the top of her head, he said, 'We are not going to worry about such things today. It's just you and me up here surveying the scene below – like gods on Mount Olympus. Just look at that view. Reminds me of that poem about this sceptred isle being set in a silver sea, or something like that?'

'What does sceptred mean?'

'Er, sort of regal, I suppose.'

'I'm goin' to miss all your long words and pomes and things,' she mourned. 'Look,' she pointed, 'you can see right over to the Isle of Wight, and the forts in the Solent. I wonder how they managed to build them in the water all those years ago.'

'And the Nab Tower off the end of the Island and the English Channel beyond. The moat around our castle.'

'Those cranes are the dockyard and look at all the ships, and that spire is St Mary's church.'

'I didn't appreciated that Portsmouth is so much an island,' he said as he looked down at the causeway that joined it to the mainland. 'It's all so flat, but the Isle of Wight is hilly.'

'Yes. And that's Langstone Harbour and Hayling Island

to the left and Portchester in the other direction, across the water. Look, you can see the square castle.'

'My parents live not far from the castle.'

Will I ever meet them? she wondered. Will I ever see him again after today? Pain wrenched at her heart and tears flooded her eyes, but she didn't want him to see them. Emotions like that just embarrassed men. She wanted him to remember her as a cheerful fun-loving girl – a girl he'd want to come back to.

They had enjoyed being together for these few weeks; going to the pictures, the beach, an occasional dance at South Parade Pier, or just a drink in a pub. And all the time she had been falling deeper and deeper in love with Stonewall. But she still did not know exactly how he felt about her. She told herself that he did not want to become too involved because he was going away.

But she knew what he was really after, of course. He had 'tried it on' with her a few times, and though she had allowed him certain intimacies, she always stopped him before it had gone too far. She wanted him all right, longed to make love with him, but she knew it was wrong and, far more important, she didn't want him thinking that she was 'easy' and cheap.

'Shall we sit here and eat?' he asked. They were standing just below the dark brick fort. Queenie nodded and he spread out his jacket for her to sit on. 'We don't want you getting all prickled by the grass.'

'But it'll crease,' she remarked.

'It doesn't matter. I've got to drop a lot of gear over to Portchester tonight. Mum will take it to the cleaners for me.' He flopped down beside her. They lay back with eyes closed for a while, dozing in the warmth of the sun and listening to the drone of nectar-seeking bees.

'You will write to me, won't you?' she asked tentatively, propping herself up on one elbow and looking yearningly at him.

'Why not?' he murmured sleepily.

'And send me a photo now and then?'

'Mmm.'

She sat up and opened her bag. 'I've writ down Pearl's address for you. She says you can send letters there for me. Ma would only create if they came to Baker Street. And I'll write to Able Seaman Stonewall Jackson, HMS *Barham* – where? You'll put your full address won't you?' She leaned over him, pushed the folded paper into his breast pocket, and picking a piece of grass, tickled his nose with it.

He opened his eyes and gazed into hers with a chuckle. Where they had been luminous in the sun earlier, they were now darker in her shadow. He grabbed her hand. 'Stop that, woman. Listen, if you want me to get your letters you'd better address them to *Keith* Jackson!'

'Keith! Why didn't you tell me, you mean thing?' She thumped his chest playfully. 'I thought Stonewall was a funny sort of name.'

'Naval nickname for Jacksons – after Stonewall Jackson.'

'Who's he when 'es at home?'

'An American President, you little ignoramus.'

'Well, I'm not ejucated like you, am I? *Keith*. Keith. I like it. And I like you.' She planted a kiss on his mouth. He put his arms around her and returned it enthusiastically. 'Now, now,' she laughed, pulling away. 'I know where this sort of thing can lead to. Food first.'

'And what are you promising for afterwards?' He sat up grinning.

'Have to wait and see, won't you,' she said with a provocative pout.

'You're an awful tease, Queen of the May.'

'I know, it's part of my charm.' She lifted a parcel of sandwiches out of the basket. 'Ham. That all right? I managed to wangle the day off with Fred, but Ma'd kill me if she knew I was up here with you today.'

'Why haven't I met your Ma? Anyone would think you were ashamed of me.' He bit into a sandwich.

'Oh, no! I'm proud of you. Really, really proud. It's just that . . . well, it doesn't matter now does it? When you come back it will be all right. I'll be . . . older then, won't I? Ow,' she wailed, 'how am I going to live without you for two whole bleedin' years?'

Keith reached out and stroked her bare leg from her knee to her ankle. She thrilled to his touch. 'You'll survive, Queen of the May, that's what you're good at. Mmm. Sun-toasted flesh. I could eat you.'

'Have another sandwich, cannibal.' Laughing, she thrust one between his teeth. 'Will you think about me while you're away?'

He studied her while he chewed. 'I'll remember you just as you are today, in your blue dress that matches your lovely eyes. And your hair – in the sun it's got a sheen on it like a blackbird's wing.'

'Coo, you do say nice things.' She looked at him shyly from under her lashes. 'You make me feel all googly.'

'I wonder what else I could make you feel, given half a chance?'

Queenie threw him a saucy glance before pulling out some biscuits, apples and a bottle of ginger beer from the basket. When they got to the apples, they shared one as they had done on Sally Port beach a few weeks previously, their heads close together, nibbling at it, exchanging juicy kisses in between.

Keith unbuttoned his shirt and pulled it off. Taking a silver flask from his hip pocket, he grinned at her as he unscrewed the top and, throwing back his head, took a long swallow from it. Queenie, her breath quickening, watched his throat working, ran her eyes over his shoulders and chest, wanting to stroke his smooth skin, to be naked with him. He offered the flask to her. She wrinkled her nose. 'What is it?'

'Rum. Coming from a naval family, I'd have thought you were brought up on it. Go on, have a drop.'

It was horrible. 'You trying to get me tipsy?' she spluttered.

'Of course – so I can have my wicked way with you.' His hazel eyes held hers captive, sent a message tingling through her, to lodge in the core of her body with an aching sweetness that begged for relief.

Her heart beast fast. She felt giddy. Tomorrow he was going away. She had so long to wait, and there was a strong chance that she might never see him again. And if she didn't, she might never meet another man who made her feel her like this. It was wrong, she knew, but perhaps if she did . . . it would make him want to come back to her. She swallowed. 'I wouldn't mind . . .'

The world stopped turning as they stared at each other, and the air became charged with sexual tension. Keith moved towards her as if in a dream and bore her back onto his jacket. He lowered his head to hers and kissed her deeply, then his mouth roamed over her face and throat, sending more of those delicious tingles through her. Her hands caressed his upper body. He moved himself onto her and she welcomed his weight, wishing absurdly that he would crush her into the chalky soil of this hillside and leave her imprint here forever.

'Queenie,' he muttered against her throat.

'Will you come back to me?' she cried, opening her eyes into the unfathomable depths of his.

His answer was another kiss that ravaged her senses. Moving his weight off her, he unbuttoned her bodice, pulling her brassière down off her breasts and suckling her nipples. Queenie moaned in fearful delight, wondering what was happening to her body. His hand smoothed up the length of her thighs and between them. She parted her legs and, through the daze felt him rip off her knickers, felt his weight upon her again, and gave a little shriek of pain as he entered her. 'You will come back to me?' she implored before all her sensory perceptions combined in quivering response to his assault.

A feeling of unbearable pleasure was just beginning to escalate within her when he gasped and collapsed upon her. Coming down to earth, Queenie was puzzled. What had happened – or what had not happened? 'That was lovely,' Keith muttered against her neck. It had obviously been all he had expected and that was all that mattered. Her heart swelled with pride at the pleasure she had given him. 'I love you, Keith Jackson,' she murmured, running her fingers through his hair.

'I promise I'll write,' Keith assured her, taking Queenie's hand as they paused outside St George's church where he had walked with her after getting off the tram.

'Take care of yourself,' she said brightly, 'and don't do nothin' I wouldn't do.'

'I won't.' He smiled gently. 'Well, I'd better be off. Be happy, Queen of the May.' He bent and kissed her quickly on the mouth and she knew that he was relieved she was not going to be clinging.

'I'll try,' she said in a strangled voice, knowing that if he didn't go immediately she would embarrass him horribly by dissolving into the floods of tears that she was struggling to hold back.

He walked away – taking her dreams with him. At the railway arch, he turned and waved briefly before disappearing from view. Not only had he never *hinted* at marriage, he had not even told her that he loved her. Even after making love to her in the grass, he had not said 'I love you'. He had promised he would write, but for how long? The man she would die for had walked away from her with no promises for the future.

Her throat aching with suppressed sorrow, Queenie let herself into the church. She couldn't go home in this state. A quick glance round showed her that she was mercifully alone. Leaning against a pillar, she enclosed her face in her hands and gave way to a storm of grief. Eventually the sobs that racked her body subsided to an intermittent shuddering, and she raised her blotched face with its swollen eyes. She'd have to think up a good excuse for going home looking like this.

She loved Keith Jackson with every ounce of energy in her body, yet she had known from the beginning that he was going away. Perhaps she had just been a fool, but there was nothing else she could have done. She had felt that it was fate that had brought them together and she still did. *Of course* he would come back to her.

Meanwhile, she had to soldier on, pretending at home that he had never existed, and waiting for his letters. How was she ever going to get through the next two years? If she could be sure that he felt the same way about her, she could just about bear it. She had given him all she had to give – her heart and her body, yet he had never even said that he loved her.

'Oh, Dad,' she sobbed. 'I've lost you, and I've lost the only other man I'll ever love.'

# · Seven ·

At her mother's call, Queenie dragged herself miserably out of bed. Her stomach immediately revolted against the vertical position and she pulled out the chipped chamber-pot from under her bed and vomited into it.

Sitting on the edge of her bed, she wiped her clammy face. She felt awful and had done for weeks. Catching sight of herself in the splotched mirror over her chest of drawers, she saw that she looked awful too. Ghostly white, dark shadows under her eyes from worry and lack of sleep, and stringy hair.

She put her hands on her stomach. It felt normal, but ignorant though she was about most of the facts of life, she was pretty sure about her condition – and she knew she could not hide it much longer.

'Ma will *kill* me,' she told her reflection, and she began to shiver. 'Oh, why did this 'ave to happen? Why did I let him do it?'

Such terrifying results from so little. She never meant to have a baby from it, and that was all his fault. Keith Jackson was the one who ought to have known better. He was a sailor, a man of the world and five years older than she was.

And it wasn't as if she had even enjoyed it that much. No. It was a big disappointment. It had hurt at first and then, just as she was beginning to experience some pleasure, it was all over. And so messy!

It wasn't her fault, was it, that no-one had explained the facts of life to her properly? The little she knew she had learned from snippets she had overheard, and the whispered sniggers of her friends. She couldn't expect her older brothers to explain such an embarrassing subject, but how could Ma be so prudish after all her pregnancies?

And Vera, Billy's wife – she could have explained things when *she* got pregnant. Queenie had hoped for great things when Vera married into the family – a sister, a confidante. But her sister-in-law was a spiteful, stuck-up cow. Jealous, that's what she was.

Tears trickled down Queenie's cheeks and she wiped them away fiercely with the back of her hand. Where was *he* – the cause of her distress – now?

He had promised her letters and she had been overjoyed at receiving one from Gibraltar. Pearl had brought it to work with her and they had pored over the enclosed photo together – Stonewall with a beard, standing with two shipmates on the deck of HMS *Barham*. They were dressed in white tropical uniform and looking very dashing. He was smiling and her heart had swelled with love and pride.

But there had been no more letters. Every day for weeks she had gone hopefully to wrok, her heart in her mouth as Pearl came in, only to have her hopes cruelly shattered when Pearl shook her head. Keith Jackson had thrown her love back at her – unwanted – and now he was enjoying himself in some warm, exotic place, while she shivered, scared stiff, in her cold attic room.

Her eyes moved over the few miserable bits of furniture, the damp stains on the wallpaper under the window, the threadbare rug at the side of her bed, the faded and torn curtain at the little window set in the roof. The downstairs rooms were nicer, but she had chosen to move up here after Billy had moved out, for its privacy and the glimpse of the harbour from the window. She had always intended to do it up, but when it came to it she'd preferred to buy clothes and a little bit of make-up with the pittance she was allowed to keep out of her earnings.

It didn't matter now, anyway. Ma was probably going

to chuck her out. But where could she go? How could she look after a baby on her own? She was only sixteen. Fear gripped her, adding to her nausea.

It was Saturday, her one in four off, thank goodness. But Ma was at home, and she was going to have to sneak the poe past her to the lav. She held it in the crook of her arm, and, draping a towel over both, shakily negotiated the two flights of stairs.

'Not dressed yet?' Beatie Ellis threw her a sharp look from where she stood at the kitchen table, cutting towards her the loaf of bread held against her aproned chest.

Queenie swayed and leant against the door-frame hazily surveying the familiar room – the hub of the house. The table, covered with oil-cloth whose pattern had almost worn off, with an assortment of wooden chairs around it. Two shabby brown armchairs sagging either side of the black range, protected from greasy heads by hand-worked lace antimacassars, a rag rug on the patterned lino between them. Cream-painted cupboards, housing crockery and pots and pans, were built into the recesses on either side of the range. The mantelpiece was cluttered with tins, ornaments, a box of spills, letters, the old wooden clock. Last year's flower calendar hung on one wall and a picture of *Christ, Light Of The World* on another. The battered high chair resided in a corner, awaiting the next little Ellis bottom. Through the window, a view of the yard and a high brick wall. This is what I wanted to get away from, Queenie told herself, but now she'd give anything to be allowed to stay.

'Get a move on,' chided Beatie, 'I want you to go up the Landport Drapery Bazaar and get some of that crinkly wool that Lil got. I'll knit a nice little suit for Vera's Ronnie.'

Queenie doubted very much that the same offer would be made for *this* baby when Ma found out about it. It was on the tip of her tongue to say that she wasn't well enough to go, but then she would have to answer akward questions. She went down the yard to the lav to empty the poe, rinsed it under the outside tap and washed her face and hands in the scullery.

Coming back up the step into the kitchen, the room suddenly swam before her eyes and she staggered against the wall.

'What on earth's wrong with you?' her mother cried. 'You look like death warmed up.'

Queenie, groaning, sank onto a chair, one hand supporting her drooping head. 'Must be somethink I've ate. Don't feel well.'

'You better have a cup of tea.' Beatie poured her one from the ever-brewing brown teapot with the coloured rings around it, spooned some sugar into it and tipped in a dollop of condensed milk from a tin. Stirring it, she passed it to her daughter. 'This'll settle your stomick.'

Queenie's stomach rejected the strong brew and the chamber pot received its second offering that morning.

'My word, you are bad! Better get back to bed.'

At the unaccustomed sympathy Queenie almost blurted out her problems – but could not quite find the courage. Her throat hurt from the need to cry, but determined not to give way to tears, she sat with her elbows on the table and her face hidden in her hands.

Eventually, her mother's unnatural silence clamoured at her consciousness. She raised her eyes slowly to encounter the appalled suspicion in Beatie's black eyes. 'Been 'aving your monthlies regular, 'ave you?' she asked sharply. A year ago, Beatie would have known. She would have seen her daughter boiling up her rags once a month, but since she'd been earning more money, Queenie had been buying those new-fangled Kotex Towels. Girls had fancy ideas these days. 'I'm askin' you a question.'

Queenie's eyes fell. The game was up. She shook her head. 'I've missed three,' she muttered.

'Oh, my Gawd!' Beatie's voice rose in a wailing crescendo. 'Oh! You-wicked-little-slut!' Emphasising each word. 'As If I haven't got enough troubles on me plate. Who was it?' She grabbed a handful of the girl's hair and shook her by it. 'Who you been with? I didn't even know you was seeing anyone.' Slapping her daughter about the head and face, she screamed, 'I'll swing for him, so help me God!'

Queenie raised her arm in an attempt to fend her off. 'I couldn't help it, Ma. He *made* me.'

'I'll give you – ' Another blow fell. '*Who was it?*'

'He's ever so nice, Ma. He's a sailor – '

'A *sailor*?' she shrieked. 'That's all we need. Did you tell 'im you was only sixteen?'

Queenie shook her head.

'You little fool. How could you? You was brought up respectable.' Her mother was shaking with rage. 'I'll soon fix 'im.' She walked towards the door. 'I'll get Lil, she'll know what to do.'

'Oh no, Ma. Can't we keep Lil out of it?' Once their neighbour knew, it would be all over the street before you could say fish and chips.

Beatie rounded on her furiously. 'Lil's my dearest friend. Been by my side through thick and thin. I don't know how I would have managed without her. The things she's done for me! Laid out your poor, dead feather – '

'I know, Ma, I know. She's a good friend. It's just that I'd rather she didn't – '

Arms akimbo, Beatie rasped, 'Well, that's too bad, ain't it. What makes you think you're in any position to make demands?' She went to the back door, opened it and screamed for Lil.

'What is it, Beat?' Lil's anxious voice wafted over the wall of the back yard.

'Get in here, for God's sake.'

Two minutes later, Lil came stampeding through the door like a runaway elephant.

At the same moment, a sleepy-looking Jimmy appeared,

pyjama-clad, in the kitchen doorway. 'What's going on? What's all the shouting about?' he asked.

'Get out,' yelled his mother. 'It's women's business. Go and get Josh up. Go on!'

Scowling, he went, his mother following him to the door and giving him a cuff round the ear when she found him outside it. 'No eavesdropping,' she yelled and he fled.

'Fer Chris'sake, Beat, what's 'appened?' Lil shouted.

Lil always shouted. Anything less would have been inappropriate to her size and her sense of drama. Now she brushed back her ever-untidy, bleached hair with an impatient hand.

Beatie waved a hand at her daughter who sat rocking back and forth, her hand nursing her stinging ear and red cheek. 'Can you believe it, Lil? This little madam has got herself . . .'

Reading her friend's eloquent expression, Lil's mouth dropped open. 'You don't mean she's . . .?'

Beatie nodded and sank down, deflated, onto a chair.

'Oh my God, Beat,' Lil shrieked. 'As if you 'aven't got enough on your plate!'

'Exactly what I said.' Beatie, undone by her neighbour's rough sympathy, gave way to tears.

Lil, patting her much smaller friend on the back, glared accusingly at Queenie. 'I always said *you'd* come to a sticky end, my girl. Too big for your boots, that's you.'

Queenie tossed back her hair and narrowed her eyes at her. Being their neighbour since long before any of the Ellis children had been born, Lil always thought she had the right to speak her mind – but this was none of her damned business. Queenie knew Lil had had it in for her ever since she refused to go out with her nosy son. Queenie loathed Dick – 'Spotty Dick' they called him because of his acne – who, from an unattractive and sly boy, had grown into an even less attractive youth.

'Sit down, Lil.' Beatie sniffed wetly and wiped her hot

cheeks on her apron. 'Pour yerself a cuppa and tell me what should I do?'

It was apparent to all three present that Beatrice Ellis needed no-one's help. The hardships life had thrown at her had not vanquished her, but had served only to reinforce her determination to overcome all obstacles and make the best she could of the little she had. Nevertheless, it was a relief to pour her troubles into a sympathetic ear. 'It's some bloody sailor she's been goin' out with. I never knew nothink about it – sly little cow. But he's going to pay for this.'

'I should think so – the rotten bastard! But *you* should have known better,' Lil shouted at Queenie, her pale eyes sparking.

Queenie's lips tightened. 'Known better? *I* didn't know nothink, did I?' She looked accusingly at Beatie. 'Nobody ever *bothered* to explain the facts of life to me.' Her mother's face reddened.

'Thought the stork brought them, did you?' Lil laughed nastily, spooning sugar into her tea.

'No – they grow under gooseberry bushes, don't they?' Queenie flared at her.

'That's enough of that! Show some respect,' Beatie said fiercely. 'How many times did it 'appen?'

'Only the once . . . The day before he went away.'

'That makes it all right, does it?'

Queenie was suddenly anxious to exonerate herself. 'No, Ma, but I thought it would be all right, din't I? Billy and Vera had married for over a year before she fell.'

'That's because they was careful. They didn't want kids straight away.'

'What d'you mean?' A frown creased Queenie's brow. 'How was they careful? You mean they didn't . . . do it?'

'Bit bloody late for a lesson in birth control, ain't it?' blustered Beatie, who, after several miscarriages and nine live births, of which six survived, had plucked up the courage to go with Lil to the Co-op Guild to hear Dr

Marie Stopes talk about 'family planning'. An exercise which had nevertheless failed to prevent the birth of two more children. 'I'll go up the Navy authorities, that's what I'll do. And he'll 'ave to marry you – that's all there is to it.'

'Hallelujah!' This being Lil's favourite word for expressing agreement, joy or exasperation.

'He can't!' Queenie wiped the perspiration from her brow.

Beatie's hand went to her mouth. 'Oh, my God – he ain't married already, is he?'

'No, he ain't. He's only twenty-one.'

'Old enough to know what to do with it, and old enough to know 'e shouldn't,' observed Lil sagely.

'He's gone away on his ship.'

'Where to?' Beatie shrieked.

'The Mediterranean.'

'The Med? For Chris'sake! He'll be away for at least two years. How we goin' to manage when you have to give up work, I'd like to know. It's difficult enough now.'

Beatie and Lil exchanged a horrified look.

'I'll manage – somehow.' Queenie looked more defiant than she felt.

'Well.' Lil lowered her voice conspiratorially. 'There's always the other alternative. *You* know . . .'

Beatie's eyes widened. 'No! I wouldn't dream of it. Apart from the fact that I can't find that sort of money, it's too bloody dangerous. Look what 'appened to Liz Parkins, and Mrs Browne's daughter. Betty was only fifteen, poor little kid.'

'What?' Queenie's eyes went from one to the other. 'What happened to them?' Having been excluded from the whispered scandals, she had never found out what horrible thing those two had died from. But she *had* gathered that it was illegal – though how you could die from something illegal, she had never fathomed.

'Never you mind.' Beatie and Lil's expressions were guarded as her mother dismissed her question.

'Adoption, then?' Lil suggested. 'There's that nice place up Mile End where girls can go and – '

'No!' Queenie interrupted, surprising herself. She had not yet really thought this thing through, being too worried about the discovery. But now that it was all out in the open, she knew suddenly that whatever happened, she was going to keep this baby. It might even be a girl. Unexpected joy flooded her and she placed a hand on her stomach.

Witnessing this, Beatie nodded in agreement. 'No adoption. We always look after our own in this family. You'd do the same, Lil, you know you would.'

The daughter met her mother's eyes with a rare look of gratitude. 'I – I'll write to him, Ma. And to his mother. I found out her address in Portchester.'

'Portchester,' Beatie exclaimed. 'We'll go and see 'er, then. *She'll* see that justice is done.'

'I wouldn't count on it,' Queenie's face was red with embarrassment. 'I haven't met her but from what I've heard, she's . . . a bit posh.'

'Oh. Posh is she? My daughter ain't good enough for 'er? I'll give 'er posh. What does the father do then?'

'He's a commercial traveller.'

'A bloody salesman! What's she got to be so superior about?'

'His grandfather's a tailor. Quite well-off. He's got a Gentleman's Outfitters in Derby – '

'You mean a shop, do you? You've got all bloody posh too, lately, haven't you?' smirked Lil.

'As I was saying before Lil put her oar in – his father left the firm because of a family row.'

'Couldn't your sailor-boy 'ave worked for 'is Grandad then?' asked Lil. 'Better prospects than the Navy, I'd 'ave thought.'

'He din't want to feel trapped.'

'Well, he's trapped 'isself now, all right,' sneered their neighbour.

Queenie's eyes smouldered at her.

'Right!' Beatie's mind was made up. 'We'll go over there this afternoon.'

'No, Ma!' Queenie begged. 'There must be somethink else – '

'We're going. He'll 'ave to pay up while he's away, face up to his responsibilities. Can you come with us, Lil?'

Their neighbour smiled happily. 'I wouldn't miss it for anythink.'

Queenie's temper erupted. She jumped to her feet. 'Shall we ask Shirley from number fourteen if she'd like to come? Why not invite the whole bloody street while we're about it? They'll all know soon enough anyway.' She threw Lil a venomous look.

'Don't you give us any back-chat, you little madam,' Beatie shouted. 'I suppose you're proud of yourself?'

Queenie stared at her mother for a moment, almost with dislike. 'I'm not *proud* of myself.'

'She's got that look of 'er father's,' offered Lil. 'I always said Joshua spoiled her.'

'*You* leave my Dad out of it,' Queenie snapped, but Lil couldn't have paid her a greater compliment. She threw back her head. 'No, I'm not *proud* of myself, but I'm not *ashamed* neither.'

'Hallelujah!' exclaimed Lil, shocked.

Stiff-backed, Queenie walked with great dignity from the room. Past her goggle-eyed, listening brothers in the passage where the washing was strung up to dry because it had rained yesterday. Up the shabbily-carpeted stairs to her room under the eaves.

Throwing herself on her bed and beating it with her fists, she moaned, 'Oh Dad, why did this 'ave to happen?' She was too angry to cry and after a few minutes she got up and stomped over to the window. The little glimpse of the harbour between the roofs and chimneys held no enchantment for her today. In a month or two, this little window would be glazed with frosty patterns, and she'd be huddled up in bed with her stone hot water botttle giving her chilblains. And *he* was carefree and happy in the sunshine!'

She went to her chest of drawers and took out from under her clean knickers the little photograph he had sent her enclosed in the only letter she had received from him. 'A life on the ocean wave'. All right for some! Swanning around the Med in the sunshine, while she was facing the music on her own in Pompey in grey November. And this afternoon she had to go and bloody well break the news his Mum.

'You rotten *sod*!' she shrieked, tearing up the photograph and stamping on it.

# · *Eight* ·

Queenie sat miserably behind the two gossiping women on the long motor bus jouney to Portchester, watching their hats bobbing towards each other, but too busy with her own worries to listen to her mother and Lil. She felt sick, but had no way of knowing how much was due to pregnancy and how much to nerves.

Ma and Lil had dragged her round to Nurse Hebdon that morning to have her sins confirmed by the midwife's probing fingers. A pleasant and discreet woman who had been involved in most of Beatie's pregnancies, but for Queenie, the examination had been shameful. Fanny Hebdon had given her some advice on diet and told her when to go back for a check-up.

At last, after a change of bus at Cosham, they arrived at Portchester Castle. Beatie and Lil had asked directions to Sea Lane when they alighted, and now Queenie followed them along a pleasant tree-lined avenue of semi-detached houses – a far cry from the narrow, crowded streets of Portsea.

Queenie wished they had come without their neighbour. She was sure she would only be an added embarrassment. She watched with fascination as the vast twin orbs of Lil's rump jostled for room under her tightly-stretched coat. The woman was enormous. Next to her, Ma, although a plump little thing, looked quite dainty.

They slowed down, searching gates and doors for numbers. On reaching number thirty-one, smartly white-washed, and bay-windowed with those little stained-glass friezes at the top, her mother turned to her. 'This is it, then.' Only the sheen of perspiration on Beatie's face showed that she was nervous, out of her element in this smart residential area.

They walked up a path between neat flowering borders and smooth lawns and into a little porch. Beatie pressed a bell beside the oak door. Queenie's knees were knocking and she was sure she was going to throw up at any moment. But no-one answered.

Her mother lifted the wrought-iron handle and knocked. They waited. 'Oh, my gawd, we've come all this way and had all this expense for nothin'.'

Queenie was faint with relief.

Beatie stepped out of the porch and looked anxiously up at the top windows, as if expecting to see someone peeping down from behind the curtains. Then she put one foot into the flower border, her other leg held out behind her like an arthritic ballet-dancer, and placing her hands at the sides of her eyes to shut out the sunlight, she peered in through one of the bay windows.

'Ma-a!'

'You should see the furniture they've got,' her mother grumbled. 'They're not short of a bob or two.'

'*Excuse me!*' said a cultured voice. 'Can I help you?' They looked up to see a neighbour eyeing them suspiciously over the hedge.

'We want to see Mrs Jackson,' Beatie informed her.

'She's out shopping – hasn't been gone long. Can I do anything to help?' Terribly genteel.

'Well, I think we'd better wait,' Beatie said. 'It's about her eldest son.'

'Ma!' warned Queenie.

'He's away at sea,' the neighbour said.

'We know that, that's why we come all the way from Portsmouth to see 'is mother. He's got my girl into trouble.'

'Oh, Ma!' Queenie's face flamed.

'Into trouble?' asked the woman, apparently uncomprehending.

Delicately, for so large a woman, Lil stepped over the flower border. Leaning confidentially over the fence, she imparted the nature of the trouble. The woman's eyes grew round and she raised her hand to her mouth. Queenie stared defiantly at her.

'You'd better come in and have a cup of tea.' Suddenly friendly – no doubt curious to hear a bit more about the misdemeanours of her neighbour's son. 'You can't stand out there all afternoon.'

Beatie and Lil needed no second bidding and were up her path before she could say Jack Robinson. They were shown into a front room crammed with large chintz-covered furniture and ornaments.

'Do sit down. I won't be a jiffy.' She left the room to make the tea.

Beatie and Lil looked critically around the room.

'I don't like those china dogs on the mantelpiece,' Beatie observed in a stage-whisper. 'Pekes, ain't they? I think them white plaster Alsations you brought me back from Petticoat Lane are much nicer, our Queen.'

'Why did you have to tell *her* our business, Ma? Mrs Jackson might not have wanted her to know.'

Her mother shrugged. 'She knows what *she* can do then! *I* feel better for getting it off me chest.'

The neighbour returned with a tray of dainty cups of tea and some biscuits. 'Help yourself, do.' She held the tray in front of Lil, who spooned in several scoops of sugar and took a fistful of biscuits.

When they all had a cup of tea in their hands – Queenie's rattling in the saucer with nervousness – their hostess sat down and looked from one to the other with an eager expression on her face. 'What a dreadful thing to happen. Always was a bit of a lad, that one.'

Queenie sat pale and tight-lipped as her mother elaborated on the 'dreadful thing'. Between slurps of tea and with her mouth full of biscuit, Lil added a few frills. Queenie noticed with distaste the livid mottled scorch marks on Lil's legs, from always huddling over the fire.

After about half an hour and a change of topic to the scandalous cost of living, their hostess, who had been keeping her eye on the window, jumped up. 'There's Violet now,' she announced with barely suppressed excitement. 'Perhaps I'd better come out with you.'

Queenie wanted to die all over again. They followed the woman out through the door. 'Violet,' she called gaily, waving her hand with little rapid movements.

The middle-aged woman in the next garden looked up from her examination of a flower bed.

'I've been looking after some of your visitors, dear. They've come such a long way – so sad. I couldn't leave them on the door step, could I?'

Violet Jackson, a slim, good-looking woman, dressed in cream and brown and a cloche hat, raised her eyebrows. 'I suppose not. But I don't believe I know . . .?'

The neighbour stuck her face forward, saying confidentially, 'It's er, rather a delicate matter, dear.'

Mrs Jackson frowned, then shrugged. 'I really can't imagine . . . You'd better come round then.' She picked up her basket and preceded her uninvited guests to the front door. Leading them inside, she put her gloves on the hallstand, lifted off her hat and patted her brown Marcel-waved hair, then opened the door to the front room, standing aside to let them go through. Once through the door they all stood looking at each other.

'I'm sure I've no idea what you have come about. I've never met you, have I?' Queenie quaked inwardly at her cultured tone and the very superior expression on her face. She looked them over, with hazel eyes so like her son's, as if she had no great desire to meet them.

'It's about my girl,' Beatie began bravely, though the perspiration was back on her face. 'She's a good girl, Queenie is. But your son – he's got her into trouble.'

'Trouble?' The fine eyebrows drew down into a frown.

Good God, thought Queenie, don't they speak the same language in Portchester?

'He's got her in the family way.'

Violet's eyes opened wide. She looked at Queenie, horrified. 'You're pregnant?' she asked.

''Fraid so,' Queenie mumbled with downcast eyes.

Violet's mouth hung open for a moment. 'But,' she spluttered, 'I refuse to believe that my son is responsible.'

Queenie's head snapped up and she blazed indignantly. 'He bloody is.'

Violet Jackson recoiled slightly, then with compressed mouth she allowed her eyes to sweep slowly over Queenie, from the top of her head to her bare legs and high-heeled shoes. Bare legs in this weather! Then then up to her face again, making no effort to disguise her look of utter disdain. Queenie drew herself up and looked her defiantly in the eye.

'And she's only sixteen,' added Beatie.

'And 'ow's 'er poor mother going to manage – 'er being a poor widow-woman?' put in Lil. Queenie gritted her teeth.

Violet's eyes took on a dangerous gleam and she took a step towards them. Her guests took a step backwards. 'Now just you look here. I don't know you people from Adam. You come to my house making wild allegations against my boy – '

'Now don't go gittin' all aireated,' advised Beatie. 'It won't help nothin'.'

'Aireated! What proof have you that my son is the – that he is responsible for this. Your daughter' – pouring scorn into the words ' – looks to me like the sort of girl who has lots of – boyfriends.'

Queenie's eyes flashed. 'I never – '

'How dare you suggest such a thing,' shrieked Beatie. 'My Queenie's a good girl. She's been brought up respectable. And she's still a child. It's *your son* what's to blame.'

Violet shook with indignation. 'It's your word against his, and I know whom I shall believe. And if what you say *is* true – then she did it on purpose – '

'What a wicked thing to say,' interposed Lil. 'I've known little Queenie since she was a babe in arms, and there ain't a sweeter girl – '

Queenie broke in. 'It isn't going to help anything, going on like this. I'm sorry to upset you, Mrs Jackson – it must be a shock, but it's true. Nobody meant for it to happen, but it *was* your son. I never . . . I haven't been with anyone else.'

'And what do you expect me to do?' asked Violet witheringly.

Beatie wagged an indignant finger under the taller woman's nose. 'You write to 'im and tell 'im that if he don't face up to 'is responsibilities, I shall get *him* into trouble – with the Navy. I'll get him discharged for misconduct.'

'I shall write to him, have no fear.' Violet's lips were thin with anger, her cheeks red with distress. 'We'll get this business sorted out as soon as possible.'

'Unfortunately,' Lil said with a thoughtful air, 'babies can't be sorted out so easy. They don't just go away. They have to be looked after for *years*.' Lil had missed her vocation on the stage.

'That's right,' Beatie agreed, cottoning on to her friend's wavelength. '*I* can't afford to bring up a ill-er-gitimate child.'

'I can see perfectly well what you're after.' Violet's look of disgust encompassed them all. 'I must ask you to leave now. I intend to say no more on the subject at present. But rest assured,' she threatened, 'Mr Jackson will have plenty to say about it.' She strode to a desk in the corner and came back with a notepad and pencil which she held out to Beatie with a shaking hand. 'Kindly leave your name and address.'

Beatie passed it to her daughter. Queenie licked the lead

before laboriously writing the information down. Her eyes locked with Violet Jackson's in mutual anguish and dislike as she handed the pad back.

They were shown out, their reluctant hostess watching them with mistrust as they walked down the path and giving a great sigh as the gate clicked.

'Everything all right, dear?' came the falsely sympathetic voice of her neighbour, who had miraculously appeared from behind the separating hedge.

'You know very well it is not!' cried Violet, storming into her house and slamming the door.

'How d'you like yer perspective mother-in-law, Queenie?' asked Lil with a sneer as the three unwelcome visitors made their way down the road to the bus stop.

'Stuck up bitch! Lady Muck! No shrinking violet, her,' raged Beatie. 'Who does she think she is with her pewter and distempered walls. Give me a nice flock wallpaper any day.'

Queenie was amazed that her mother had picked up such details during the heated exchange. She didn't know whether she felt more like giggling at the absurdity of it all or weeping with relief that the ordeal was over. She succumbed to the latter.

'Bit late for that now,' Beatie said roughly, but threaded her arm through her daughter's.

'"United we stand",' quoted Lil, linking her arm on Queenie's other side. 'Don't you worry, luv, we'll get it sorted.'

Bernard Jackson returned wearily from his week of travelling that evening, to find his wife in a dreadful state of nerves. Amid tears and fury, she recounted the tale of the afternoon visitation.

'Keith's been sowing some wild oats, has he?'

'For heaven's sake,' Violet cried, detecting the note of admiration in his voice. 'Is that all you can say? Isn't that just like a man! It's a matter for pride is it that I am accosted in my own home by that dreadful, common little woman and her tarty daughter. Saying dreadful things about our son.'

'Was she tarty?' her asked with interest.

'Bold as brass. Bright red lipstick and her eyelashes stuck together with mascara. Bare legs, in this weather. And only *sixteen*. The trollop. But the worst thing of all,' she gulped, 'was that they told the whole pack of lies to Madge. Everyone will know in record time. How will I hold up my head again in the neighbourhood – oh, the humiliation!'

'Better get on to the boy, old girl. It won't do him any good if a complaint is made. Though how he'll prove it isn't his, I don't know.'

'They are demanding maintenance! It's blackmail, isn't it?'

Bernard rubbed a hand around his jaw while he thought about it. 'Reckon he's got no choice. He'll have to pay up and sort it out when he gets back.'

'How perfectly dreadful! Well, I tell you here and now, I shall never speak to that girl again, and I will certainly never acknowledge the child.'

Bernard threw himself into a chair and groped in his pocket for his pipe. 'Make me a cup of tea, old girl. I've had a hard day.'

Violet jumped to her feet. 'And I haven't, I suppose! Can't you show more concern over this shameful business, Bernard Jackson? All you care about is your pipe and your snooker.'

'Give over, mother. It's nothing new. Happens all the time – ' he paused meaningfully ' – doesn't it?'

Violet's cheeks flushed scarlet. 'That was different . . .'

'Was it? Lust is lust. Same the whole world over, if you ask me.' He grinned half-heartedly.

'You'd know, of course! Your son takes after you, obviously,' she said with a prim mouth and her little retroussée nose stuck up in the air.

'One thing I've noticed,' he said conversationally as he tapped tobacco into the bowl of his pipe. 'The sun shine's out of those boys' backsides as far as you're concerned. You ruined them while I was away at war. When I came back from France I couldn't get a look in – '

'Oh, we've been over this hundreds of times. You were jealous of your own sons and you didn't like the fact that I'd become so independent. Well, we women had to be, we wouldn't have survived – '

'Yes, yes. I know. But what I was going to say was that those boys can do no wrong in your eyes, but on the occasions that you have to face up to the fact that they're not perfect, it's always me that they take after.'

Violet flounced from the room.

Bernard sighed and leaned back with his lids closed over pale grey eyes, rubbing a hand absentmindedly over his thinning grey hair. By God, he was tired.

Weary of this way of trying to eke out a living, with Violet resenting the fact that he had left his father's firm and feeling he should have done better.

She just couldn't understand how he felt after his experiences in the trenches. After watching so many of his mates gassed, mutilated or dying, nothing else seemed to be important. He certainly wasn't prepared to put up with his father's petty tyranny again.

And now this!

If the lad had got this girl pregnant he was going to have to do the decent thing by her. Just as he had. It seems you have to pay for your pleasures in this world – but sometimes, if you knew the price beforehand, you might think twice.

'You look glum, tonight, Stonewall. Glummer than usual, that is.' Leading Seaman Bob Parker, overweight and sweating in spite of his lightweight tropical uniform, came to lean against one of the gun-turrets of HMS *Barham* with his shipmate.

'Mmm,' agreed Stonewall, gazing out through the entrance of Grand Harbour, Valetta, to the blue Mediterranean beyond, his handsome bearded face dour.

'Trouble at home? Girlfriend gone off with another bloke? The hazards of being a matelot!'

'Yes and no. I wish she had!' Usually rather taciturn about his private affairs, Stonewall felt like confiding in someone, and Parker was a discreet sort of bloke. 'A girl I met in Pompey just before we left claims I've got her pregnant.'

'But you couldn't 'ave because you never touched her – is that it?'

'I'm not denying that, Parky, but it was only once. What are the chances of getting a girl pregnant on one occasion, I ask you?'

'Pretty high, even standing up, I've heard tell – unless you took care not to.'

Stonewall's cheekbones above the fuzz, reddened. 'It just . . . sort of happened.'

'That's what they all say, shipmate!'

'Yes, but if she did it with me, how do I know how many others she's been with? How can I believe it's my child?' My child – the words struck him like a blow. A terrifying responsibility and one he had not intended to take on for many years.

'What sort of girl is she?'

Keith considered. 'What sort of girl is Queenie?' A picture of her came into his mind as she had looked on that last day. So much had happened since leaving Pompey that he had almost forgotten. 'Well, she's very lively, pretty, cheeky, flirty. And a bloody liar. She told me she was eighteen, and it turns out she was only sixteen.'

'Whew! Almost a hanging offence that! Was she a virgin?'

'I assumed not. She would have resisted, wouldn't she?'

'No signs. No blood?'

'I didn't notice,' Keith mumbled, embarrassed, remembering how he'd given her his handkerchief to clean herself up with behind a bush. It all seemed very sordid now.

'So what's the score?'

'My mother has written to me. They're demanding maintenance until I get back – then God knows what.' He snorted humourlessly. 'I gather she's not exactly my mother's cup of tea.'

'My advice is not to argue the toss – you don't want a lot of trouble. With a bit of luck she'll have taken up with someone else by the time you get back to Blighty, and you'll be off the hook.'

'Yes. Maybe. Thanks, Parky. I got into a bit of panic over it.'

'One thing I guarantee, shipmate.' Bob Parker laid his pudgy hand on the young seaman's shoulder. 'Next time you dip your wick, you'll be more careful. You won't allow yourself to get carried away again.'

'You're right there. It's a bloody stupid and expensive mistake to make.'

'Come on, let's go ashore and paint the town red.'

'Not tonight, Parky, thanks.'

'You're going to stay and dwell upon your sins?'

'Something like that.'

It hadn't seemed sinful, Keith reflected as he watched Parky waddle off. Just the culmination of the pleasant times they had enjoyed together in the previous weeks. Queenie had played unexpectedly hard to get up till then – probably trying to get a ring on her finger – so he had been pleasantly surprised when she had suddenly given in.

'I love you, Keith Jackson,' she had said afterwards, and he wished she hadn't. But girls were like that, always making a drama out of everyday events.

And now she was claiming innocence – that he was the only man she had done it with. Was it true? It was obvious she wasn't as experienced as Sylvie, the waitress from

Portland, but . . .? For God's sake, she *was* only sixteen, so it probably was true. He'd never have touched her if he'd known that. Had she done it deliberately, to snare him? The little Jezebel!

Damn and blast it all to hell! He had no wish to be saddled with the responsibility of a wife and child. *A child!* It was terryifying.

Responsibility was something he had always avoided. He just wanted to go to Art School and travel when he'd served his twelve years. He had all sorts of plans for his future into which a girl like Queenie May and a child just would not fit. He had been a bloody fool – ruined his life for a few minutes of pleasure.

And what of her life? his conscience asked – to be quickly suppressed.

Parker and some other shipmates were going down the gangway. Going to the jetty in the launch. He looked over to the old buildings crowding down to the harbour – soft cream and ochre in the evening sunlight. He'd paint that before they left Malta. His mates were impressed with his little paintings and sketches.

Parky looked up and waved at him. They'd be going to the Gypo Queen on the corner of Strait Street, or the other bar where Bobby, a brilliant pianist, entertained. They'd get pissed, pick up a few whores in The Gut and have a good time. Something he was normally reluctant to take part in because he was particular where he dipped his wick.

What the hell! He had better enjoy his freedom while he still had some left.

'Hey. Wait for me, Parky,' he called.

# · *Nine* ·

Beatie struggled down to the harbour against driving rain, a headscarf about her head and an old umbrella giving poor protection. The cold wind cutting across the pier tugged at the umbrella, threatening to blow it inside out. By the time she was standing in the early morning queue for the ferry to Gosport, her legs and feet were wet and cold and she felt thoroughly miserable.

One of the little tug-boat-shaped ferries came in to the pontoon. A young chap dropped a thick warp over a bollard to make it fast before opening the barrier and checking the tickets and passes of the passengers as they moved through. Thankfully, Beatie stepped aboard and made her way below to the comparative comfort of the little forward saloon furnished with portholes, yellow-painted steel walls and hard benches made from strips of varnished wood.

These were occupied by huffing, complaining men. Beatie sagged wearily against a support column.

''Ere Missus, 'ave a seat.'

'Oh, ta,' said Beatie gratefully to the hulking fellow who stood up. Squeezing between two men with early-morning pallor on their faces, she was glad of the warmth from their thighs. There was only one other woman in the cabin and Beatie wondered where she was going at five-thirty in the morning.

Already, smoke from a dozen or more cigarettes was polluting the air, and several passengers were coughing. In fine weather, even if it was a bit cold or windy, Beatie preferred to stay up on deck and breathe in the fresh, salty air. On calm mornings the harbour looked beautiful beneath pearly or rosy skies. Windy days were exhilarating as the little ferries ploughed through the waves. Occasionally it was foggy and then the timetable went to pot. The boats would creep across, their foghorns answering the mournful hoot of other vessels, and fumbled around at the other side until they found the jetty.

Beatie gave a great sigh and leaned her head back, closing her eyes. She didn't feel at all well today, with that awful, dragging ache again, low down in her belly. She had been hoping that the pain would go away, but she knew she ought to see a doctor. Where would she find half a crown for the fee? But the truth was that she was scared stiff of having to have an operation. A lot of people she had known had gone into hospital and never come home again. Her greatest fear was that she would die, leaving the kids to fend for themselves. Like she'd had to. She'd just have to do something about it.

Her own father and mother had died within a year of each other and she had been left, at the age of fifteen, to act as parent to eleven-year-old Ethel, Danny who was ten, and eight-year-old Arthur. My God, she'd had to grow up quick and no mistake!

In addition to going out to work, she'd managed to wangle a few bob from the PAC people, the 'Poor Relief'.

She had tried to carry on as her Mam had done, tried to feed the kids properly, but at the end of the week they were always on bread and marg. Until she decided to keep chickens and rabbits in the yard, then they would have an egg for breakfast most days, and she'd take the old chickens, and a rabbit occasionally, round to the butcher in the next street to be slaughtered. That was a rare treat. Sometimes she'd swop a rabbit or a chicken for a pig's head – you could make good brawn from that, and it made a change from tripe, offal, and cow-udder.

She kept the kids clean inside and out, like her Mam

used to, by giving them a bath every Friday night, and a dose of liquorice powder to keep them regular.

Her mother's sister, Aunty Tildy, used to pop in now and then and give them advice, cast-off clothes from her own brats, and a few bits and bobs, but she was hard up, too.

The engines of the ferry started to throb and Beatie felt the sway of the boat as it moved away from the jetty. Soon be there and she'd have to leave the steaming cocoon of the cabin for the rain again.

Recalling how she'd had to manage on her own, she sighed. The only way she had kept number twelve Baker Street on was to take in two of her cousins as lodgers. They were dockers, like her dad had been. But that hadn't worked for long. Micky started to pester her, apparently thinking that board and lodging gave him entry to her bed, too. And even after she'd chucked *him* out, Bob kept bringing his tarts to the house.

But then, at seventeen, she had met Joshua Ellis and it seemed her worries were over.

A smile twitched at Beatie's mouth as she remembered their first meeting.

She was working at that time in the kitchens of the Sailor's Home Club. That particular day, she had gone out into the yard with some peelings for the pig bin and, tired out, had somehow managed to drop it all over the place.

She'd been up with Arthur and his bronchitis during the night. He'd been too ill to go to school today and was at home on his own. She was worried about him, had just quarrelled with the cook and this was the last straw. She stood there bawling with her fists in her eyes like a child.

'What's all this then?' asked a cheerful male voice. 'There's worse things happen at sea, you know. Come on, I'll help you clear it up.'

She had looked up at this good-looking bloke, and the

first thing she noticed were his marvellous violet-blue eyes. A sailor he was, just come out of the Gents, and he looked so nice and friendly that she blurted it all out. With sobs in between.

'You poor kid,' he said, and in the most natural way in the world, he put his arms around her and patted her back. Starved of affection and support, it was just what she needed.

He helped her pick up the rubbish. 'What you need, my girl, is a night out. You're coming to the Hippodrome with me on Saturday night. There's Music Hall on. Just what you need – a bit of music and fun in your life.'

She'd never had a date before and she wanted to go so much. 'Oh . . . I don't know. My cousin, Bob, goes out every Saturday night and I can't really leave the kids on their own, specially if our Arthur ain't well.'

'Course you can. Haven't you got a neighbour you can ask to keep an eye on them?' So she put herself first for a change and asked her neighbour's daughter, Lil, to come in with her young man.

And what a mate Lil had been over the years. Always a step ahead of Beatie, she had married first and given Beatie advice on what to expect on her wedding night and during pregnancy. She was with her and Nurse Hebdon for most of Beatie's confinements.

They'd shared tears – lots of them – and laughter. Laugh! Like the time they'd gone along to consult that woman who was supposed to be able to talk to the dead. They'd been shown into a cold front room by a maid and sat there giggling nervously, hearts thumping, wondering what they were going to hear from their dear departed parents. They hoped they wouldn't *see* anything. Lil's mother, Daisy, had looked a fright when she was alive – God knows what she'd have looked like after being dead for years!

'Madame Montague' came in, middle-aged and dressed all in black, against which the jet beads of her necklace sparkled, like Beatie's mother's had done. The maid closed the heavy curtains and put a match to two candles on the table. Lit by the flickering flames, the woman looked like a witch, and she and Lil had clasped clammy hands under the table.

The medium started to ask them questions in a low, throbbing voice that added to their unease. They whispered their hesitant replies, their hands locking together.

Suddenly a bell rang.

They both screamed and jumped up, and Lil galloped out of the room, dragging Beatie behind her. They burst out of the front door, canonning into the woman on the doorstep who had rung the bell, and they landed in a heap on the pavement.

Beatie and Lil were in hysterics, tears running down their cheeks. She looked up and saw Madame M and her maid staring down at them from the open door with puzzled expressions on their faces. Laugh! She'd nearly wet her knickers. Beatie chuckled silently. *Hallelujah*! as Lil would say, that was a scream, that was.

But she had been remembering Joshua.

The evening out with Josh was magical, sitting beside him in the plush red seats of the Hippodrome with her best hat on. The straw with the blue ribbons and flowers that the kids had given her on her birthday. Saved up for months, they had, the three of them, doing any odd job that came their way, for a ha'penny or so. She had been really touched.

There was a lovely atmosphere at the Hippodrome, everyone happy and joining in the fun. There were comedians, dancers, and acrobats. And that lovely Master of Ceremonies with his hammer and long words they all 'oohed!' over. They performed a medley of songs from

*The Merry Widow*, which was all the rage in America. But the bit she liked best was when they all swayed in their seats and sang the good old numbers together like 'Down By The Old Bull And Bush', and 'Daisy, Daisy'.

She thought she was in heaven sitting beside the bloke with the twinkly eyes, and Josh bought her a pie afterwards and kissed her goodnight ever so nicely. He was such a good man. Handsome, amusing, full of easy charm.

Beatie couldn't believe her luck when, a few months after they met, Josh asked her to marry him. She had looked at him in disbelief, not understanding what he saw in her. 'You know you'll 'ave to take on the kids as well?' she asked roughly.

'That's all right, Jenny Wren.' He used to say she was like a little wren with her small frame, quick movements and dark eyes. Later, when she became round as a barrel with all her pregnancies, he called her 'Jenny Hen'. 'We'll be one big, happy family.' And he had never tried *anything* on with her while they were engaged.

Cousin Bob was given the push and Joshua moved in. He paid for their modest wedding. His parents, coming down from London for the event, clearly thought he could have done better for himself than take on the responsibilities of an orphaned family. She'd never got on well with them, and when his mother died and his father remarried, they lost touch altogether.

Joshua Ellis. My Josh.

Married life was wonderful at first. She discovered a well of untapped sexual passion in herself, and Josh was a good lover. Fortunately, her sister and brothers adored him. But the harshness of Beatie's life after the death of her parents was replaced by different hardships. The frequent miscarriages before the birth of Billy four years after their marriage. The difficult years when her husband was away at sea and she had to manage on her own. Sailors didn't earn enough to keep a family on, and she tried to work when she could and was always scrimping in order to pay the rent and rates.

Then, after Billy, little Samuel was stillborn. Nine months of discomfort and being careful, to have nothing but grief at the end of it.

Eddy was born two years and another miscarriage later; a sickly baby but he had survived. His club foot made him feel inferior, she supposed, because he was always a strange boy. Very secretive, but never any trouble. Living at home still, he came and went as he pleased, hardly noticed, and his mother still had no idea what made him tick. But his contribution to the family income was vital.

John was her favourite. Bright, good-natured and affectionate. Doing so well in the Marines, and she'd never had to speak a cross word to him. Now he was happily engaged to Phyllis, who was a lovely girl.

Then the war came – the Great War they called it – and Josh was away for over three years. A relief from continual pregnancy, but oh, she did miss him. And always there was the fear that he might not return.

Joshua had been leading stoker in one of the three submarines sent to the Baltic by Admiral Jellicoe at the start of the war. They were to attack German battleships as they made their way out of the Baltic ports. She didn't know that at the time, of course, or she'd have been even more frightened for him. The *E11* had to return after some damage, but the *E1*, Josh's boat, and the *E9* had carried on with their hard and dangerous mission.

Poor Josh. He had come back exhausted physically and mentally, a shadow of his former self. His lungs were weak and the slightest infection turned into a bad cough. It took the death of his mother, some months later, to open the dam gates of his pent-up emotions and release all his sorrow.

'You can't imagine what it's like being cooped up in a tin can with the same men month after month after bloody month, Jenny Hen,' he told her, cuddled up against her in the safety of their big bed. 'All good mates – I'd 'ave died for any of them – but there were times when we came close to *murdering* each other. When we wasn't taking appalling risks, that was!'

'I *can* imagine. Oh, Josh, I've always hated those subs. Why did you 'ave to go in them?'

'You was grateful for the extra money, I seem to remember. Don't like your old man being called "The Trade" by the boys on the surface, is that it?'

'I don't care about that. It's the bloody danger! Even when there ain't a war.'

'Danger's part of the excitement of the job, Beat. I'm never more alive than when I'm facing danger.'

'That's all right for you!'

'Had a bit too bloody much of it in the Baltic, though. By Christ! the tension when we was creeping along the bottom, looking for Fritz! And the bottled-up fear when we was trying to escape after we'd fired a tin fish and given our position away. We could have shit ourselves with fear, Beat, but apart from a little flicker you saw now and then in a mate's eyes, you'd never have known it.'

'My poor love. Still you're 'ome now.' She stroked his hair as he got it out of his system.

'Bad food. Bad hygiene. And breathing air, Beatie, so thick you could cut it with a knife – foul with oil and gas fumes. Dying for a tickler, we'd be, but you couldn't light up in those conditions.'

'That's why your lungs is bad, Josh. It ain't right!'

'Then there was the mines – '

'Ooh, don't Josh.'

'*E18* – she came out later – she was lost to a mine. They was good men, Beatie, the very best – all lost.' He sniffed wetly. 'What a bloody waste.'

'It's criminal, Josh. Why do people want to make war? Life's 'ard enough as it is, without all that. But you did a good job, didn't you? Got a bleedin' medal from the Tsar!

You can be proud of yerself – I'm proud of you. My hero, that's what you are.'

He went on as if he had not heard her. 'You know what they say, Beat, about thirteen being an unlucky number? Well, *E13* ran aground on Danish territory. By international law she had twenty-four hours to get herself off, before being interned by a neutral country. But along come a sodding German destroyer and . . . you won't believe this, Beat . . .' He couldn't go on, he was crying.

'Don't upset yerself, love.'

'But Beat,' he wept, 'I've got to tell you. That bastard shelled our stranded sub and set it alight. And then . . . then he opened fire on the crew as they . . . tried . . . to swim for it. It was cold-blooded murder.' Josh was sobbing, and Beatie cried with him.

'Oh, Josh, darlin',' she said at last, 'try not to think about it. You're home and safe. I prayed for you every night, you know.'

They cried together for the thousands of men who didn't come back, for the cruel futility of war, for all they had gone through, and the relief it was all over.

'One good thing has come out of it though, Beatie, my love. Everyone's learnt their lesson. There will never be another war like it.'

'Never,' she agreed tearfully, and she tried to comfort him in the only way she knew how. They had never been so heartbreakingly close and she felt sure that Queenie had been conceived that night.

Beatie sighed and wiped a tear from her cheek.

Queenie, her father's darling, his 'Little Queen of the May'. She was Josh's favourite but Beatie and her daughter had *never* seen eye to eye. Perhaps because they were too alike. Not that Queenie would ever admit that. Oh no. She only wanted to be *Josh's* daughter. Anyway, she was the opposite of Eddy: always in trouble, cheeky and resentful, but most people found her irresistible. Particularly men. She always had an eye for the men, sitting on their laps when she was little and flirting with them.

A lot of it was Josh's fault. He spoiled her and filled her head with nonsense – all that rubbish about her being an escaped Russian countess or something. It fair turned the child's head and she went around with that fantasy for years, until at last she had to face the truth because the dates didn't fit.

And now Queenie was pregnant! How would Josh have coped with that if he'd still been alive? His little Queen slipped off her pedestal.

Beatie knew that her daughter thought she was a hard and unfeeling mother. Queenie would not understand if she tried to explain it to her. She didn't really understand it herself – only that over the years she had built a protective shell around herself. Afraid of weakening, losing control, she dared not give way to emotion in front of her children. She had been forced to be strong ever since she had to take on the upbringing of her sister and brothers. Then all those miscarriages, coping alone when her husband was at sea and having to carry on unaided after his death.

She knew she was being unfair but she couldn't help blaming Josh for all that – the hardships. She loved him, but it was his fault, after all, that she'd had fifteen years of childbearing. Billy, Eddy, John and after Queenie there had been Henry, dying at a few days old.

Then little Hannah. That didn't bear thinking about. A sweet baby, nearly a year old before she died of diptheria. Beatie shuddered as she remembered the horrible grey film at the back of the baby's throat, making it difficult for the child to breathe. Queenie, who had adored her tiny sister, had to kept away from her because it was so catching, and she had been as upset as her parents when little Hannah died.

Jimmy was born two years later and 'Little Josh' – thankfully the last – when she was thirty-five.

By this time her husband had been invalided out of the Navy with his bad lungs and the onset of epileptic fits. He only served eighteen of the twenty-two years he joined up for, so he did not qualify for a pension. Neither did he receive disability pay because he wasn't able to prove that his epilepsy was brought about by a blow to the head when something came loose under pressure in the submarine. The family was in dire straits for years. They'd had to apply to Poor Relief to pay the rent. Poor Josh. He was a proud man and he'd risked so much for his country, but he had to go through all that humiliation. It was criminal.

The Means Test! That nosy little ferret of a man, coming round from the Authority and asking questions. Looking over the house to see if they had anything worth selling, so that the PAC people wouldn't have to fork out so much. She'd hidden her crystal under a pile of dirty washing when she heard he was coming.

It was bloody criminal! She'd had to work all the hours there were to earn a bit to make ends meet – and they seldom did. All those years of hardship. Yes, she'd had to be tough and to bring her daughter up to be tough too. A woman's life was bloody cruel and Queenie might as well get used to it. It would be even harder now as an unmarried mother. Harder for both of them.

And that bloody sailor. Ooh, if she could get her hands on him!

A rough masculine hand shook her shoulder. 'Wake up, Missus, or you'll be back in Pompey.'

Beatie opened dazed eyes. 'Oh, thanks. I wasn't asleep. I was just . . . day dreaming.'

# · Ten ·

Every Thursday before going to work, Queenie had to go by bus to the Guildhall. There she would go to one clerk to pay the rates – somehow they always managed to scrape the money together – and to another clerk to pay in her uncle's maintenance for his illegitimate daughter.

Apparently Uncle Bert had been 'visiting' a widow who had proved more fruitful than Auntie Ethel – embarrassingly so. Not knowing what else to do, he had confided this difficulty to his sister-in-law. Beatie, anxious to spare her sister the pain of discovering her husband's adultery, had offered to make the payments on his behalf. Or rather, had offered that Queenie would undertake this errand. So every Sunday, when he came to tea, he left an envelope behind the tea-caddy on the kitchen mantelpiece.

Queenie, loathing Bert with good reason, had been wildly rebellious about this at first, but after a couple of clips around the ear from her mother, had been forced to become resigned to it.

Now, added to these two tasks was one on her own behalf – the collection of a weekly sum of money from Keith Jackson. This was a great source of satisfaction to her – let the bugger pay!

Life for the young mother-in-waiting was subdued, her mother often angry yet at other times roughly sympathetic. But Queenie found a surprise ally in her older brother Eddy, whom everyone tended to ignore as he was so innocuous, limping quietly in and out of the house.

'You've really gone and done it this time, our Queen,'

he said one day, after the discovery of her plight, and finding her crying in the kitchen after another row with their mother. He patted her shoulder awkwardly. 'It's a pity, girl. *You* could have made something of yourself. You've always had more spirit than the rest of us put together. Except Ma. You take after her, you know.'

'After Ma!' Queenie was indignant, her pretty face splotchy with tears and her eyes red-rimmed. 'I bloody well hope not.'

'Yes, you're just like Ma. She couldn't have kept goin' like she has, unless she was damned tough. I don't say much, I know, but I notice things.' His pleasant, nondescript face was flushed with the embarrassment of self-revelation. 'I know how hard you and Ma work. I'd 'ave moved out years ago, but I knew she needed my money. Don't think too hard on her, Queen, she's had a rotten life.'

'Has she?' Queenie had never given it much thought, usually too busy with her own grievances. 'Well, she needn't take it out on me.' The tears started again.

Eddy put his arms around her and she clung to him, weeping as he rubbed her back.

'I'm frightened, Ed.' Her voice was that of a little girl. 'I'm frightened of . . . birthing the baby, frightened it might die, and I'm scared of having to look after it till it's growed up.'

He stroked her hair. 'The way I look at it is this, our Queen. It's every woman's lot to 'ave babies – something you just have to do, so you got to grin and bear it. But you're a healthy girl – Ma always fed us well – so you shouldn't have no problems. And I'm goin' to look after you and the nipper. So will Ma, make no mistake. Her bark's worse'n her bite, you know that.'

Queenie had never heard him make such a long speech before and she looked up, wide-eyed, into his burning face. 'I know,' he mumbled, his black eyes sliding shyly away from hers, 'I'm a queer old cuss but . . . I do love you, Queenie. And I'm goin' to take care of you.'

'Oh Eddy.' She threw her arms around his neck and kissed his red cheeks and ruffled his dark hair. 'You're such a nice, kind old bugger. I feel ever so much better now.'

His eyes twinkled at her. 'That's all right then, ain't it? Come on, dry your eyes. I'll make us a cuppa tea.'

Queenie watched him as he went through the familiar tea-making routine. She'd never really got to know him, had she? Poor Eddy, so easy to overlook, but perhaps he was really lonely inside. She'd never thought about it. He had always been kind to her when she was little, bringing her sweets and picking her up and cuddling her if she fell over and hurt herself.

Dad was fond of him, she remembered. She was sometimes jealous of the way her father used to talk to him. Eddy must miss Dad almost as much as she did. Yes. He'd always been a good brother to her.

'Ed,' she said, as she stirred her tea, throwing him a quick, shy glance. 'I love you too, you know.'

He turned away quickly. 'That's all right then, ain't it.'

Her brother took to meeting her at night from work and they would walk home arm-in-arm, not saying much, but happy with each other. He took over the heavy chores, even though Queenie knew he considered them 'women's work'. Sometimes he brought her sweets and once, with a bashful expression, a bunch of flowers. And he stuck up for her when Beatie was bad-tempered.

'You know, Queen, Ma don't look at all well,' he said once when Beatie had flounced out to the yard after an argument.

'Don't she?' Queenie, busy with her own problems, a lot of which she considered were caused by her mother, did not give her a great deal of thought.

'No. I'm a bit worried about 'er. And you know, if you

didn't back-chat 'er so much, things would be more peaceful round 'ere for us all.'

She gave him a belligerent look but took note of what he said and tried to be more tolerant of Beatie's moods. Life grew marginally more peaceful.

Queenie, in her advancing pregnancy, found another friend in John's fiancée, Phyllis. When John was away, Phyllis often came round on her own and occasionally spent the night. Beatie was always welcoming and sweet to her future daughter-in-law, which peeved Queenie until she decided that jealousy would hurt no-one but herself, and she liked Phyllis too much to hold it against her.

Even so, she could not help envying her new friend's slim figure, while her own waist was thickening and her stomach beginning to bulge. She felt so lumpish and awkward. But she was still pretty and, having got over the morning sickness, her complexion had taken on a becoming bloom. And she still had her lovely hair. The two young girls would try out new hairstyles and make-up in the kitchen, and drool over the latest fashions in Queenie's second-hand *Woman* magazines, while Beatie sat knitting by the range.

'What about all this stuff about the Prince of Wales and this American woman?' Phyllis read out an article about how he had been squiring a Mrs Wallis Simpson around.

'She's no better than she ought to be,' snorted Beatie. 'A tart's a tart, even if she comes from society. And bringing our future King into ill-repoot, too.'

'What a waste,' said Queenie. 'Why does he want to go chasing some old tart, when there are all us lovely girls for him to choose from.'

'We want a lergitimate heir to the throne, if yer don't mind,' laughed her mother. 'And it won't be long before Edward is on the throne by the sound of it. I heard on the wireless that old Georgy-Porgy is very ill. Poor old boy. He's bin a good king.'

Queenie and Phyllis went to the pictures when they could afford to, and walking back from the bus-stop they would sing the popular songs together, like 'I Got Plenty Of Nuthin'' and 'Begin The Beguine'. The latter accompanied by a tango-like glide along the pavement – Queenie's distended belly between them – and ending in a storm of giggles in someone's doorway.

They clung to each other and cried their eyes out over the newsreels of the King's funeral in January. In March, Hitler's troops jack-booted into the Rhineland against protestations from Britain and France. But it all seemed very remote to Queenie who didn't understand politics at all and was much more worried about her own problems. Often she wanted this baby with intense joy, but at other times she resented it for causing her increasing unattractiveness. Sometimes a chap would ogle her or whistle after her as they had always done, but quickly look away when they registered her condition. She did not like to dwell too much on how the child was going to curtail her freedom. She was too young to be tied down. And would any man want her once she was saddled with an illegitimate child?

In mid-April, Queenie worked her last midday shift at Fred's Fish Shop. Fred gave her a bonus, and his wife gave her a hand-knitted shawl.

'I warned you about sailors, didn't I?' was Fred's parting remark.

Queenie put on a mock-tragic expression. 'I know Fred and I should 'a listened to you.'

'Bring the baby to see us,' smiled Mrs Fred.

'Good luck, Queenie,' added Pearl. 'This place won't be the same wiv'out you. Don't do nuthin' I wouldn't do, now.'

'Bit late for saying that.' Queenie laughed. 'You watch yourself, Pearl, and take Fred's advice. Don't get caught like what I did.'

As she walked home, her stomach thrusting ahead of her, two small boys kicking a ball in the road stopped and looked at her, whispering behind their hands. 'Been eating too much new bread, missus?' shouted one and they fell about giggling.

'Cheeky little sods,' she called back with a grin. A couple of weeks to go and she'd be a mother! Queenie's heart beat faster with excitement and fear. She was all ready. She had moved down to a bigger bedroom and Eddy and Ma had re-decorated it with pretty rose-patterned wallpaper. And she had painted up the old cot that so many Ellis babies had started life in. And some of them had died in. But she had bought a new mattress for it. She had a little 'layette' ready for the baby – she'd got that word from *Woman* magazine. It sounded ever so posh.

What a pal Eddy had turned out to be. She had never known, or been particularly interested in what he was thinking, but since that speech in the kitchen, he really had looked after her. And was it her imagination or *was* Ma a bit softer these days? Eddy was right, the old girl didn't look too well. After she'd had the baby, they'd do something about Ma.

And Keith Jackson. Did he ever think about her and his forthcoming child?

After her claim that he was the father of her unborn baby, she had heard nothing more from him or his family. Just received an official letter telling her to collect the maintenance each week. She supposed he need not have started paying it until the baby was born, but he obviously didn't want the Ellises kicking up a fuss. She had saved a bit each week from the money and bought the things she needed for the baby.

Funny. She couldn't really remember what 'Stonewall' looked like any more. She had often regretted tearing up the only photograph he had sent her. She remembered him as being handsome and clever, and that she had been madly in love with him. She had imagined he was going to take her away to a better life. How could she have been such a fool! He had hurt her so much.

The baby kicked in her womb and she put her hand over the movement, her eyes glowing with excitement. Nurse Hebdon reckoned on it being born early in May. She remembered telling Keith Jackson that everything good happened to her in May. Perhaps her baby would come on the first of May – her own birthday. Just think, if it was a girl, it would be her own little 'Queen of the May'.

Queenie turned seventeen on Friday, the first of May, 1936. Normally, there would have been a bit of a family 'shindig' on the following Sunday to celebrate, but with the baby so close and Uncle Arthur and her brothers, Billy and John, away too, it was to be just a small get-together.

Late on the Friday afternoon, Queenie and Beatie were in the kitchen baking some cakes for Sunday tea when Queenie pressed the palms of her hands into the small of her back and groaned.

'What's up?' asked Beatie, alarmed.

'I've got an awful back-ache, Ma.'

'Oh my God! It's started.'

'The baby?' gasped Queenie, her eyes wide with fright.

'Nothin' to worry about,' said Beatie, looking thoroughly alarmed. 'I'll send Jimmy for Fanny Hebdon.'

'What d'yer want 'er for?' the boy asked.

'Never you mind!' Beatie aimed a swipe at his ear which he skilfully ducked. 'Jest go and git 'er.'

It took Jimmy nearly an hour to locate the midwife, as she was at another house on a similar mission.

'Early days yet,' said Fanny after a quick examination. 'I'll give you a draught to take, dear, to get it goin'. First babies take ages. Just carry on as normal.'

'Carry on as normal!' groaned Queenie, doubled up with a painful contraction. She drank the foul concoction of caster oil and something bitter that the nurse gave her. 'Ugh – that was 'orrible!'

'Get you going, that will,' repeated Nurse Hebdon, picking up her bag. 'I'm round at Sheila Griggs' in Butchers Streets. She's just about *there*, so I'll be back as soon as I can. Get to bed when the pains are coming every five minutes.' She laughed. 'I don't need to tell *you* that, Beatie, do I? We've been through this so often.'

Beatie shook her head but still looked worried. 'I'll get water boiling and everythink laid out,' she said.

The draught certainly got Queenie 'going' – down the yard to the lavatory several times.

'Ooh, Ma, I do feel awful,' she said a couple of hours later. 'These pains . . .'

'All right, luv. I'll get rid of the boys and you can 'ave a nice warm wash-down by the stove. Then we'll git you to bed. You'll feel better then.' She asked Eddy to take the younger boys out.

'Good luck, our Queen.' He gave her a wink.

'Where's Nurse Hebdon?' Queenie gasped at about ten o'clock. She was sitting up in bed with her arms crossed over her stomach. 'These pains are coming ever so fast, Ma.'

'Don't worry,' said Beatie, white-faced. 'She'll be here any minute. I'll send Eddy up Butcher Street as soon as 'e gits back with the boys . . . But I think I'll get Lil in – just in case.'

For once, Queenie didn't argue.

Lil came up to the bedroom and started bustling bossily around. 'You go and make us a nice cup of tea, Beatie,' she said, 'while I check we got everythink we need. Make sure there's plenty of water on the boil . . .' she called unnecessarily. She came over to Queenie. 'How you feelin', luv?'

'Frightened,' whispered Queenie, her eyes huge with exhaustion and fear.

'No need to worry, luv,' said Lil, surprisingly gentle,

stroking her sweat-soaked hair back off her forehead. 'It's all in a day's work for a woman. Tell you what, I'll plait yer hair – it'll be cooler without all that round yer neck.' The bed sagged under Lil's weight. Queenie found that the big woman's nimble fingers soothed her agitation. She wasn't a bad old thing, really. 'Thanks, Lil,' she smiled gratefully before doubling up with another contraction.

'Come on now – breathe like this, it'll relax yer.' Lil's demonstration resembled the output of a giant bellows. 'Me and yer Ma have been through this how many times? Reckon I know as much about birthing a baby now as old Fanny Hebdon.'

'I hope so,' gasped Queenie. ''Cos I don't think she's goin' to be in time.'

Beatie came in with a tray. 'Eddy says there's been complications round Butcher Street – the doctor 'ad to be called.'

'O-oh!' wailed Queenie.

'It's all right,' soothed Lil. 'Sheila Griggs always 'as trouble with her birthings. But you're a strong, healthy girl.'

'Aah! It's comin',' shrieked Queenie and gave a grunt like a constipated pig.

'She's pushing, Beat!' yelled Lil. 'Hallelujah! That's it, Queen. Push down when you feel like it.'

'Yer doin' well, darlin',' encouraged Beatie, calm now that the crisis had arrived and she had the stalwart Lil with her. 'We'll pull the bed out from the wall, Lil, so's we can both get at her.'

Queenie thought she was dying. She had never known that there could be such pain – she was drowning in it. But through the dizzying waves of agony came the thought that her poor mother had been through this nine times – quite apart from the miscarriages. 'I'm sorry, Ma,' she cried. Sorry for so many things.

The baby was born just after midnight. With its cry, all

the pain faded away, and Queenie subsided into joyful peace.

'It's a little girl,' crooned Beatie, laying the wrapped child in her arms.

'Hallelujah,' murmured Queenie softly, looking at the crumpled little face under its fuzz of dark hair, at the wailing mouth and quivering tongue, at the tiny fingers waving like the tentacles of a sea anemone. She felt the vibration of a life now separate from hers. It was a miracle.

'Ugly little bugger, ain't it?' said Lil with a fond chuckle.

'G'arn, she's beautiful,' murmured Queenie with tears rolling down her cheeks. She sniffed. 'You was nearly the most wonderful birthday present I've ever had, but you didn't quite make it for the first, did you, pet?' She looked up at the two women bending over her. She belonged to a special sisterhood now. 'Thank you, Ma. Thank you, Lil. I'm goin' to call her Hannah – if that's all right with you, Ma?'

Beatie's eyes filled with tears. 'I'd like that,' she answered in a choked voice and bent forward to embrace her daughter and her first granddaughter.

Just then the front-door bell rang.

'I'll answer it, Ma,' called Eddy from outside the bedroom door.

'Eddy, I've got a little girl,' called Queenie.

'Well done, our Queen.' She could hear a smile in his voice. 'I'll see my niece in the morning.'

Nurse Hebdon came puffing through the doorway. 'I hear you've done it without me.' She leaned against the door-frame, her plump body shaking with laughter. 'I must say I'm very grateful – I'm knackered.'

'Is Sheila all right?' asked Lil.

'She'll live. A little boy, it was. What've we got here, then?' She approached the bed, took the squalling baby, unwrapped her and moved her limbs around. Queenie thought Hannah looked like a newly-cooked shrimp. 'She looks healthy. Is the after-birth out?'

Beatie nodded, pulling back the sheet to reveal the liver-coloured mass lying in a bowl. 'We was just wondering if we ought to cut the cord, but we was a bit worried about it, Fanny.'

'I'm glad you left it to me – we don't want a pokey-out belly button for a little girl, now do we?'

There was a commotion outside the door. The door bell and voices on the stairs had obviously woken Jimmy and Josh who had slept through the rest of the drama, but were now demanding to know what was going on. Eddy was trying to get them away. 'I ain't goin' till you tell me,' shouted Josh in a strangled voice, which suggested that his elder brother had him by the pyjama collar.

'Our Queen's had a baby, if you must know. A little girl.'

There was a moment's silence. In the bedroom the four women looked at each other.

'I did wonder,' said Jimmy. 'I noticed she'd got ever so fat.'

'She *can't* have had a baby,' came ten-year-old Josh's answer. 'It must be Ma's! But . . . it can't be Ma's neither, 'cos she hasn't got a husband – '

Eddy gave an audible groan. 'Look, come with me and I'll try to explain.' They shuffled off.

Beatie stood there red-faced, her hand to her mouth.

Queenie started to giggle. 'They've got to learn the facts of life some time, Ma. Then they might not get some poor girl like me into trouble.'

# · *Eleven* ·

When Queenie Ellis registered Hannah's birth under her own name, she was upset with the instruction to leave Column 6 blank – Rank or Profession of Father. The child *had* a father even if he was not interested. And it wasn't as if *she* had been with several men and didn't know who was responsible for her pregnancy. It made her feel like a tart.

'One day I hope I'll be able to explain it all to you,' she whispered to the baby.

Hannah yawned. She didn't care.

Queenie had never been so happy as she was the month following her baby's birth. She adored Hannah who was breast-feeding and developing well, and she had no thought for anything else. She went to St George's to be 'Churched' – mother and child blessed and thanks given for a safe delivery.

The young mother was spoilt by everyone, all the relatives bringing gifts for the baby, but Eddy brought her a gift for herself. A lovely little marcasite brooch in the shape of a swallow in flight.

'I've never had anythink so beautiful, Eddy, 'cept Hannah of course,' she said with tears in her eyes. 'I'll always treasure it.'

Her brother held his tiny niece, jiggling her up and down. 'She's lovely, our Queen, and she's special to me, 'cos I don't expect . . . I mean I won't have any children of my own.'

Queenie's eyes widened. 'Why ever not, Ed?'

His face reddened and he studied the baby's hand carefully. 'Well, no girl's goin' to want to marry *me*, is she?'

'*Why not?*'

'You know . . .'

'You don't mean because of your bleedin' foot? You idiot, Edward Ellis! You don't know nothin' about girls, do you? Most girls would rather have a kind, gentle bloke like you, with a bit of a limp, then Cary Grant or Errol Flynn. Look where it got me, falling for a pretty face. The girl what gets you, Eddy, is goin' to thank 'er lucky stars. I mean it.'

He looked at her then, his eyes bright and his mouth compressed with the effort not to grin his pleasure at her words.

She leant forward and kissed him. 'I mean it, you silly old fing. Ma loves my little Hannah too, you know,' Queenie went on. 'She's been a different person since she was born. It's sort of . . . brought us together.'

'I'm glad about that, Queen. Now, you've got to tackle Ma and find out what's wrong with her.'

'She has been looking awful tired . . .'

But there was so much to do with the baby that Queenie forgot all about it until she received a shock one Sunday morning on finding her mother sagging against the kitchen table with a face as white as a sheet and pinched with pain.

'What's up, Ma?' She rushed forward and eased Beatie down onto a chair.

'It's me stomick, Queen,' moaned Beatie, holding her hands over it and rocking back and forth. 'It's been paining me something awful for a long time – and I've been losing a lot of blood. And I . . . I'm frightened.' Her face crumpled and she reached out to her daughter.

Queenie pulled her mother's head against her middle and rubbed her shoulders, feeling awkward at this reversal of roles. 'You should've said! But don't worry, Ma. We'll get you to bed and call the doctor. I'm sure it's somethink that can be put right in no time.' But she, too, was beset by fear at the possibility of her mother dying. People did die at her age. What would they all do without Beatie?

She put her mother to bed with a hot water bottle and sent Jimmy for crusty old Doctor Monroe, who only ever entered the houses of Portsea in the direst of emergencies.

'Mmm. Fibroids, I believe, Mrs Ellis, and a dropped womb,' he announced after an examination. 'Not to be wondered at after all the pregnancies you've had, eh? Now, I'll give you something for the pain and we must make an appointment for you to see a gyneacologist.'

'Will it mean an operation – in 'ospital?' whispered Beatie, wide-eyed.

'It will, but don't worry. It's done all the time – very routine.'

'But what will it *cost*?'

'You leave that to the family, Ma,' said Queenie firmly, and tackled them all about it that afternoon when they came to tea.

'Beatie's never 'ad a day's illness in her life,' said a surprised Ethel, after Queenie had told them all about it. 'Apart from lyin'-in and miscarriages.'

'She's never let us see it!' exclaimed Queenie. 'And we're all too busy gettin' on with our own lives to notice. But Eddy saw there was something wrong, din't you, Ed?'

Eddy nodded. He avoided these family get-togethers when he could, but Queenie had collared him this time and insisted on his support.

The members of the family looked from one to the other in consternation, as much from worry about how they would manage without Beatie, the hub of the family, as for her own sake.

'We'll all club together to pay for any treatment she needs,' said Bert.

Queenie looked at him in amazement. He was the last one she expected co-operation from.

'Beatie's always been very good to me,' he said, looking his niece straight in the eye.

'Yes, she has,' she agreed, and they both knew what that meant. Bert went up slightly in Queenie's estimation.

They further decided that Beatie should give up getting up so early and going across to Haslar. They went up to her bedroom to put their suggestions to Beatie, who was lying there like a queen giving audience. She was to give up her job immediately and her brothers and brother-in-law would subsidise her until after her operation. Then, if she felt fit enough after convalescence, and would be prepared to stay at home and look after her grandchildren during the day, Vera and Queenie would find employment. Vera would pay her a wage and most of Queenie's money had always gone to her anyway.

Beatie agreed with surprising alacrity but insisted on keeping her evening job of cleaning the baker's shop. 'I wouldn't feel right, not working,' she said, as though looking after a toddler and a baby all day was nothing at all.

Over the anxious period of her mother's stay in hospital and convalescence, Queenie weaned the baby from breast to bottle. To her relief, the operation made a new woman of her mother physically. But more than this, the genuine concern of the family, by whom she had always felt taken for granted, was uplifting to Beatie's spirits.

And before Queenie started work – she had found a waitressing job at the Sailors' Home Club in Queen Street, off the Hard – Hannah was christened. Hanna Loretta Ellis. This event had been put off until Beatie was feeling well again. A proud and pink-faced Eddy was her godfather and an equally proud Lil was her godmother, along with Aunt Ethel. Queenie cried a little during the service, sad for her little girl who didn't have a father at her christening.

One day, before she went back to work, Queenie put Hannah in the old family pram and walked her up to Kingston Cemetery where the remains of Joshua Ellis lay. Just a mound which had grassed over, indistinguishable from the other mounds around it. *She* could tell it from the others, but one day her children would not know where to find their grandfather's grave. But then, they wouldn't have known him, so would they care?

Queenie cared, and stood looking at it with tears in her eyes. 'It's a crying shame, Dad, that you ain't got a headstone,' she whispered. 'But *you* understand, don't you, that Ma couldn't find the money for one. "I always did my duty by him when 'e was alive," she says, "but food for the kids is more important than flowers and headstones on graves".' Queenie gave a little chuckle. 'Ma says that if she could bring you a bottle of beer and watch you enjoy it, that would be a different matter. But I've brought you somethink better than flowers today, Dad.'

She lifted Hannah out of the pram. 'I've brung your first granddaughter to see you, Dad. I've called her Hannah after your little girl what died. Isn't she lovely? I hope you're as proud of her as I am, even if she ain't got a proper dad, poor little sod. But Eddy, Ma and me are goin' to take good care of her and I promise she won't want for nothing.'

Queenie stood rocking the gurgling baby in her arms in the late summer sunshine, telling Joshua things in her head, reminding him of the lovely times they had before he was ill. And how, when he *was* ill in bed, and Ma was at work, she used to go out and scrounge cigarettes for him, even though he wasn't supposed to have them.

'What does it matter, my little Queen of the May,' he

used to say, coughing his lungs out. 'Might as well die happy.'

She wouldn't tell anyone she'd been to see Dad today. She never did – it was her secret. But she smiled as she thought about the secret they would all know about one day. She had saved a few pennies every week when she was working, and now from Hannah's maintenance, going without things she would have liked, to do so. It was mounting up nicely in her secret hiding-place. She wasn't going to let Ma get her hands on *that*.

Hannah started to whimper. 'Got to go now, Dad. I'll come and see you again soon.' She put the baby in the pram, then turned and winked towards the grave. 'One day, Dad, I'm goin' to buy you a lovely headstone – all engraved. And that's a promise. I would have like one of them angels with the outspread wings to stand over you, but you know I ain't a bleedin' millionaire!'

November and December were full of speculation over whether or not the as yet uncrowned King, Edward, would marry the now divorced Mrs Simpson. But there was opposition to it from every side. On 10 December he abdicated and went into exile.

Queenie and Phyllis thought that it was very sad, when he had been so dashing and popular. They cried their eyes out listening to his speech on the wireless.

'But isn't it the most romantic thing you can imagine, Queenie? A King giving up his throne for the woman he loves.'

'Coo, makes you go all goosepimply just thinking about it, don't it? And now Albert's going to succeed to the throne. They say he's ever shy and he stutters, and he's going to be called George – George the sixth. What's wrong with Albert, I want to know?'

'But Elizabeth is gorgeous. She din't expect to be Queen, did she? Just imagine.'

'It's even better than that film we saw,' murmured Queenie in a dreamy voice. 'You know, where the girl gets carried off on a great white horse into the desert by that sheik. That had us going for weeks.'

'Ooh!' The girls shivered in ecstasy.

# · *Twelve* ·

It was Sunday, Hannah's first birthday, and most of the family were coming to celebrate.

Beatie and Queenie had been busy preparing since early morning. Sandwiches had been made and jellies set and the decorative pink icing had been added to the cake. Now they were in the scullery washing the cockles and winkles bought live on the doorstep from the tradesman.

Apart from being Churched after the birth of the baby, and Hannah's christening, they had rather lapsed in Sunday worship. Eddy never went to church anyway, but the two younger boys still attended Sunday School in the afternoon, even though Jimmy now complained that he was too old and it was 'sissy'. Queenie had it on good authority that they usually scived off but *she* wasn't going to shop them.

It was a good excuse to get rid of them for a couple of hours so that Beatie could go to bed for a rest before the usual Sunday onslaught of family. Those precious two hours of solitude had, Queenie remembered with a smile to herself, another purpose while her father was still alive. Before he became too ill. She recalled how she found out when she was about eight.

'Pay attention *Ellis* child,' Miss Sidebottom – pronounced, she insisted, *Sidee-bott-ome* – said nastily, poking Queenie with a bony finger. All the Ellis children had passed through 'Miss Silly Bum's' Sunday School but Queenie considered that was no excuse, and *she* wasn't going to stay there and be poked and insulted by an old witch who couldn't even be bothered to remember the name of the only girl amongst them. The old cow could go to hell!

Ma and Dad were upstairs resting when Queenie returned home. Still smarting with indignation, she ran up to tell them about nasty Miss Silly Bum, and forgetting to knock on the door, she burst into their bedroom – and got an awful fright.

Dad was bouncing up and down on top of Ma, and it must have been hurting her or at least squashing the air out of her, because she was gasping something awful. Why was he doing it? she wondered, because from the way he started groaning, it was obviously painful for him too. What could she do to help them? 'Whats-a-matter?' she cried out in fear. She would never forget the look on their red faces as they swivelled their heads in her direction and both yelled, 'Get out!'

She ran shrieking down the stairs and cowered in the kitchen. 'Don't ever burst in on us like that again!' her mother yelled at her when she came down, and gave her a clip round the ear. 'And don't you dare run out of Sunday School again.'

'But . . . what was you *doing*?' Queenie cried.

'Never you mind. It's private.'

'Leave her alone, Beatie. It wasn't her fault.' Her father came in at that moment, looking a bit sheepish, and ruffled her hair. 'You'll understand when you're grown up, Queen of the May.'

It had left her with an uneasy feeling and it had been many years before she *had* understood, albeit hazily, what went on between men and women. Even after her own little skirmish on Portsmouth Hill, it was *still* a bit hazy.

Reflecting now on her mother's amazing good humour these days, Queenie said, 'Things could be a lot worse, couldn't they, Ma?'

'We ain't starving, if that's what you mean.' Beatie was 'feeding' the cockles with flour, grit coming away with the flour as they spat it out.

'No, I mean you seem much happier now you've given up the laundry job to look after Hannah and Ronnie. It's working out all right, ain't it?'

'I s'pose so. I 'aven't got that horrible pain any more, and I do enjoy the babies.' Life was a good deal happier for everyone now that Beatie had found her forté in life – as grandmother. Relieved from years of parental responsibility, actual and surrogate, she was now allowing herself the luxury of adoring her grandchildren, and being paid to do so into the bargain. It had seemed the best solution all round after Hannah's birth. Queenie certainly was not one to be stuck at home all day.

'Vera and I bringing some money in, and you with your evening job, Eddy paying his whack – we've never been so well off. And then there's Hannah's bit of maintenance – '

'Humph! "Bit" just about describes it, don't it? *He's* gettin' away with it lightly, if you ask me. The sooner that swine comes back and faces 'is responsibilities, the better.'

Queenie wasn't sure what *she* felt about Hannah's father. She had just become accustomed to things as they were. The situation wasn't perfect, but she was happy in a low-key way. Her baby absorbed all her spare time from her waitressing job in the Sailors' Home Club and she felt she did not need any more complications.

Her problem was that she liked men. She knew she had the reputation for being a bit of a tease down the Club, because flirting was second nature to her, but she never meant anything by it. She basked in the admiration of the sailors but resisted the passes they made. She really hadn't got the time or the inclination for more these days.

Besides, there was always the possibility . . . No, it didn't do any good dreaming. She'd had hardly a word from Keith Jackson for over a year. A brief note from Port Said, hoping that 'mother and child were both doing well', when she wrote and told him that he had a baby daughter. One or two postcards from exotic-sounding places like Tangier and Famagusta, acknowledging the photographs of Hannah that she sent him. She always wrote on the back, 'To my daddy, from Hannah'. Followed by a kiss.

She would send him a copy of the studio portrait she and Hannah had just posed for at the Empire Studios in Commercial Road. The baby was dressed in a little cream cotton frock with sprigs of flowers on it, her dark hair in a fringe almost down to her little eyebrows and a slight smile on her open lips. Like a little doll, she was. And *she* looked good too, with a cream beret pulled down at one side with that marcasite bird-brooch Eddy had given her pinned on. And a smart, striped jacket over her blouse. If he still didn't want to know them after a picture like that ... Well, he knew what he could do!

She might never see him again, she mused, just continue to receive maintenance until Hannah was of age. It probably would never have worked out between them anyway. What did she really know about him? Perhaps, one day he would become a well-known artist and she would tell Hannah about her famous father. And pershaps she would die an old maid! Like hell, she would!

'What yer laughing at?' Beatie asked.

'Oh, nothin'.'

The winkles had cooked and were now draining in a colander while Beatie plunged the cockles into a pan of boiling water on the Larbert range. 'Poor little things,' Queenie shuddered. 'I'm glad they don't make that horrid hiss that lobsters make when you put them in.'

'G'arn, that's your imagination.'

'They do! There's only these to put into vinegar when they're cooled and the tables to lay, Ma.'

They were reckoning on the usual eighteen to twenty for tea, counting the kids. So they had carried the table from the kitchen into the dining-room to extend the one already there, getting it with difficulty on its side through doorways and along the narrow passage. They were both now covered with snowy damask cloths.

Queenie whistled the melody 'Whistle While You Work'. She and Phyllis had been to see Walt Disney's *Snow White and the Seven Dwarfs*, and she thought it was ever so clever how those moving pictures came from someone's drawings. Keith had been good at drawing. She still had that picture he did of her at Sally Port. She sighed. That day she had been hoping for so much. Never stopped hoping, if she was honest. Wistfully she sang Snow White's song about how she was wishing for her Prince to come and find her today.

'You'll be lucky!' Beatie sat down heavily.

Seeing that her mother looked tired, Queenie said, 'You go and have yer lie down before the hordes arrive.'

Half an hour later, the tables laid and everything checked, Queenie opened the double doors between the front room and the dining-room. She sighed thankfully, about to go up to her room to change into the new dress she had treated herself to on her birthday – the day before Hannah's – when the door-knocker sounded.

'Oh, bugger!' she muttered, annoyed at the thought of someone arriving over an hour early. She went along the passage to answer it.

On the pavement outside stood a bearded sailor with a large, white, toy cat under his arm.

It was fully a minute before Queenie recognised him. Then her mouth dropped open with astonishment.

'Hello, Queen of the May. How are you? I just managed to make it for Hannah's first birthday. Bit of luck.'

She stood there, red cheeked, wide-eyed, and speechless for a change. She had forgotten just how handsome Keith Jackson was, and now, sun-bronzed and bearded, even more so. Her heart was knocking in her breast.

Keith grinned. 'The *first* time I saw you, your head was done up in a turban like that.'

He *would* catch her looking like a charwoman. Half an hour later and she would have been all dolled up. She wasn't sure how to behave. Should she be indignant and tell him to get lost? But the sight of him had her in a tremble of excitement – just like the first time she had set eyes on him.

'I s'pose you better come in,' she muttered, standing aside to let him go past her. He took his cap off as she showed him into the front room. His hair was shorter than when she had last seen him, but still wavy.

They stood looking at each other awkwardly.

'We wasn't expecting you back for ages,' she said bluntly.

'Nor was I. We've come steaming back from the troubles in the Med for His Majesty's Review of His Fleet after the Coronation. *Barham* is playing host ship to a Russian warship. But we've only got a couple of weeks and we're off again. I've come straight away – haven't been home yet.'

'Oh.' What was she supposed to make of that? 'I was just goin' up to get changed for Hannah's birthday party.' She indicated the laden tables, saying hesitantly, 'If you want to stay, you'll meet all the family.'

He looked worried. 'Would I be welcome, do you think?'

She shrugged. '*I* don't mind. Me mother'll probably kill you, but if you want to take the risk . . .'

'I'd . . . like to see the baby.'

She saw the appeal in his eyes and pleasure flooded through her. 'She's out the back. Come through if you like.' She led the way down the passage to the kitchen and pointed to the open door to the yard. He nodded, setting the toy cat down in the high-chair. She saw that he was waiting for her to go.

'I . . . I'll just go and get tidied up then. If she wakes up you can lift her out – but she'll probably have a wet bum.'

But instead of going up the stairs, she went into the dining-room which had a window looking out into the yard. She just *had* to see how he reacted to his daughter. She peeped round the curtain.

The young sailor approached the pram hesitantly, then bent his slim frame over it. Hannah was obviously awake as Queenie saw him smile and his lips move, though she could not hear his words. She saw the baby's chubby fist reach up and he lowered his hand gently so that his finger could be grasped, and smiled again. Hallelujah! It looked as if it was going to be all right.

With tears in her eyes, Queenie fled up the stairs. Automatically, without really knowing what she was doing, and in a feverish hurry, she pulled the scarf off her head, took the bobby pins out of whirls of hair and brushed it out. It was longer than when he had last seen it and fell in loose waves to below her shoulders.

Pulling off her overall, she puffed some talcum powder into her armpits and slipped into her new satin, all-in-one camiknickers. All the rage. What would he say if he saw her now? she wondered, suddenly unbearably excited because she knew that, in spite of the periods of hatred and bitterness she had felt when she had thought about him these last eighteen months – in spite of all that – she had been hoping and hoping. And he *had* come back. She giggled; her prince had come and found her today.

She slipped the brightly-flowered rayon dress over her head. This new material was just like silk, the tulip-shaped skirt clinging to her satin-clad hips and accentuating her slim waist.

Spitting on the solid block, she rubbed the small brush on the black mascara and applied it to her lashes. 'Damson Blush' on her lips, a dab of perfume behind her ears and between her breasts, a dusting of powder on her nose, and she was ready. Looking at herself critically, she saw that her colour was high and her eyes sparkling with excitement. She looked absolutely gorgeous! She hadn't felt so alive for over a year, and now, surely, she was in control of her own destiny once more.

Keith was sitting in the kitchen with his baby daughter on his lap, Hannah burbling and pulling on his lanyard as he held her clasped awkwardly between his two brown hands. The toy cat was watching them from the high-chair. Keith looked up as Queenie came into the kitchen . . . blinked . . . and went on looking.

Pretending unawareness of the surprised approval in his eyes, she tossed back her head. 'Well,' she challenged truculently, one hand on her hip. '*Is* she your daughter?'

He nodded. 'I never really doubted it. And to prove it, she's even got the Jackson little finger – '

'The what?' she laughed, trying not to reveal how delighted she was.

'The Jackson little finger.' He held out the baby's hand. 'See how it curves inwards? Like my father's and his father's. She's beautiful . . .' His voice broke. He swallowed and looked up at Queenie. 'Like her mother,' he added softly, his eyes damp.

Queenie's smile was radiant, tears of joy adding lustre to her remarkable eyes. Keith stood up and they moved slowly towards each other, he with the baby on one navy serge arm, held secure with his other hand, and she drinking him in.

He looked more mature. The beard, not dense or bushy, neatly followed the line of his jaw, leaving two unadorned areas beneath his lower lip. She liked it but she missed the cleft in his chin.

'Queenie,' he began softly and her heart skipped a beat. 'I just want to say how sorry I am . . . I, um, I've been a real bastard . . .'

She bit on her bottom lip, sharing his embarrassment,

both of them knowing that his stammered statement was totally inadequate; that no words could compensate for or excuse his doubt over her integrity, his failure to acknowledge his child. Yet she knew she had forgiven him.

Hannah bent towards her mother with arms outstretched and Keith relinquished her. 'Do you like your Daddy, Hannah?' Queenie asked, jiggling her up and down, and looking up at him from under her lashes in the devastating way that had captivated him before.

'I suppose,' said Hannah's Daddy, 'that we had better get married.' Not the way Cary Grant or Errol Flyn would have proposed to their leading ladies – but it was good enough.

# · Thirteen ·

Beatie came down a little later to a surprise introduction to her future son-in-law. Her mouth gaped for a moment. 'Better bloody late than never, I suppose!' she exlaimed roughly. But Queenie could see from the glint in her mother's eye that she liked the look of Keith Jackson. 'When you goin' to make an honest woman of our Queenie, then?'

'I'm sorry to say it can't be until this tour is over, Mrs Ellis. *Barham's* off again after the Review . . . for another year.'

'Oh well. Gives us plenty of time to prepare for the wedding, don't it?' Beatie, dressed in a polka-dotted brown dress with detachable lace collar, had a pleased smile on her face, but Queenie was momentarily crushed with disappointment. Then she thought of the past eighteen months when she had not known what her future would bring. Now she did, and a year would pass like a flash. He wouldn't be here anyway, so it didn't matter if they were married or not. But it would be something lovely to look forward to.

The various branches of the family arrived thick and fast, and on being introduced to 'Queenie's young man', were obviously agog with curiosity.

Beatie's sister Ethel had Uncle Bert in tow; he of the unwelcome advances to his niece. Their daughter Vilma was absent as she was 'courting'. Beatie's brothers,

Danny and Arthur, came with their wives and assorted children.

Billy, Queenie's eldest brother was away on army manoeuvres, but Vera came with their little Ronnie. She couldn't take her admiring eyes off the dashing sailor, which, after all her catty remarks during her sister-in-law's fall from grace, was balm to Queenie's bruised pride.

Queenie's two younger brothers and John, the marine, with fiancée Phyllis, completed the party. There was some good-natured banter between John and Keith about 'matelots' versus 'boot-necks' and Queenie was thrilled to see that Keith was fitting in so well.

'*He* was worth waiting for,' Phyllis whispered in Queenie's ear, giving her a happy squeeze.

'Where's Eddy?' asked Beatie.'Oh, well, we may as well get started. Yer never know if *he's* going to turn up or no.'

Beatie held baby Hannah, dressed in frilly white with a little palm tree of hair sticking up from a bow on top of her head, and a silver bracelet denting one plump arm. Shiny red, buttoned shoes adorned her tiny feet.

Queenie, passing plates and pouring tea, noticed with pleasure that Keith's eyes returned to his daughter again and again, and when his eyes met her own he would wink or smile at her. Soon there was a cheerful hub-bub and Keith was asked about his present tour.

'You could say we're policing the Med – it's become a real trouble spot. What a year it's been. The British Navy has had it's hands full, I can tell you. The Italians invading Abyssinia, so that we had to guard the Suez Canal. Trouble between Arabs and Jews, and ships having to stand by off Haifa.'

'Now the Spanish War,' added John.

Keith nodded. 'We watched the bombing of Malaga – defies description.'

'Oh, I'd no idea what you were going through,' cried Queenie, filled with remorse at how she had cursed him for 'swanning round the Med' when all the time he had been involved in dangerous activities.

'It's been no picnic most of the time. Since the Spanish civil war broke out we've been involved with the evacuation of British Nationals and Spanish refugees to safe ports. Nuns, babies – the lot.'

'Didn't see much of the Mediterranean fleshpots then?' asked Uncle Bert.

'Chance would have been a fine thing,' answered Keith, his cheeks colouring slightly when he remembered his visit to Malta, but no-one noticed.

'Ah, what you missed,' reminisced Uncle Arthur, the merchant seaman, small and dark-eyed like his sister Beatie. 'Those luscious Arab girls. The things they can do with a donkey!'

'What can they do, Uncle Arthur?' clamoured the younger children.

'Arthur!' warned Beatie sharply. The men guffawed as the women cast worried glances around. Queenie suspected what he was getting at, but the children exchanged exasperated looks at the grown-ups' habit of giving them glimpses of their world, and then refusing to explain.

The cockles and winkles were disappearing fast to the accompaniment of appreciative murmurs.

'Talking of donkeys, Keith,' broke in Uncle Bert, and Queenie knew just what was coming, they'd heard it so often. She and Phyllis exchanged a grimace. 'I call myself the 'Elephant Man', because it took me *seven years* to get my daughter, our Vilma. But not for want of trying, eh, Ethel?' He leered at his wife who snickered dutifully amid the groans.

And what about the other one? Queenie wanted to ask in anger. The daughter that poor Ethel knows nothing about, you dirty old man. The one that I pay your maintenance for every week – and I've heard rumours that you still visit that woman. She gave him a disgusted look and was gratified to see his florid face turn even redder.

'Have a ham sandwich . . . Keith.' Queenie passed him the plate, feeling quite shy to be using his name in front of her family, and when he smiled at her, her heart did a flip. *They were going to be married!* She felt so happy she could burst.

'What about next door's dog. You remember, Beatie,' Ethel reminded them with a laugh.'When John got the whooping cough and Lil told you to rub some meat on his chest and throw it over into Shirley's yard and her dog would eat it and take the cough off John.'

They all groaned.

'Did it work?' asked Keith with a twinkle in his eye, pleased by the Ellis family's easy acceptance of him and at their efforts to entertain him. Especially after he had treated Queenie so shabbily. His mother would no doubt describe them as rough, and she wasn't going to be very pleased when he told her he was going to marry Queenie. But he liked them.

'Well, John didn't get better any quicker, but poor old Bonzo got a very nasty cough,' laughed Beatie.

'Tell the story of the tramp, Auntie Queenie,' demanded eleven-year-old Harry.

'Oh, no,' she groaned.

'Yes, go on, tell,' the children clamoured.

'Oh, well.' Everyone waited for her to continue. Queenie grinned, happy to be the centre of attention. 'There I was, all togged up in me best knickers and me very first brazzeer . . .' She paused for the children to snigger at the naughty word, and tossed Keith a saucy look. 'And I decided I'd go down the yard to the lav dressed up in me new finery.' She placed one hand on her hip and waggled from side to side on her chair. 'I was hoping to give Spotty Dick from next door an eyeful. He's always spying on me.'

'Cheeky sod!' exclaimed nine-year-old Joannie.

'Language!' admonished Dot, giving her daughter a light cuff.

'Go on,' the other children demanded.

'Where was I? Oh, yes, I'm just mincing down the yard, all la-di-da,' her hand on her waggling hip again, she met Keith's grin and sparkled at him. 'The chickens' eyes nearly popped out of their heads I can tell you. Anyway, I get to the lav door and peep back over me shoulder and sure enough, Spotty Dick's looking out of his bedroom window. I pokes me tongue out at him, turns round and opens the door . . . and get the *fright* of me life!' She paused for effect. They all knew what was coming, but waited with bated breath for the punchline.

'A bleedin' old tramp was asleep on the lav!'

Exclamations came from her audience. Keith, the only one not to have heard the story before, raised his eyebrows.

'I don't know who was more frightened . . . him or me.'

'I wondered what all the screaming was about,' cried Beatie over the laughter.

'I come running back up the yard and trip . . .'

'Arse-over-tit . . .'

'Thank you, Uncle Bert! And fell right into the bath of cold water outside the scullery.'

More laughter.

'And the worst thing of all,' she finished, 'was that Spotty Dick was sniggerin' his head off at his window. I won't tell you what I called him.'

'That poor old tramp scooted off down the alley like a streak of greased lightnin'' chuckled Beatie. 'I'd 'ave given him somethink to eat if he'd waited.'

'What's all this, then?' Eddy limped through the doorway, a diffident smile on his pleasant face, his cheeks pink with embarrassment at coming into a room full of people, even if they were family.

'Freddie, sit on yer Mum's lap and let Uncle Eddy have your chair,' said Beatie.

'Where you been?' asked Queenie, not expecting an answer as Eddy was always totally uncommunicative in public. 'You've almost missed your god-daughter's party, and all the cockles and winkles have gone.'

'I got back in time for the cake,' he answered. 'Cup of tea'll do me.'

'This is Queenie's fiancey,' said Beatie, waving a hand in Keith's direction.

Eddy raised an eyebrow while he digested this surprising piece of information. Anger flickered in his eyes and tightened his mouth as he regarded the handsome sailor.

'Eddy.' Queenie entreated, knowing that deep passions ran beneath his quiet, shy exterior.

Eddy heard the note of entreaty in his sister's voice and saw how her face glowed and her eyes sparkled. 'The wanderer returns,' he offered at last with an obvious effort not to be unpleasant.

'Didn't have any choice in the matter, I'm afraid,' muttered Keith defensively.

'Why should he worry?' asked Uncle Bert. 'A wife in every port . . .'

'Didn't get ashore in many of them.'

'And that's not nice, Bert,' chided Auntie Ethel, her permed curls aquiver with indignation, while Queenie quelled him with a smouldering glance.

Keith nodded at Eddy. 'Afraid this is only a flying visit.'

'Where you off to then?' Eddy eyed him warily as he sat down.

'Back to the Med. Calling at the same places and a few extra ports . . . Valencia, Barcelona to pick up more refugees, Oran, Corfu, to name but a few. Plenty of shell practise. Ready for anything that might erupt.'

'Glad to hear you chaps in the pukka Navy are being kept on your toes, ready to defend us against the Hun again,' said Arthur. 'Now the War Office has signed that treaty with Berlin allowing them to build up their Navy again, I reckon we'll 'ave to watch our backs. Wouldn't trust a German further that I could throw him after the last lot.'

Keith nodded. 'I agree. We're on standby. Malta is very vulnerable if war with Germany breaks out . . .'

'All this dreary talk about war! It'll never come to that,' asserted Beatie. 'Pass Keith one of those coconut cakes, I'm famous for me coconut cakes. And Peter, stop pickin' yer nose.'

'"The war to end all wars"! That's what they said about the last one.' Uncle Danny had a cast in his eye which made it difficult to know who he was looking at. Everyone nodded in case it was them. 'But . . . I wonder.'

'My father was on the Somme,' said Keith, shaking his head. 'He came back a bitter man.'

'He was lucky to come back at all, if you ask me,' observed Uncle Bert, who had sat the war out with poor eyesight. '*Thousands* of men were killed on the Somme.'

'Nearly a quarter of a million, I believe,' amended Keith.

'All those widows and orphans,' mourned Dot.

'My old man was in the Baltic in a submarine, Keith,' Beatie informed their guest proudly.

'Queenie told me.'

'Dad was a hero,' said John.

Eddy nodded, 'You can say that again.'

'Bloody foreigners,' grumbled Arthur. 'Josh told us how those Bolshies turned against their admirals in the revolution . . . set one alight and danced round 'im, they did. You wouldn't get the British doing things like that.'

'Coo . . .'ow 'orrible,' spluttered one of the boys.

'Don't talk with your mouth full,' Beatie admonished.

'Poor old Cromie, Josh's commander,' went on Arthur, 'he stayed on as a diplomat after the men come back. And he got slaughtered by the mob on the steps of the British Embassy.'

There was a moment's silence.

'What's slaughtered mean?' asked one of the children.

'Murdered. The *bastards*!' exclaimed Uncle Danny.

'*We* wouldn't murder our lovely Royal Family, neither.' Ethel's eyes were misty.

'And long may they reign!' agreed Dot fervently. 'Those

dear little princesses. Just think, Elizabeth will be our Queen one day.'

'*Our* little Queen, here,' put in Uncle Danny with a chuckle and a sly askance look at Queenie, 'used to believe *she* was Princess Anastasia, the only member of the Russian Royal Family to escape.'

Queenie coloured. 'No I never, Uncle Dan! Not really. But Dad used to kid me that he brought me back on the troopship and that I was the daughter of a Russian countess.'

'If you was, *he* must have got his leg over,' laughed Uncle Danny. ''cos you couldn't be anyone's daughter but his.'

'Don't be crude, Danny. Josh wasn't like that!' exclaimed Beatie. The children looked from one to the other, puzzled. 'Anyway, Queenie was born *after* the war.'

Queenie looked a little sheepishly at Keith and he winked back. 'I knew there was something special about you, Queen of the May. Just hope you've got some jewels stashed away for a rainy day.'

'*No wonder* you've always acted so superior,' sneered Vera.

'I have not!'

'Leave Queenie alone,' championed Phyllis. 'You're just jealous because she's got some style about her.'

'Style! That's not what I'd call it.'

'Cow!' muttered Queenie, forgetting that she was on her best behaviour.

'Now then, you girls,' cried Beatie, the matriarch. 'That's enough of that. If everyone has finished, we'll cut the cake.' Keith reached out for Hannah who was banging the table with a spoon. 'Go to Daddy while I light the candle on yer lovely birthday cake.'

Beatie passed the baby to her pleased father, who settled her awkwardly on his lap and Queenie watched with a lump in her throat as he lowered his head to the baby's level to share her entrancement over the flickering flame, everyone encouraging her, by huffing and puffing, to try to blow it out. Her puzzled little eyes went from face to face.

'Shall Daddy do it?' asked Keith, proudly.

'Ere!' blurted out Freddie. 'How can you be Hannah's Dad? You ain't married to Auntie Queenie.'

There was a moment's silence.

'"Out of the mouth's of babes",' quoted Uncle Danny, disparate eyes studying the ceiling.

'For God's sake, someone go next door and get Lil,' Beatie said quickly. 'I promised to call her in when we got round to the cake.'

Keith blew out the candle.

# · *Fourteen* ·

The Ellises were a *real* family, mused Keith as he made his way back to the Sailors' Home Club. Genuine people. They didn't stand on ceremony, polite and remote like his own family. They said what they thought, quarrelled when they felt like it, but were always, he imagined, there for each other when help was needed.

Look how they had rallied round Queenie when she got pregnant. Her situation, living at home with an illegitimate child was, in spite of the extra hardships it caused, entirely accepted, whereas in a middle-class home it would have been a matter for shame and concealment.

In this case the shame was his, in the way he had treated Queenie; doubting her word and not acknowledging the child. She was worth more than that.

And Hannah!

Tears stung his eyes as he recalled his first sight of his tiny daughter. Eyelids like flower petals, closed over eyes that when opened were a dark indeterminate colour still, but with hints of hazel in their depths. The cherubic mouth, a few little teeth like seed pearls. He had never had anything to do with babies and was quite unprepared for the surge of emotion that hit him as he gazed down at her. The sudden primeval pride of fatherhood.

Yet he knew even before he saw her – had always known if he was honest – that she *was* his child. He had so often studied the photos that Queenie had sent him and was in love with Hannah from the start. Else why would he have come hot-footing it up here from the dockyard before he even thought of going to Portchester to see his parents?

His offspring. A miniature of her combined parents. Hannah had smiled up at him, trusting, knowing nothing of his baseness, and had stolen his heart. He loved the feel of her warm little body through the cool silk of her dress; robust yet fragile. She had stood on his thighs in her twinkly shoes and grasped his beard with her tiny, perfect hands, pulling his face down to hers. As his forehead made contact with hers, her two dark eyes had merged into one at close range and she had burbled happily. He adored her.

And her mother?

Although still so young, Queenie had become a woman since he had last seen her. Time and motherhood had filled out her figure, given her a new serenity and the promise of beauty in the young girl had been fulfilled. But she still possessed that infectious sense of fun.

Keith grinned to himself as he recalled how the birthday party had swelled to unmanageable proportions with nosy, brassy Lil from next door, her weedy husband and their son, 'Spotty Dick'. The children had exchanged a few sniggers over him, and Keith noticed, annoyed, that his eyes never left Queenie.

The gathering had become increasingly noisy and Hannah became fractious. 'Time for beddy-byes, young lady,' her mother told her. 'You've had an exciting day, what with your party and . . . everything.' Her smiling eyes met his. 'I'll just go and get your supper.'

'How d'yer like yer perspective son-in-law, then, Beat?' asked Lil roguishly, when Queenie had left the room.

Beatie and Keith eyed each other warily. His eyes asked forgiveness. Hers offered understanding. 'He'll do!' she said at last, and exchanged a grin for a wink.

'He's smashing!' Phyllis said, and blushed. A nice girl.

Queenie's brother, the marine, was a good bloke too. Eddy was a bit of an oddball, but likeable.

Queenie came back after a few minutes and fed the baby with rusks and a bottle of milk. 'Say goodnight to everyone.' Hannah was passed around, jiggled and kissed and only returned to her mother when she started bawling. 'You can come and see her put to bed if you like,' Queenie invited him shyly.

'I'd like that.'

'No hanky-panky, now,' leered Uncle Bert as they left the room.

'That man!' exclaimed Queenie, leading the way down the dark passage with its brown anaglypta wallpaper halfway up the wall and cream above the rail. He followed her up the stairs to the room on the first floor that she now shared with the baby.

He knew that she felt as awkward as he did when they were alone together in her bedroom. They had shared the ultimate intimacy of sex, yet they were almost strangers. She thrust the baby at him.

'What a pretty room you've got, Hannah,' he observed, holding her while Queenie busied herself with closing the thin floral-patterned curtains, getting together nappies and so on. The nursery end of the room was furnished prettily with a miniature dressing-table, complete with mirror, and some sort of chests, all covered in frilled pink taffeta to match the bedding in the cot. Two nursery-rhyme pictures hung on the walls.

'Ma made that furniture – from orange boxes.'

He pulled back a drape to see that it was indeed an orange box turned on its end, the partition making a shelf that was lined with paper and bore piles of little garments. A stack of clean nappies was on the bottom. 'Amazing! I like your mother – she's a good sort.'

Queenie looked surprised. 'She has 'er moments, I s'pose. Come to Mummy, pet.'

Hannah rubbed her little fists in her eyes and whimpered

while her nappy and dress were being changed on Queenie's bed. He watched, fascinated. 'All ready for sleepy-byes. Say goodnight to . . . Daddy, Hannah.' Keith held the baby for a few minutes, dressed in her cotton nightie and smelling of talcum powder, nuzzling his face in her fine hair and against her satiny cheeks.

Her mother bent over the cot to lay her down and crooned to her for a few moments. Standing close to her and a little behind, he suddenly became excruciatingly aware of Queenie's body. The line of her hips swelling from her small waist, the sweet profile of a breast ripened by motherhood, the firmness of her buttocks and the graceful curve of her arm. Her dark hair had fallen forward to conceal her face, and a rather overpowering smell of cheap perfume surrounded her. Tenderness swept through him for the girl he had wronged, but who had come bravely through her ordeal and appeared to bear him no malice. He vowed to make it up to her.

The tenderness gave way to desire, flooding his body, stirring his sexuality. He laid his hands gently on her waist, half expecting a rebuff. He wouldn't have blamed her. But she stood up and leant back against him. Moving his hands to clasp her midriff, he felt the swell of her breasts overlap his thumbs. Like Hannah's, her flesh felt warm under cool, slippery material. Silk whispering on silk. They stood like that for a few moments, his face buried in her hair.

The baby's eyes were closed and her head was moving from side to side as she sought sleep. 'She is so beautiful,' he murmured. 'I am proud to be her Daddy and I hope . . . I hope her Mummy will be able to forgive me?'

Queenie swivelled round in his arms till her firm breasts were pressed against his chest. Linking her arms around his neck, she looked up into his eyes, her own hazy in the dim light with the same desire that was pulsing through him.

'What've I got to *forgive* you for? You gave me Hannah,' she said softly.

He lowered his lips to hers, gathering her tightly to him and they were breathless when they drew their faces apart.

'Whew!' he said.

'No hanky-panky, Uncle Bert said.' She grinned. 'But what Ma says is true – 'kissing a man without a beard *is* like eating an egg without salt.'

'Let's try it again.' The forbidden, hesitant passion of eighteen months earlier gave way to a stronger rage now that they had committed themselves. His hands cupped her breasts, and his lips moved over her arched throat. He desperately wanted to lie on the bed with her but he felt it was more than he deserved. He had been a selfish bastard and would have to wait now until they were married. He linked his hands on her buttocks and looked down into her eyes.

'You'll have to come and meet my parents.'

She grimaced. 'I've met your mother don't forget, and I think she's going to be bleedin' pissed off about this.'

'She will be if you use language like that,' he laughed. 'She's all right really. It's her strict up-bringing. I expect it was a bit of a shock for her.'

'I'll say. My Ma wasn't too pleased, neither. Gave me a thick ear.'

'Poor little Queenie. I'm so sorry – '

'Well, it's all in the past now. Does your Mum and Dad know . . . about this?'

'I'm going home tomorrow to tell them – '

'Coo, there'll be fireworks and no mistake.' She giggled.

'I expect so, but I'm a big boy now. Make my own decisions. I'll spend a couple of days with them, and come back, say Tuesday or Wednesday?'

'I get Wednesday afternoons off.'

'Good. We'll go out and buy a ring – make it official.' She smiled in delight. 'Then I'll take you home to tea next weekend.'

'I can't wait!'

Laughing at her comical expression, he kissed her again

before they went downstairs. He had a couple of beers with the men and shared some dirty jokes and talk about the unrest in Europe, while the women chatted in the kitchen over a cup of tea and the kids played in the yard. Eddy, obviously shy in the company of women, was not backward in expressing his opinions in the presence of his own sex.

Keith had the feeling that life with Queenie and her family was going to be far from dull. But there *was* going to be a war, and he would be in the forefront of it. Fear knotted his gut, shivered down his spine. What sort of security could he offer Queenie and Hannah after all?

Sitting on the front seat on the top deck of the bus to Portchester to have tea with the Jacksons, Queenie remembered her last visit and her stomach churned.

Hannah looked adorable in the new dress her Daddy had bought her, and her red shoes. Queenie knew she was looking good, too, in her cream beret and jacket and the rayon stockings Keith had bought her. Just like silk they were. The cluster of garnets on a slender gold band that she had chosen from a jeweller in Commercial Road, glowed on her left hand.

Her arm, shoulder and thigh were thrillingly welded to Keith's as she watched him rolling a cigarette. She loved the movements of his hands, his handsome profile – everything about him. He put the tickler between his lips while he replaced the packet in his pocket and took out his lighter. She and Hannah watched the small flame flicker under the end and smelled the puff of smoke.

Suddenly aware of her scutinity, he turned his head and his mouth curved into the suggestion of a smile, his eyes warm.

'Did your mother like your beard?'

'No, she hated it. That's why I'm going to keep it.'

'What if *I* asked you to shave it off?'

'Then I would, of course. Your wish is my command.'

'I like salt with my eggs.'

'You like "salts" – full stop.'

'You know I've always liked sailors, but now there's only one for me.'

Their eyes held dreamily. Queenie felt Keith's gaze reach deep inside her, touching a sensitive spot somewhere within that blossomed into sweet desire. He bent his head and brushed his mouth against hers. She didn't mind if the people sitting behind them were watching. She hoped they were. She was proud of him and in love all over again.

Keith carried the baby up Sea Lane and Queenie clung to his other arm, teetering slightly on her high heels as she tried to match his stride. 'Oh, I feel sick,' she said as they neared number thirty-one.

'Just don't throw up on my mother's precious Persian rug,' he advised as he held the gate open for her. 'She'll forgive you, in time, for anything but that.'

Queenie took several deep breaths in the porch as they waited for their knock to be answered. She'd show them! What had she to be ashamed of? All right, she didn't speak posh but she was Joshua Ellis's daughter, and he had been every bit as good as they were.

Keith's father opened the door, his forehead puckered anxiously but with half a smile on his wide mouth and lighting his grey eyes.

'Hello, Dad. This is Queenie.'

Bernard Jackson nodded briskly and held out his hand. His grasp was firm, his eyes appreciative. 'Come along in, lass. Mother,' he called, unnecessarily, 'they're here.' Then staring at Hannah, his eyes moistened. 'Hello, little 'un. You're a lovely little maid.'

Queenie relaxed slightly, taking an immediate liking to her future father-in-law. But it wasn't *him* she was worried about – she could always get round men.

'Take Queenie through to the lounge, Keith.'

Lounge! In their house it was the bloody front room.

The lounge door was slightly ajar and Keith pushed it open and walked in ahead of her, for which she was grateful.

Violet Jackson, dressed in a beige knitted suit and lacy blouse, rose to her feet from an armchair, her handsome face set into an unsmiling mask, her short hair immaculately waved.

'Mum.' Keith kissed her cheek.

'Hello, dear.' Her glance swept coolly over Queenie, then went back to him and fixed on Hannah. 'The dear little mite!' she exlaimed and smiled an unexpectedly sweet smile. 'Will she come to me?' She held out her arms and Hannah, a sociable baby, coming from such a large family, responded by leaning towards her.

With her grandchild in her arms, Violet turned to Queenie. 'Do sit down,' she invited stiffly.

'Thanks. How . . . how you been keeping, Mrs Jackson?' Queenie sat on the settee and folded one ankle over the other in what she hoped was a ladylike pose.

'As well as can be expected – all things considered.'

'Hrmm. I'll put the kettle on, then,' said Bernard from the doorway where he had been hovering anxiously.

Violet sat down too, and started talking to the baby. 'Who's a pretty little girl then? Look at those smart red shoes.' Hannah reached up and grasped her grandmother's pearls. To Queenie's horror the strand broke and, to the accompaniment of Violet's shriek, the pearls shot in all directions.

'Oh – I'm ever so sorry!' cried Queenie, dropping onto her knees and frantically picking the beads up off the 'precious Persian rug'.

Keith got down on his hands and knees too, shuffling towards her with a mock-horror expression on his face which made her dissolve into nervous giggles.

'I don't think it's funny,' said Violet frostily. 'They are quite valuable.'

'You'll have to teach our daughter better manners,

Queenie,' said Keith with a wink. 'How many were there, Mum?'

'How can I possibly know that? They were all graded in size, so I suppose we should be able to lay them out and see how many are missing. Take the baby so that I can find the ones in my lap.'

Queenie took Hannah and prised several beads out of her tight little fist.

'What's going on?' asked Bernard, wheeling in a laden trolley. Then the front-door bell rang and he had to go and answer it. There were voices in the hall before a handsome young man, slightly shorter than Keith and with the same cleft in the chin, but with his father's grey eyes, came through the door. 'Hello, Mum.'

'Michael!' Violet's eyes shone and her face softened. Queenie saw that she had been a very pretty girl. 'You made it after all.' He bent and kissed her cheek then turned to Keith.

The brothers grinned at each other, clasped right hands and patted each other awkwardly on the shoulder with the left.

'How's the Navy, old sport?'

'Could be worse. Exotic ports, Mediterranean sunshine. Why should I grumble? What's that miserable weed growing under your nose?'

Michael smoothed a finger along his narrow dark moustache. 'Makes me look more mature, don't you think? Anyway it's preferable to that fungus that's decorating your ugly phizzog!'

'Naval tradition, old boy. Had to ask the captain for "Permission to stop shaving". Hear you've passed the cookery classes. Have they given you an apron yet? You're going to make someone a lovely little wife.'

'Ha-bloody-ha!'

Queenie smiled in delight at the affectionately teasing exchange.

'Michael's a *qualified chef*, Keith,' Violet admonished.

'Don't belittle him. And one of the reasons we asked him to come up today was to tell you some exciting news – '

Keith raised an eyebrow and interrupted. 'And the other reason, I suppose, was for him to meet my beautiful future wife and my lovely daughter, Hannah.' Queenie was thrilled to hear pride in his voice. He put an arm around his brother's shoulders and turned him towards them. 'And this is my perfectly horrible little brother.'

'I think he's lovely!' she was unable to resist a flirtatious smile.

'Wow!' said Michael, coming forward to clasp her hand, and holding onto it while she looked up him from under her lashes. 'I can quite see why – '

'Bring the trolley over, Bernard,' Violet ordered sharply.

Queenie had some difficulty keeping her little finger crooked like Violet did when she raised her tea-cup to her mouth. The contents of the cup were disgusting – like cat's pee. She liked her tea strong enough to stand your spoon up in. The sandwiches were tiny, with the crusts cut off. Blimey, you'd never get Ma being that wasteful. Lovely cakes though – that sponge was as 'airy as a fairy's fart', to quote Uncle Danny.

For Queenie, it was an uncomfortable hour and her nervousness made her garrulous. She just could not keep her mouth shut, even though she could see Violet was getting more annoyed by the minute. Keith egged her on with winks and laughs, and his father and brother kept exchanging delighted looks. She was amusing *them* all right.

It was a relief to Queenie when the conversation turned to the forthcoming coronation on 12th May.

'I wonder why he wants to be known as George the Sixth,' mused Violet. 'King Albert would sound rather grand. We've had a King Alfred, but never an Albert have we?'

'Victoria's husband, Albert, was a German. Not a popular idea at the moment,' suggested Bernard. 'But this chap's a chip off the old block. He'll be good for the country.'

'And he's a respectable married man,' Violet nodded, 'with a fine wife and family – '

'Those little princesses are gorgeous.' Queenie interrupted Violet, who looked at her with pursed mouth. 'Hannah's my little princess, aren't you, pet?'

But Hannah was bored and started to play up, clambering from one person to the other and whingeing. Michael gave her some keys to play with. 'Albert is a bit of a dull chap,' he said, returning to the previous conversation.

'Edward would have made a more interesting king,' agreed Keith. 'Is this one going to be strong enough when – if we go to war?'

'Edward is a weak and selfish character,' sniffed Violet, 'or he would never have put himself and his . . . pleasures before his duty. He would have brought the monarchy into disrepute – he was nothing but a playboy. That *dreadful* American woman.'

'An absolute floozy,' agreed Keith. He and Michael exchanged a grin.

'It's just like the films though, ain't it?' Queenie's fine eyes had a dreamy look. 'Giving up his throne for the woman 'e loves. Ever so romantic. Would you do the same for me, Keith?' She threw him an arch look to which he responded with a wink.

'Irresponsible I call it,' snapped Violet. 'Thank goodness his true nature was exposed before he actually became King. He would have dragged this country's – this Empire's – good name through the mud.'

'That's a bit strong, Mater,' interrupted Michael. 'He had his good points – '

'So did Henry the Eighth! And *he* had six wives.'

'Lucky old him,' laughed Keith.

'One's enough for any man if you ask me,' said Bernard with a wry grin. Violet threw him a sharp glance.

Queenie changed the subject. 'Have you seen *Gone With*

*The Wind*?' No one had, so she told them all about it with enthusiasm. 'I'm sure I'd be like Scarlett O'Hara if there was another war. I wouldn't let the Germans beat *me*.'

Keith laughed. 'Just let them try.'

'That's the spirit, lass,' said Bernard and received a disdainful look from his wife.

'And I'd look after the family through thick an' thin,' Queenie continued. 'Phyllis says I look like Scarlett – I mean Vivien Leigh.' She tossed back her hair and grinned at her fiancé. 'But she can keep old Clarke Gable – I'd rather have my Keith any day.'

Violet, with pursed lips, banged her cup down.

'Steady on, Mum, that's your Crown Derby,' smirked Michael.

Hannah had by now resorted to crawling on all fours and, reaching a little table, she pulled herself up against it and grabbed hold of a little china basket of flowers that sat on top with various other trinkets.

'Put that down, you little sod!' Queenie leapt up, smacked Hannah's hand and then, wanting to console the bawling child, asked desperately, while trying to remember her aitches at the same time, '*H*ave you got a buttered crust she could suck on, Mrs Jackson? It'll keep *h*er quiet until I give *h*er a bottle.'

Violet's nostrils were stretched wide in disapproval, but she went out, returning a minute later with the crust. 'Would you mind not letting her have it on my Persian rug – I don't want butter on it.'

Keith reached for the baby and Queenie passed her over and, taking a bib out of her handbag, tied it round Hannah's neck. The child's face and hands were soon greasy from the butter, and bits of soggy bread fell onto her father's navy-clad knee. 'What's this exciting news you mentioned earlier, Mum?' he asked, picking off the crumbs and putting them on his plate.

'I've been waiting to get a word in edgeways.' Violet threw Queenie an exasperated look, before turning to her son with an eager smile. 'Your father and I are taking over a guest house in Cornwall. Porthleven is the name of the village – on the south coast. It's a lovely house, isn't it, Bernard?'

'It is that, Mother.' Bernard smiled enthusiastically.

'Tremayne. Don't you think that's an attractive name?'

Keith nodded but looked nonplussed by the news.

'It's a white house with Georgian windows – you know, those little panes. There's a glass conservatory at the side and a verandah across the front.' Her dainty little hands made descriptive movements. 'Across the little road is a whitewashed wall with a gate in it, leading down to a private garden below.' She smiled as she recalled. 'And from there you look down into the outer harbour and the sea beyond.'

'It sounds really posh,' breathed Queenie, thinking again that Violet was a pretty woman when she relaxed and wasn't looking as if she had something painful stuffed up her bum.

Violet continued. 'There's a lovely plant growing at the foot of the wall and in the crevices – deep pink spikes of flowers with pale, fleshy leaves. What's it called, Bernard?'

'Valerian, wasn't it?'

'That's it. And waves of graceful orange montbretia swaying in the sea-breeze.'

Queenie was entranced by the description. She could see it all in her mind. 'You're ever so clever with words, Mrs Jackson. Just like Keith.'

'It comes of having an education.' Violet sniffed and Queenie looked crushed.

'We don't all have the same opportunities, Mother,' Keith commented sharply.

Violet ignored the criticism. 'But I haven't told you the best part – ' pausing for effect ' – Michael is going to cook for us!' Her hands were held up in a gesture of delight.

Keith turned sharply to his brother with an amazed look on his face. 'Is that a good idea, old chap? I mean – ' he amended quickly, 'don't you want to get out in the world on your own?'

'Now don't interfere, Keith,' his mother said quickly. 'It's all decided.'

Michael smiled and nodded his head. 'Suits me.'

Keith frowned then turned to his father with a worried look. 'What about you, Dad? What will you do down there?'

Bernard smiled enthusiastically. 'There's plenty for me to do. Odd jobs, gardening, book-keeping. I'm looking forward to it. Make a nice change from slogging round trying to sell something to people who don't want it. Soul-destroying, that can be.'

'But . . . listen you people. Don't you realise *there's going to be a war!*'

Bernard shook his head. 'After the last fiasco, they'll never let that happen again. Anyway, Lord Halifax has been to talk with that German dictator and we've got this policy of appeasement now, haven't we?'

'I wish *I* could be so sure.' Keith looked down mournfully at Hannah who had fallen asleep in the crook of his arm.

'My uncles say there'll be a war,' added Queenie.

Violet raised her fine eyebrows as if to suggest that the opinions of Queenie's uncles were of no account. Her superior air goaded her future daughter-in-law into launching forth into a speech about her father's contribution in the last war.

Queenie warmed to her subject when she realised that she had the full admiring attention of her male audiance. She told them how her Dad had been in one of the first submarines sent to Russia and about the hardships he had suffered. She got to the point where the Germans had offered a prize for the capture of the British submarines.

'My Dad said that Fritz reckoned as 'ow a British sub was worth more than a Russian battleship! After they'd scared the bleedin' Germans out of the Russian ports, they sank the merchant ships what was carrying iron-ore and stuff to Germany to make ammunition and stuff for the war. But – my Dad said – they always made the crew get into lifeboats, or they put them ashore before they blew their ships up. Don't you think that's *bloody* marvellous?' she asked with shining eyes. The three captivated men nodded.

'*I* think,' said Violet, rising to her feet and placing the back of her hand theatrically against her forehead, 'that I am getting the most awful headache. Will you please excuse me?' She swept from the room.

# · Fifteen ·

Violet drew the curtains in her bedroom, unbuttoned her beige kid shoes, took off her skirt and long knitted jacket, and lay down under her counterpane.

Sighing, she closed her eyes and massaged her temples. Tension brought on these dreadful attacks, screwing up the muscles in the back of her neck and causing a throbbing pain in her head. She always had to take to her bed.

Sometimes she couldn't name the exact cause of the spasms, but today she knew the source of her anxiety very well. She was so disappointed in Keith! Getting that common girl pregnant and now insisting on marrying her. How could *she* be expected to get on with a girl like that? The very name – Queenie – said it all, didn't it?

The baby was a dear little mite, and although she had vowed never to acknowledge the child there was no doubt that she was Keith's daughter – and her granddaughter. Her heart had been instantly captivated.

She could be such an influence for good on her granddaughter, teaching her manners and how to speak well. But now they were moving to Cornwall, she doubted that she would see much of her. It was such a long journey, and the fare so expensive. It used to be something like twenty-five shillings return for an adult from London when she went on holiday as a child, but was no doubt more than that now.

Cornwall – the name wove a magic of its own. She smiled to herself. She would think about Cornwall and perhaps her headache would go away.

Her family had enjoyed such lovely holidays on the south-west coast and she was thrilled to be going back to the county of so many happy memories. Her parents, herself and her younger sister, Ruth, used to go down to Falmouth from Paddington Station on the Great Western Railway. Mama, looking lovely in a summer-straw hat, would have packed a nice lunch and they would play 'I Spy' and charades, and imagine that the train wheels were saying things like, 'I'm get-ting you there, I'm get-ting you there'.

She and Ruth would be exhausted by the time they reached Falmouth Station, but quickly revived on the short walk up the hill and into Melvill Road, where they always stayed with plump Mrs Hocking at her guest house, 'Melrose'. Their luggage would be brought up to the house later by horse and cart, after they had enjoyed the first delicious Cornish pasty of the fortnight.

Then Mama would take Papa's arm, he looking very dashing in a straw boater, linen blazer, and swinging a cane, and they would walk through Princess Pavilion Gardens to the Promenade, breathing in the sea air. They'd walk along and watch the sun go down over Falmouth Bay, turning the silver sea to blazing orange or blood red. As it darkened they would see the cheerfully twinkling lights from the portholes of the great cargo ships anchored out in Falmouth Bay.

St Mawes was Violet's favourite place in the whole world. She adored the little Tudor castle at the entrance, the twin to Pendennis Castle on the headland at Falmouth. She loved the white, cream and grey cottages and houses that peeped over the high wall above the sandy beach. The boat would round the arm of the little harbour and tie up at the quay. Such a peaceful place. The roads were so steep and rough that they hardly saw even a horse and cart. Lovely semi-tropical plants and palm-trees grew in the gardens, and everywhere, wild flowers and butterflies.

'When I'm grown-up,' she told Mrs Hocking one day,

'I'm going to have a guest house – in St Mawes. You'll have to show me how to make these wonderful pasties, 'cos they'll bring people back year after year.'

And now she was getting her childhood wish. A guest house in Cornwall. Unfortunately St Mawes had become very fashionable and expensive these days, so they had been forced to look further afield.

She had fallen in love with Tremayne the moment she saw it lit by the evening sun, its windows glowing orange, and seagulls keening overhead. It had six guest-bedrooms, and a delightful dining-room and lounge looking out to sea towards the Lizard.

What a challenge it was going to be. Just what Bernard needed.

*What was the matter with her husband?* He had become increasingly lethargic over the last few years – depressed and old before his time. He was only forty-seven, for heaven's sake.

He should *never* have left his father's business. They would be in clover now if he had stayed on. His moroseness when he had returned from the war and his decision to cut loose from the family firm had nearly finished their marriage. She thought it so irresponsible. She would have left him if she'd had anywhere else to go and any other means of support, but both her parents were dead by then.

Keith took after his father. A lovely boy but lazy, just wanting to drift through life. And look what he had drifted into now! A pretty face had been the undoing of many good men. And a pretty face was all *that* girl had to offer.

Violet sighed. Had her marriage been a failure? How sad. She and Bernard were certainly not happy together, but she had done *her* best, hadn't she? Her head throbbing, Violet found herself thinking back to the scorching summer she had met Bernard. She had been idling at home after two years at finishing school in Switzerland, wondering what the future held in store for her, when she received a letter from her schoolfriend Sybill Jackson, inviting her to Derby for a summer holiday. There followed some discord between herself and her parents over it.

'It is not correct,' said her mother, 'for a young girl to pay an extended visit to a family that her parents are not acquainted with . . .'

'Oh, Mama – Sybill's family is very respectable. Her mother is a concert pianist and Mr Jackson is a Gentleman's Outfitter.' Her argument did not seem to be having the necessary effect so, following her mother's example when she wanted her own way with her husband, she covered her face with her hands and sobbed.

'Plee-ase, Mama.'

And, just as he always gave in to Mama's tears, Papa said she could go. He put her on the train and Sybill's brother, Bernard, had come with his sister in the pony and trap to meet her at the other end. Sybill had spoken of her older brother on a number of occasions, and Violet was full of pleasurable anticipation now she was to meet him.

And she was not disappointed.

Bernard Jackson was the most dashing young man that she had ever met – but then, she had not met very many. Tallish, fairish, with laughing grey eyes, he was as immaculately dressed in spats, striped blazer and straw boater as one would expect from the son of a 'Gentleman's Outfitter'.

And she was looking very attractive she knew, in a new blue and white striped dress with little bows down the bodice. Her pretty straw hat, trimmed with blue flowers, was tipped forward to allow her ringlets to be gathered with a ribbon at the back of her head.

Bernard took her gloved hand and helped her up the steps of the vehicle. 'I do like to see a neat ankle,' he said roguishly as she lifted her skirt with one hand. She blushed and her bosom rose and fell rapidly with an excitement that was quite new to her. Sybill had exclaimed primly, 'Oh, Bernard!'

It had been a magical few weeks. Croquet on the lawn,

picnics and boating on the river, singing around the piano in the evenings – palpitating hearts and stolen kisses.

Bernard's mother was a superb pianist. 'You have a sweet, true voice, Violet,' she told her young guest with a fond smile. And Violet quickly came to love Gertrude Jackson, who became such a friend to her in her disgrace . . . She was devasted when Gertrude died a year later. By that time Violet and Bernard were married and had Keith. But she would *never* get over the shame. The shame of the speed with which the marriage had to take place.

Violet's head throbbed violently. Why did she keep allowing her thoughts to wander to this painful subject when she was supposed to be thinking about Cornwall? But the shame was always lurking . . . It was the cross she had to bear in life.

Unused to the approval and flattering attention of young men, she immediately fell in love with Bernard, and those summer days had been spent in tremulous longing for something she barely understood.

One afternoon the three young people returned early from a walk as it was so hot, and finding a note to the effect that Gertrude had been invited out to tea, decided to take a jug of lemonade to the summer house in the garden. After a while Sybill innocently retired to the house to write a letter.

The knowledge that no-one would disturb them for some time hovered tangibly between Violet and Bernard as they played draughts. Her hands were damp with nervousness and her heart was thumping madly in her maidenly breast. As soon as Bernard won the game, he rose and sat beside her, knocking over the wooden board and scattering the pieces in his haste.

'Bernard,' she breathed, offering only a token gesture of resistance as he embraced her. The hitherto fleeting caresses now gave way to torrents of passion. She swooned in his arms, allowing him to fondle her breasts, to undo the buttons of her bodice, and unlace her camisole. Her young bosom jutted alloringly over the top of the tight stays and Bernard groaned with desire as his lips roamed over them.

Alarmed, she struggled somewhat as his hand went under her skirts, but soon gave in, and between them they removed her pantaloons and pulled down his trousers and the lower halves of their bodies were pressed thrillingly together. She was rather embarrassed at the sensations she was experiencing – a sort of desperate, liquid wanting.

She had no idea what a naked man looked like and was truly frightened by the size and heat of the large male thing that throbbed against her. What was it supposed to do? Where was it supposed to go? 'Bernard,' she shrieked as he moved upon her, but the thing seemed to find its own way and was suddenly, with very little pain, inside her body and pulsating. It was delicious as he moved it in and out, and they both cried out as they experienced the most shattering sensations.

Afterwards they wept together as they really weren't sure what they had done. 'Oh, Bernard,' she sobbed, shaking like leaf, 'We shouldn't have done that. Have I given you my maidenhead?' She had read that in a novel but not understood.

'I reckon you have, lass.' He wiped his eyes and adjusted his lower garments. She dared not watch. 'And it was lovely, wasn't it? We don't need to feel ashamed about it. We can do it every night when we're wed.'

She had blushed from the roots of her hair to the tips of her nipples, which her lover kissed again before helping her to lace up, button up, and pull on her pantaloons.

So the bastions of her purity had been besieged and crumbled rapidly under assault by her ardent suitor. Added to her profound shame was the knowledge that she had profoundly enjoyed it. And she enjoyed it twice more before she went home and came to her senses.

Her parents' disgust with her when her pregnancy was discovered not only caused the beginning of what threatened to be a lifelong guilt complex, but nipped her blossoming sexuality in the bud.

The guilt she experienced made it very hard to meet Bernard halfway – to respond to his love-making once they were married. She had no way of knowing if his . . . appetites . . . were excessive or not. He was patient with her, she had to admit, but she knew he was frustrated . . . in that way. But she could not help it – he had sullied her.

Violet stirred and sighed, fiercely denying the feeling of arousal she was experiencing from the recall of her deflowering, and resolutely pushing from her mind any suggestion of a thought that her situation had been similar to that of Queenie Ellis. Or that she had been older than that girl. *There could be absolutely no comparison.* In her own case it was ignorance and Bernard that led her astray, while she was quite sure that her future daughter-in-law knew exactly what she was about when she trapped Keith into marriage.

Violet forced herself to think of Cornwall – and Michael.

As her younger son came to the end of his training, this wonderful idea had come to her, that he could join them in their venture as their chef. Bernard, surprisingly, had jumped at the idea. Surprising because he was normally so unenthusiastic about everything. 'Let's put it to him,' he had agreed. 'It could solve some of our problems.'

There was one problem that she knew would never be resolved – the intimate side of their marriage. It was far too late. But maybe, if they could get other things right . . .

Anyway, if Bernard lived at home, he wouldn't have the opportunity to go sneaking off to any of his women. When he had flung this at her in one of the rows he was always picking with her, it had made her physically sick.

'You're telling me that you "go" with other women?' she had almost shrieked, she was so appalled.

'Well, what am I supposed to do – married to a professional virgin – '

'That's not fair!'

'I'll tell you what's not fair, Violet Jackson,' his handsome face twisted in a sneer. 'Leading a man on to get him to marry you and then showing your true nature – frigid as bloody ice.'

'It wasn't like that at all! You seduced me!' She was shaking so much she had to sit down. 'I was a pure girl when we met and you took advantage – '

'Don't give me that. You couldn't get your bloomers down quick enough – '

'Ugh! You're disgusting – '

She had cried bitterly and from that time there had been nothing physical between them – and she was glad. She had insisted on separate rooms. The pressure of her husband's expectations was lifted from her, but strangely it was about that time, wasn't it? that the headaches started.

Michael had looked flabbergasted when she put the idea of the guest house to him. Violet assumed it must have been the surprise that made him stand up and walk to the window, to look out in brooding silence.

'Michael,' she prompted.

He turned, biting on his lip. 'I don't know, Mum. Dad. I had thought of going into the Navy.'

'Whatever for?' she had asked, aghast. It was bad enough to have lost Keith in this way.

'Well . . . you know, to see something of the world. A chance to grow up a bit.' He shrugged. 'Keith enjoys it.'

'What sort of reason is that? And look what it has led to.' she had said, rather sharply perhaps, but . . . 'We need you, Michael. We don't think this venture will work without you. I cannot be expected to do all the cooking as well as everything else, and hired help is so . . . undependable.'

'What part are you playing in this venture, Dad?' Michael had asked, an almost derisive note in his voice.

Bernard had looked quite excited.'I'll keep the books, see to the business side of things, do a bit of gardening, general handyman – I'm good with my hands.'

Michael had scuffed at her Persian rug with his foot. 'Don't do that, dear!' she reminded him.

'I don't know. I'll need some time to think it over – '

'We haven't got time, Michael darling.' She had gone to him and laid her hand upon his arm. 'We've come to the end of our rental agreement on the house. We'll have to renew it, or move out.'

'What about Aunt Sybill. Couldn't she come and help run it?'

'You know she has to look after your grandfather – there's no one else to do it.'

Michael had stared at her with a hard expression on his face that she had never seen before. He had always been such a biddable boy. 'It's not fair to spring this on me so suddenly, Mum.'

She couldn't stop her lips from trembling. Was that all the gratitude she got for all her years of caring and love? Was he just as selfish as his brother? His father?

'Tell you what, old boy,' Bernard said. 'Why don't you give it a try – say a year. Then, if you don't like it . . .'

Michael shook his head. 'I'm sorry, but I feel it would do me good to – '

She had covered her face with her hands and sobbed. She just could not help it. Well, then he had seen how much he had upset her and he changed his tune. He agreed to give it a year.

'Oh Michael, darling.' She had dried her tears and smiled at him to show she had forgiven him. 'We shall have such fun together.'

And they would. It was so exciting. And perhaps he would meet and marry a nice, sensible Cornish girl, who would come and live with them and help run Tremayne.

As for Keith. Well, he had flown the nest and he was past redemption. And that *dreadful* girl! Violet had noticed the lascivious way they had all looked at her this afternoon. Even Bernard.

And that little trollop had sat there revelling in the attention she was getting from those three gawking men, crossing and uncrossing her legs, and fluttering her eyelashes at them.

And she never stopped talking, though her speech left much to be desired. By the end of the afternoon she had given up even trying to be polite, and most of her adjectives began with a 'b'! Showing off – about looking like a filmstar and how wonderful her father had been.

The sooner they got to Cornwall the better, though she supposed they would have to travel up to attend the wedding planned for next year. That would be an unwelcome expense. Money was going to be very short until they got the new business going.

There was a tap on the door and Bernard poked his head around it. 'Feeling better, old girl?'

'A little . . .'

'Keith and Queenie are just going – d'you want to say goodbye to them?'

Violet shook her head and moaned. 'I don't think so. Ask Keith to come and see us again before he goes back to his ship. And tell him to come on his own next time.'

# · Sixteen ·

'Here comes the bride. Tra-la-la-la. How do I look, Ma?'

Beatie turned to look at her daughter.

Queenie stood in the doorway of the front room in a long turquoise dress in crêpe de Chine with softly puckered leg o' mutton sleeves. The fitted bodice had a lace inset and a little ruched frill just below the round neckline, to one side of which she had attached her marcasite swallow brooch. A similar frill adorned the bottom of the fairly straight skirt.

Crowning her dark head was a plaited headdress made of silver lamé, below which her hair fell in glossy curls. No veil. Silver sandals in the same material adorned her feet, and in her right hand she carried a bouquet of white carnations, lilies and asparagus fern. The fern trailed almost to the hem of the dress with an occasional flower and a few bows.

The colour enhanced the brilliance of her eyes, and excitement lent a natural bloom to her cheeks. Her eye make-up and lipstick were unusually discreet. And her face bore a radiant smile. 'Well?' she asked, twirling round.

Beatie swallowed and nodded. 'Knock the bleedin' Jacksons fer six you will, our Queen.'

Queenie went to her mother and bent and kissed her cheek quickly. 'You look ever so nice in that blue and the buttonhole's pretty. Orchids – posh, eh?' With her spare hand she re-arranged the silk-trimmed ruffles that fell in the place of lapels on her mother's grosgrain coat. 'That hat could 'a done with a feather in it, I reckon.'

Beatie looked up at her reflection in the mirror and tweaked at her deep-crowned hat, decorated with a satin ribbon and a buckle. 'I'd 'a liked a bigger brim, but you know where you can stick yer bleedin' feathers!'

They were laughing as Phyllis joined them, having put the final touches to her own toilette after helping Queenie dress.

'Here she is, my blushing bridesmaid.'

'Always a bridesmaid and never a bride,' quipped Phyllis, looking very pretty in ice-blue taffeta, similar in style to the bride's, but with short sleeves, her fair hair adorned with a little coronet of silver leaves.

'P'rhaps today will persuade John to agree to the date,' replied Queenie. John had gone ahead to the church with the younger boys. 'I'm dyin' to see Hannah all dressed up. Hope she's behavin' herself with Vera. Ooh, I'm ever so nervous – suppose Keith don't turn up.'

'I'll kill 'im if 'e don't.' promised Beatie.

Soon Billy, who was going to give Queenie away in place of her father, arrived looking very smart in his khaki sergeant's uniform. He poured them all a port and lemon to give them 'Dutch courage'. It was only a few minutes' walk to the church.

Queenie, holding her skirt raised elegantly with her left hand, stepped down the red doorstep of number twelve Baker Street for the last time as an Ellis. As she walked along on Billy's arm a cheer came from the people further up the street who weren't coming to the wedding. Most of them had known her all her life. It was the same in Butcher Street – shopkeepers standing on their steps, cheering her on.

'You look beautiful, Queenie,' they said, and 'Good luck, Queenie', and 'You must be proud of 'er, Mrs Ellis'. They were all smiling and the kids were beaming and polite for once, and she really felt like the Queen of the May. They had chosen the first of May for the wedding because it was her birthday – her nineteenth – and because it was her lucky month.

'Thank Gawd the sun's shinin',' she said to Billy, giving a little shiver in the shade of the houses.

'It could have been raining and you'd have turned up looking like a drowned rat.' Billy gave her a fond smile. She glowed up at him, proud of her big brother who was aiming for a commission in the Army.

'These new shoes is pinching something awful,' complained Beatie, 'I've brought me old ones to change into at the reception.' Queenie giggled at the brown paper bag tucked under her mother's arm.

The vicar, or the 'Amen-wallah', as Billy called him, met them at the open church door in dog-collar and cassock at eleven o'clock on the dot. They could hear the organ droning away inside. Queenie gave Mr Kerr a nervous smile though he didn't seem to have any objection to performing a marriage-ceremony for the girl who had last attended his church to give thanks for her illegitimate baby.

His thin face creased into a answering smile. 'You make a lovely bride, Queenie. It would appear that everyone is here – including the bridegroom.'

'Thank Gawd for that – oh!' Queenie bit her bottom lip and looked up at him nervously.

He raised his eyebrows. 'My sentiment exactly, Queenie. Come, Mrs Ellis, let me escort you to your seat. As soon as you hear the 'Bridal March' start up, Billy, bring Queenie in – slowly.'

'You all right, Phyllis?' Queenie looked over her shoulder, her whole frame shuddering, and not just with cold.

'Of course. You concentrate on what you're doin' and don't worry about me.'

'At least I haven't got a bleedin' train for you to trip over.' They both giggled.

And then the familiar strains of the Wedding March

floated out to them. 'Ready?' Billy asked her, baring his teeth in a nervous smile. She bared hers back and nodded.

The church, with sun filtering through the stained glass windows and throwing patterns on the stone floor, seemed almost full. The locals loved a wedding and many would be up in the gallery with the choir that Billy and John used to belong to. When she was young, the kids used to have a good time in the gallery, responding with nervous giggles to the Bible-thumping sermons of the previous vicar, particularly when he used to mount the steps to the third tier of the pulpit which put him on the same level as the gallery. Waving his arms about and glaring – he was like an avenging angel.

She saw a couple of sailors up near the altar, standing with their backs to her, and then people started to turn their heads and smile at her as she walked towards them. She swivelled her eyes from side to side to smile back. She hoped she was smiling, her mouth seemed awfully jerky to her.

She caught sight of Lil, resplendent in sugar-pink – a colour which did nothing to diminish her size. The little frothy hat of feathers and net sat incongruously on her brassy curls. Queenie gave her a fond wink.

Her eyes swept proudly over her own family filling the first three rows of boxed pews on the left, and then her stomach knotted as she saw the three Jacksons alone in the front row opposite. She looked away as her bridegroom turned and smiled at her – and nothing else mattered.

She recalled how she had imagined this nearly three years ago, only in her dream she had been dressed in white. At that time she had hardly seen Keith smile, but now she knew that he did quite often, with a droll sort of humour, appearing to stand back and chuckle at life and the way people behaved. He accepted people as they were and never criticised. For a long time she had thought she hated him – but now her heart swelled with love. They were going to have such a lovely life together.

'Mummy,' Hannah's baby voice called from where she sat on her Uncle Eddy's lap. Queenie gave her a quick smile, hoping she wouldn't play up. Beatie had tried to persuade her to leave Hannah with a friend, thinking it a little improper that the guests should be reminded of the necessity for the wedding. But Queenie had insisted that she should be there. And dressed like a tiny bridesmaid.

The bride smiled up at her handsome husband-to-be, home from the Mediterranean in February, tanned and clean-shaven again. His eyes met hers softly, proudly. He was wearing a white ribbon below his lanyard in addition to the customary 'black silk' and in the bow was tucked a white carnation. She turned and handed her bouquet to Phyllis.

The ceremony passed in a blur for Queenie. Keith made his vows in a strong voice and she spoke up as best she could, her knees knocking together, but giving him a saucy wink when she promised to 'obey'. He winked back and the vicar raised an eyebrow.

Then they went to the vestry to sign the Register. Violet Jackson took Queenie by the shoulders and briskly kissed her cheek, but her eyes avoided contact. Violet and Beatie shook hands and dipped their heads to each other. Bernard Jackson followed suit but with a warm smile. 'You look grand, lass,' he kissed Queenie with enthusiasm. 'How do you do, Mrs Ellis.'

Queenie was awed by her new mother-in-law's elegance in a dove grey, knitted-silk suit with satin trimmings. A matching satin, wedge-shaped hat with a big bow at the back, swept down to a peak tipping saucily over one eye. But oh, if only she would relax.

On the way out, Phyllis took toddler Hannah by the hand to follow her parents. The little girl was dressed in the same ice-blue taffeta as Phyllis, but with a flounced skirt, and carried a small Victorian posy.

They were to adjourn to the church hall for the reception, but first there were the photographs outside the church, the confetti and the well-wishing of the guests. The church bell tolled from its open, domed tower with the weather-vane on the top. The sun shone and the unfurling buds were tender green on the trees around St George's Square – for Queenie's wedding day.

The bride and groom, Beatie, Billy, and Violet and Bernard Jackson stood in line to receive the guests.

Queenie felt some sympathy for the Jacksons, only the four of them, swamped by her noisy family and friends. Keith was stationed in *Vernon* again, having volunteered for training in the Torpedo School, and had been engaged in MTB trials off Spithead and torpedo testing at Stokes Bay. His parents and brother had come up from Cornwall the previous day and were staying in Totterdell's Hotel opposite the church for a couple of days.

'This is the first time in my life that I've envied my big brother,' grinned Michael, kissing her on the lips. 'Pity you haven't got a sister. Your bridesmaid looks rather tasty, though.'

''Fraid she's engaged to me brother. Might be able to fix you up with Pearl, though. She's the blonde over there in the cerise dress.'

Michael looked. 'Er, thanks, but perhaps not.'

Keith grasped his brother's arm and muttered, 'See if you can get some drink down Mum. Get her to let her hair down a bit.'

Michael grimaced. 'I'll do my best, big bruv.'

The last guest was greeted and the hall, which they had cheered up with flowers, paper chains and bunches of balloons, was bubbling with voices and laughter. There was a crowd around the table where the gifts were displayed and Phyllis was busy unwrapping those that had just been brought by guests.

Several trestle tables had been put together and covered with white cloths for the buffet wedding-breakfast. The women members of the family and the neighbours, Lil and Shirl, had been cooking for days, making pies, sausage rolls, cakes and desserts, and they had been up late the night before making the sandwiches, and early this morning laying it all out.

There was a table for the drinks – a keg of beer and spirits for the adults, lemonade for the children. Small tables and chairs had been set around the room to eat at, and many guests were already laying claim to them, putting handbags on the table and jackets on the chairs. The middle of the room was left clear for dancing.

Eventually, Lil, the habitual organiser of every event from births, weddings through to funerals, suggested that the bridal party should occupy the long table set for them, so that everyone else would settle down.

Queenie, laying her bouquet on the table in front of her, sat between Keith and her new father-in-law. Beatie, obeying Lil's instructions, sat on the other side of Bernard with Michael to her left, and Violet between Keith and Able Seaman Parker, the best man. Phyllis was placed between him and Billy. Satisfied that everyone was in their proper place, Lil returned to her table immediately in front, where she had positioned herself so that she could control the proceedings.

'Ain't it marvellous, Keith,' smiled Queenie, 'all these people have come to share our day.' And all the uniforms: sailors, soldiers, her Marine brother.

He looked around. 'Your Ma has done us proud, I must say.'

'We saved up like mad this last year. Ma said she'd 'ad enough doom and gloom and we was goin' to have a really posh do. It was a relief that you paid for the booze though, or we might have had to pawn the family silver.' She gave him a playful dig in the ribs with her elbow. 'If we had any, that is.'

Keith leaned forward and looked past her and his father to where Beatie sat. 'You've done us proud . . . Ma.'

Beatie beamed back to him. 'I only got one daughter, so I wanted to do it proper.'

A lump constricted Queenie's throat. This was the only time that she could remember her Ma actually sounding proud of her.

Lil gave them a nod of her frilly hat and Queenie led the way to the food table. Soon everyone was queueing up to load their plates and then tucking in. Keith took his mother another drink. Queenie waggled her fingers at Hannah who was being fed tit-bits by Eddy.

Eventually Lil teetered over on her high heels, wobbling like a pink blancmange, and told Able Seaman Parker it was time for the speeches. He groaned. 'Quiet everybody,' she bellowed, and everyone fell into a surprised silence. She nodded her gracious permission for him to speak, before waddling back to her seat again.

The sailor stood up, looking a bit embarrassed, ran a hand over his short brown hair and cleared his throat. 'Unaccustomed as I am to public speaking – '

There were good-natured groans.

'I don't intend to say much – '

Cheers and catcalls from the other shipmates who had come as Keith's guests.

Parker grinned. 'I've known young Stonewall here for the two years we've served together on the *Barham*. I've always considered him a good lad – '

Their shipmates drummed their heels on the floor.

'On this occasion, however, he "put the cart before the horse" in a manner of speaking, becoming a father before he became a husband. Anyway, now he's done 'is duty in true naval tradition. All that remains for me to do, is to wish the happy couple all the luck in the world, to hope all their troubles will be "little ones" – the patter of tiny feet and all that, and just one more thing. I'd like to assure the new Mrs Jackson, that all those rumours about sailors aren't true.'

Laughter and shouts of 'Oh, yeah' and 'Pull the other one'.

Parker raised his glass. 'Please rise and drink to the happy couple.'

Glasses chinked and there were echoes of the best man's good wishes. He read out a few telegrams of good wishes from Keith's side of the family, notably messages from his grandfather and his Aunt Sybill. Then there were cries of 'Speech. Speech,' to the bridegroom and Keith stood up looking bashful.

'Er . . . hrm. I just want to thank Parky for his kind words and doing me the honour of being my best man, and particularly to thank Mrs Ellis – Ma – for this wonderful party. I appreciate my family coming all the way up from Cornwall to be here with us. It's lovely to see everyone enjoying themselves. Thank you all for your gifts – they've really set us up.'

He looked down at Queenie. 'I know that there's only one thing missing for Queenie. She would have loved it if her father could have been here today. She was so proud of him, and he would have been equally proud of his beautiful daughter . . .' He stopped and swallowed. They gazed at each other.

There were tender murmurs from the audience. Queenie blinked away tears. Fancy him knowing that – she had been thinking of her Dad on and off all morning.

'But most of all,' he went on, 'I want to thank Queenie for becoming my wife and . . . for giving me a lovely daughter. Bring little Hannah over, will you, Eddy,' Keith requested.

Eddy limped up and put the doll-like child into her father's arms. He kissed her. The guests applauded. Then, reaching down, Keith took his bride's hand and announced, 'I promise Queenie that I am going to make it all up to her, the waiting and . . . and the uncertainty. And I'm going to cherish her and little Hannah.'

Everyone clapped and called out for a speech from the bride. 'Oh no!' she shrieked, but they would have it. Keith hauled her to her feet. Red-cheeked from embarrassment and one drink too many on an empty stomach, Queenie swayed against him. 'I just want to say,' she giggled, 'I just want to say that this is the happiest bleedin' day of my life!' Keith kissed her.

When the formalities were over, the cake cut and enjoyed, the vicar departed, Uncle Danny got out his accordion. The groom led his giggling bride onto the floor and they shuffled round in a fair rendering of a waltz. Keith was not much of a dancer but Queenie had attended many Saturday-night hops at South Parade Pier with Phyllis. Bernard and Beatie executed the dance in a natty fashion together – fish-tails and all. Beatie and Joshua used to go dancing whenever they could in their younger days and, despite her plumpness, she was light on her feet.

Michael dragged a stiff Violet out to join them, Parky followed with Phyllis, and soon everyone was enjoying themselves. Those who weren't dancing were tapping their feet, and the children were rushing around misbehaving themselves.

But for the bride and groom, everything was secondary to the thrill of being in each other's arms. They gazed dreamily into each other's eyes. 'How soon can we get away?' he whispered in her ear.

'Ow's it goin', down in Cornwall, Mrs Jackson?' Beatie asked Violet during a pause in the proceedings.

'We're enjoying it very much, thank you.' Violet appeared to be making an effort to be pleasant. 'We've had a quiet season this year of course – some of the old regulars had booked already but others were wary of a change of ownership. But most of this year's guests have booked again for next summer, and we shall advertise, of course.'

'If there's no war,' intoned Bernard gloomily. Even he had begun to fear that it could happen again.

'It's workin' out with yer youngest son, is it? He's a nice lad – well, they both are. I think I'm goin' to be very fond of my son-in-law.'

Violet's nostrils flared and Beatie realised she was jealous of having to share Keith with the Ellis family. 'Michael is enjoying putting his training into practice and he loves Cornwall.'

'I ain't never been further west than Torquay,' said Lil, who had been hovering. 'Always wanted to go to Cornwall. We'll be all right, now, won't we Beat?' She dug her friend with her elbow. 'Perhaps we could hire a charabang and all go down.'

Violet looked as if she might faint.

Lil laughed. 'Got you goin', that did, din't it, Mrs J? Don't worry, I'm a town body, meself. Can't stand it when it's too quiet.'

Uncle Danny was having a rest from the accordion. Keith came up to the women with Queenie hanging on his arm. 'Mum. Come and play the piano for us.'

'Oh, I couldn't!'

'Come on, Mrs Jackson,' wheedled Queenie. 'We can have a sing-song.'

'I doubt whether I can play *your* sort of song.'

Everyone clamoured, so blushing prettily, Violet allowed her son to lead her onto the little stage where the piano stood. 'There's plenty of music,' said Queenie, pointing out a pile of scores. 'We often have a concert and a sing-song 'ere of a Saturday night.'

Violet looked through the music and selected a few pieces. 'I don't know . . .' She sat down and tinkled her fingers along the keyboard. She played a few pleasant little melodies, though many people were busy talking.

'Don't you know nothin' we can sing to?' asked Queenie.

Violet gave her a challenging glare and launched into 'Daisy, Daisy'. This was followed by 'It's A Long Way To Tipperary', 'Bye, Bye, Blackbird', and 'You Must Have Been A Beautiful Baby'. Almost every adult in the hall was singing.

Violet riffled through the scores. 'Here's one for you, Bernard. "Ol' Man River".' After the opening chord several voices started up but were hushed by gestures from those around the piano. Bernard continued alone in a pleasant baritone voice, stretching his arms wide at the end, and was warmly applauded.

'Give us "Stormy Weather", Mother,' he nodded encouragingly to Violet.

'Oh, I couldn't . . .' said Violet uncertainly, looking as if, with a bit of encouragement, she might.

Everyone implored her. Violet took a hasty gulp of gin and tonic from her glass on top of the piano, where Keith had strategically placed it, and played the introduction. She started off rather hesitantly, but then, as if deciding that if she was going to do it, she might as well do it properly, her voice strengthened and rose and fell with throbbing intensity as she sang about the long time she and her man had been apart.

Something in her delivery sent a shiver down Queenie's spine and the audience was spellbound – there was more to Violet Jackson than met the eye. Violet looked flustered but pleased at the applause. Keith squeezed his mother's shoulder and she looked up at him with a soft smile.

Beatie and Lil, both very merry by now, were only too happy to perform 'Sally, Sally' in a shrieking parody of Gracie Fields. Uncle Danny joined in with the accordion. 'Come on,' cried Beatie at the end, 'let's 'ave some fun.' She scampered off the stage. 'Come on, Dan. Give us "Knees up Mother Brown".'

Soon almost everyone, including the children, was

stomping up and down. If a few of the women lifted their skirts a bit too exuberantly and showed their knicker elastic, it made it all the merrier. Eddy, with a sleeping Hannah in his lap, was sitting it out with several of the men who seemed more interested in the beer than dancing.

Queenie's cheeks were aching from laughter, but she noticed it was too undignified for Violet, still sitting on the piano stool, even though the toe of one smart grey shoe was tapping. Keith and Michael, after a whispered consultation, rushed on-stage and lifted down their protesting mother. But she was laughing, and joined in the 'Hokey Cokey', and the 'Conga' that snaked in and out of the tables and out into St George's Square. Violet Jackson had finally 'let her hair down'.

# · *Seventeen* ·

Keith carried his bride over the threshold of their new home in Victory Road.

Beatie had found the little terraced house for them a few doors down from the Victory pub. It was small, but to Queenie it was lovely. Her very own place. It suited her to go on working to help pay the rent, and the 'never-never' on the bed, and she wasn't one to stay at home anyway. She could drop Hannah off round the corner, to spend the days with her grandmother as usual.

Her new husband set her on her feet and they clung together. They had kissed many times on the short walk along, when they weren't laughing over Lil, exclaiming over the amount of booze that had been consumed, and at the way Violet had joined in at the end.

'My mother is a frustrated woman,' explained Keith. 'I often wonder if there isn't a lot of untapped passion under that cool exterior. If Dad only knew how to release it . . .'

Queenie didn't quite understand what he meant, but she had more important things on her mind. 'Just think,' she murmured, 'two whole days to ourselves.'

'Whatever will we find to do?' he murmured against her mouth. She giggled.

He straightened. 'Do you think Hannah will be all right with Ma?'

''Course she will. Ma is 'er second mother, ain't she? D'you want a cuppa tea?' Her eyes gleamed at him.

'I can think of much more exciting things to do than drinking tea!'

Queenie blushed and a tremble went right through her.

Keith took her hand, and drew her up the stairs after him and into their bedroom. They had lain on the double bed a few times in the previous week when they had brought their possessions to the house, but their love-making had stopped short of consummation. Queenie had been aroused and eager, sensing that it would be so much more satisfying than their first fumbling encounter on the hill, but now the moment had arrived she felt very shy.

Gently, Keith lifted the plaited crown from his wife's head and ran his fingers through her hair. Then he undid all the tiny buttons down the back of her turquoise dress and helped her step out of it. She stood before him in her lace-edged, satin camiknickers, suspenders and stockings, blushing and ducking her head. He kissed her tenderly.

Queenie was fascinated watching him discard his tunic, collar, dicky front and bell-bottom trousers. All the trappings of a sailor's uniform. Standing in his white underwear, he laid it all neatly over the back of a chair.

This completed, he turned to her with a smile, sat on the bed, and pulled her down beside him, and with his long fingers he stroked her hair, caressed her face, her shoulders, the length of her arms to the tips of her fingers. He lifted her hands one at a time and kissed the palms.

Queenie shuddered, then shyly she reached out to him, tracing his features, following the muscles of his shoulders and chest with her fingertips. Then. greatly daring, she took his hands and placed them over her breasts. Surely he must feel the thudding of her heart?

Their breathing became ragged, and clasping each other tightly, they stretched out on the bed. Their rising passion led them through the divesting of their remaining underwear, the further exploration of each other's bodies and through a dizzying spiral of sensation to the final union.

'Oh,' cried Queenie as she toppled back to earth, 'I never knew . . .'

'You're lovely,' said Keith, gazing down at her. 'More lovely than I remembered.'

Later, Queenie watched him get up and fold his uniform. Turning the trousers inside out he re-folded them into the seven creases. 'For the Seven Seas,' he said.

'For the seven days of the week,' she added, sleepily.

He lifted his side of the mattress and laid the trousers carefully under it, before letting it down again. 'Can't let my standards go, just 'cos I'm a married man,' he grinned.

'Come back to bed.' She held out her arms to him.

He slipped his pants back on. 'First, I'm going to make that cup of tea. With lots of sugar – to give me strength.'

Queenie giggled. 'I could get used to this sort of treatment, you know. Oh, we're goin' to have a lovely life.'

He looked at her solemnly for a long moment. 'God willing.'

She raised herself on one elbow. 'Don't sound so sad. Anyway, you don't believe in God.'

Back at Totterdell's Hotel, Bernard Jackson, sitting on his bed in his pyjamas, waited as nervously as any bridegroom for Violet to come back from the bathroom.

It was the first time they had shared a room for several years, but Violet had insisted that if they had to, in the interests of economy, it would have to be a twin-bedded room.

She had been pretty tipsy and giggly when they walked back to the hotel. Hanging heavily on his arm, she sang 'Stormy Weather' again. It had been a little embarrassing getting her past Reception and up the stairs.

Once in their room, he had helped her off with her skirt and jacket. The sight of his wife in her petticoat had aroused him immediately and he had found it necessary to slip along to the bathroom to cool off.

He found Violet in a silk dressing-gown on his return – one that he had not seen for many years. When they passed on the landing these days, she was always muffled up in a woollen or towelling robe.

She left the room without a word, but something in the almost smouldering look she had given him, made him very hopeful . . .

Violet sidled back into the room and busied herself at the dressing table for a few moments. Then, dropping her towel and sponge-bag on the chair, she turned and came towards him.

She could have gone to the far side of the bed and so avoided him, but she came between the beds and stood before Bernard, her face flushed and her lower lip caught between her pretty little teeth.

Gazing up at her almost fearfully, Bernard saw, with an ache in his loins, the outline of her breasts and the thrust of her nipples under the thin material.

Holding his gaze with shining hazel eyes, Violet slowly untied the sash of her dressing gown. She was naked underneath.

'Oh, my lass,' gasped Bernard as, rising in every sense of the word, he clasped his wife in his arms and kissed her as he had wanted to over all the wasted years.

# · Eighteen ·

Queenie was peeling potatoes and listening to the wireless when Keith came back from some mysterious mission he had been on.

He waved an envelope. What it contained was obviously making him very happy. 'Dry your hands, Mrs Jackson, and come and have a look at this.'

While Queenie opened the envelope he scooped Hannah up off the floor where she was playing with a wooden zoo he had bought her. He watched, smiling, as his wife, with puckered brow, tried to make sense of the document she had removed from the envelope.

'It's . . . is it another birth certificate for Hannah?'

'Yes, but it's different from the one she has already, isn't it?'

Queenie continued to look at it. 'Oh!' she shrieked, 'You've made our Hannah legal. Father, Able Seaman, HMS *Vernon* – and your name in the next column.' Her face was radiant. 'Ooh, I do love you, Keith Jackson.'

'We're a proper family now.' With Hannah in his arms, he bent to give Queenie a lingering kiss on the lips and with their daughter held between them they pranced around the little kitchen to the strains of Benny Goodman.

'Now I can't call you a little bastard any more when you're naughty, can I?' Queenie laughed at her daughter, then seeing Keith's frown, she amended, 'Not that I ever did.'

Keith was a model father, happy to bath Hannah, feed her, play with her and take her out in the pram for walks when his duties permitted him to be at home. When he was on leave and Queenie working, he was perfectly content to be left in sole charge. And when they were both at work, Hannah was dropped off at her grandmother's at number twelve Baker Street.

This arrangement was not to Beatie's liking to begin with and she had gone storming round to Victory Street, with little Ronnie and big Lil in tow, to give her son-in-law a rollicking.

'To what do I owe this pleasure?' asked Keith, not looking overjoyed at the intrusion as he showed his visitors into his sitting room. Hannah was having her afternoon nap and he had just settled down to enjoy his only extravagance, the magazine, *The Artist*. Then he was going to do some drawing.

'Only good enough to look after your daughter when it suits yer, am I?' Beatie shouted, arms akimbo and bright spots of angry colour on her cheeks.

Lil imitated her stance. 'You tell 'im, Beatie. After all you've done for his child . . .'

Feeling rather intimidated – he wasn't used to shouting women – Keith raised his eyebrows, hoping he looked nonchalant. 'Calm down, Ma. What's this all about? If it's the money you're worried about, then of course we'll pay you each week whether you have her or not. I'm sorry, I should have realised.'

'It ain't the money,' she shrieked angrily. Little Ronnie was peeping round her, sucking his thumb. 'And, what's more, you din't come round to tea last Sunday.'

Suddenly realising what was behind this tirade – a simple matter of jealousy – Keith attempted to give Beatie a hug, but she shrugged him off. 'Sorry, Ma, I should have thought. You've been a second mother to Hannah – '

'That's right, she has.' Lil nodded vigorously. 'And this is all the thanks she gets.'

Keith shot her a look of annoyance. 'As I was saying, Ma, you've always looked after her up till now, and of course you miss her when I'm minding her. But try and see it from my point of view, will you? I want to be with her while . . . when I get the chance. I've missed the first two years of her life, haven't I?'

'Whose bloody fault was that!'

'Yes, whose?' parrotted Lil.

'I know, I know.' He raised his hands in a gesture of supplication. 'But if I hadn't been posted to the Med I would have taken responsibility for it straight away, wouldn't I?'

'How do we know that?' Beatie was calming down a bit. 'You wasn't exactly fallin' over yerself to acknowledge yer daughter.'

'No, you bloody well wasn't,' agreed Lil. 'When I think what poor Beatie and little Queenie went through. The struggle they've 'ad – '

'I think my mother-in-law and I can sort this out between us,' Keith flared at Lil.

'Don't think you can bully *us*,' she cried.

'I wouldn't attempt it,' he answered wryly. 'And we're frightening Ronnie. Look, Ma, I admit I was mistaken and I've been a louse. But I'm determined to make it up to Hannah and Queenie now. You know that. And I just wanted them to myself for a bit. We don't get much chance to be together, now do we?'

'Oh, well . . . if that's all it is.'

'That's all it is. Don't go thinking I'm not grateful to you. I am – more than I can say.'

'All right, then,' mumbled his mother-in-law, embarrassed now that she'd calmed down.

'All *right* then,' said Lil, crossing her arms across her vast bosom.

'What you doin' there?' Beatie asked, in order to change the subject, pointing to the paper and equipment on the table.

Keith showed her the sketches he had made of Queenie and Hannah, and how he was translating some of them into pen and ink portraits.

'Look at these, Lil. Ain't they clever? I seen that drawring you done of Queenie when you went to the beach – '

'I'll give you a couple of them when I've finished,' he said quickly before she remembered that he shouldn't have been with Queenie on the beach. 'Here, Ronnie. You come and sit up with this pencil and here's a bit of paper. Do me a nice drawing while I make your Gran and Lil a cup of tea.'

He escaped to the kitchen. 'Whew!' he breathed as he filled the kettle. He just wasn't equipped for a full-frontal female attack of this nature. He could cope better with the more subtle psychological ploys used by his mother to get her own way.

However, half an hour later the two women and Keith parted the best of friends. 'I reckon our Queen's got a lovely lad there,' he heard Beatie tell Lil as he shut the door behind them.

Queenie was in seventh heaven and could hardly believe her luck. She was in love with her husband, she had an adorable child, and a dear little house to keep sparkling clean. And she was a good cook and home-maker after all the practise she had had in Baker Street.

Her prayers had been answered. She had, after all, escaped from Ma.

But it wasn't all plain sailing for two people from such different backgrounds. There were disagreements over the upbringing of the baby, when Queenie would remind her husband, none too politely, that for the first two years of her life, Hannah had been her sole responsibility. There were arguments over the housekeeping money. And Queenie sometimes suspected that her husband thought her lacking in intelligence, so she would tell him, 'I might not be as ejucated as you, but I'm not bloody stupid you know.'

Their first real row took place a few weeks after their

wedding. Keith, sometimes calling into the Sailors' Home Club for an off-duty drink when Queenie was waitressing, frequently objected to her flirting with the customers.

'How many times have I told you I don't like it?' he asked her angrily on this occasion when they were walking back to Baker Street to pick up Hannah.

'And how many times have I told you – it don't mean nothing,' Queenie answered truculently. 'I'm just bein' nice to them 'cos they're away from home.'

'Far too nice! I don't like it. I know what they're like – give them an inch and – '

'G'arn, you're jealous!' she accused in delight, giving him a little push.

He was unreasonably angry. 'Of course I'm not *jealous*. It's just that you're a married woman, now, and it isn't the way to behave.'

Queenie's chin went up. 'Hang on! What about you a couple of years ago? You didn't care as long as you got what *you* wanted. Well, they're not all like you, thank God! I had to fend for meself until you decided you wanted your daughter. I didn't 'ave to marry you, you know.'

'Why did you then? Saw me as a meal-ticket for the rest of your life?'

Queenie drew in her breath with a hiss. 'You rotten bastard!'

'Stop behaving like a tart, then.'

They had reached number twelve. Queenie opened the door, and stepped inside. Turning, she barred his entry. 'You go to hell, Keith Jackson,' she shouted. 'Hannah and me are stayin' here.' She slammed the door in his face.

'What's goin' on?' Beatie rushed out of the kitchen, Hannah in her arms.

Queenie burst into tears. 'We've just 'ad our first row, that's what.' And why wasn't he banging on the door – begging her forgiveness?

'Don't be a fool, gal. Go after 'im. Go on!'

Her mother pushed past her, opened the door, and

grabbing her daughter's shoulder, she thrust her through the doorway. But Keith was halfway up the street, walking in quick angry strides. 'Keith,' yelled Queenie. He did not look back.

'There you are!' she stormed at her mother. 'I ain't runnin' after him, not after what 'e said to me. He'll 'ave to come crawlin' back and apologise before I go home with 'im again.'

'Fer Chris'sake!' shouted Beatie. 'You should be grateful for what you got there. He's better than you deserve.'

Queenie was open-mouthed with amazement after the names her mother had called him when he was in the Med.

'Anyway I could do without this sort of thing,' Beatie grumbled. 'First Billy and now you.'

Queenie shared her mother's bed that night, borrowing one of her flannelette nighties, because her old room had been taken over by Billy, who had also left the matrimonial home in a huff. In his case, his mother-in-law's house.

'I couldn't put up with it any longer, Queen,' he admitted as he, Eddy and the boys ate the 'Twopenny Suppers' of faggots and mushy peas that Queenie had gone to buy from Mrs Russell's in Butcher Street. She and Beatie were making do with bread and dripping. Queenie loved it spread thickly and sprinkled with salt, and it was especially tasty if you could dig up the amber jelly from the bottom of the bowl.

'Vera's under her mother's influence,' Billy mourned, 'and when the two of them get on at me . . .'

'What about Ronnie? Will she still bring him round to Ma?'

'Oh, don't mind me!' exclaimed their mother. 'Everyone's convenience, that's Beatie Ellis.'

Billy shrugged. 'Her mother goes out to work.'

'You should move out, Billy,' his sister advised. 'Get a place of your own. It's no way to start married life – livin' with yer mother-in-law.'

'I know. But I'm away so much and Vera's scared to be in a house on her own – '

'Silly cow!' said Queenie.

He snorted. 'What about you, then! Married two minutes and already you're back home.'

Queenie looked down. 'Yeah, well . . .'

'Marital bliss!' Eddy chuckled. 'What a lucky escape I've had.'

'By the way,' said Beatie. 'I've put me name down for one of those new Council flats up the other end of the Square. I don't need this big place now. Eddy says 'e don't mind gettin' a place of his own, and John's away and gettin' married anyway – one of these fine days – so there's only the boys and me.'

'But Ma,' protested Queenie with a laugh. 'There won't be room for us all to come home when we've 'ad an argy-bargy.'

But later, in bed, kept awake by her mother's little grunts and snores, Queenie wasn't laughing.

Hot tears coursed into her hair and wet her pillow. 'How *could* he say those things to me?' she asked herself. 'Callin' me a tart! I've never been with anyone but him, or even wanted to. Why don't he trust me? But I meant what I said, Keith Bloody Jackson. I'm not goin' home with you till you come crawlin' round here on your belly and beg me to forgive you. So there!'

The next afternoon Keith was waiting outside the Club when Queenie finished work. They took one look at each other and Queenie rushed into his arms. 'I'm sorry, darling,' he muttered into her hair. 'You were right. I was just jealous and being unreasonable. I missed you last night.'

She raised tearful eyes. 'You silly sod, Keith Jackson.' She sniffed. 'Don't you *know* you're the only man I've ever fancied?'

He grinned down at her. 'Oh yes? What about Errol Flynn and Gary Cooper? Tell you what,' his eyes darkened with desire, 'why don't we go home for a while before we collect Hannah and you can show me how much you fancy me.'

Queenie compressed her lips and gave him a push, but they turned and walked arm in arm towards Victory Road.

# · *Nineteen* ·

The news from Europe over the months which followed was alarming.

Keith read bits out of the newspapers to Queenie. The government's policy of appeasement in trying to bring about settlements of the German disputes in Europe was in jeopardy. The likelihood of England's eventual involvement in a repeat of 1914 seemed high. According to Keith, that was, who could not understand – if the opinion polls were anything to go by – that the majority of the public still believed that Britain could stay out of any European war.

Discreet re-armament had been going on since 1934 when Mussolini broke the British, French and Italian *entente* and invaded Abyssinia. But, after a protracted recession there was opposition to the cost of such a policy, particularly from the Labour Party. And opposition also from the Dominions, reluctant to become involved in a war that they did not see as their business.

Keith was often away on exercises in the English Channel, and when he was at home tended to be preoccupied and morose, wanting to lose himself in his hobby of drawing and painting, while Queenie wanted to go out and have some fun in her spare time. Quite often she and Phyllis would go to the pictures while he stayed at home and looked after Hannah.

The Munich Crisis in September of 1938, with Hitler threatening to invade Czechoslovakia, caused widespread panic. Where would he stop? Gas masks were issued. Civil

Defence strengthened, and the building of air-raid shelters speeded up. If this war materialised, there would be devastation from the air.

Keith had to remain in base most of the time because, although the future role of motor torpedo boats was not yet clear, the Navy had been mobilised.

Then Chamberlain returned from Germany victorious, having effected a settlement with the aid of the French.

'Eddy said old Neville would stop it,' said Queenie, the eternal optimist, when her husband returned home for a few days' leave. 'No one in their right mind wants a war.'

'The last thing you can say about Adolf Hitler is that he's in his right mind,' growled Keith, sunk in an arm chair and peeling off his boots and socks. 'No one in their right mind rounds up and murders their own citizens just because they're Jews.'

'Ow, don't be so gloomy.'

'I don't know what you've got to be so cheerful about,' he said, noting that she had a glow about her.

'Well, the *Daily Express* says it'll be all right now. Anyway it's nothin' to do with us. But in any case I've got – '

'Don't you believe it,' he interrupted. 'Hitler's a psychopath! A Nazi megolamaniac, bent on dominating Europe. And it's only a matter of time before he sets his sights on Britain, if you ask me.'

Queenie didn't know the meaning of the big words, but she got the idea. 'But the Navy'll never let him in. We got the best bleedin' Navy in the world.'

'Well, they've got the "best bleeding Navy in the world" digging bleeding trenches in *Vernon*. The Royal Navy – digging bloody trenches! We even had a race to see which team could finish it quickest, and the fuck— the effing band was playing to encourage us. I ask you! I'm knackered, Queen. Light the copper for a bath, will you?'

'Arf a mo! I got some news.'

He cocked his eyebrow at his coyly smiling wife.

'Hannah is going to have a baby brother or sister. What d'you think of that?' Queenie watched several expressions play across his face, not one of which appeared to be pleasure. 'Ain't you pleased?' she wailed, bitterly disappointed.

Keith passed a hand across his eyes, then looked up, making an effort to smile. 'Of course I'm pleased.' He held out a hand and Queenie went to him and took it. Pulling her down onto his lap, he kissed her. 'You're a clever girl, aren't you. And you're keeping well?' She nodded, smiling. 'No morning sickness?' She shook her head.

'I am pleased, Queenie. I'd love another child. It's just that I wonder – ' He swallowed as if something was caught in his throat. 'I wonder if we have the right to bring children into the world with all this uncertainty.'

Queenie cradled his head against her shoulder. 'Life's got to go on, darling. Everything will be all right. You'll see.'

Queenie and Keith's second baby, another girl, was born in March of the following year –1939– just as Germany broke the Anglo-German agreement drawn up in Munich, and jack-booted troops marched into Prague and occupied the whole of Czechoslovakia.

Queenie went home to Baker Street for the birth, to Ma and Nurse Hebdon. It was as straightforward as Hannah's had been but less painful because Fanny Hebdon had a young trainee with her, and now, if there were two of them present, they were allowed to administer 'gas and air' to women in labour, to give some pain relief.

'I think she takes after your mother,' Queenie told Keith as he cuddled his new daughter. 'Would it please her if we called this one Violet?'

They had not seen his parents since the wedding, but Queenie wanted to keep in with them. Keith and his mother corresponded and Violet admitted to being anxious about the guest house business in the event of war. They sent her an occasional photograph when they could afford it, and she always asked after Hannah's progress. Occasionally she would put a polite little message in her letter for Queenie.

'Violet.' Keith grimaced. 'It wouldn't please me very much. Or your Ma, for that matter. But we could have it as her second name, I suppose. What about Emma? I've always liked that.'

Queenie smiled. 'We'll call her whatever you like as I chose Hannah Loretta.'

'Where did Loretta come from?'

'Loretta Young, the film star. Haven't you ever seen her? Real pretty, she is.'

Emma Violet was a contented baby. Her hair was lighter than Hannah's, her lips fuller and her dimpled hands and feet very dainty. Hannah was not too happy about this interloper who nuzzled at her mother's breast, but her father and grandmother paid her as much attention as ever, so she came grudgingly to accept her little sister.

England committed herself to fighting on Poland's behalf against German aggression if it came to that, and the same guarantees were given to Greece, Romania, Holland and Denmark. The Russians signed a non-aggression pact with Germany in August. King George and Queen Elizabeth undertook the visit to Canada that had been planned for so long. Then they went on to the United States of America, who were maintaining their neutrality in the European struggle. At home conscription was brought in and more air-raid shelters dug. There was a big one in St George's Square.

But for Queenie and her family things went on much as usual. St George's church was to host two more Ellis family events. Emma was christened in May and Phyllis put pressure on John to bring their wedding forward to

July. So, for the women, the anxieties were offset by the fun of preparation.

Phyllis and Auntie Dot were Emma's godmothers and Michael came up from Cornwall to be her godfather. 'I won't be sorry if there's a war,' he told Keith. 'I can't wait to get into the Navy.'

'Don't talk bloody daft,' said Keith angrily. 'You can join the Navy without a war. Anyway I'm not surprised if things aren't working out between you and the parents. I tried to warn you. You've got to get away.'

'I must. You know what Mum's like! Wants to control your every breath. And I can quite see now how things went rotten between Dad and grandfather. Parents can't accept that their children become adults. A son needs independence. Things are pretty fraught down in Porthleven, with Ma frequently throwing prima donna acts, worrying over the cancelled bookings, and Dad threatening to join the coastguards. The way things are going, the guest house won't support *them*, let alone me.'

John's wedding, imminent for so long, was now hurriedly arranged. It was to be a simple one in the circumstances, with a bit of a shindig in the church hall afterwards. No honeymoon, and the young couple were to live with Phyllis' parents to begin with.

'That's a mistake,' advised Queenie.

'I'd prefer not,' agreed Phyllis, 'but John's away so much that it seems a waste of money me paying another rent to be on my own most of the time.'

'At least you can wear white, be a proper bride.' Queenie briefed her friend on the physical side of marriage. 'Wish I'd had someone to tell *me* all this,' she laughed. 'I had to find out the hard way.'

'Was it very hard?' asked Phyllis innocently.

Queenie's twinkling eyes belied her serious expression. 'Well, put it like this – you don't get nowhere if it's soft.'

'Oh, you are awful!'

They both giggled.

Queenie hugged her friend. 'I hope you'll be as happy as I am, Phyll.' And seeing the expression of adoration in her brother's eyes as he watched his bride approaching the altar in her simple white gown and veil, Queenie knew that, just like in the favourite fairy stories, John and Phyllis were going to 'live happily ever after'.

At the end of August, Hitler invaded Poland.

Britain procrastinated for a day or two. The *Daily Express* said there would be no war. On 3 September, 1939, the Ellises, sitting round the wireless in the kitchen of number twelve, were stunned to hear Neville Chamberlain announce that Britain was at war with Germany.

'I never thought it could 'appen again, not after all Josh went through,' said Beatie, unashamedly crying. 'Our Billy, our John and your Keith will all be in it. Oh, my Gawd.'

Eddy exchanged a horrified look with his sister and fear snaked through Queenie's vitals. People they loved could be killed and maimed, their homes could be bombed, their children were in danger. 'That bastard Hitler!' she cried. 'Keith said 'e was a madman.'

'I'd like to get my hands on him,' Eddy said with compressed violence, banging his fist on the table. 'Why was I born a bloody useless cripple?'

Eddy had never mentioned his affliction before that Queenie could remember and this outburst was so unlike him. She went to her brother and pulled his head against her middle. His arms went around her hips.

'Don't talk like that, Ed. In any case if your poor old foot keeps you safe at home, I'm glad you was born like it. And you've got a very important job down the dockyard. We need people like you to keep things going here while the boys are fightin' – '

Beatie got up and went through the ritual of tea-making, the cups and saucers rattling in her shaking hands.

Jimmy and Josh came running in, bright-eyed and shouting. 'We're at war! We're at war.'

Beatie cuffed Jimmy and grabbed Josh and shook him. 'It's not a bloody game, you boys. We might all be killed.'

'Or have the Germans swarming all over us,' added Eddy, lighting himself a cigarette. 'How would you like to be slave-labour for the Germans, while they build their new world?'

There was a tap on the back door and Lil and her husband Sid came in. 'Well, after all they said, it's 'appened,' Lil said in a sepulchral voice, her large face unnaturally pale. 'Who'd 'a believed it. My Dicky'll 'ave to go.'

Queenie bit her lip. She'd never liked 'Spotty Dick', but now a wave of affection for him washed over her. Emma was asleep upstairs but she lifted Hannah out of the high-chair and hugged her. The child knew there was something wrong, her anxious eyes going from face to face.

'I'm goin' to enlist for the ARP. Might as well do something useful,' said Sid, who had been unemployed for years.

'Good fer you, Sid,' nodded Beatie before wailing, 'oh, Lil, our poor boys.'

Lil sat down heavily. 'And 'ow many German mothers are sayin' the same thing, Beatie?'

Her friend nodded. 'It's these bleedin' politicians. If it was up to women, there'd be no wars. Do we 'ave sons just to fight?'

'The King, God bless 'im, is speaking in a few minutes,' Lil told them. Beatie switched the wireless on again and poured them all a cup of tea.

They sat silent and still, only the ticking of the old wooden clock on the mantelpiece accompanying their monarch's occasionally stammering voice, speaking to them simply, 'as if I were able to cross your threshold and speak to you myself'. He asked them to stand firm and united, for the sake of all they held dear. To stand united in defence of liberty, peace and justice.

'Amen,' said Lil when he had finished and they all sat with bowed heads. The younger boys exchanged looks of fearful excitement.

Later, after Lil and Sid had gone home and the Ellises had eaten a scrappy supper, and the babies were put to bed, Beatie, Eddy and Queenie continued to sit around the kitchen table. Each was submerged in their own thoughts of what this war might mean to them. Jimmy and Josh were playing a subdued game of Ludo.

The inner kitchen door opened and Phyllis walked in from the street. No sooner was she through the door than she burst into tears. Queenie went to her and, putting an arm around her, led her to the table. Beatie patted her hand.

'I'm so frightened,' wept Phyllis. 'I've only been married two months and this has to go an' happen.' No-one could think of anything comforting to say. Queenie's chin trembled but she was determined not to cry.

'We'll stick together,' said Beatie eventually, as though that would be enough to save them.

Then Keith arrived, coming into the kitchen with a grim face. Queenie ran to him and he held her close. 'We wasn't expecting you,' she mumbled against his serge tunic.

'Ain't it awful, Keith,' said Beatie.

He nodded. 'We were on deck when we heard. The news came wafting out from the porthole in the captain's cabin. Everyone stopped what they were doing and stood as still as statues. The captain came out and just looked at us – didn't have to ask if we'd heard. But I've known it was going to happen for a very long time.'

'You always said it would,' said Queenie, raising frightened eyes to his. 'What's goin' to happen now?'

'I've got to be back in base for briefing at six tomorrow morning. A lot of the blokes won't be able to get home to see their families. I'm lucky – I've got time to take action.'

Queenie's brow furrowed. 'Action?'

'I'm taking you home to pack, my girl. The babies can stay here tonight if it's all right with you, Ma?' Beatie nodded. 'You're off to Cornwall tomorrow, Queenie.'

'To your mother?' shrieked Queenie, pulling back from him with blazing eyes. 'I bleedin' ain't!'

He gripped her shoulders and gave her a little shake. 'Portsmouth is going to be a number one target. I want you and my children out of it.'

'I couldn't – I just couldn't!'

'You can – and you will. I've sent a telegram.'

'You go, our Queen,' said Beatie. 'It'll be a load off my mind to know *someone's* safe.'

Phyllis and Eddy agreed.

'But I can't just go and leave everyone 'ere to face the music without me. What will happen to Jimmy and Josh?'

'I'll send them to Aunt Tildy in Cowplain,' said Beatie, brightening up. 'They'll be safe over the Hill.'

'I know you think you can organise most things, Queen,' said Eddy with a wry chuckle, 'but you being here won't make any difference to our chances, and you can't take us all with you.'

'But . . . I can't just leave my job – '

'I'll fix that,' said Keith. 'They'll understand. These things are bound to happen when there's a war on.'

Phyllis started crying again. We'll miss you, Queenie,' she sobbed. 'You always manage to cheer things up, however bad they are.'

'It'll be awful,' wailed Queenie, beseeching her husband. 'I'd rather stay here and take my chances with old Hitler than live with your Mum.'

# · *Twenty* ·

The long train journey down to Cornwall was an ordeal. Apart from the anxiety of travelling on her own, sorrow at leaving her husband and family, and fear of having to cope with Violet Jackson, Queenie had the added problem of Hannah's travel sickness. She had to keep leaving baby Emma in the care of a woman in the compartment while she raced Hannah along the corridor to the toilet, trying to keep their balance against the swaying of the train. And not always getting there in time.

When they arrived at Helston, Queenie was exhausted, the baby crying, and Hannah looking thoroughly wretched and smelling of vomit.

Her father-in-law was there to meet her with a waiting taxi. 'Hello, lass.' Bernard greeted her with a kiss and a sympathetic smile that almost had her weeping on his shoulder. She was glad to relinquish Hannah and the luggage into his capable hands.

'I hope Mrs Jackson don't mind us turning up like this at such short notice?' she asked anxiously in the taxi.

Bernard turned from the front seat and gave her a wink. 'Don't you worry, lass. You're very welcome as far as I'm concerned. Violet – ' He paused. 'If you have any problems – of any kind – I want you to promise to tell me.'

Grateful at finding an ally in what she perceived as hostile territory, she smiled and nodded. 'I bloody well will, don't worry.'

Queenie hardly noticed the scenery so preoccupied was she with the coming meeting with her mother-in-law. Oh, how she wished Keith was with her. Her eyes stung with tears as she remembered their passionate love-making last night. It was almost as if they feared they wouldn't see each other again. But she mustn't think like that.

The taxi turned a hairpin bend that revealed a breathtaking evening view of the sea, and stopped in a little road outside the imposing double frontage of Tremayne.

Bernard opened the door and took Emma from Queenie's arms, so that she could take Hannah's hand and draw her out of the car. The salt-laden wind caught at Queenie's long hair and spun it about her face as they walked to a door set in a side conservatory.

It opened to frame Violet Jackson.

Violet's eyes swept over the bedraggled trio.

'Poor little mites,' she said kindly, bending and holding out a hand to her eldest granddaughter. 'Hello, Hannah.' Then she straightened up. 'And this is little Emma. Let me take her from you, dear, you must be very tired.'

Queenie, sighing with relief, followed Violet upstairs to a bedroom with two single beds and a cot, Bernard bringing up the rear with the battered suitcase and bags. 'I hope this will be all right for you, dear. The bathroom is next door. Now do you need any help with the children?'

'I can manage, thanks. We all need a wash, Hannah particul'ly 'cos the poor kid's been so sick on the train. Then I must feed Emma.'

'Come down when you are ready. In about half an hour? Michael is cooking a nice supper for us.'

Her unexpected kindness almost undid Queenie. She blinked tears away. 'Thank you, Mrs. Jackson. I do hope we're not goin' to be a bother to you. Keith insisted . . .'

Violet's eyes also moistened. 'Families must stick together in times like these.'

'That's what Ma said.'

'How is your mother?'

'Worried about Billy and John.'

Violet nodded. 'Our poor boys. I don't know how long

it will be before Michael gets his call-up.' She compressed trembling lips. 'Call if you need any help, dear.'

Perhaps it was going to be all right, after all, thought Queenie thankfully as she undressed Hannah and washed her in the bathroom. Violet was not as intimidating as she had been on previous occasions and now they had a common bond with their worry over Keith.

Queenie looked wide-eyed at the white bath with silver taps, the sparkling wash-basin and the *inside* toilet. They had bathrooms down at the Sailors' Club, but she'd never seen anything like it before in a private house. Ooh, she couldn't wait to get in that bath. There seemed to be some sort of complicated water-heater thing on the wall. She'd have to ask how that worked. Meanwhile Emma was bawling her head off in the bedroom, but was fortuntely tired enough to drop straight off to sleep after her feed.

It was a relief to have someone of her own age around, thought Queenie, as she watched Michael carve a joint of beef. He had been delighted to see her too. It surprised her, coming from a household where the women were the skivvies, how domesticated the Jackson boys were. Keith could cook quite well and would turn his hand to the ironing if necessary – but that was partly the result of being in the Navy.

The meal was beautifully cooked and the vegetables presented in bowls. She helped herself sparingly to the carrots and cabbage as there didn't seem to be much of either. Ma always cooked several vegetables and heaped the plates with food, straight from the saucepans.

'What're those?' she asked of little, lightly-browned whirls on a plate.

'Duchesse potatoes,' said Michael with a smile, handing her the gravy boat.

'You'll 'ave to learn me how to do spuds like that, Michael,' Queenie enthused. She cut up Hannah's meal, and the child, obviously fully recovered from her wretched journey, ate it enthusiastically.

'Coo,' Queenie exclaimed. 'My Uncle Danny would say that this Yorkshire pud is as airy as a fairy's f . . . – Er, it's lovely. You're going to 'ave your work cut out giving me cooking lessons.'

There was lemon meringue pie with clotted cream to finish and Queenie and Hannah had second helpings. Michael and Bernard washed up afterwards, insisting that the two women should rest. Queenie was amazed. Men never washed dishes in her home.

Violet, holding Hannah on her lap, read some stories to her from old books that she told her had belonged to her daddy. Longing for Keith overwhelmed Queenie again. Where would he be sent now, and what dangers would he have to face.

After putting Hannah to bed, Queenie, tired out, asked how to go about having a bath. Surprised at such a question, Violet demonstrated the vagaries of the geyser, and Queenie discovered to her amazement that it wasn't the only bathroom in the house.

Luxuriating in the first proper bath she had ever had, Queenie reflected on her lot. In spite of her misgivings, she had been kindly welcomed and elegantly if sparingly fed. 'I could get used to this life, you know,' she told herself.

Beatie sent Josh and Jimmy over the Hill to Cowplain to stay with Aunt Tildy, an arrangement which pleased no-one. Vera and Ronnie were dispatched to a grandmother up north, Phyllis took a job at Eastney, training to service locomotives now that so many men had been called up.

Beatie, missing her grandchildren dreadfully and quite unable to be idle, wondered what on earth she was going to do with herself now there was just her and Eddy. She could not take in any lodgers, as that would jeopardise her place on the housing list for a new flat, so she took an additional cleaning job.

'Oh, Beatie,' Lil came drooping into the kitchen one afternoon with tears running down her cheeks.

'Whatever's the matter, Lil?' Beatie asked concerned.

'I've lost Moggy.'

'E's run off? He'll come back,' said Beatie, knowing how fond Lil was of her rangy old tom cat.

Lil shook her head. 'I've 'ad 'im put down. Didn't you read the pamphlet?'

Beatie shook her head.

'Said we 'ad to 'ave domestic pets put down because of the difficulty of feeding them with a war on. So I took 'im down the PDSA and . . .' she sobbed, 'brought 'im home in a little brown sack. Sid's burying 'im now in the yard.'

This was the start of things to come, thought Beatie grimly.

Down in Cornwall, Queenie soon became bitterly miserable, frustrated and home-sick. She had never been away from her home or Portsmouth for more than a week at a time, and then the occasions could be numbered on one hand. Panic had gripped everyone when war was declared – they rushed around and evacuated as if Hitler's hordes were about to swarm ashore immediately. But it had all quietened down and the expected bombings had not happened and it was being called 'The Phoney War'. Everyone was fine in Portsmouth, her younger brothers had gone home, and she couldn't understand why Keith insisted she stay put.

She was kept very busy, although there were only two remaining guests at Tremayne. Several people had cancelled for the following Easter after the declaration of war. Porthleven was charming. She loved the sea-views and the sunsets from the windows of Tremayne. But, oh, it was so quiet.

She loved taking the dinner scraps over the little road and scraping them off the plate onto the wall for the gulls who came screaming overhead. 'If I tied a message to yer leg, would you get it back to Ma for me?' she called to them. Yes, she actually missed Ma.

Violet had managed to borrow an old pram for her, so Queenie often wheeled the children around the harbour and up the other side towards Looe Beach. But it was getting late in the year and cold, and there were often days of unremitting 'mizzle', as the light drizzle was called locally.

She spent a lot of the time in the kitchen, taking cooking lessons from Michael, spending much of the time in hysterics over shared jokes and culinary disasters. But in spite of the fact that Queenie helped all she could with the housework, tried to keep the children quiet, and was continually watching her 'ps and qs' – except that they were mostly 'bs' in her case – Violet was frequently wound-up and snappy, often taking to her bed in the afternoons.

Her mother-in-law had a way of making little snide remarks, finished off with a sarcastically intoned 'dear' which made Queenie feel ignorant. And she never called her by her christian name. 'Well, of course, *you* would, dear'. 'Naturally, *you* wouldn't know that . . . dear'. Queenie found herself constantly on the defensive and her confidence became undermined. She often had difficulty controlling her temper and her tongue.

Bernard joined the coastguards and was away for long periods, but he seemed happier now that he had a contribution to make. He was unfailingly humorous and kind to her, warning Violet off her sly digs when he was there.

Michael was a friend, also frequently helping her out of awkward spots, playing with the children and sometimes accompanying her on her walks. Although they had little in common – even less than she and Keith had – they were easy in each other's company. Yet, she guessed, living at home with a mother like Violet, he had little experience of girls. But quite often he and Bernard went down to the

Ship in the evenings for a drink and a jaw, and she was left with Violet. Very occasionally she was able to see an old Arthur Askey film or similar at the village hall, but she missed the cinemas of Portsmouth.

'If it wasn't for you, Michael, I'd go bleedin' potty,' Queenie told her brother-in-law one evening as they played Rummy. 'I get so bored. When I'm here with your Mum on our own, she plays Patience – God give me patience – or she dozes off, and I'm sitting here listenin' to that bloody grandfather clock tick-ticking away, until I could scream. Or else she's got that high-brow music on the wireless, that drives me *mad*. Give me jazz any day.'

'Poor old Queenie.'

'Don't get me wrong. I know it's hard for your mother. She's trying her best to be nice to me, but we'll never really get along – not in a month of Sundays.

'She's improved since you first met.'

'You could've kidded me. No, I s'pose she has.'

'Your wedding seems to have been the turning point. She doesn't get so many headaches now, and she and Dad appear to be er, co-habiting again.'

'Co-what?'

'Er, sleeping together.'

Her eyes opened wide. 'You mean they . . .?'

He nodded. 'I've seen him coming out of her room and occasionally they exchange hot glances.'

'Gor blimey! At their age.'

'Life doesn't end at fifty, you know.'

'It does for some,' said Queenie, thinking of her own dear father. 'I thought that sort of thing finished earlier, though.' She gave a secretive little smile. 'Best news I've had for a long while.'

Michael grinned. 'Keith's a lucky bugger.'

He got up and twiddled the knobs on the wireless till he got some swinging music. Queenie jumped up in glee and started to wiggle her hips and gyrate round the room. He joined in and they laughed at each other. After a few lively numbers, the tempo changed to the rhythm of ballroom dancing and they drifted cautiously into each other's arms.

Their mutual attraction and the seductive music drew them closer together. Queenie gazed up into Michael's grey eyes, unlike Keith's, and roamed over his face to the cleft chin that reminded her of her husband.

'You're sweet,' Michael murmured. 'Old Keith is a lucky dog.'

The sensation of his arms warm around her awakened a longing in her. 'I'm missing him,' she mourned.

Michael nodded. 'I'll bet he's missing you, too. If I was him I couldn't bear to let you out of my sight.' His eyes sent delicious messages thrilling through her and she could not resist giving him a languorous look in return which had them both breathing quickly.

Suddenly Michael pulled away, strode to the wireless and turned it off. 'I don't think this is a very good idea, do you? I promised to take Mum up some cocoa. Want some?'

Queenie shook her head and he went out. She sank onto the settee. If he hadn't pulled back then, what might have happened? She was shaken by the force of the attraction she felt for him. Shaken by the knowledge that she was susceptible to another man, while being in love with her husband. How easy it would be . . .

Michael avoided her after this, even avoided meeting her eyes, and she felt even lonelier. A week later he announced that he had joined the Navy and was being posted to Plymouth in three days' time.

Violet pressed the back of her hand against her mouth and her eyes beseeched him.

'I've got to go sooner or later, Mum, you know that. The holiday season's finished. You might get a few bookings over Christmas, but you've got Queenie here to help.' He gave his sister-in-law a quick glance and she knew that she was part of the reason for him going. 'You can manage without me.'

Violet jumped up and ran weeping from the room.

'Christ!' exclaimed Michael.

Queenie bit on her bottom lip.

'Don't worry about it, lad,' said his father. 'Nothing much is happening at the moment, but it will. You'd have got your call-up papers soon, anyway. No-one wants to see their sons going off to fight a war, but she'll have to face up to it like every other mother.'

Queenie said goodbye very formally to her brother-in-law three evenings later and left him with his parents until the taxi came to bear him away to an unknown destiny. She went out to look over the wall at the sea, pulling her cardigan around her and crossing her arms against the cold. Her hair was tied back, but the fierce wind tore strands of it out of its confining ribbon and whipped it, stinging, across her eyes. She shuddered.

This bloody stupid war! Families being split up – and it wasn't just the men. All those kids evacuated from London and Portsmouth and other cities, their mothers not knowing who they were going to and if they'd ever see them again. She'd seen the pictures in the paper. Little kids with gas-masks slung over their shoulders and labels tied onto their coats. She supposed she should think herself lucky that she was able to be in a safe place with her babies, but . . .

The taxi arrived and Queenie went in to tell them, meeting Michael on his way out through the conservatory. They stopped and stared at each other. Seeing tears on her cheeks, he said, 'Don't cry, Queenie.'

'Oh, Michael,' she wailed, throwing herself into his arms. He kissed her forehead, her wet cheeks and finally her mouth. Tearing himself free he marched out to the car.

'Trollop!' The word was hissed behind her, and she spun round to look into Violet's furious face – a face pale and twisted with a mixture of disgust, jealousy and hatred. The words she spat out matched these emotions. 'You've been working on him, haven't you? Setting your cheap, sleazy snares to catch him. He's a decent boy – he'd never dream of – but you, you trashy little tart! Brothers, fathers, it doesn't matter, does it? One man wouldn't ever be enough for your sort, would it?'

Queenie's eyes had stretched wide at this amazing and undeserved tirade. 'Now just a minute,' she said at last, trying to keep her voice level though her heart was thumping violently. 'Just because I kiss me brother-in-law goodbye don't mean nothing. There's nothing between us. I'm fond of him, that's all. *I love Keith*. And just what d'you mean about "fathers"?'

'I've seen the way you lead them all on, giggling, flirting, promising them things with your eyes – '

The spite and injustice of Violet's words stung Queenie to fury.

'You evil old *witch*,' she yelled. 'You're jealous! Want to keep your sons to yourself. Well, that's twisted if you ask me. I pity your poor husband – '

'How dare you!' Violet's voice rose correspondingly. She took a threatening step towards her daughter-in-law and Queenie gritted her teeth and squared her shoulders.

'What the devil's going on?' Bernard appeared in the conservatory doorway. 'What the hell are you two shouting about?'

'Ask her. The old cow!' Queenie thrust past them, then turned. 'I'm bloody well going home tomorrow. War or no war, I ain't staying here to be insulted.' She ran up the stairs and started throwing things into the old family suitcase. She didn't have to worry about the kids – nothing short of a bomb would wake them once they were asleep. She was shaking with fear, fury and wild elation, because now she had a good excuse to go home.

Queenie waited several days in their little house in Victory Road for her husband to come home. She did not even know where he was. She cleaned the house which was only a little untidy, and went around touching his belongings tenderly, burying her face in his sports coat and inhaling that faint mixture of tobacco and sweat that was uniquely his. She longed for him and kept herself pretty at all times in case he suddenly turned up.

There had been a tearful reunion with her family. Queenie was pleased to see that they had all missed her almost as much as she had missed them, but of course they had all been together while she had been in exile. Jimmy and Josh had come home from Auntie Tilda's after a few weeks.

Hitler hadn't invaded England yet, the panic had subsided, and perhaps it would all be over before it began.

To Beatie's sorrow, Queenie had left Hannah with her paternal grandmother. What a scene there had been on the morning of her departure from Tremayne.

Violet had appeared with puffy red eyes and Bernard drew her forward by the arm, prompting, 'Go on, Mother.'

Sensing a moral victory, Queenie looked at her, tight-lipped and stony-eyed – unprepared to give an inch. Bernard and Violet must have had a hell of a row last night for Violet to appear so crushed and Bernard so firm.

'Violet,' he persisted.

Violet's mouth opened and closed a few times like that of a fish out of water. 'Please try to forgive me for the things I said last night . . . dear,' she said with difficulty. 'It was just that – I was so upset.' There was a moment's silence. Queenie did not want to forgive her because then they might try to persuade her to stay.

Bernard cleared his throat. 'We were all upset last night. Seeing young Michael going off to God knows what and Keith already away somewhere. *War is upsetting*.'

'Please don't go,' begged Violet. 'Keith will never forgive me. He sent you to us for safe-keeping.'

'I can't stay,' mumbled Queenie, knowing that it was the fear of her son's disapproval that was prompting Violet's humility. 'I've got to go home.'

The Jacksons exchanged a worried look. 'Then please, at least leave Hannah with us,' pleaded Violet, picking the child up and hugging her to her. 'You know we'll look after her and she'll be safe here. We'd like to keep Emma too, but with you still feeding her . . .'

'It makes sense, lass,' added Bernard.

Queenie bit her lip. She did not want to part with her daughter, but she knew Keith was going to be angry with her anyway. Perhaps he would be less angry if one of the children was in a safe place. Hannah was quite happily settled here, blooming with health, and her grandparents loved her and would bring her up nicely. And it would be some comfort to Violet who had now lost both her adored sons.

So she agreed.

Violet visibly relaxed. 'And I'm sure, dear, that you didn't mean those things you said to me, either.'

She wanted an apology! Queenie's eyes sparked at her. 'Oh yes, I did, Mrs Jackson. I meant every bleedin' word.'

Queenie heard Keith's key in the lock, late on the fourth night, and jumped out of bed to run down to greet him. She was nervous about his reaction to her homecoming but joy was the more powerful emotion as she threw open the door to the sitting room.

Keith was not alone. He was standing close – far too close – to a woman with dyed red hair and heavy make-up.

## · Twenty-one ·

Queenie's breath stopped in her throat and her heart beat in heavy thuds as she stared at her husband and his companion. Keith, looking momentarily shocked, soon got himself under control.

'Good God, Queenie, what are you doing here?'

She could not answer. She could not move.

'Keith turned to the woman. 'We'll . . . er, we'll have to postpone that drink, Thelma . . . and you can tell me all about it some other time.' He picked up her coat, thrust it at her and manoeuvred her past his wife, into the hall and out of the front door.

Queenie moved into the middle of the room, shaking violently now, and so upset and enraged that it crossed her mind that if a knife had been at hand she was capable of plunging it into him.

He came back into the room and closed the door. 'That's the girl who took over your job at the Club,' he told her with heightened colour but coolly under control. 'I was just seeing her home and she was a bit upset about her boyfriend being posted, so I asked her in for a night-cap.' He indicated a bottle of whisky on the table.

There was a moment when she might have believed that was all there was to it, but the whisky was the final straw. They never had spirits in the house – they could not afford it on his pay. And to bring a bottle in with a woman could only mean one thing.

Jealous fury mobilised Queenie. 'You rotten bastard!' she screamed, rushing at him with fingers clawed to rend her fury on his face. 'You sent me away just so you could – '

'Listen to me. Listen!' He caught her wrists and held her off, perspiration beading his forehead –

'You pig. You filthy, rotten pig! I bet you go and visit Pompey Nell up the other end of the road as well. Charge much, does she?' She kicked at his shins with her bare feet.

'Stop it. Stop. There was nothing in it. I promise you. Just a friend – '

'I'll give you friend!' she shrieked. 'I trusted you. I thought you loved me and all the time – '

He gave her a little shake. 'Stop yelling like your mother.' His own voice rose, 'What are you doing here, anyway? I sent you and the kids away for safety. How *dare* you disobey me.'

Queenie stopped struggling and gave him a scornful look from flashing blue eyes. 'Oh. Throwing *my* marriage vows at me, are you? What a laugh, 'cept it ain't bleeding well funny. Don't think you can turn the blame onto me – whatever you think, I'm not a fool.' She pulled out of his slackened grasp. 'But, in case you're int'rested in *anything* I do, I couldn't stand it with your so-and-so mother any longer. She's got a nasty, poisonous mind.'

Shivering violently with cold as much as with emotion, she clasped her arms with her hands. 'You're cold.' Keith attempted to put his arms round her, but she shrugged him off furiously.

'Don't touch me, Keith Jackson.'

'This is ridiculous.'

'We agree there. It's bleedin' ridiculous that I ever thought I could trust you again after the way you deserted me when I got pregnant – '

'Oh, for Christ's sake – I was posted.'

'Very convenient. And how many women did you go with while you was abroad?'

Keith ran his hand over his mouth and jaw. 'Look, Queenie, let's try to straighten this thing out. I admit I like women. It's my most regrettable weakness. But I was ... lonely while you were away, and we aren't living under normal circumstances, are we? It's all a bit of a strain – waiting to see where you're going to be sent, what you're going to be asked to do. Can't you see that?'

Her expression softened. She wanted to believe him, she wanted to forgive him. He looked young and tired and so sad. Her mouth and chin trembled and her eyes filled with tears.

He hesitantly reached out a hand to her. 'I am a bastard. I don't deserve you. I know that. But *you* know, don't you, that you and the children ... are the most important things in the world to me.'

It was the break in his voice that did it. Queenie flung herself at him and they rocked together, clasped in each other's arms. 'Forgive me,' he murmured in her ear. 'I promise it won't happen again.'

They kissed frantically, tasting each other's tears. She felt warm and safe again, and decided to ignore the smell of the other woman's perfume on him. 'Promise!' she whispered.

'Promise. Come on, my darling, let's go upstairs.'

Their lovemaking was heightened by their quarrel and the relief of coming together again. 'It gets better and better,' she murmured contentedly when they were both sated.

He supported himself on his elbows over her, smiling down into her eyes, a lock of hair tumbling over his forehead. 'Now, young lady, what brings you home?'

Queenie told him – colourfully. He groaned and flopped down on his back beside her. 'My mother! What *is* wrong with that woman?' He turned and looked at her with a grin. '*Sure* there was nothing between you and Michael?'

'Course not!' But Queenie blushed, recalling how easy it would have been to succumb to temptation, just as Keith had done.

*

Queenie had come back to a city which virtually closed down as soon as darkness fell. There had been blackout of course, in Cornwall, but she hadn't noticed it there because they never wanted to go out after dark anyway.

In Portsmouth the kerbs had been painted white to show up in the dark, the trees and lamp-posts had been marked with white, and even her mother's red doorstep had now been whitened. At this time more civilians were being knocked down and killed and injured by motorists in the dark than by enemy action. A twenty mile an hour speed limit was imposed after dark.

Cinemas and dance halls were closed for a while and the New Year's celebrations at South Parade Pier had to be curtailed by ten o'clock. Christmas and New Year celebrations were very muted anyway. The usual revels in Guildhall Square did not take place. Church bells hung silent in their belfries, having been forbidden to ring since the outbreak of war. Ships' sirens, usually sounded to celebrate the incoming of a new year and other momentous occasions, were silent in Portsmouth Harbour.

January also saw the introduction of food rationing.

'How we goin' to live on about a pound of meat and a couple ounces of cheese a week?' asked Lil, scandalised.

'It's the tea and sugar what I'm goin' to miss,' grumbled Beatie. 'At least we've got eggs, Lil. And we ain't goin' to miss the bacon – '

'Cos we couldn't afford it anyway.'

'Maybe we'll git nice and slim.' They both laughed at that.

The Phoney War was well and truly over. London was being systematically bombed, and now the enemy were turning their attention to the naval ports. For reasons of security the tallies on sailors' caps now bore only the letters HMS.

In May, Keith was to be transferred to Felixstowe on the East Coast where things were still quiet, but before that he went down to Cornwall on his own to see his parents and bring back Hannah, reckoning that Felixstowe would not attract much German interest.

It was a matter for rejoicing to have the little girl back again. She looked well, was talking a lot and had good table manners. 'It's done you good, being with Grannie Jackson,' Queenie admitted grudgingly. 'How was the old – dear?' she asked Keith.

'Not quite so wound-up as she usually is. She and Dad seem to be getting on much better these days. For years her bedroom's been sacrosanct but I actually saw Dad coming out of her room on one or two occasions and I'll swear there was a saucy smile on his face.'

She laughed. 'Michael told me that too. Think we'll still be doing it when we're their age?'

Keith grinned. 'Middle-aged passion. Perhaps like wine it gets better the older it is.'

'Something to look forward to.'

He kissed her nose, saying seriously, 'I hope so, darling.'

'Oh, don't,' knowing that he meant that he hoped they would have the chance.

'Mum sends you her best wishes, by the way.'

'Like hell!'

Shortly after his arrival in Felixstowe, Keith found accommodation for the family and sent for them. It was apparently easy to find rented accommodation as so many inhabitants of the small town had evacuated. He would spend most of his time at the base but get home as much as possible. Queenie gave up the house in Victory Road, excited at the prospect of a change, knowing it was safer for the children too.

Now that Hitler's troops had invaded Holland, the motor torpedo boats were proving their true worth in patrolling the North Sea on the look-out for enemy convoys. With their speed of attack, and a heavy hitting power for their size – in spite of being out-gunned by the German 'E' boats' – the MTBs became the equivalent of seaborne bombers.

Queenie found Felixstowe attractive, though with an east wind off the sea, colder than Portsmouth. They rented a maisonette in Sea Road which looked out across pleasant gardens and the Promenade, enjoying magnificent ocean views. The model yacht pond and the pier were to the left, and in the other direction, Landguard Fort lying in the entrance to the River Orwell, and beyond, the Naze headland.

On 14 June almost every wireless-set in Britain had tuned in to Alvar Liddell on the six o'clock news to hear that Paris had fallen. The enemy was just across that stretch of water . . . But old Winston had made that marvellous speech saying, 'We shall never surrender' and Queenie remained convinced that the Navy would never let them get across.

Everywhere there were posters saying 'Careless Talk Costs Lives', and Ministry of Information pamphlets warning that the enemy might infiltrate the population disguised as anything from nuns to boy scouts.

It was just a shame they couldn't get onto the beach because of the concrete anti-tank blocks and barbed wire that had been erected to keep Hitler out. But it was the same in Portsmouth, and there, Southsea Common had virtually been given over to vegetable growing. 'Digging for Victory' they called it. And there were ack-ack stations and searchlights on the common. Not to mention some of the fifty barrage balloons that floated over the city and Gosport. 'Look. Elephants,' Hannah had cried when she first saw the great silver balloons with a trunk-like shape at one end.

HMS *Beehive*, the coastal forces base, consisted of little more than the depot ship *Vulcan*, a hangar at the air station, and a hotel taken over for offices and the billeting of naval officers and Wrens. It was just along the coast road and across to Felixstowe basin, so Keith was able to get home quickly, but life was slightly more difficult with him needing to sleep in the day when the boats patrolled at night.

On the morning of 7 September they were woken by the pealing of church bells. Queenie lay sleepily puzzled. 'What's that all about? It isn't Sunday.' She suddenly remembered that church bells and hooters had been banned since the beginning of the war. Only air-raid sirens were heard these days.

Keith leapt out of bed and started pulling on his clothes.

'What is it?' Queenie asked, sitting up, frightened by his grim expression.

'It's come – the bloody invasion is under way.'

'What?'

'It's the pre-arranged signal. All leave cancelled. All forces mobilised.' He stopped and looked at her. 'You'd better get the kids up.'

She jumped out of bed, grabbing clothes, fear washing through her in waves. 'But what shall I do?'

He gave her a distracted look as he pulled on his boots. 'Pack some things quickly. Get up to Ipswich and down to Cornwall.' He got up and gave her all the money out of his wallet and the emergency fund out of the drawer. She stood staring at him with huge, frightened eyes. He grasped her by the shoulders, saying roughly, 'Pull yourself together now, my girl. It's my job to go out and fight – it's yours to get the children to safety.'

Queenie wanted to scream, to cry out that she might never see him again, that something unthinkable was about to happen to them all – but she blinked her eyes, gritted her teeth and nodded. Throwing on some clothes she went to the front door with him. They embraced fiercely. Keith kissed her mouth with bruising force and was gone. She watched him marching briskly away from her.

She had a dreadful time trying to get onto a crowded train and stood squeezed in the corridor for the journey, holding Emma in her arms and with Hannah sitting on their case. There were no rail connections available at Ipswich for civilians and she had to book into a hotel for the night, terrified of what might be going on at the coast and whether she would get the children away before the Germans reached Ipswich.

But it turned out to be a false alarm. There was no invasion. The signs of enemy activity on the other side of the Channel had been misread. Queenie and the other stranded wives cried tears of relief as the news came over the wireless.

The bells rang out all day along the south and east coast of England because no-one had arranged a signal for them to stop, and by the evening everyone's nerves were at screaming point.

Queenie returned home with the children the next day on a slightly less crowded train, as some of the women had decided to go on to their original destinations, supposing it was bound to happen again sooner or later. But Queenie was full of joy – they had been given another chance.

She saw Keith waiting at the barrier as they alighted from the train – saw his solemn face break into a smile. He pushed past the ticket collector and ran towards them, gathering them all in his arms and kissing them. 'I've met every bloody Ipswich train for hours,' he said with a grin.

'I thought I'd never see you again,' she wept.

He kissed her tears away.

At dusk, one autumn evening, the engines of five motor torpedo boats swelled to a roar that echoed round Felixstowe Basin. A sound familiar to local inhabitants.

'Let go for'ard,' shouted Lieutenant 'Dicky' Dickinson, the officer-in-charge of Keith's boat. 'Let go aft.'

The boats slipped away from the jetty one by one, and once clear of the harbour they formed up in the shape of an arrow head, Dickinson's boat keeping station on the starboard quarter of the leading MTB. The coastline faded behind them as they set out on the long cruise across the North Sea to where enemy convoys or merchant ships might be encountered.

Keith and one or two other ratings went below and stripped off their heavy oilskin overalls.

'A fiver says we bag one tonight,' said Geordie, rolling a cigarette. 'What d'ye say, Stonewall?'

'I'd rather keep my fiver. We might not even get a sighting.'

'I hate it when nothing happens, man. When we drag back the next morning dead tired and fuckin' fed up, and I'm wondering where that little blonde barmaid who I could have been shacked up with, has spent the night. But you, of course, are a respectable married man.'

'S're you.'

'Yes, but what's the use when the old woman's up in Durham? What the eye don't see . . .'

'Well, I don't know about you, Geordie, but I'm not too keen to meet up with old Fritz. I'm all for a quiet life. But if we do – it's a perfect night for a battle.'

Sometimes the wind would rise and the waves steepen so that they would be forced to lie in wait in an uncomfortable swell, the crew often becoming sea-sick. If it became too rough to engage the enemy, the boats would be unable to fire with accuracy and they'd have to turn back for home port after an unpleasant and wasteful trip. Nonetheless glad to be alive.

The coast loomed menacingly ahead, always with the possibility that at any moment a salvo of shells might erupt from enemy shore batteries. The officers on the bridges were keeping a relentless watch.

They were a good crew, thought Keith, all pulling together in times of stress. Lieutenant Dickinson and most of the crew might be the 'Wavy Navy' – reservists called up – but they commanded respect. After midnight, cocoa and sandwiches were passed around.

'Enemy in sight to port!' was the sudden galvanising call from the bridge of Keith's boat. The men below scrambled into their oilskins and steel hats. Dickinson hailed the other boats. All eyes strained to port. Yes, there were three darker shapes emerging from the gloom. Hopefully unaware of them as yet. Everyone was ready at their posts.

The shape of the targets indicated a large ship, probably a merchantman, two escorting trawlers and three E boats. Taking bearings and plotting the enemy's course and speed, Lt Johnny Smith, the commanding officer, ordered the manoeuvre into position.

Keith experienced a surge of adrenalin, the familiar visceral sensations of excitement and dread gripping him. But now there was work to do.

'Ready both,' ordered Lt Dickinson, staccato-voiced, having the merchantmen square in his sights. Keith, the seaman torpedoman, rendered the missiles ready for instant firing. 'Away both!'

The starboard torpedo jammed. 'Damnation!' Keith lifted the mallet and struck the impulse charge a sharp blow. The torpedo fired and leapt forward with a whoosh. The second one was loosed.

The merchantman was unaware of its danger until the missile hit it amidships. There was a flash and an explosion. Ammunition exploded in sparks. Two of the other boats fired torpedoes at the accompanying trawlers, which missed. However the tracks of the 'fishes' were sighted by the enemy and gave away the positions of the little boats, and the enemy opened fire with all they had. Star-shells burst overhead and showers of red and green tracer bullets poured towards the MTBs, lighting the scene with a terrible beauty.

'Christ, it's better than fucking Guy Fawkes night, man,' joked Geordie. The motor torpedo boats turned and made off at high speed, later regrouping and creeping back for another attack, the burning merchantman leading them to the scene.

More torpedoes were loosed from the English side and one of them scored a bulls-eye on a trawler. In the light of the star-shells from the other trawler the English boats saw the stricken vesssel halt. But now they were too close for comfort to the attacking E boats with their superior gun power, and there had been some British casualties. The sky was brightening to the east. It was time to get out of there and go home. Run away – to fight another day.

The five boats returned to HMS *Beehive* exhausted but triumphant. 'A good night's work, chaps,' called 'Dicky' Dickinson, his arm in a sling and his face grey from a serious bullet wound. He had stopped only long enough to have it dressed, passing command to Petty Officer Coburn, his number one, before returning to the bridge.

The men stood around in little groups swapping tales of the night's events. Dickinson and three casualties from other boats were taken off by ambulance.

Keith experienced the 'high' feeling he always had after a successful sortie, but with a strange underlying sorrow. Germans had been killed. Young chaps just like him, who had no choice but to fight. One night it might be his turn.

The crews boarded *Vulcan* for breakfast. Queenie would wonder where he was, but he was too wound up to go home for some time yet.

# · *Twenty-two* ·

Over the months Queenie received news of Portsmouth and cuttings from the papers from Eddy and Phyllis. London and naval ports were being bombed with a vengeance. She was in tears on more than one occasion when Keith returned from a night at sea.

'They've been bombing the shops in broad daylilght,' she reported in August. 'Saturday afternoon. A hundred and seventeen people killed. Sixty bombs! Where's the sense in that?'

'Terror tactics – disrupt ordinary life, lower the morale of the civilians.'

And in January of the following year: 'One hundred and seventy-one dead, Keith. Churches, cinemas, the Eye and Ear Hospital, Hippodrome, dockyard, Clarence Pier. They knocked out the electric power station just outside *Vernon*. There's been no electric for days in Vernon and Portsea, and the dockyard and the harbour railway station have been closed.'

In March, one hundred personnel were killed in a moonlight raid on HMS *Vernon* when Dido Building was destroyed.

The fire blitz – incendiary bombs to light pathways to targets and to destroy indiscriminately by fire – was a new terror.

'Eddy says that a mate of his was coming down Portsmouth Hill and it looked as if the whole city was burning. They dropped twenty-five thousand fire bombs!'

Keith shook his head in disbelief.

'Our lovely Guildhall burned out. Oh – but this is nice!' She gave him a smiling glance. 'King George and Queen Elizabeth visited Pompey. Lizzy looks gorgeous in that little beret-style hat, all up at one side. And all those pearls.'

'Very appropriate,' Keith commented dryly.

'Listen to this. Someone shouted, "Are we down-hearted?" and everyone yelled back "No!" Ain't that bleedin' marvellous?'

'Marvellous.'

'Oh, don't be sarky. They're very brave down in Pompey. Anyway Lizzy said,' Queenie put on a plummy voice, "I think you are wonderful people. I am proud of Portsmouth."'

Keith snorted. 'Some consolation, I suppose.'

Queenie's mood changed back to one of gloom. 'Ow, what's going to happen to my fam'ly?'

She was soon to find out, because circumstances changed and sooner than she expected she found herself staying with her mother while she looked for a flat. For Keith had been posted to Portland in November, with a brief stop-over at Hornet, the Coastal Forces base at Gosport. Before he went, he took the children off down to Cornwall again for safety.

Beatie had now moved into a top floor Council flat in St George's Square and she was thrilled to bits. Even if it *was* tiny and had only two bedrooms, it had a little balcony overlooking the square, and a bath in the kitchen with a wooden worktop over it. And best of all – an inside lavatory. Beatie thought it was smashing, and so easy to keep clean.

'And d'you know what, our Queen?' She laughed. 'They put me stuff in this lorry and drove it round for a couple of hours, foomigating it. So we ain't brought our Baker Street bugs with us.'

Beatie's only regret was that Lil still lived down the road. 'I hope she don't have to wait too long for one of these flats. Number twelve is a bloomin' old doss-house now, but they're goin' to pull all that lot down after the war. If it ain't been bombed down by then.'

Queenie was amazed at her mother's cheerful stoicism. Jimmy and Josh were over at Aunt Tildy's, and as it happened, Beatie had good reason for being grateful that Queenie was with her at that time.

The second night of Queenie's stay she was woken by 'Moaning Minnie'.

'I don't always bother to go down the shelter when the boys are away,' admitted Beatie as they threw their coats on over their nightdresses.

'You *should*, Ma. What'll the boys do if anything happens to you? Come on, let's get going.'

'Born under a lucky star, that's me. Grab a cushion – them seats are bleedin' hard.'

Neighbours were streaming down the street with them as they hurried along and the dimly-lit shelter was already half full when they arrived.

'Beat. Queenie.' Lil's shriek rose over the chatter. They pushed their way through to where she was sitting with Shirley. Lil threw her arms around them both. 'How're you then, Queenie, luv? What you want to come back to this hell-hole for?' She sat down and indicated that people should shuffle along and make room for her friends.

'Nice to see you, Lil,' grinned Queenie. 'Keith's been posted to Portland, the kids are down in Cornwall with 'is Mum, so I've come home to dear old Pompey and the bombs. I'll be looking for a flat. How're Sid and Dickie?'

'Sid's 'aving a *lovely* time fire-fighting with your Eddy. There's plenty of *them* every night. Our Dickie's in the army, itching fer a chance to git at them Jerries.'

Soon most people were chatting cheerfully, many with young children asleep across their laps, discussing the bombing, their jobs, whose son had been lost at sea. Queenie's stomach knotted as she thought of Keith on his

MTB, and Michael who was now somewhere on a destroyer.

The Italian shopkeeper had brought packets of Garibaldi biscuits from his shop to hand round. 'Good bloke, old Val is. He had a bit of trouble from 'ooligans last year when old Mussolini declared war on us,' confided Beatie to her daughter. 'Put a couple of bleedin' bricks through his winder, they did.'

'Bloody disgusting,' agreed Lil. 'It isn't as if he's really Eyetalian. He come over as a little lad with his parents and grandparents.'

'That bloody traitor Musso,' said a man sitting opposite. 'Sold the poor old Eyeties down the river, he did.'

There was murmured agreement.

'That was a terrible raid in January, our Queen,' said Beatie. 'Commercial Road and all that posh shopping area round King's Road and Palmerston Road – all ruined.'

'Bleedin' Jerries,' spat Lil. 'I know what I'd like to do to the lot of 'em.'

'The only good German is a dead one!' someone agreed.

'What about the fuckin' Japs attacking Pearl Harbour?'

'Just before Christmas too!'

'At least it's brought the Yanks in at last.'

''Spose they'll say they won the war when it's all over.'

'That's what I like to hear – something positive,' said Lil. 'As far as I'm concerned anyone is welcome to win the war, as long as it's our side. Hallelujah!'

'Yes, but how many more ships are going to be lost before that happens?' asked Queenie fearfully.

'The *Repulse* and the *Prince of Wales* sunk by the Japs,' mourned Beatie. 'All those boys.' Several of the women wept.

'And now the unmarried girls being called up.'

The conversation turned to less weighty matters.

'The price of fresh veg these days!'

'When you can get it – '

'Wouldn't it be lovely to have an orange? Haven't seen one since war was declared.'

'Kid's wouldn't know what a banana was if they saw one.'

'We'll all 'ave to grow beards if we can't get any razor blades.'

'Never mind. It'll keep you warm in winter when the coal runs out.'

Mrs Kelly, sitting opposite Queenie with three of her brood of thirteen, the rest evacuated to God knows where, leant across and asked Queenie if she'd like to buy some clothes coupons. 'I don't need them, you see. With so many kids, there are always hand-me-downs. I'd rather have the money.'

It was illegal to sell coupons but Queenie was tempted. She needed some new clothes – not that she could afford to buy any at the moment. Her conscience was salved by the knowledge that she would be helping poor Mrs Kelly. She agreed to visit her in the morning.

A muffled explosion not far away caused a shocked silence. Mrs Kelly crossed herself.

'Some poor blighter's home has gone,' said someone.

'Hope they wasn't in it,' muttered Lil.

'I hope our Eddy's safe,' whispered Beatie.

Queenie was feeling sick with fear and impotent anger. The thick air in the shelter and the smell of so many bodies didn't help. 'How can humans do this sort of thing to each other?' she asked furiously.

A man whom they knew from Baker Street started to play a mournful tune on his mouth organ.

'Let's 'ave "Rule Britannia" fer Christ's sake, Sam,' someone shouted. 'Britons never, never, never shall be slaves . . .' Their voices filled the shelter with triumphant spirit.

Then came 'Land Of Hope And Glory', 'Jerusalem' and 'Eternal Father Strong to Save', which made Queenie cry for Keith and all the other sailors she knew.

Then they launched into 'Roll Out The Barrel' and 'Lili Marlene' – never mind that it was a German song – until they were interrupted by the 'All Clear'.

'Hallelujah!' shouted Lil.

'I really enjoyed that,' said Beatie as they came out of the fetid air of the shelter into a crisp, starlit night. 'Trouble is though, it don't 'arf knacker you for the next day. Good thing it's a clear night. We 'ave hell of a job sometimes finding our way home in the dark.'

'Sweet dreams, girls,' said Lil. 'I'm off 'ome to me Fry's cocoa. Only sixpence a tin, and Fry's tell us it's got as much goodness as twenty-one eggs. Believe it if you like.' They embraced and went their different ways.

Beatie and Queenie, walking arm in arm, each with a cushion under the other, shivered with cold and distress as they saw fires down two of the streets. 'Poor sods,' tutted Beatie. Then she suddenly shrieked, 'Oh, my Gawd!'

'What, Ma?' cried Queenie, her hair prickling on her scalp.

'The flat. Me flat's on fire.'

Queenie thrust her fist against her teeth as she looked towards the block of flats. Orange light flickered from the front window of number fifteen.

The two women ran hand-in-hand, stumbling up the stairs to the top floor. Queenie took the key from her mother's trembling hand and shakily inserted it in the lock. She opened the door cautiously and acrid smoke drifted out. The door to the living room had an orange glow around it and they could hear the ominous sound of crackling flames.

'What shall we do?' cried Queenie. 'Find a fire-fighter?'

'There's no time fer that. Git the bucket of water from the kitchen – I'll git the stirrup pump. Perhaps we can put it out.'

Queenie dashed to the kitchen and grabbed the pail of water from under the sink with both hands. It was always kept full in readiness and the water slopped over her feet as she ran. Beatie grabbed the pump.

They exchanged a worried look outside the living room door. 'Stand back, Ma, and get ready to run,' instructed Queenie. Gingerly, she turned the Bakelite handle and eased the door open. Smoke belched out, making them cough and stinging their eyes. She saw through the crack that the fire was over near the window, past the dining-table. 'I think it's only just taken hold,' she spluttered, pushing the door wider.

They crept into the room, hands over noses and mouths as if that could stop the fumes going into their lungs. Beatie snatched the smouldering chenille table cloth off the table, one leg of which was burning, and started flapping at the flames.

'Stop it, Ma, you're making it worse,' Queenie's shriek turned into a coughing fit. The stirrup pump had two nozzles. Forcing herself to keep calm she tried to recall the instructions she had read on a Will's cigarette card, which these days were full of wartime advice.

Thrusting the spray nozzle into her mother's hands, she shouted, 'Play that on the bomb while I pump.' It was difficult to get the pump started but at last, after furious effort, they managed to put the fizzing device out of action. Just a tube it seemed to be, twelve to fifteen inches long and only about an inch in diameter, with four fins. 'That's got you, you bastard!' shouted Queenie.

The square of carpet was burning and had set fire to a couple of chairs, the curtains and window frame. But their retreat was clear, so Queenie ran back to the kitchen to refill the bucket, and Beatie turned the stronger jet onto the fire. Some neighbours turned up with buckets of water and pumps and after a few minutes they had put the fire out. They all breathed huge sighs of relief, though Beatie and Queenie's legs were trembling in shock.

'What a mess,' mourned Queenie, looking at the hole in the ceiling, the smoke-blackened walls and the burnt window frame. 'We'd better open the windows and let this foul smell out.'

'Oh, my G-a-w-d!' shrieked Beatie for the second time in half an hour.

'What's the matter?' Queenie cried, her nerves a-jangle.

'Me bleedin' crystal!'

Beatie's pride and joy, her mother's crystal that graced the window-sill, had melted into long icicles of glass.

Queenie started to giggle and held on to Beatie. Soon they were both howling with laughter, though Beatie was crying at the same time. And that was how Eddy found them when he came panting up the stairs.

'Heard you was on fire,' he gasped.

'All under control,' chortled his sister.

'Let's 'ave a bleeding cuppa,' breathed a soot-blackened Beatie. Her neighbour went to put the kettle on. Beatie sank onto a chair, the burnt leg of which gave way and she collapsed onto the floor. They all laughed hysterically, Beatie wiping her eye on the hem of her nightie. They perched on the undamaged furniture while Beatie's neighbour brought in a tray.

'They'll have to rehouse you, Ma,' said Eddy.

Beatie sipped her tea noisily. 'Old Lord Woolton came up trumps anyway, with 'is "Christmas Box", didn't he? I never thought I'd see the day when two extra ounces of tea and four of sugar would mean more than a bloody fortune to me.' She raised her cup with a grin. 'Now we'll all be able to drown our sorrows and no mistake.'

'Hallelujah!' said Queenie in imitation of Lil.

Queenie did not need to find a flat in Portsmouth after all because the Portland posting was brief and Keith, Queenie and the children were back in Felixstowe before Christmas, having found a little flat in Orwell Road, just off the seafront.

Keith, inwardly happy to have his family with him, was

outwardly rather morose and distant. His working hours were so erratic that Queenie gave up expecting him at any particular time and was just welcoming when he did return. But she got bored, and decided, with Keith's approval, to look for a job. Hannah having started school, she arranged to leave Emma with another rating's wife, Peggy Hill, whose husband was an electrical artificer at HMS *Beehive*.

Peggy was a pleasant woman in her forties with only a twelve-year-old girl at home now. She loved children and needed something to occupy her, so the arrangement suited her well. Her daughter Sally enjoyed mothering the younger children and took Hannah to school with her and brought her home in the afternoons.

Queenie quickly found a position as lunchtime barmaid at the Harbour Hotel and the short-staffed landlord was delighted that she could start that same day. She knew that Keith would be pleased that she was getting out to do something, and bringing in some much-needed money, but unable to let him know where she was as he was not back after his night patrol, she ran home and left a note for him.

The proprietor of the Harbour Hotel, a cheerful, red-faced man in his sixties, was delighted to engage such a pretty and cheerful barmaid. Queenie picked up the business very quickly during her first lunchtime stint and had a cheeky comment and a smile for the customers.

That was until a particular customer came in. Her husband – with a woman on his arm.

It was a few minutes before Keith saw his wife behind the bar, and in those minutes Queenie saw that he knew his partner very well. It had been a long time since she had seen him smiling so cheerfully and chatting so freely.

They came up to the bar – and Keith froze.

Queenie stared at him rigid-faced, feeling murderous rage building up inside her.

‘What’re you doing here?’ His face portrayed a mixture of anger and embarrassment.

She could not speak through her gritted teeth, though she was thinking plenty while her heart thumped in slow, sickening thuds.

Keith’s companion, a good-looking woman in her thirties, and by no means a tart with her upswept hair and her fashionable though utility-cut suit, looked from one to another, puzzled.

Keith gave the woman a quick glance and said, with hateful studied casualness. ‘Cynthia, meet my wife. It seems she’s just got herself a job here.’

The woman’s plucked eyebrows rose. She looked at Queenie and back at Keith. ‘You’ve made a right cock-up, haven’t you, darling?’ she drawled. ‘Well, that’s it, then. I’m off.’

‘I should – if you don’t want your eyes scratched out!’ Queenie hissed, her cheeks scarlet with fury.

‘Shut up!’ snarled Keith, glancing around the bar, embarrassed at the scene which was likely to erupt.

‘It’s *his* eyes you want to scratch out, dear,’ Cynthia drawled. ‘He’s the one who’s deceiving you.’

Queenie gave her husband a malevolent glare. ‘I’ll deal with him, don’t you worry.’ She noticed Cynthia’s wedding ring. ‘Where’s your old man, then?’ she asked through stiff lips.

‘He’s out flying a bomber at the moment, dear. Somewhere on the other side of the Channel.’

Queenie gave her a look of utter contempt. ‘So while your husband is risking his life for his country, you go out to play – with other women’s husbands! You – you’re disgusting. I’m faithful to me marriage vows, I am.’

‘Stop it at once, Queenie,’ interjected her husband.

Cynthia smiled patronisingly. ‘Don’t worry, I don’t want him permanently, my dear, but one’s got to amuse oneself somehow in this dead hole. I’m from London, you see.’

'Well,' Queenie jabbed a finger at her. 'I should get back there if I was you. Make yourself useful with some war-work.' Her voice rose. 'You certainly ain't wanted round here.'

'I'm warning you . . .' groaned Keith ineffectually.

The landlord came up to them. 'Is there a problem, Queenie? This gentleman is one of our regulars.'

His new barmaid turned her flashing eyes on him. 'That's obvious. And you know where you stick your rotten job, don't you? Encouraging men to bring their tarts to your hotel.'

'Excuse me, sir,' he said to Keith, his face a few shades redder than normal. Taking her arm, he drew her away from the bar. Furiously she twisted from his grasp. 'I don't know what's got into you, Queenie,' he muttered. 'It's none of our business who the customers come in with.'

'Oh yes, it is,' she yelled. 'He's my husband!'

'Oh, my God!' He put his hand to his mouth. 'Well, I'm sorry, my dear – '

'So'm I.' She stepped back to the bar, took a nearly-full glass of beer from a customer who had been listening to the interchange with fascination, and whooshed it up into Cynthia's face.

'Oh,' the woman screamed, golden drops dripping off her nose, her hair and the little fox fur thrown so casually round her shoulders. 'You – you *absolute* bitch!'

Queenie's eyes sparkled with satisfaction.

'Get your coat,' barked Keith at his wife, looking as though he would like to murder her, while trying ineffectually to mop Cynthia up with the tea-towel passed to him by the crestfallen landlord.

Queenie gave a bitter laugh and flounced off to do as she was bid. She left by the back door. Keith caught her up, grabbing her arm.

Furiously, she shook him off. 'You bastard!'

The cold east wind tore through them, carrying their

words away. 'You made a real exhibition of yourself there, didn't you,' Keith shouted, his face suffused with anger.

Queenie thought he might hit her now they were away from the bar. She almost needed him to – it would give her an excuse to scratch his eyes out. But violence wasn't in his nature.

Frustrated, she shrieked, 'Go on – try to make me feel bad when it's you that's at fault. How could you *do* this to me again?' She was walking backwards facing him, her knees bent and her fists clenched at thigh level, her body bent almost Z-shaped with impotent fury. 'I should never have believed you before. No wonder you come home so bloody late and we're always so short of money. I want a divorce.'

'Don't be so bloody stupid.'

'What's stupid about it?' She stood and faced him, arms akimbo, shouting. 'I can't trust you further than I can throw you, Keith Jackson. Well, if you must have other women, you can have them. But you ain't bleedin' well having me and the kids as well.'

'There's a bloody war on, woman,' he shouted back. 'Get your priorities straight.'

'My first priority is my fam'ly – and that's what yours should be.' People had stopped to stare at them. 'Had an eyeful?' she screamed scornfully at the spectators, her hair plastered to her face with the driving rain. 'Never seen anybody having a row before?' She stuck her tongue out at them, immediately hating herself for her childish petulance.

'Don't make matters worse.' Keith grabbed her arm and dragged her along.

'Worse! Could they be?'

'Let's get in and discuss this sensibly.'

'Sensibly!' she shrieked, raising her arms to break his hold. She ran sobbing up the steps ahead of him. The row continued indoors, Keith bullying and pleading and promising her that he would never do it again.

In the end, utterly weary, Queenie agreed that she would not press for divorce – not while there was a war on anyway. But she told him that she would never trust him again.

Eventually, blotchy-faced, she went to collect the children, stopping off to send a telegram to Phyllis on the way, requesting her friend to get leave and come up for a few days. Short of leaving him, she needed someone to put some distance between her and her husband.

# · Twenty-three ·

The motor torpedo boats were skimming along on a glass-like sea on a pre-dawn February patrol. The weather had been so foggy for days that they had been confined to harbour, so this run from Felixstowe to Dover was in the nature of an exercise.

Keith stood for'ard of the bridge. The slipstream was bitterly cold on his face but his oilskins and the thick jerseys underneath kept his body warm. The fourth winter of the war, if you included the winter of the Phoney War, had been hard in terms of the bitterly cold weather, the fighting and exhausting forays.

This winter had also seen the threatened breakdown of his marriage.

Now the sun was rising, lightening the grey sky and making a pinky-orange fairway on a lake of silver. Slowly the heavens turned into a symphony of lemon, turquoise and rose, which was reflected in the sea, and Keith felt a wave of spiritual awe at the beauty of the scene.

It didn't seem possible that on a day like this they would run into the Hun. It would be sacrilege to fight the enemy against such a breathtaking backdrop.

And in spite of Geordie – today he was happy.

It was Geordie who had brought him and Queenie together again.

Queenie had been almost impossible to live with since he had walked into the Harbour Hotel with Cynthia. Moody, weeping, sulky. Screaming at him for the smallest thing. Not that he could blame her in any way. But what rotten coincidence that she should have got a job there. What she hadn't known, after all, would never have hurt her. Geordie's philosophy.

He had been taking Cynthia to the hotel occasionally over a period of a few weeks. Just for a roll in the hay. She was bored and he needed the release, the dubious excitement of illicit sex to let him down slowly between the exhilaration of returning safely from a night of danger, and his normal life. That was all there was to it really. He was intrigued by Cynthia's cool sophistication, her casual attitude to sex, but she didn't mean a thing to him emotionally.

A wry smile creased his face. She was just the sort of woman his mother would have liked, but fancy being married to a two-timing bitch like that. Huh! Who was he to talk? But it was different for a man, wasn't it?

Things had been unbearably strained between him and Queenie for several weeks, though he'd tried very hard to make it up to her, to convince her that his little escapades meant nothing. She would not allow him to touch her and he became desperately frustrated.

'You'll *drive* me into the arms of another woman. Is that what you want?' he challenged.

'Why should I care? It didn't make no difference when I was . . . being nice to you.'

The children sensed the atmosphere, little Emma often crying, and Hannah, who had just started school, watching them nervously. God – he loved those children. He didn't believe in God – or he thought he didn't – but somehow they seemed like a divine gift. It was a privilege to have children. He swore to himself that he would never again do anything that might threaten their happiness and security.

And he loved Queenie.

She had her faults, could be infuriating at times like these, when she acted on gut reaction instead of logic. But her good points outshone the bad by about a million to one. She was intensely loyal. He knew without a doubt that she would not go with another man. He *had* been a bastard – but never again.

His thoughts turned back to Geordie and he sighed deeply.

A sudden message had come through from the RAF that two German warships with a full complement of escorts, including fighter planes, were on the move in the Channel.

The little ship flotillas – motor torpedo boats and gun boats – rushed out of the harbour with their steel-helmeted crews cheering madly. That they might all be going to their deaths against the fearful odds did not seem to dampen their enthusiasm for a real battle. They had been longing for such an opportunity and the British fighting spirit was roused.

It had been a terrifying and magnificent moment when the enemy warships with their escort of destroyers and E-boats were sighted through the mist, under a cloud of Messerschmitt planes. The little British boats sped forward to engage, accompanied by Swordfish aircraft and the Fleet Air Arm.

After the initial shock of daylight attack from sea and air, the enemy put up a dense smoke screen, so it was difficult to see how effective the onslaught was, but certainly a lot of damage must have been done. Six Swordfish aircraft were shot down and most of their gallant crews lost, but some survivors were picked up by the MTBs. Those returning claimed to have shot down more Jerries, and done serious damage to a warship. One of the MTBs also claimed a hit.

The British ships, all having spent their torpedos, were finally put to flight by the appearance through the smoke of a German destroyer.

'There's a lot of shit flying around the day, man,' grinned Geordie as the outgunned boats bore away from the scene of battle. Then, as Keith glanced at him, an Oerliken shell went straight through Geordie's body.

To everyone at base, it was a miracle that all the little ships returned. Keith, sickened by his friend's death, had gone straight home after breakfast at base, as he always did these days.

Queenie was having trouble with a fractious Emma and with Hannah refusing to go to school, and had taken out her frustrations on him. Dog-tired and racked with grief over his friend, he went silently to bed.

That evening, a thick sea fog meant that the crews were on shore-leave and the sea-planes from the local airfield were grounded. The children were in bed and Keith was sitting at the table doing some pen and ink work. All he wanted was to lose himself in his art-work and clear his mind of all the clutter of war and domestic life.

Queenie had kept up a barrage of complaints for some time, about lack of money and any sort of social life. 'I never even get out to the pictures any more, let alone a dance.' There was a pause. Her voice rose as she launched into a tirade about him and his women, finishing with, 'You aren't even listening to me, are you?'

He threw down his pen in exasperation, the ink flying off it in blots to ruin what he had been working on. Furiously he tore the page in half. 'I've had enough of this!'

He took several deep breaths, trying to keep calm. He felt as if he were about to topple into a pit of despair so deep that he would never be able to climb out again. 'I've told you they meant nothing. If you can't forgive me, than I'd better go and stay at base.'

'Yes, perhaps you'd better,' she spat back, her pretty face twisted in a scowl. 'Then you can go whoring as much as you want.'

Keith turned and glared at her, causing her to flinch

slightly from the desolation in his face. But she squared her shoulders and stared back defiantly.

Rising, he went into the bedroom, changed into his uniform and stowed his gear in a kitbag. Hoisting it under his arm, he went into the children's room. Their little faces, relaxed in sleep, wrung his heart. How could he leave them? They were part of him.

Queenie came out of the kitchen as he left the children's bedroom and saw him brushing away the tears that were running down his cheeks.

'What's the matter?' she asked, her chin and mouth trembling.

He swallowed and answered in a strangled voice, 'I'm amazed you have to ask.'

'Why don't you try telling me? You never talk to me any more.' Her eyes were bright with unshed tears. 'You're always in a bleedin' foul mood.'

'For Chris'sake, Queenie.' His voice was thick with despair.

Hesitantly, she held out a hand to him. Hesitantly, he took it and she drew him into the sitting-room. Wrenching his hand from hers, he threw himself into an armchair, covering his face with his hands. 'Geordie . . . Geordie was killed yesterday.'

'Oh no!' Queenie flung herself on the floor beside him and threw her arms about him. 'Oh, darling, I'm so sorry. I'm so sorry. I know what you felt about him.' She was crying too as she held him.

Eventually he cried himself out. 'I don't know how I can go on like this,' he said brokenly. 'These runs – never knowing if I'm coming back or not. No home life, and now to leave the kids . . .'

'Oh,' wailed Queenie. 'What a wicked cow I am, only thinking of myself as usual. I should've realised what you were going through. Forgive me . . .' She broke off in a storm of weeping.

Keith held her to him and, when she had quietened, he

took her by the shoulders and they gazed at each other with crumpled faces and wet eyes. He tenderly pushed back a strand of her hair that was stuck to her wet cheek. 'It's me that need forgiveness. Oh, Queenie, my love, it isn't too late, is it? Don't let it be too late. We can start again. Make allowances for each other. Let's try again, Queen of the May – for the children's sake?'

'And for our sakes?' She wiped her running nose with the back of her hand and sniffed like a child.

'And our sakes. I'm know I'm a miserable bastard at times, difficult to live with, but it's the war. I do love you, you know.'

She gazed into his eyes. 'Do you? I wasn't sure. Those women – I couldn't understand it. I know we have our problems but I thought . . . at least *that* was good between us.'

'It wasn't that I lacked anything, my darling. I just needed a bit of excitement or relief to . . . to offset all the strains, I suppose. Sounds a weak excuse.'

'I believe you.' She kissed his lips, stroked his hair. 'I want to believe that it won't happen again. I couldn't bear it. Let's go to bed, shall we? Make up . . .?'

And they had shared a night of passion deeper than either had ever thought possible. 'It's almost worth having a row, if this is what making up is like,' Queenie had whispered with shining eyes.

The next morning Keith wrote a letter to Geordie's wife, telling her how bravely her husband had died, and that the last words he had spoken had been about her. Not strictly true, but still . . . And she need never know that her old man had been unfaithful to her.

Queenie leant over his shoulder, her face against his, to read the letter. His fingers caressed her hands.

'That's beautiful,' she whispered, turning to press her

lips against his cheek. 'Come on, Emma's having a nap. Let's go back to bed.'

Those few days of bad weather had given him more time at home and allowed them the opportunity of rediscovery, of finding depths in one another that they had never plumbed before. They were blissfully happy.

But the weather had improved and now the boats were on the prowl again. A pre-dawn practice patrol.

Keith felt fortified by the few days' leave and the discovery of how much he loved his wife.

He had not wanted to marry, to be tied down, but then, a few years ago, he had had no idea what true love was. How it meant wanting the happiness of one's partner above all else, putting oneself second, as he was determined to do in future. He hoped he would be capable of it, because in this selfless love, he recognised true fulfilment.

He usually took Queenie a cup of tea in bed if she woke up when he was going off in the middle of the night. But this time she had got up and insisted on using her week's bacon ration and a precious egg to give him a good send-off. He had turned in the street and seen her standing at the window, and she had blown him a kiss. He felt blessed – this was how married life should be.

Keith smiled, imagining Queenie now, probably snuggled back in the warm patch they had left in the bed, until it was time to get Hannah up for school. He had done some nude sketches of her in the last couple of days. She was a good model. Although a little too heavy in the hips and thighs, she possessed a natural grace, and lovely tip-tilted breasts with nipples rosy as this dawn. She smiled softly at him as he drew. One day he was going to paint her in oils, just as he would paint a dawn like this.

'You're very quiet down there, Jackson. Not asleep are you?'

'No *sir*!' he called up to Petty Officer Ray Coburn who

was at the wheel, looking mature and piratical with his dense, black beard. He was a regular Navy man, not a reservist. Difficult job being coxwain – the link between officers and men – but Coburn was a tactful bloke, and dependable. They were *all* good blokes. One positive thing that war did was to bring people together in a common cause.

An incredibly young Sub-Lieutenant Godfrey was today's officer-in-charge on Keith's boat, which was cruising in second position, Lt Dickinson still being confined to base with his wounded arm. The young officer's voice, cracking with excitement, suddenly announced, 'Enemy sighted on starboard quarter.' Everybody's eyes slewed to the right.

There they were, still a long way off, the patrol consisting of two armed trawlers and three E boats. What would the Germans do? It had been noted that they tended to alter course and avoid confrontation unless, presumably, they considered it a worthwhile target.

The English commander, Lt Johnny Smith, was under no such compunction. He gave orders for the boats to manoeuvre into position for assault. Keith, holding on tight as the boats picked up speed, went aft to his battle position. The officer in charge of the third boat answered through his megaphone. 'They appear to be bearing away, sir.'

'All the more reason to take them by surprise. For-w-a-r-d!' The commanding officer waved his arm in a forward-sweeping gesture as his boat leapt into action.

'Christ! Old Smithy thinks he's leading the Charge of the bloody Light Brigade,' Keith shouted up to the bridge.

Petty Officer Coburn shook his head dubiously as the distance between the English boats and the Germans diminished rapidly.

'Bugger,' muttered Keith to himself. 'What a day for heroics.' He never liked the idea of an engagement in full daylight, when you could see all too clearly that the enemy you were fighting were just men like yourselves. Darkness made it more impersonal. All he wanted was to get home to Queenie and the kids. A picture came into his mind of his wife's face, soft with pleasure, eyes slumbrous with desire . . .

The enemy were clearly procrastinating, and so made a sitting target for the first pair of torpedoes fired from the lead boat. There was an orange glow as one of the trawlers was hit and began to list to port.

Suddenly the enemy galvanised into action and the four sound boats grouped together and raced towards their attackers at high speed. In such calm weather and clear visibility they could not miss, and Godfrey's boat was holed on the water-line. There was a dreadful shudder and it seemed to Keith that the crew was suspended in slow motion for a long moment, mouths open with shock, movements laboured.

'Curse it!' The young officer shouted an order to turn to starboard. The other English MTBs also turned to manoeuvre for a second attack. They soon outstripped the damaged boat, not immediately understanding why it was going round in a circle.

The engineer called up through the voice-pipe, 'Starboard engine knocked out, Skipper.'

Keith momentarily pushed the grim reality of the situation from his mind and allowed Queenie, Hannah and Emma in.

Now the English commanders realised that their second boat was in trouble and sped back to the rescue, but the Germans were nearer and made a quick concerted attack on the crippled craft, causing further damage. The little fleets engaged in a mini Battle of Trafalgar, guns blazing at each other and shells sounding like whiplash as they streaked overhead. And all the time the thought of Queenie burned like a bright star in Keith's head. He repeated her name over and over again.

The crippled boat, out of action now, had slewed round

to face the enemy and was wallowing. Godfrey saw a chance for revenge, a chance to score a hit on the second trawler which was beam on and engaged in battle.

'Ready – both,' shouted the young officer.

But Seaman Torpedoman 'Stonewall' Jackson did not obey the command.

He was lying on his back behind the bridge in a huddle of oilskins and a pool of blood, the pearly dawn sky imprinted on his sightless eyes for the rest of eternity.

# · Twenty-four ·

Queenie wet the middle finger of each hand with the tip of her tongue and with these fingers gently smoothed down her husband's roughened eyebrows, as she had done so often when he was alive. Just as she used do to her Dad.

Keith's unmarked face was a pale blur through her tears. She blinked and the water that was trapped by her lower lids cascaded down her cheeks in warm drops and dripped into the coffin. She wiped them from her face with the back of her hands.

'He looks . . . peaceful,' murmured Phyllis standing opposite. 'Just as if he was asleep.' She took out her hanky and blew her nose.

Queenie nodded and drew in a shuddering breath before she began to sob again. Phyllis came round and put her arm around her. 'I'll wait outside till you . . . till you're ready.'

Alone with him, Queenie cried on, stroking her husband's wavy hair, and tracing his features gently with her fingers. He was so good-looking. Had been. She recalled his hazel eyes gleaming with laughter, looking at her with love. His mouth twisting in that wry grin of his.

'Why did this have to happen?' she whispered. 'Just when we'd really found each other. It isn't bloody well fair. We really fell in love with each other those last few days, didn't we? Really got to know and understand each other.' Well, at least she had that to be thankful for. How could she have lived with it if they had not had the opportunity to make up after that awful quarrel.

She stroked his hands, the long slim fingers that had caressed her body; that had, with pencil, pen and brush, made so many lovely pictures for her to keep. That had also serviced missiles of death. There was a band of paler flesh on his wedding-ring finger, where they had cut off his signet ring to return to her. It lay in her pocket now.

'I don't know how Hannah, Emma and me are going to manage without you,' she murmured, feeling frightened at the uncertainty of the future.

Then, with her usual resolution, 'But we'll be all right. Don't you worry, I'll get a job and there'll be a little bit of a pension from the Navy, I hope. I'll be like Scarlett O'Hara.' She could see Vivien Leigh kneeling in the parched earth and raising her arms against a vivid sunset, vowing she would never go hungry again. That was how she would be – she wouldn't let *her* children go hungry.

She whispered 'goodbye', kissed his marble lips, and said she would be with him tomorrow when they buried him. Horrible. Horrible to think of him going under the earth in a closed box. Never to be seen again.

Out in the wintery sunshine of Dover, the port her dead husband had been returned to and where for the sake of expediency he was to be buried, Queenie took her sister-in-law's arm. 'Thank you for coming up, Phyllis. I don't know how I would have managed without you. Is Ma very upset?'

'Very. She loved your Keith, didn't she? She sends you her love and said to tell you to go home any time you want to.'

'I've decided I'm going to stay in Felixstowe for a bit. It's safer for the kids. With so many people away and all those troops stationed there, I'll get a job, sort meself out. We'll manage for a bit until I can decide what's for the best.'

Phyllis squeezed her arm. 'Eddy said he'll get the time off somehow, and come up tonight.'

'I'd like that. I don't know if the Jacksons will get up from Cornwall. It's a long way and difficult with the war and all. Let's walk along the sea-front, shall we, before we go back to the guest house?'

The early March wind tugged at their coats, whipped colour into their cheeks and cooled Queenie's swollen eyelids. Even the gulls were having difficulty keeping on course. 'It must be nice here in the summer,' observed Phyllis, looking at the smart hotels along the Promenade and the white cliffs at the end. 'Wish we could afford to stay in one of these.'

'We'd be like fish out of water. It's bad enough staying at Harbour View Guest House. One of these hotels, I forget which one, Keith did tell me, has been given over to Coastal Command. HMS *Wasp*.'

Her eyes scanned the wide harbour encircled by stout walls with one or two breaks. Keith's crippled boat had been towed back through one of those entrances, Petty Officer Coburn had told her. Into Wellington Dock, because Dover had been nearer than Felixstowe.

A nice man, Ray Coburn. He was nothing like her father, of course, but he *was* fatherly. Big and bluff with warm brown eyes. When he had kindly come to the flat to tell her about Keith's death, she had wanted to throw herself into his arms, to cry against him. She was glad she had resisted the temptation – that would have embarrassed the poor man.

'How's our John?' Queenie asked Phyllis as they turned into the more sheltered street of the guest house.

'Last I heard of him he was somewhere in the Med. Terrible isn't it, Queen? Waiting and praying for them to come home safely.'

'And then, one day, they don't,' muttered Queenie with clenched jaw.

*

Eddy turned up after supper – not that Queenie had been able to eat anything – and it was a relief to have a good cry with him. He held her in his arms for a long time. Just stroking her hair. Not saying anything. There was no need.

Later the three of them sat in her room with cups of cocoa brought by the sympathetic landlady, whose guests too often, these days, were newly-bereaved young widows. Queenie told them what Ray Coburn had told her.

'He said Keith had been killed instantly. I'm so glad about that.' Had her name been on his lips as he died? she wondered, as he had written to Geordie's wife. That sort of thing always happened in films.

'Apparently, as well as having an engine knocked out and a hole in the hull, the boat was on fire down below. The other MTBs held the Jerries off with gunfire until Keith's boat could get away. Then they caught up with her and took her in tow.'

Phyllis was gnawing on her knuckles. Eddy shook his head.

'Several blokes had been wounded and they got them off onto the boats and managed to put out the fire. Three of the boats went back to *Beehive* but Keith's was towed into Dover by a gunboat, because it was nearer and they was afraid she might sink.'

'He was a good man, our Queen,' said Eddy, holding her hand. 'You had a few happy years together. You hold on to that. And remember he was a hero. He gave his life – '

'Don't give me that, Eddy,' she interrupted angrily, her cheeks flaming. 'He no more wanted to give his life than thousands of other poor young sods. They don't have any choice, do they? All he wanted was to be with his fam'ly, paint pictures, see something of the world . . .'

'War is just bloody wicked,' Phyllis agreed with spirit.

'Is Keith's "sacrifice", as they call it,' Queenie's lips twisted in bitterness, 'and it's *my* sacrifice too, don't forget, going to make a scrap of difference to anything or anyone – except the people who loved him?'

The little funeral party gathered in a sheltered alley below Dover Castle next morning to lay to his last rest Keith Jackson, Able Seaman, RN P/JX 133985. Queenie, Eddy, Phyllis and Keith's grim-faced father, who had turned up at the chapel that morning, having travelled all night. Queenie's heart bled for him. He had clasped her to him tightly and whispered that Violet was too ill with grief to come.

At St James's Cemetery, below the Castle, they had walked past the rows of greying headstones of the First World War graves, the coffin borne on the shoulders of naval pall-bearers, to the area given over to receive the dead of the Second World War. They were obviously expecting there to be a lot of them. There were several rows of graves already – mounds marked by temporary wooden crosses. Who knew how many more there would be by the end of this war. What a terrible, terrible waste. And for what? Queenie wondered. Was the world going to be a better place at the end of it?

The group was joined by another and it took a while for Queenie to realise what the second coffin was doing there, covered like Keith's, with a Union Jack. He was to share his grave with another sailor. She recalled now that the other party had attended the same service in the church, the heavily-veiled woman – wife or mother – being almost carried out of the church ahead of them. Well, at least they'll keep each other company, she thought.

A bald-headed vicar and a couple of naval representatives of some sort were present, one of the latter having assured her that the cost of the funeral would be borne by the Ministry of Defence.

'I should bloody well think so,' she had spat at him unfairly.

The poor man had turned the colour of a beetroot. 'You do have my sympathy, madam,' he stuttered and had been rewarded with a scornful look.

Queenie was dry-eyed, carefully made-up, and smartly dressed in a short rabbit-fur jacket with a matching, cheeky, pill-box hat.

'You can't go to your husband's funeral dressed up like a dog's dinner,' exclaimed a shocked Phyllis when Queenie had come down the stairs that morning, herself having put on her one and only green coat.

Queenie looked truculent. 'I'm not going in my scruffy old coat, and I couldn't afford to waste money on another one – I've got kids to feed, remember. And I might have to face me mother-in-law this morning. I don't want to give her any excuse for looking down her nose at me.'

'All the same.'

'Keith won't mind. He'll be – he'd be pleased to think I was looking my best for him.' Queenie was obviously not going to be influenced by any silly conventions. 'I borrowed this from Peggy who's looking after Hannah and Emma. And I think I look rather good in it, don't you?'

Phyllis gave a wan smile. 'You look lovely, Queenie. Doesn't she, Eddy?'

Eddy nodded and they left in a taxi. All through the church service, Queenie had sat, her throat aching with the need to cry, but determined not to. Keith had been so brave, going out night after night to fight the enemy, and she wanted to be worthy of him today.

But she was too choked to join in the hymns that she had chosen when the vicar had kindly called at Harbour View the night before. 'Abide with me', Joshua Ellis's favourite that had been sung at his funeral thirteen years earlier, and 'Eternal Father, Strong to Save'. But the Eternal Father had not saved her husband, had He? Keith had been an atheist and Queenie was inclined to agree with his views. What was the point in praying and singing hymns to a God who did not care enough, or who did not have the power to save you when it came to it?

Not comprehending the vicar's droning words at the burial, Queenie's mind went to her father's grave in Kingston Cemetery in Portsmouth. Still an unmarked mound. She had promised him a headstone, but her savings had melted away on everyday necessities. The guilt of that almost broke her iron control, but she resolutely blinked the tears away. Today was for her Keith.

The little service passed in a blur for Queenie. She allowed her mind to wander – it was less painful that way. She was pleased it was such a lovely spot, sheltered from sea gales and with those tall pine trees on the slope. Seagulls overhead. Dover Castle keeping guard on top of the hill. Bet that old fortress could tell some tales – Romans and all that.

'Dust to dust . . .' the vicar was saying. Two sailors ceremonially removed and folded the flags from the coffins. The gravediggers, who had been keeping a respectful distance, now came forward and lowered the coffins into the grave. Queenie kissed the sheaf of daffodil buds she was carrying and dropped them down onto the plain wooden lid, to be buried before they had come into bloom – just like Keith. Bernard scooped up a handful of earth and let it trickle into the gaping hole as he said a silent farewell to the son he had loved for only twenty-seven years.

Phyllis sobbed, Bernard and Eddy stood with bowed heads, but Queenie, with grief threatening to strangle her, gazed calmly out to sea as half a dozen sailors gave the rifle salute.

Bernard Jackson, looking grey-faced and ill, went back to the guest house with them. The landlady had kindly offered to provide a light lunch before they all went their separate ways. Conversation was at a minimum over the meal. Queenie chewed and chewed on the sandwiches but had difficulty swallowing them.

After a cup of tea, Eddy and Phyllis went to their rooms, apparently to get their bags, but Queenie knew they were tactfully giving her and Bernard a little time together.

Bernard cleared his throat nervously. 'We'd like you to come down to Cornwall for a few weeks, lass. Mother would love to see the children. I'll come back to Felixstowe with you, help you pack.' Seeing her hesitancy, he added, 'And I'll pay the fare of course.'

Queenie bit her lip and thought about it. She did not want to go, she had enough to cope with, without taking on Violet's grief as well. However well-meaning Violet was feeling at the moment, it would all turn sour, she knew it would. What would Keith advise her to do?

'It would help Violet a lot,' Bernard coaxed.

Queenie shook her head. She had to do what would be most helpful to herself at the moment if she was going to keep going. 'I *can't* come. But if it would help, if it would give her comfort, perhaps you could take Hannah back with you for a while? I'd like to keep Emma with me and two would be too much for Mrs Jackson anyway.'

'That would be capital if you really feel you can part with her,' Bernard agreed and Queenie detected relief in his face. He too, knew that it wouldn't work for long with Violet and Queenie under the same roof.

When Phyllis came down, Queenie told her of the plan and that she need not go back to Suffolk with her, as previously arranged. Phyllis promised to get up to Felixstowe the next time she could take time off work and spend a few days with her. The two girls hugged each other, trying not to cry, and Phyllis and Eddy left to go back to Portsmouth.

Queenie and her father-in-law got to know each other a bit better over the two days he spent with her in Felixstowe. Away from Violet's disturbing influence, Queenie liked him a great deal, and could see a lot of Keith in him.

He insisted on giving her some money which she knew, with the guesthouse business failing, he could ill-afford.

Hannah seemed confused to be going to Cornwall to see her grandmother. She had been told that her Daddy would not be coming home again, but at six was too young to really appreciate what that meant. She had not spoken about it at all and little Emma was blithely unaware.

After she and Emma had bid a tearful farewell to Hannah and her grandfather at the railway station, Queenie bought the local paper to scan the 'Situations Vacant' column for a job.

Vowing to be strong, Queenie went through her daily routine like a robot, her grief held fiercely in check, though at times she felt she would drown in it. But three months later, the Ellis family were to mourn again: the death of her brother John, husband to Phyllis and Beatie's favourite son. 'Missing at sea'. No body brought home to be buried in a tranquil spot in the country that he had laid down his life for.

It was only then that Queenie, leaving Emma with Peggy, shut herself away and was able to howl out her grief. For Keith. For John. For all their ruined lives.

# · *Twenty-five* ·

Pilot Officer James Mallory, his straight brown hair falling forward from his brow as he strummed his guitar, sang 'Danny Boy' in a pleasant tenor voice.

His companions, young pilot officers and flying officers from the nearly depleted RAF Station, yodelled along with him in the lounge bar of Homeward Bound, as they had renamed the Barley Mow. The whole of the Marine Aircraft Experimental Establishment had moved upcountry at the outbreak of war. Now there was a small unit of young men and Walrus Seaplanes for limited air-sea rescue – along with high-speed launches – plus a maintenance unit for visiting Sunderlands and other planes.

'Come on, Jimmy, old chap,' one of them demanded when he had finished. 'Let's have 'Deep In The Heart Of Texas'. Soon they were all singing and waving their tankards to and fro, pretending to be as merry as hell. There was another round of drinks and they gradually lapsed into a gloomy silence, punctuated by an occasional remark.

Jimmy glanced over at the pretty barmaid. She was a looker all right, with that cloud of dark hair and blue eyes with a hint of violet in them. Voluptuous figure too. Didn't smile much though, and that wedding ring on her finger meant no messing. The landlord had warned them to leave her alone when he took her on, or he would never allow them into the pub again. There was to be no familiarity. But you never knew . . .

Once or twice over the last few weeks Jimmy had

detected a twinkle in the barmaid's eye when one of the lads said something. He deduced that she did have a sense of humour lurking somewhere beneath that touch-me-not exterior and that she would be a right little smasher if she let herself go. It was his ambition to make her really smile. That was all – honest.

He picked up his guitar and started on 'You Are My Sunshine'. After a few notes he got up and ambled, tall and gangling, to the bar, strumming as he went. Leaning one elbow on the counter, he sang to her that in spite of grey skies she made him happy.

She gave him a straight look. 'Skies look pretty grey over there with your mates. What's up, then?'

He sighed, pushing back his lightly greased hair, his light blue eyes clouding over. 'One of our kites bought it last night. Two of our mates. Suppose with so few of us, we notice it more.'

She wiped spilt beer off the bar with furious movements, her lips tightly compressed. 'Bloody war!' she said at last in a shaking voice, looking at him with passionate anger sparking in her eyes. Extraordinary eyes, he thought. Long black lashes.

'I don't know how you Air Force and Navy boys keep going out night after night.' She shook her head wonderingly.

He put on a comical face. 'Stiff upper-lip and all that. Wouldn't miss the excitement for the world, don't you know! Let me buy you a drink. It's my birthday.'

Her smile was tender. 'Happy Birthday. All right, thanks, I'll have a lemonade.' As she poured herself one he found himself looking at her rounded arms, the shape of her full breasts, the line of her throat. *Luscious*. She raised her glass to him. 'Happy Birthday, then. How old are you?'

He drew himself up with mock afront. 'Madam, it is impolite to ask a gentleman his age.' He wasn't going to admit to being only nineteen when she was obviously a few years older.

'I like that moustache that you've just about managed to grow on your stiff upper-lip.'

He stroked it. Moustaches, pipes and Brylcreemed hair were the badges of office of young RAF officers. 'Think it makes me look – old enough?'

'Old enough for what?'

That twinkle was definitely there. 'Why to fly a kite, of course,' he said, playfully indignant. 'What else could you have thought I meant?'

'Have you got a nice girlfriend waiting for you, where you come from?'

She seemed interested in him. Just sympathy, no doubt. Trying to cheer up one of the 'Brylcreem boys' before he went to his almost certain death in a prang over the North Sea. It was only a matter of time, after all. If it didn't happen here, it would be in a bomber over Germany. He was due for a posting.

'I come from Norfolk. Norwich. I've left droves of pretty girls pining for me up there. Receive dozens of love-letters every day. Can't make up my mind between them.' He leaned over the bar in a confidential manner. 'There's Molly, but she's cross-eyed. Tess, but she's got hairy legs. Um . . . Clara, but she looks just like the horse she's *really* in love with.'

His voice dropped lower and he glanced from side to side as if to make sure no one was listening, then beckoned her closer. She leant towards him with gleaming eyes, till he could detect a trace of perfume from her warm skin, the tickle of a few wayward curls against his cheek. 'The real contest,' he murmured, 'is between Gloria and Priscilla. Trouble with Gloria is that she's frigid. And Priscilla,' he rolled his eyes, 'she's just the opposite – a raving bloody nymphomaniac.'

She drew back, laughing. 'You should be so lucky.'

He grinned. 'I've achieved an ambition tonight. I've made you smile.'

Her face closed up immediately.

'Sorry, I didn't mean to be . . .'

She shook her head and sighed. 'I haven't had much to smile about lately. My husband was killed beginning of March. On one of the MTBs.'

Jimmy felt the colour flood his face. 'Oh Christ. I've really put my foot in it. I'm so sorry – '

She reached out and touched his hand. 'That's war, isn't it? What's your name, birthday boy?'

'James Mallory. But you can call me Jimmy. I only allow that familiarity to my best friends.'

'Thanks. You can call me Queenie if you like.'

'There – I thought you looked like a queen. Medieval – '

'Evil! Thanks very much.'

'No. *Med*ieval – you know, from the middle ages. Castles, tournaments, lovers' trysts. To me you shall be Queen Guinevere.'

'Who's she when she's at home?'

'King Arthur's wife.' She still had her eyebrows raised. 'King Arthur and his round table?'

'Oh, that King Arthur. I thought you meant the other one.'

Jimmy laughed until he saw by her embarrassed expression that she had not meant to be funny. She just did not know anything about King Arthur. 'I shall be your Sir Lancelot. He was Arthur's favourite knight until he discovered that he was having it off with Guinevere – '

'Go on. I think you should keep your affection for Priscilla, you'll get a lot more joy out of her.' She gave a saucy laugh and moved up the bar to serve some locals who had just come in.

Jimmy went back to his seat, smiling.

'You look like the cat that's been at the cream,' said one of his friends.

Jimmy grinned and played 'Bewitched, Bothered And Bewildered' on his guitar, singing the words softly as he looked over at Queenie.

Whenever the weather was nice, Queenie took Emma out shopping in the afternoons or for a walk along to Landguard Common. Past the old Martello tower, towards the even older Landguard fort, which sprawled on a point of land into the mouth of the Orwell and Stour. It now housed a garrison of soldiers and had two six inch guns pointing out to sea. With much of its population evacuated, Felixstowe was in effect a garrison town occupied by the three services, with the RAf greatly in the minority.

Throwing a ball to her little girl on a warm afternoon in early June, Queenie wondered how Hannah was getting on in Cornwall. How long would her grandparents want to keep her? Emma was pining for her sister. Queenie missed her too, but it was much easier with just one child while she was working at the pub lunchtimes and evenings. Emma slept at Peggy's now, sharing Sally's room and spending the mornings with Peggy. This arrangement took quite a chunk out of Queenie's wages, but she had to admit that she liked the freedom. She loved her kids but wasn't one for being shut up in the house with them all day. It used to drive her nuts when they were little.

Emma grew bored with playing ball and sat on the grass to pick daisies. Queenie sat beside her, showing her again how to thread them into a chain. Looking out over the North Sea, her heart ached with loss and her eyes filled with tears. She missed Keith unbearably.

Petty Officer Coburn called to see her now and then. He was kind, and she guessed he was lonely away from his wife and three children. He told her how he had met Marjory, a local farmer's daughter, at a dance while he was stationed in Plymouth. She was back living on the farm now.

Queenie lay back and shut her eyes. The sun on her face and the drone of insects reminded her of the day on Portsdown Hill. The day that Hannah had been conceived. Hannah had been six in May – had it really happened such a short time ago? She felt a hundred years older than that silly, skinny young girl who had thought she had found her dream, only to have it so cruelly shattered.

She couldn't regret any of it now, though. She had the children. She had some lovely memories. She and Keith had been through some bad patches, but they had also had such happy times. Marriage had changed them both – learning to give and take.

She had been so ignorant when she first met him and he had taught her a lot that had been lacking due to her poor education. She took care how she spoke now with people outside the family and she felt much more confident in herself. She hoped she had done him some good too.

Tears pricked behind her eyelids and she clenched her fists in impotent anger. Why did he have to die? Why did she have to suffer so? If *only* they could have had more time together . . .

A shadow came between her and the sun and Emma said, 'Mummy', in an uncertain tone of voice. Queenie opened her tear-misted eyes and looked up the distorted length of an airforce uniform tapering to a small face. She frowned. Once she would have instinctively flirted, but now she was annoyed at being accosted.

'Hello, Guinevere.' The long legs suddenly bent and brought the face nearer.

She sat up, pushing back her hair self-consciously, thinking he had mistaken her for someone else. Then she remembered where she had heard the name before. 'Oh, hello . . . Jimmy. Got some time off?'

'They let us off the camp for a few hours now and then, you know. Otherwise it's rather like a prison. And who is this delightful little lady?'

'This is Emma. Say hello to Jimmy, darling.' The child

smiled in delight. She was an open, affectionate child, unlike Hannah, who was nervous and moody. Emma liked people, particularly men, and Queenie thought she took after her in character, while Hannah was more like her father.

Jimmy sat on the grass beside them and Emma climbed over her mother and on to his lap. He tickled her and made her giggle. He and Queenie talked a bit about themselves, with him doing most of the talking. She learned that he was the son of a London doctor. Jimmy had started medical training before the outbreak of war and had intended to join the family practice.

Queenie studied his profile as he spoke; clean-cut, handsome, so very young in spite of the brave moustache. 'Don't suppose I'll ever join the firm now.' They both knew what he meant.

'Heard from Priscilla lately?' she asked, to lighten the mood.

'Who?' he turned to look at her, desolation in his eyes.

'You know – the nympho.'

'Oh, her.' He suddenly laughed, then jumped up. 'A figment of my imagination. Come and play ball, Emma.' Queenie watched them playing for a while, the gangling youth throwing the ball gently at the child's level. The tiny girl, no higher than his thigh, her face alight with laughter, stretching out her plump arms with fingers splayed, with not a chance of catching it. Then he picked the child up and swung her, screaming with excitement, round and round.

Queenie stood up and brushed down the seat of her skirt. It felt a little damp from the grass. 'Time for Emma's tea.' He asked if he could walk a little way with them. Queenie hesitated, not wanting her privacy invaded, not wanting to be involved with him even superficially. But he looked so young and lonely.

She told him a bit about her life with Keith, and her difficulties as a widow. He sympathised as he carried

Emma who plainly adored the attention. They walked along the Promenade, separated from the beach and a tranquil blue sea by barbed-wire and concrete anti-tank blocks.

Opposite Orwell Road Queenie reached out for Emma. 'It's been nice talking to you, Jimmy. Might see you in the pub tonight?'

He looked so heartbreakingly young and lonely.

'Want to come home for a cup of tea?' she asked.

It became quite a habit; Jimmy meeting her on the common when it was fine and going home for a cup of tea.

'Please don't tell the other boys,' she had asked that first afternoon as he left the flat. 'You do understand, don't you?'

'Mum's the word,' he had promised. 'It's our secret.'

'Now don't go getting any ideas,' she warned, worried that he might be reading all sorts of things into it. 'It's just an innocent . . .' She was making matters worse. 'I mean – '

He took her hand and raised it to his lips. 'Don't worry, Guinevere, I know you're just being kind to a lonely young chap.'

And he cheered her up. It was nice to have a young fellow fancying her again.

In the pub, she could see how difficult Jimmy found it to keep away from her. She read the gleam of suppressed excitement over their secret meetings in his eyes. Perhaps she had made a mistake taking him home but it was perfectly harmless, wasn't it? If it gave him a little pleasure to think about her between his dangerous missions then she was glad. She smiled to herself. He was part of her war effort.

She relaxed more with the other boys now. They were such a nice bunch of fellows. They had heard Jimmy calling her Guinevere and, assuming it was her name, called her by it too. There was often a group of them at the bar with Jimmy, chatting her up. She found herself indulging in a little harmless flirting. It made her feel more like her old self.

One of them, Ossie they called him, was older and obviously more experienced with women. Oily. He really fancied his chances. Kept trying to get her on her own and asking her to meet him. Making suggestive remarks.

'I only like sailors,' she told him with a twinkle in her eye. 'I've been warned about you "Brylcreem boys".'

'Time you set your sights higher,' he told her one night. 'We're much more sophisticated. Know how to treat a woman.'

She shook her head. 'I like my men rough and ready. Give me a Jack Tar any day. There's something about those bell-bottom trousers . . .'

'It's what's in them that's important,' he leered suggestively. 'Come on. Let me see you home – '

The smile left her eyes. 'No! Now get off back to your mates . . . sonny.' That fixed him. Giving her a baleful look, he rejoined the group. Jimmy had been watching the exchange, and made some remark to Ossie which obviously infuriated him. He lunged at Jimmy who stood up and the two faced each other like a pair of fighting cocks.

Queenie, watching from the bar, bit her lip. 'There might be a bit of trouble over there,' she told the landlord. He went over and gave them a warning and they simmered down. 'You'll have to be a bit more distant with them, Queenie,' he told her on his return. 'You're an attractive young woman and they don't get much opportunity to get into town and meet girls.'

She agreed. She didn't want to lose her job.

Looking apologetic, Jimmy wished her a wistful goodnight. After clearing up, Queenie changed into slacks, put on her short coat and went out of the back door to get her bicycle as usual.

In the yard, she put the bag containing her dress and high-heeled shoes into the bicycle basket. Resting one foot up on a box, she bent to fix her bicycle clip around her trouser leg.

Suddenly she was grabbed by the waist from behind and gave a little scream as the lower part of a recognisably male body was ground against her buttocks. She knew who it was immediately.

Struggling she gasped. 'Let go of me, you filthy bugger, or I'll scream – '

He did let go of her – very suddenly. She heard the crack of bone against flesh, and realised he had been wrenched off her. Two figures struggled and grunted in the murky light.

'Is that you, Jimmy,' she hissed. 'For Chris'sake stop it, or I'll lose me job.'

There was another nasty crack and a moan and one of them fell to the ground. 'Come on, let's get out of here,' said Jimmy, grabbing her arm with one hand and her bike with the other.

'Oh, Jimmy, what the hell d'you want to do that for?' she asked when they were clear of the pub and walking along the road together. 'I could've dealt with that . . . twerp. Now there'll be trouble for you back at the camp, won't there?'

'I saw him go round the back when we left. I guessed he was going to try something, so I waited as usual. It isn't right for a girl to have no protection at this time of night.'

'I'm all right. It's only a few minutes to whizz home on me bike. Here, what do you mean . . . as usual?'

He scuffed his feet. 'I . . . I always cut back when we get to camp, just to see that you get off home safely. The fellows don't know.'

'You what? You mean . . .' She started to laugh. 'Well, you are my knight in shining armour and no mistake.' She linked her arm through his. 'Well, Sir Lancelot, if you're going to see me home, I'll reward you with a cup of cocoa.'

Accompanied by giggles, Jimmy pushed the bike with her seated on the saddle, her arm thrown across his shoulders.

After leaving the bike outside in the porch, she took him up to her flat and bathed his sore eye with cold water. 'You're supposed to put steak on a bruised eye to stop it going black. I've got a bit of liver for tomorrow's dinner,' she laughed. 'Think that might do the trick?'

He grimaced. 'It'll be all right. I don't think Ossie will give me any more trouble, either. He's got a big mouth, but he usually backs down when there's an argument. I'm just glad we don't fly together.'

They talked for a little while over a steaming cup of cocoa, then she said, 'You'd better get going. It's ever so late. Tell you what – take the bike. Drop it off at the pub tomorrow evening. I don't mind walking to work, but I don't like walking home on my own in the dark in this bleedin' blackout.'

She saw him to the door. 'Tss, you're going to have a shiner there, Jimmy.' She touched his face tenderly. His arms went round her and his mouth claimed hers.

After a shocked moment, Queenie struggled out of his clasp. 'Don't Jimmy!' She backed away. 'You must never do that again, do you hear? We can't ever be more than friends – '

'I love you, Guinevere.' He held out his arms to her, an expression of longing on his face.

She shook her heard. 'No, you don't. You think you do, with all this romantic nonsense about Guinevere and Lancelot. But I'm just Queenie and you're just Jimmy. And well, to put it bluntly, Jimmy,' she blushed, 'it's just sex . . . not love.'

He shook his head.

'Yes, it is. If times were normal, you'd be going out with lots of girls of your own age. Having fun, a bit of loving, finding out what it was all about.'

'Things aren't normal though, are they?'

'It don't make no difference where I'm concerned,

Jimmy. I'm sorry, but you know my position. Perhaps I shouldn't have encouraged you, but I never thought for one moment that . . . Look, I don't want you to come here again. For your own sake. You should try to get into the town a bit more – meet a nice girl . . .'

He nodded, turned his face away, but not before she had seen the gleam of tears. 'G'night then Guin – Queenie. I'll leave the bike at the pub for you.'

'Goodnight, Jimmy. I won't forget my Sir Lancelot.'

I've been a fool, she told herself when he had gone. Done that poor young bloke more harm than good. She could still feel the imprint of his lips on hers. She touched her mouth gently. Moaning, she leant against the door-frame. For a moment back there she had wanted to let go, to respond, to take him to her bed and make love to him. Especially when she saw how upset he was. Oh, God, she was so lonely too.

Queenie cried herself to sleep.

Jimmy did not come to the pub next evening, though he had left her bicycle in the back yard. Ossie did not turn up, either, for which she was grateful.

'Where's Jimmy Mallory?' she asked one of his mates after a few evenings of absence. 'Going into town these nights, is he?'

'No. He's a bit moody, these days. Just hangs around the camp. He and Ossie had a bit of a dust-up. Over some bird, I shouldn't wonder.' The way he looked at her made it obvious that he knew it was over her.

She flushed. 'Give him my best wishes, will you? Tell him we're missing his guitar.'

Queenie's heart skipped a beat when Jimmy turned up again. He behaved very formally with her, but strummed his guitar and sang his songs much as usual. She was glad she had made him see sense.

At the bar, the boys were talking about the bombing

raids on German cities. Now that Gemany was occupied with its assault on Russia, the Airforce had gone on the offensive.

Queenie thought about the ordinary families in Germany, running to the shelters, losing their homes, their lives. Most of them probably not wanting this war any more than most British families. It was that bleeding Hitler's fault. Look what he had done to English cities. Dear old Portsmouth in ruins. And something like thirty thousand people killed in London in the worst of the Blitz. You just couldn't believe it. It was downright criminal.

Jimmy was sitting on his own near the bar, playing his guitar and humming an old tune. What was it? He looked up and their eyes met. He looked older tonight, more of a man than a boy. And sad. 'I did but see but see her passing by,' he sang. 'Yet will I love her – ' his voice rising on a sweet note ' – till I die.'

Queenie turned away, blushing. She tried to ignore him for the rest of the evening, but whenever she glanced in his direction, he was watching her. She felt quite flustered and a little excited.

Later, as she padlocked her bicycle to the porch, a figure appeared in the moonlight behind her. She jumped, a strangled scream in her throat.

'It's only me. Sorry I frightened you.'

'Oh, Jimmy,' she breathed in relief. 'What're you doing here?'

'I've come to say goodbye. I've been posted. I'm off to Grimsby tomorrow.'

'Oh.' Disappointment flooded her and fear for him. No doubt he'd be going on more dangerous missions. 'I'll miss you.'

'Aren't you going to offer a last cup of cocoa to the condemned man?'

She hesitated. 'Oh all right, then. Just a quick one.' He paced round her little living room like a captive tiger and finally picked up her wedding photo.

'You looked lovely.'

'We were married on my nineteenth birthday, first of May. My dress was turquoise – '

'Your husband . . . looks a good chap?'

'He was lovely. Sit down, Jimmy. Your cocoa's getting cold.'

'Tell me about him.'

She began hesitantly, then losing herself in her memories, she talked as if she would never stop, unaware of how wistfully he was watching her.

'What was the row about?' he asked eventually.

'Oh, he had a bit of a fling with some woman. It was just the war – you know how it is. She wasn't a tart, mind. I was hopping mad, but somehow, after we'd had it all out, it brought us closer together. Those last few days were wonderful. We really thought . . . and then – ' Her face crumpled and she buried her face in her hands.

Jimmy went to her and knelt on one knee beside her chair, stroking her shuddering back. She turned her face into his shoulder and he stroked her hair. When her grief had subsided, she raised swollen eyes to his. 'I'm sorry, Jimmy. I shouldn't have embarrassed you like that.'

He held her chin while his mouth came down on hers in a gentle caress. Queenie pulled back abruptly. 'Gawd, is that the time? You'd better get going, Jimmy. You don't want to be tired out for your journey tomorrow.'

'Don't make me go . . .'

Their breathing grew rapid as they stared at each other. Uncertainty clouded Queenie's mind. She wanted him to stay. How lovely it would be to be comforted by this sweet young man and she could give him something in return. She could transform the boy into a man. But it was too soon for her . . . and it was too important for him.

'I wish I could let you stay, Jimmy,' she said softly, 'but . . . I'm not like that. I wouldn't feel right about it. We can't let the war be an excuse for everything, can we?'

'Queenie . . .'

She shut her eyes. If he said what they both knew – that he might never have the opportunity to discover the joy of making love – she knew she would succumb. Tears squeezed from under her lids and trickled down her cheeks. Jimmy kissed them away and stood up.

'I respect you for that, Guinevere,' he said resolutely, standing up. 'Right, I'll be off. Take your bike again? I'll drop it off as I go past the pub.'

She nodded, standing too, telling him with a watery smile, 'I'll think about you, Jimmy.'

'Can I write to you?'

'I don't see why not. I'm not much good at writing, though. Never had much of an education.'

'Just a few words, now and then? Would you . . . give me a photo?'

'Of course.' She went to the drawer of the sideboard, rifled through an envelope and took one out. 'You don't want one of an old married woman. This is me when I was fifteen, all dressed up as the Queen of the May.'

He looked at it and smiled. 'I wish we'd met then – before life got so complicated.'

'Go on, you'd have only been about twelve or thirteen then,' she laughed.

'I was a very precocious boy.'

'Not half so precocious as I was, I can tell you.' Was there really so little difference in their ages? She felt at least ten years older. She was a mother while he was probably still at school.

He went to the door and she followed him. 'Goodbye, Guinevere.' He kissed her quickly and went.

'I'll pray for you, Jimmy,' she murmured to herself. She had to admit she had wanted him desperately. But that would have been selfish, wouldn't it? It was better this way.

She would always be Guinevere for him now, a pure girl in a white dress with a wreath of May blossom on her head.

# · Twenty-six ·

Ray Coburn shaved, combed his hair and shrugged into his naval jacket. He had slept for several hours but was still feeling rather shattered from the night's abortive run. You didn't mind coming back exhausted knowing you had achieved something. But going all that way just to wallow around feeling sea-sick, lying in wait for an enemy who did not turn up, when you just wanted to be tucked up in bed – bloody soul-destroying.

He had just had lunch and decided a brisk walk along the sea-front would do him good. As far as the pier and back. He might just look in on young Queenie Jackson as he went past. Poor kid. The war might make heroes, but the unsung heroines were the widows who struggled on, bringing up the children, coping with bereavement, loneliness, shortage of money and rationing.

He had not visited this particular widow for a while and he knew why if he was honest. Missing his own wife, Queenie upset his equilibrium. She was too attractive for his peace of mind.

But he *had* promised to call again to see if she was all right, if she needed anything. There might be something he could do for her. Perhaps she would be out, as she had been once before, and he could slip a note through her letter-box to say he had called – conscience salved and temptation avoided. He picked up a couple of bars of chocolate that he'd been saving to take home and put them in a bag.

Queenie opened the door to him and he was startled as

always by her beauty: the rose and white complexion, the lustre of her dark hair and the incredible purply-blueness of her shadowed eyes. A quick appraisal revealed that she had lost weight, but it only added emphasis to her features.

She smiled a little hesitantly. 'Oh, nice to see you, Mr Coburn. Come in.'

'I was just passing . . . What a lovely summer's day.' He crouched down to Emma's level. 'How's my pretty girl then?' The child put her arms around his neck and pressed her cool cheek against his. Missing his own children, he felt a prick at the back of his eyes.

Emma pulled away, chuckling from contact with his beard. 'It tickles.'

'I know, I'm like Father Christmas, aren't I? and I've brought some choccy for you and Mummy.'

'Oh, you shouldn't have,' said Queenie as he straightened up with a groan, rubbing the small of his back.

'Getting old,' he grinned. 'Tiring night.'

She nodded, understanding.

'How've you been?' He saw the misery deep in her eyes. 'Silly question, I suppose.'

Queenie shrugged. 'Mustn't grumble. I'm enjoying the job at the Barley Mow and the money's quite good.'

'Is that the pub up near the airfield?'

'Yes. All those nice young blokes. You just get to know them and they get posted, or worse.' She looked away. 'Would you like a cup of tea?'

'If I'm not stopping you from doing anything?'

'No. We were just going out to do some shopping, but there's no rush. Go through to the sitting room. I'll put the kettle on.'

Emma brought him various dolls to admire. He picked her up, enjoying the closeness of her plump little body, and took her to the window. Lovely view and in the middle of a raging war, so peaceful. Walking around the room, he examined the few bits and pieces that made a personal statment upon the rather dreary contents of a furnished, rented flat. Some ornaments, several small pen and ink animal pictures signed KJ, and framed in *passé par tout*. Emma's toys, some pink knitting, and a few cheap women's magazines. A small pile of a more expensive magazine called *The Artist*.

Ray picked up the photo of Stonewall Jackson on the mantelpiece. All that wavy hair, face crinkled in one of his rare smiles. He'd been a bit taciturn but a good bloke. One of the best.

'Where's my Daddy?' asked Emma, bending to kiss the cold glass just as her mother came in with a tray.

As Queenie put it on the coffee table, he replaced the picture quickly. 'I miss him something awful,' she said with a break in her voice as she straightened up.

Ray was embarrassed. 'He was a good man. Things'll get easier as time passes . . . my dear.'

She shook her head. 'How many more . . .? Bloody stupid war! I tell you I'd rather have old Hitler over here, bossing us about,' she said passionately, 'and still have my Keith.'

Ray nodded. 'I understand how you feel. But we've got to stop that Nazi, whatever it takes. You know that. Look what's happening to the Jews. He has taken Holland and France. We've got to stop him.'

She bit her lip and nodded, sitting down and pouring him a cup of tea. 'What's been happening at the base then?'

'Young Godfrey's been killed.'

'The officer who was with Keith when . . .?'

He nodded.

'Poor little sod! He wasn't married, was he? His poor mother. Is Dicky Dickinson back?'

He nodded. 'Fighting fit.'

'Worse luck for him.'

They talked on for half an hour before he took his leave; about what had been happening in the North Sea, about how she was going to Cornwall soon to fetch Hannah back. 'Phyllis, my sister-in-law, says I ought to. Hannah's been down there for months, and Phyllis says she'll be forgetting who her mother is.'

Ray told her about about his three children, Will, Clive and Penny. 'I miss them dreadfully. But at least I feel they're safer on the farm.'

'Will you come again?' she asked wistfully at the door.

'When I can,' he smiled, knowing it would be unwise.

Queenie shut the door and leaned against it.

She hadn't wanted Ray Coburn to go. He was such a big, comfortable bear of a man. Larger than life. Thick brows, big nose, crooked teeth, laughter lines around his kind eyes. Gentle.

She would have liked him to cuddle her like her Dad used to.

Why were people so polite? So careful of each other's feelings? How would he have reacted if she had told him the truth when he had asked her how she had been? What if she had answered, 'Lonely. Frightened. Mourning my husband. Missing Jimmy Mallory. So angry about this stupid war that I could scream – and never stop.' He'd have run a mile.

She had received two love letters from Jimmy. One was a poem to his Queen Guinevere. She wasn't sure what some of the fancy words meant, but they sounded nice. It was good for her self-esteem but she hoped, for his sake, that he would soon forget her. She thought it wouldn't take long for him to get tired of her boring, badly-written letters. She had put one of Emma's drawings in with the last one.

Queenie and Violet Jackson faced each other across the hall of Tremayne for a few minutes before Violet's face crumpled and Queenie ran and enfolded her in her arms. The two women rocked together and wept.

Bernard picked up his daughter-in-law's bags and went quietly up the stairs.

'Is Mummy here, Grandad?' Hannah was kneeling on the landing, looking through the banisters. Holding back.

'Yes, little lass.' He reached the landing, leaned down and helped the child to her feet. 'We'll give Mummy and Grandma a few minutes, shall we? They've got a lot to say to each other. Come on, take me to your room and show me what you've been doing.'

Hannah obediently led him to her room. Always obedient, quiet, never showing her emotions. She wasn't a normal child, but there, like so many children, she had gone through things that no six-year-old could understand. Several times he had questioned his wisdom in bringing her away from her mother and sister.

Both women had needed the comfort the child could bring, but he had thought that Violet needed it most – Queenie still had Emma. It had certainly been of benefit to his wife, made her pull herself together. She couldn't lie in her room all day with a young child to look after. She had been forced to put on a brave face and her health had rapidly improved.

His own grief lay heavy in his chest like a lump of iron, its rust permeating his heart, mind and soul. Once or twice on the lonely coastal vigil he had given way to it. Thought of his dear son and the dangers he had faced – and how he had died. The present grief was tangled with the unshed tears for his comrades of an earlier war. He prayed nightly for Michael.

But had it been fair on Hannah? She was getting on well at the local school. The teacher liked her – well who would not like a polite, amenable little girl? One of the children at school had discovered that the top edge of Hannah's right ear went into a little point, and had christened her

'Pixie'. So she had become Pixie to everyone in the village. And there was something fey about her.

Hannah showed him her drawing. A playground scene. Children running around on their little matchstick legs, skipping, throwing balls. Happy, happy. Not like the first drawings she had done when she arrived. Fierce black and red scribbles. He was no phychiatrist, but even he could see that they showed her confusion, her fear.

Then he saw in the drawing the little girl in the corner, with long black plaits and rivulets of fat tears streaming from her eyes.

'What's the matter with her?' he asked pointing. 'Has she hurt herself?'

Hannah shook her head. 'That's Pixie. She's always crying 'cos she had to go away and her Daddy's not coming back.'

He had noticed that she talked about Pixie in the third person more freely than if she was asked a question about herself. He lifted the child on to his lap and cuddled her. Poor little mite. What was going in that head of hers? It would be good for her to be with her mother again.

In the lounge Queenie and Violet sat talking quietly. Bernard heard the conversation as he and Hannah approached the open door.

Queenie was saying. 'He was under a lot of strain. Those night runs, never knowing if he was going to come back.' She sniffed wetly. 'But it might help you to know that we were very happy together – always.'

Violet's voice, unnaturally subdued. 'I owe you such a lot of apologies, dear. I'm afraid I'm not always . . . very kind.'

'I know you thought he could have done better for himself. Oh yes, and he could, I know that. But perhaps it was better that he had some married life before he . . .'Cos he wasn't really the marrying kind, was he?' She gave a little chuckle. 'He did warn me at the beginning, you know. But I never set out to trap him – it just happened.'

'Well, I'm sure you're right.'

Bernard led his granddaughter in. The two women looked over to the door. 'Hannah!' Queenie leapt up and ran to the child. Falling to her knees, she took Hannah in her arms, the little girl allowing herself to be embraced and kissed but not reciprocating. 'How are you, darling? Have you been a good girl?'

The child nodded. 'Pixie's been good, too.'

Bernard explained.

'Where's Emma?' Hannah asked, looking past her mother.

'She's waiting for us at home, darling. Auntie Phyllis has come up for a little holiday to look after her.'

Tears filled the child's eyes. 'Pixie wants Emma.' Her mother, wondering how best deal with her, embraced the unresponsive little body.

'Time for tea,' said Violet.

Over the meal, Bernard told her how they were moving to Coverack along the coast. 'Even with our lodger, Mr Johnson, we can't afford to keep this place on.'

How disappointing for you after all your dreams.'

'More important things have been shattered, lass,' Bernard said sadly.

'It's a nice enough little coastguard cottage,' said Violet bravely, 'but Bernard will have a long walk to Black Head to do his watch.'

'Do me good, Mother. I'm not an old man yet. Am I, eh?'

He saw that Queenie caught the look that passed between Violet and himself and, from the twinkle in her eye, he realised that she guessed the meaning. She was a bright one. She might not have been the wife that Violet would have chosen for Keith, but in *his* eyes she was a grand lass.

The Jacksons made sure that Queenie enjoyed her week with them. Occasionally, Violet would forget herself and lapse into her old ways, pulling the girl up on something, disagreeing with her, complaining about an inadvertently dropped expletive, but Bernard always pulled her up sharp.

Much to his continual amazement, Violet took more notice of him these days than she had ever done. Ever since Keith's wedding. She must have realised, as he had, that something that had almost been lost – thrown away – was retrieved that night in Totterdell's Hotel.

'Who is it?' Queenie's muffled voice came from behind her closed door.

'Ray Coburn,' Ray answered, puzzled.

The door opened a crack. 'Excuse me if I don't ask you in, Mr Coburn. I'm not feeling well.'

'Where's Emma?'

'Peggy's got both the kids . . .'

Surely, he thought, she would have been in bed if she was so unwell that she could not look after the children, and there was something about her voice . . .

He pushed against the door. There was little resistance. She stood before him red-eyed and draggle-haired.

'What is it, Queenie? Has something happened?'

Her breath drew in on a sob. 'It's Jimmy.' The tears started again.

He reached out and gently held her shaking shoulders. 'Jimmy who?'

She began to wail, hanging in his grasp, her mouth open and tears spurting from her eyes. Startled, he pulled her against him and held her shuddering body in his arms.

After a few minutes she quietened a little and with an arm about her, he led her into her living room. Pulling a dining-chair from under the table he sat down and settled her on his lap, placing his peaked-cap on the table. She lay passively against him, sniffling and sobbing.

He reached in his pocket and gave her his handkerchief and she blew her nose. 'Sorry about that,' she muttered, obviously overcome with embarrassment.

'Want to tell me about it?'

She gave him a purple flash from her reddened eyes, then looked down at the hanky she was twisting in her lap. 'It's this stupid bleeding war. Where's it all going to end. K'Keith gone. John, my Marine brother, blown up in the Atlantic. No survivors, no body brought home. At least I know where my Keith is . . .' She cried again. 'P'poor Phyllis, hardly married any time at all. Don't know if it was a good thing they didn't have kids. They were waiting for a better time – makes you laugh, doesn't it?' she asked bitterly. 'And poor old Ma. Our John was her favourite. Heartbroken she is.'

Ray pushed her damp hair off her cheeks. 'And Jimmy?'

'Jimmy Mallory. He was a young pilot from the airfield. We were just f'friends. Both lonely. He was only nineteen or twenty. He was so sweet and rom'romantic. Used to play the guitar and sing. He beat a bloke up one night because he grabbed me. Called me his Queen Guin – '

She got off Ray's lap and went to the window, looked out for a moment, then stood in front of the mantlepiece with her back to him. 'Where's the sense in it?' she asked in a low, furious voice, beating the side of her clenched fist against the marble shelf. 'Where's the sense in all these young boys being killed? A friend of Jimmy's wrote to me. His plane went down in flames over Germany. Oh, I hope it was quick for those poor boys.' Her voice broke again on a sob. 'He had all his life in front of him, poor baby. And I feel so *guilty*,' she ended on a high, frenzied note.

Ray went to her. Held her shoulders. 'I can't imagine what you've got to feel guilty about, girl. Come on, now, be sensible.'

She twisted round to face him and grasped his lapels. 'Damn you! Don't tell me to be sensible,' she yelled. 'I was being sensible when I sent him away on that last night, wasn't I? He wanted to stay. I wanted him to stay. He'd never . . . been with a woman. It wasn't much to ask in the circumstances, was it? I had nothing very precious to offer him. But I was *sensible* and sent him away.' She thumped her fists impotently against his chest, then fell against him, weeping hopelessly.

'Cry it out, my lovely. You can't take everyone's problems on your shoulders, can you? Such little shoulders.' He was talking nonsense, but what could he say? Little defenceless creature – didn't even come up to his chin. He stroked her back, her hair. Held her in his arms.

'Sorry,' she murmured at last, pushing back her hair and looking up at him with tear-streaked face and swollen eyes. 'I shouldn't have gone on at you like that. You were only being kind.'

What could he do but bend his head and kiss her trembling mouth and swollen eyelids?

They looked at each other, startled. She raised a hand and tentatively stroked his bearded jaw, let her fingers steal up around his neck and pull his head down to her. They kissed again – and again. He held her tightly and she clung to him.

'Please, oh please.' She hardly knew what she was begging for. Something to blot out all the misery.

Ray bent, put an arm behind her knees and scooped her up. She linked her arms around his neck, buried her face against him as he carried her out of the room, across the hall and pushed against a half-open door which he took to be her bedroom. It was dimly-lit as the curtains were drawn, the bedspread crumpled where she had lain crying.

He ripped back the covers before laying her down, pulling off his jacket and dropping it on the floor, dragging off his tie and his shirt. She watched him as he removed his trousers, kicked off his shoes. Undoing her skirt, she wriggled it down her legs, and unbuttoned her blouse.

Ray fell panting on the bed beside her, helped her out of the blouse, kissed her neck and shoulders, bit at her nipples through her slip and brassìere. Roughly, he dragged her knickers off, pushed up her slip – and entered her with desperate haste.

Queenie gasped and raised her hips to meet his thrusts, crying out at the climax they rapidly reached together. Ray rolled off her and lay breathing quickly. After a few moments of confused thought they turned their heads to look at each other, eyes glowing in the semi-dark. He raised himself on one elbow, looking down at her. 'Are you all right?'

She nodded, tracing his nipples with her fingernail, running the palm of her hand over his hirsute shoulders, the matted hair on his chest, and down his stomach. It was exciting. Ray was big, hairy and heavy, carrying a little too much weight really.

Keith had been slim and hard and only his limbs had been hairy. But she shut her mind to memories of Keith – to comparisons. She only knew that she had been starved, and now . . .

'You've still got your socks on,' she giggled.

Shyly, daring, her hand delved lower, feeling the evidence of Ray's re-arousal. Sitting up, she pulled her slip over her head, unclipped her brassière and turned to him.

'We'll take it slower this time,' he murmured, his mouth covering hers as he rested over her, taking his weight on his elbows. Queenie caressed him with her hands, tenderly imprisoning his thighs with her legs, and returning his kisses. This time he entered her like a key into a well-oiled lock and together they broke through terrestial barriers for a brief glimpse of paradise.

Later, Queenie awoke to find herself curled inside the curve of a man's body, his legs bent behind hers, his arm thrown heavily across her. She went hot and cold as she remembered.

'Ray,' she said urgently. 'Wake up. What's the time? Haven't you got to get back to base?'

'Mmm?' he grunted against her neck, then coming

suddenly awake, he raised his wrist to peer at his watch in the semi-dark. 'Half-past four. You had me worried then, girl. Time for a quick cup of tea, but first – ' He pushed up hard against her.

'Oh, you couldn't, surely . . .' Queenie giggled.

'Couldn't I?' It was all too evident that he could.

'Coo, Tarzan – old Johnny Weismuller, hasn't got nothing on you.'

Queenie, in an old tie-round wrap, had just put the kettle on in the kitchen when Ray came in dressed with his jacket over his arm. She looked round to see a big, darkly-bearded *stranger*. That she had just shared the most intimate acts possible with him was suddenly terrifying.

Her eyes were huge and frightened as she said, 'I know I'm to blame for what happened, but please, I don't want you to come again. It was a mistake.'

His brows drawing down in a brief frown, he shrugged. 'I understand. It was too soon for you. I'm sorry.' He pulled his jacket on. 'I'll get my cap and be on my way.'

She was standing with her arms behind her, leaning against the sink, when he returned. Biting her lip and her cheeks red with embarrassment, she said, 'I'm sorry if I've hurt your feelings. You're such a nice man. But you do understand, don't you? It was wrong . . . for me.'

He nodded. 'I wouldn't like you to think that I go around seducing women, either. I've had one or two one-night stands when I've been away on a long commission. What Jack hasn't? Navy life is hard on married couples, isn't it? But I've never had an affair, or wanted one – till now. Goodbye then, Queenie.'

He went to her and she stiffened, looking down, afraid he was going to embrace her, weaken her resolve. He lifted her chin with gentle fingers. 'What you gave me was very precious. You're a lovely girl. But try not to feel guilty. Life must go on, you know.'

'We can always blame it on the war, can't we?' Deliberately flippant.

'It has a lot to answer for.' He placed a gentle kiss on her forehead. 'If you *need* me at any time, if you have any difficulties I can help with, you know where to find me.'

He let himself out.

Queenie went through the motions of making the tea and sat sipping it thoughtfully. She had behaved like a real tart. She burned with embarrassment. He must have thought she was easy. But she didn't want to go pinching other women's husbands, she remembered how she had felt over Keith and his women – the ones she knew about. She would always wonder how many there had been – not that it mattered any more.

And yet, the worst thing of all was that she had betrayed Keith, and so soon after refusing poor little Jimmy something that would have given him a happy memory amongst all the horror he had gone through. She had given herself shamelessly to Ray Coburn without a thought for the consequences. Her body was still throbbing from him.

Christ, suppose she got pregnant?

'Oh, my God,' she moaned, dropping her head into her hands. But she hadn't had the curse since Keith's death. Shock, the doctor had said. Still, what a bloody stupid risk to take.

Eventually, washed and dressed, she went to collect the children from Peggy. She was irritable with Hannah and Emma when she got them back home and relieved when it was their bedtime. Poor little sods, she thought, as she kissed them goodnight. It wasn't their fault their mother was a tart.

She sat in the evening gloom, too distraught even to listen to Tommy Handley in ITMA.

Scenes of her and Ray played through her mind, exciting her unbearably. Was she in reality a whore? Now she had slipped, would she go from bad to worse? She had always liked men, flirted with them. She must give out some sort of message. There had always been boys around her when she was young. That time with Uncle Bert.

How had she attracted Keith when he could have had a more suitable girl? And she had let him do 'it' without even any talk of marriage. What about his brother Michael? She'd never meant that to happen.

Always men swarming around her at the mess dos. Then Jimmy. Now Ray. She had really gone and done it this time, hadn't she? But what else had a girl like her to offer any man? But perhaps, in this case, as they had *both* given and taken, it made it all right.

In bed she stroked her body, thrilling over memories of the afternoon of love – lust would be more correct. She groaned. She had been lost in misery over Keith and her brother. Then Jimmy. But now she had the unsettling feeling that Ray Coburn could help her to forget. No, never forget. But he could help to ease the pain.

# · *Twenty-seven* ·

It was her day off. Queenie looked up and saw Ray Coburn watching her across the toy shop. Colour flooded her face and she went weak at the knees. She had thought about him so often over the last three weeks – had tried to put him out of her mind. Now he was coming over to her, smiling, seemingly at ease.

'Hello there. Hello, young ladies,' he addressed the children. 'And this must be Hannah.'

'Uncle Eddy sent us some money,' said Emma excitedly, 'to buy sumfink nice. I got paper dolls – '

'And Hannah is trying to make up her mind about which jigsaw puzzle to have,' said Queenie nervously, her face burning. Hannah looked at the bearded man suspiciously, not being the outgoing child that Emma was.

'I've just bought a model kit for my eldest boy. He'll be twelve next week,' said Ray.

'Will you get home for his birthday?'

''Fraid not, and it's so long since I've seem them. How have you been?' he asked softly, his brown eyes gentle. 'I've been worried about you.'

'Keeping busy. This and that.'

'I'd like to talk to you. Come next door for a cup of tea.'

Queenie shook her head.

'They got cweam cakes, Mummy,' begged Emma who had pressed her nose to the café window before they came into the shop.

'You can't turn down a cream bun in times like these,'

Ray said with a determined grin. 'Might not see another for months.'

'Just a quick one, then.' She was torn between the desire for his company and the doubtful wisdom of it.

In the cheerful little café with its red and white checked tablecloths and curtains, they sat over a pot of tea and cream buns for the children.

'You're looking very pretty today, Emma and Hannah. So's your Mummy.' Ray's warm eyes caressed her.

Queenie blushed and glanced up at him from under her lashes. What she used to call her Marlene Dietrich look. It was second nature to her but she mustn't do it.

'I've been wanting to see you,' his deep voice rumbled. 'We can't leave things as they are. Or I can't, anyway.'

'There's no other way for them to be. It was a mistake. It shouldn't have happened.'

'But we can't just pretend that it didn't,' he reached over the table and touched her fingers.

'Can't we?' Queenie asked, thrilling to the touch and not removing her hand as she knew she ought to.

'Why you holding Mummy's hand?' asked Emma, synethetic cream all round her mouth. Hannah looked from one to the other with a puzzle expression on her face.

'Because I like your Mummy. And I think she likes me?'

'I like you very much, but that doesn't make it all right . . .'

'I like you,' said Emma, licking her lips.

'Is there any right or wrong?' he asked. 'Two lonely people caught up in abnormal circumstances – '

'Oh yes, we could find any number of excuses but it still doesn't make it right, in here.' She touched her other hand to her breast. 'You've got a wife and children.'

'That's my problem. A matter for *my* conscience. You know as well as I do that I might never see them again.' Queenie blinked at the bald statement. 'What's the point in being noble . . . You regretted sending that young airman away, didn't you?'

She flashed him an angry look and took her hand away. 'Emotional blackmail now is it? Next thing you'll be suggesting that it's every single woman's duty to comfort the troops. The poor lonely boys away from home.'

He laughed. 'Not a bad idea.'

She smiled reluctantly. Their eyes held, the messages in his sending delicious tingles through her. She certainly wanted this lonely man, this pirate of the seas to comfort her. She had thought of little else since their last meeting, but remembering how she had felt when Keith had betrayed her, she could not encourage Ray to do the same thing to his wife. But she needed him so much.

Obviously reading the softening of resolve in her eyes he said, 'Can Peggy have the children for an hour or two?'

She blushed again. 'Probably – but we mustn't.'

'There'll be plenty of time for regret, Queenie, and maybe we'll regret the opportunities we *didn't* take more than the things we did.'

'You've got the gift of the gab.'

'What does that mean, Mummy?' asked Hannah.

'It means I can persuade your Mummy to do what she really wants to do,' said Ray with a conspiratorial grin. Queenie gave up trying to resist.

They dropped the children off at Peggy's and as soon as the front door closed behind them, the shopping was dropped on the floor and they were in each other's arms, pulling at each other's clothes, shedding garments all the way to the bedroom. They made love with passionate haste, then more slowly.

'I could get used to this, you know,' said Queenie stretching contentedly on his hair chest.

Ray lit himself a cigarette. 'I couldn't have kept away much longer.'

They smiled into each other's eyes as the smoke curled lazily from his lips. Queenie resolutely pushed thoughts of his wife and children our of her mind. She would worry about that later.

The Airforce were bombing German cities. The Japs had bombed American ships in Pearl Harbour and the USA had joined the Allies. American troops were pouring into Britain. It was now November and Montgomery had won the Battle of Alamein. Rommel, the seemingly unbeatable Desert Fox, was in retreat. The allies, under Eisenhower, landed in Morocco and Algeria. British morale was raised.

Whenever he was free, Ray came to Queenie. Several times she had tried to break off their relationship, but he talked her round, promising he would not get her pregnant and they were very careful about contraception. But she knew that as far as she was concerned there was more to it than her guilt over his wife, or fear of conception. Whether it was on the rebound or not she could not tell, but she did know that she was falling more and more in love with him, and knew also that in the end she was the one who was going to be hurt most.

Peggy or Sally used to babysit now in the evenings until Queenie came back from work. Occasionally, if the weather was wild or foggy, Ray was able to spend the night at the flat. The children came to accept his presence though Hannah always seemed puzzled if he was there for breakfast and Emma sometimes asked where her Daddy was. Queenie used to tell her he had gone to be with Jesus. She hoped he had – hoped that atheists were accepted in Heaven.

Sometimes, on a pleasant afternoon, after making love, they would collect Emma from Peggy, meet Hannah from school and take the children to the common. Apart from this, Queenie's bed was their haven, couching their passion, receiving their confidences. They found so much to talk about, lying contentedly in each other's arms. Ray was much more on Queenie's level than Keith had been, more down to earth.

Queenie told him all about her hard childhood, her marriage, and her father. 'You remind me of him, you know. You're my father and my friend and my lover all rolled into one. I love you.'

He told her about his childhood in Somerset, his apprenticeship to a small furniture-making firm and how eventually the lure of the sea had been too great for him so he chose a career in the Navy. He told her about his family. There were snaps of the children; two dark-haired, jolly boys and a little fair girl with the gappy-toothed look of a six-year-old.

He showed her a photograph of Marjory laughing against a summer sky, her fair hair blowing back, large breasts thrusting against a checked shirt.

'She's attractive.' Queenie felt her insides twist with jealousy. Marjory as a word she could cope with, but as an image . . .

Ray took the picture and studied it. 'Yes, she's handsome, and as good as gold. But you know,' he turned his gaze on Queenie, 'it's like comparing . . . the gleam of gold to the glitter of diamonds.'

Queenie's eyes sparkled. It had been a compliment to her and his wife, but she liked her bit best.

'See what you've done?' said Ray, embarrassed, 'you're turning me into a bloody poet.'

Even so, she couldn't leave it at that. 'You love them very much, don't you?' she asked wistfully.

'I adore my children. Of course I love my wife, but we've been married thirteen years and you know how it is, the excitement wears off. We're easy with each other, we know each other so well. She's a good maid and I wouldn't want to do anything to hurt any of them, but . . .'

She dared not press him further. She had no rights. She just had to enjoy him while she had him.

*

But all Queenie's good intentions fled when she learned that Ray had a short leave and was going to Devon for Christmas. 'Oh, we'll have to spend Christmas on our own. It will be miserable.'

Ray looked unhappy. 'I know, girl, but you understand that I must see my family, it's ages since I've been home. I want to see my kids.'

'And Marjory?' Queenie's eyes sparked, the poisonous venom of jealousy coursing through her veins.

'And Marjory – of course.' He took her by the shoulders. 'It won't make any difference to us, my lovely. Look, why don't you go home to Pompey for Christmas? It's been much quieter lately.'

She shrugged him off. 'I won't be able to bear it, wherever I am – knowing you're with her.'

'She's my wife! Don't you think she's been missing me? What do you want me to do? Refuse to sleep with her?'

'Well, you needn't come back to me if you do,' she shouted passionately, knowing that she was testing him too recklessly. Ray's expression darkened with a mixture of emotions. She could see he was angry and perplexed. She hoped he was also full of the fear of losing her.

'You're being thoroughly unreasonable. Admit it. You knew the situation from the off. I've never promised you anything – '

'Go home then. Go on. Get out!'

Ray's face looked thunderous. 'Don't do this to me, Queenie. Don't do this to us. You know I love you, but what can I do?'

'*You can tell her about us.*' She stood glaring at him, arms crossed over her breasts, shaking with a mixture of anger and despair. Hating herself.

'It isn't the right time – '

'We've got to wait till the end of the war to sort our lives out then?'

'Look, our future is so uncertain.' He spread his hands in supplication. 'Let's wait and see. There's no need to rush into any hasty decisions. I'll be with *you* while I'm stationed here. Can't that be enough for you at the moment? Don't tear me in half.'

She could not stop. 'I won't tear you in half. You can make a choice. Her or me!'

'No, Queenie, no. I'm not ready to make this decision. I love you, but . . .'

'I mean it, Ray.' Her eyes gleamed hard at him. 'Don't come back to me unless you've told her about us. Unless you've asked for a divorce.'

He could give her no such assurance and they parted bitterly. After she had calmed down, Queenie was shocked at her hysterical demands. Ray had told her that he loved her but had never made her any promises. But now it was too late, he had gone and she could not undo what she had done. How could she have behaved so wickedly? Why couldn't she just have left things as they were – even though she knew what they were doing was wrong? She knew what it felt like to have a husband who strayed and she couldn't wish it on another woman.

If Ray came back to her she would know that she had selfishly and wickedly broken up a happy family. She wouldn't want that on her conscience. If he did not come back, she had only herself to blame. She cried herself to sleep.

The old farmhouse looked the same. Slightly battered, set in a muddy yard. Welcoming.

Ray shut the gate and, trying to avoid the puddles, approached the front door. Before he reached it, it was thrown open. Marjory stood framed like a picture, her face glowing, her hair twisted up on her head in a new sophisticated style. Before a greeting could be passed between them, the three children came yelling out from behind her.

He hugged Will and Clive, holding their heads against

him and kissing their gleaming hair. Picking his daughter up, he gazed with delight at the more mature little face smiling shyly at him. Penny put her arms hesitantly around his neck and hugged him.

Putting her down, he went to Marjory and they stepped into each other's embrace, fitting together like two pieces of a jigsaw. There was no need to speak.

There was little evidence of war-time hardships on the farm. Plenty of food. The landgirls were a novelty though, the normal hands having been called up. Two of the girls were billeted on the farm, living in what used to be groom's accommodation over the stables. They ate with the family, which meant, with Marjory's parents and her ancient grandmother, six adults and three children. And that was without Ray.

It was lovely being part of his own family again in that warm old house. He was as welcome to his in-laws as any son. Yet at times, recalling the fear and the horror of the war he had been in contact with, he felt alien. He had blood on his hands.

And at the back of his mind there was always Queenie, glowing like a jewel through the thin fabric of his attempted obliteration.

The first night, having been apart for so long, Ray and Marjory were a little shy with one another. She came to him like a buxom milkmaid, in a flannelette nightie and with her hair in two pale gold plaits. Wholesome. The opulence of her body was an exciting re-discovery as she stood before him, passively allowing him to run his hands over her fulsome curves.

*The gleam of gold and the glitter of diamonds.* He tried to put the comparison out of his mind.

They made love so comfortably, every movement falling into its allotted place. Holding back, he allowed her to reach her climax, delighting in her gasps of pleasure, before letting himself go. Unaccountably, as he sank down beside her with a satisfied sigh, tears pricked his eyes.

'I love you,' Marjory said softly.

'I love you, too, my darling.'

'Tell me about what you've been doing?'

He told her about the night runs, the abortive missions, the successful ones. He told her about his mates, even how some of them died. But about his innermost feelings, his grief at their death, his abhorrence of the murder he was forced to commit in the name of freedom, he told her nothing. These things had no place in this tranquil haven.

Queenie had no place here either.

The landgirls went to their own homes for a couple of days over Christmas. Marjory's sister, her sister-in-law and their respective children joined them for the Christmas turkey. Her sister was running the hardware shop while her husband was away laying mines in the Channel, and the other girl's husband was in the Army. He had been rescued from Dunkirk early on in the war. So many women on their own for one reason or another, Ray thought. Carrying on, keeping things going.

What was Queenie having for Christmas lunch in Pompey? he found himself wondering, as he watched his father-in-law carving moist slices from the bird. Spam? Corned-beef hash? No, they'd have managed something. But he would have dearly loved to have her and the little girls sitting at this great table, with paper chains festooning the kitchen. The old black range was popping cheerfully away in the background, and the pudding, 'of a sort' as his mother-in-law had told them apologetically, was steaming on its top.

Queenie. His lovely girl.

Amidst the cheer and the delight of being in the bosom of his family again, he ached for her. What was he going to do about it? He miserably recalled her ultimatum, flung at him with a defiance born of desperation. Her little face alight with anger and passion. *The glitter of diamonds.*

'Penny for them, Ray.' His father-in-law interrupted his thoughts.

'No need to look to sad on Christmas Day,' said Marjory's mother. 'Forget all about the silly old war.'

After lunch, the washing-up done, the adults snoozing in front of the living-room fire, the children playing with their rather spartan assortment of new toys, Ray whispered the suggestion to Marjory that they should go for a walk.

He donned his comfortable old duffel coat and wellington boots. It was so good to be out of uniform. They wandered first round the yard, looking at the animals, then, hand-in-hand, they climbed the hill behind the farm. At the top a little circle of trees grew. Oaks and beeches. They used to call it their magic place when they were courting, newly married. Now the trees were bare of leaves and acorns littered the ground. Ray picked some up and sent them spinning out into space. He'd like to bring Queenie up here.

'What a view.' He said it every time. Plymouth in the distance. Beyond it the Sound, lying pale grey today beneath a darker grey sky. The little fortress of Drake's Island, set like a guard at the feet of a giant. And way out past the Eddystone Lighthouse and the Western Approaches to the horizon, beyond which battles were being fought. There were several destroyers and minesweepers in the harbour and more ships out in the bay, looking like small-scale models from the hill.

History had been made here all right. He loved the story of Drake insisting on finishing his game of bowls on the Hoe while the Spanish bloody Armada was sailing towards them. Typically British, that. It was that spirit that was going to make it so hard for old Hitler if he ever attempted an invasion.

'Ray.' Marjory's voice interrupted his reverie. He turned towards her. Her eyes, grey as the sky, looked frankly into his. 'What is it you want to tell me?'

# · Twenty-eight ·

Queenie arrived in Portsmouth two days before Christmas planning to stay for two weeks.

She knew that Ray would be back in Felixstowe and operational long before that, but she wanted some time to sort out her own feelings, which were in turmoil. She was terrified at the thought of facing him after her unreasonable behaviour, terrified at what she might have precipitated with her demands. She would be desolate to lose him, yet could be no happier at destroying his family if he chose her.

It was all the sadder because she loved Ray and felt he was just right for her. She felt easy with him, protected.

She had been infatuated with Keith to begin with, had hated him when he left her literally holding the baby, but had then fallen in love with him. She *had* loved him, still loved him, but there had always been that underlying mistrust. And in spite of his lower rank and his faults, she had never felt quite good enough for him. And then of course, there was his mother.

In isolation, Ray had been hers. Just him and her and her little girls. But of course she had always known this to be a fantasy. Now, through her own actions, his family had become a frightening reality.

The Ellis family were to enjoy a pleasant if restricted Christmas.

Beatie's flat – she had been rehoused in a lower one after

the bomb damage – was too small to accommodate an extended family. Jimmy, who had just joined the Navy and was undergoing training as an artificer at *Vernon*, stayed in barracks but came home for Chistmas dinner. Josh slept on the living-room settee so that Queenie could have the second bedroom, the little girls sleeping head-to-toe in one of the beds.

'Ma has aged something dreadful,' Queenie told Eddy who had called in to see her.

Eddy was wearing a new confidence that came from the knowledge that he was a useful member of society – that people depended on him. 'John's death has knocked the poor old girl sideways. She was cut-up enough about Keith, and she's always worried about you and Billy.' His kind eyes caressed her. Brown eyes always looked warm, Queenie thought, thinking of Ray. 'How're you coping, Queen?'

'Well enough. I'm hard-up and . . .' She could not say she was lonely any more but she was not going to tell the family about her lover. They would be shocked at the speed with which she had taken up with Ray. They would never understand how it had just happened. But how would she cope if he gave her up? 'Well, I'm alive, aren't I? That's something to be thankful for.'

'Yes. Let's hope we'll still be glad to be alive if we lose this war.'

'Oh, don't, Eddy!'

'Here, tell our Queen about that scare in Pompey earlier this year. You know, the parachutes,' prompted his mother, coming in with a tray.

Eddy snorted. 'Oh yes. It was like this, the bleedin' story spread like wild-fire – invasion from the air. Flashes had been seen that must be "enemy air activity". Then all the electric went off. Next thing we know there's a crowd of Jerry parachutists coming down.' He threw back his head and laughed.

'My Gawd! What's funny about that?'

'Turned out it was a bleedin' barrage balloon what had broke free, floated onto an electric cable and burst. The bits floating down were Jerry parachutes.'

'There's hope for us yet,' stated Queenie wiping laughter tears from her eyes, 'if we can have a good laugh now and then.'

Lil came up from Baker Street with a ready-plucked chicken. Beatie had passed her birds on to her neighbour when she moved, and now they shared the eggs.

Lil had not appreciably lost weight in spite of the rationing, but Beatie had; through sorrow and not wanting to make much effort any more. However, Queenie's visit had roused her from lethargy and she had made some Christmas preparations.

The three women sat around the old table in the little living-room, the one with the burned leg from the incendiary bomb. The gas fire hissed in a beige and cream tile surround. The old wooden clock, some photographs and the white plaster Alsatians resided on its stepped mantlepiece.

Apart from the chickens, Lil was also the proud owner of Beatie's prized aspidistra. *The biggest aspidistra in the world* they called it, after the Gracie Fields song. There hadn't been room in the little flat for it and though Beatie tried to grow one of its babies from time to time, they did not thrive in the gas-heated room.

This little place was convenient and less work, mused Queenie, but it wasn't 'home' like scruffy old Baker Street had been. Where they could have all the family to tea.

'Just back for Christmas then, Queen?' asked Lil. 'Why don't you come back to Pompey now you're on your own? Things 'ave quietened down lately.'

'Well, I've got my job and a nice little flat . . . and the kids are happy. I don't want to uproot them again. I'll stick it out for a bit longer – see what happens.' *See what Ray decides to do.*

'Probably for the best,' agreed Beatie. 'You never know

if the bombing's going to start up again. Lil and me have experimented with the Christmas cakes. Gawd knows what they'll taste like. Weigh a ton, don't they, Lil?'

'I reckon they'll taste all right,' laughed Lil. 'We sieved mashed spuds, Queenie, to save some of the flour, and put in chopped apple, carrot, dried apricots, and anything we could git our hands on.'

'We've left *all* the shopping till tomorrow,' said Beatie. 'We'll go up Charlotte Street Market as usual and see what Christmas Eve bargains we can get. He'll have a moan, but Josh'll come and carry some of it for us. We'll have a good Christmas, you'll see.'

'Everywhere you go these days,' said Lil, 'you've got your bloody gas-mask over one shoulder and a shopping bag in the other hand in case you see something you can buy. You join every queue automatic-like, in case there's somethink worth having. And it's not the same up the market these days, Queenie,' she mourned. 'Everything closes down early with the blackout.'

Beatie agreed. 'Remember what fun it used to be with all the stalls lit up at night with gaslights, crowds of people, everybody shouting – '

'The blokes down the pub, coming out roaring drunk.'

'Yeah, and the baked spuds and chestnuts. It just don't seem the same, gitting your bargains at four o'clock in the afternoon.'

'Where's Dicky these days?' Queenie asked Lil.

'Out in the bleedin' desert, would you believe? Poor lad, brought up in dear old Pompey, now he's out there in all that horrible sand, with those nasty camels and pyramids and things. Hallelujah! Still, good old Monty's doin' all right now, ain't he? And what about your Billy, then!'

Queenie smiled. 'Lieutenant William Henry Ellis. Commissioned. Dad would have been so proud of him. I saw our Vera yesterday. Lady Muck isn't in it!'

Tears were running down Beatie's cheeks. Queenie

reached out and patted her hand. 'It's our John, isn't it, Ma?'

Beatie sobbed and nodded, pulling up the bottom of her apron to wipe her nose. Queenie and Lil exchanged a tear-laden glance.

Lil shook her head. 'I dunno. We try to keep going, try to keep cheerful, but our darlin' boys . . . Your poor Keith, Queenie. I was so sorry. I remember him coming back all sun-burned and bearded on Hannah's first birthday when you wasn't expecting him. And your wedding day. You was both so happy.'

Queenie drew a shuddering breath. 'Oh, don't, Lil.' She didn't want to start crying. She wouldn't be able to stop, the anxiety over Ray adding to her earlier griefs.

'But your little Hannah,' Lil continued on a more cheerful note. 'Just like 'er Dad, ain't she? I noticed before Josh took the kids out. Same eyes.'

Queenie nodded. 'She's a strange kid. Never know what she's thinking.' She'd warned the kids not to say anything about Uncle Ray, but Emma was likely to blurt it out. Oh well, she'd just pass him off as one of Keith's shipmates who was looking out for her. 'I must go and see poor Phyllis on Boxing Day.'

'She's a lovely girl,' sniffed Beatie. Queenie suffered a pang of angry jealousy. Phyllis could do no wrong in her mother-in-law's eyes.

They found some good food bargains at the market by forcing themselves to hang back till the last minute when the stall-holders were desperate to clear the merchandise, even though it meant missing out on some things they would have liked. They got some bits and pieces for the children's stockings. Beatie had unpicked some old jumpers and knitted up striped cardigans for the girls for their main present. Queenie had bought them both a doll and made little garments for them out of scraps.

'Be lovely to get your hands on an orange, though,' mourned Beatie as they lugged their bargains home. Josh, carrying the heaviest bags, trailed behind.

'But what a lovely surprise to get this little Christmas tree.'

'Shouldn't be surprised if they're not black market, but the coppers are turning a blind eye 'cos it's Christmas.'

'Yeah, but it's not as if they're being brought in by ships like food is. No-one's risking their life to bring in a load of Christmas trees.' They had got one or two other little extras from 'under the counter' too.

Beatie dug out her box of battered baubles and Hannah and Emma decorated the tree. The children then sat licking the ends of gummed strips of paper that some stall-holder had dug out of pre-war stock, and linking the circles to make chains which Queenie strung from the middle light to the picture rails. She clipped old burned-down candles to the branches of the tree.

'There.' She stood back to admire their efforts as the children clapped their hands. 'No one would know there's a bleedin' war on.'

Phyllis was pale and thin. A lifeless shadow of her former self.

'I loved Johnny so much. I wish we hadn't waited so long to get married and I wish we'd had children. The worst thing of all, Queenie, is that – is that . . .' She could not finish for crying.

Queenie's mouth and chin trembled. 'At least I've got a grave to mourn over. I know where my Keith is. That's what you mean, isn't it, Phyll?'

Her sister-in-law nodded. 'I can't let go, you see. I can't really feel he's . . . gone. We was both full of hope for the future a couple of years ago, wasn't we, Queenie, and now there's nothing left. Well, you're lucky, you've got your little girls.'

And Ray, I hope, thought Queenie, feeling thoroughly guilty. 'Come to the pictures with me tomorrow. What's on up the Palace?'

'I don't know. I don't want to go anyway.'

'You should try to get out a bit. It don't do no good sitting around moping. We might *all* be dead tomorrow. Funny, wasn't it, how in the beginning everyone used to rush out of the flicks to the shelter when Moaning Minnie went? Up in Felixstowe they don't bother no more. When the old All Clear flashes on the screen, nearly everybody's still sitting there.'

Phyllis smiled wanly.

'Here,' Queenie went on. 'D'you remember when we used to tango up Baker Street in the dark?' She wiggled her hips and arms. 'We giggled so much we nearly wet ourselves.'

'With your fat belly between us it was like dancing with a kangaroo – '

'Tssht. And there was that old tramp waving his willy about under the lamp-post that time, and we chased him down the alley.'

Phyllis gave a pale laugh. 'He was afraid he was goin' to get more than he bargained for. We was daft beggars in those days. Oh, you're a tonic, you are, Queen.'

Queenie hugged her. 'I know, I'll bring the kids round tomorrow and we'll go for a walk. You can show me the bomb damage.'

'Well, that's not a very cheerful prospect. Tell you what, though, we'll go on the bus to Handley's and have tea and listen to the orchestra. My treat. I've got nothing else to spend me money on these days.'

'Handley's. It was burned out, wasn't it? Good God,' marvelled Queenie, 'don't the war stop nothing in Pompey?'

The stricken city flashing by the bus windows brought tears to Queenie's eyes. Devastation everywhere. Streets of houses decimated, the smart shopping areas ruined, 'Look at those bleedin' kids playing on the bomb sites. It must be dangerous.'

'War games. That's what kids play nowdays.'

'Sad, isn't it?'

Handley's was like something out of another, more gracious world. They wandered round, admiring the glassware, the shoes, the dresses. 'Bloody hell. Eleven coupons!'

'Even if we could afford the money.'

Under the disapproving stare of a saleswoman, they tried on hats until the children grew bored, and then went to the restaurant for tea. The orchestra was now reduced to an elderly man at the grand piano and two spinsterly ladies on violins.

Hannah didn't like the fishpaste sandwiches, so Emma ate hers as well, but they all enjoyed the scones and jam. 'Let's request a tune,' suggested Queenie. 'What shall it be?'

'"I'm Dreaming of a White Christmas,"' said Hannah unexpectedly.

'Coo, haven't we heard enough of that this Christmas?' asked Queenie. 'Old Bing crooning away every time you switch the wireless on. Go on, then, Hannah, you go and ask the nice man to play it.'

Hannah was too nervous until Emma said she would go too, so they went up, hand-in-hand, to the little dais. The pianist smiled at the children and obliged. A little later, Queenie sent them back to ask for 'That Old Black Magic'. She and Phyllis tapped their feet and wagged their heads in time to the music.

'See, you're enjoying yourself, Phyll.' Queenie's eyes shone with pleasure. 'You should get out and about more.'

'I might if you was back in Pompey.'

'Well, it might happen sooner than you think.' *If Ray gives me the push.*

'Why's that then?'

Queenie shrugged. 'Oh, I'm getting a bit fed up with Felixstowe. And things have quietened down a bit here, haven't they?' The orchestra was playing 'You Are My Sunshine'. 'Oh, this tune reminds me of a young airman I knew at the pub where I work. He used to play it on his guitar and sing it to me. Jimmy. He was killed too – poor baby.'

Queenie looked down into her lap. Keith, Johnny, Jimmy. And now, was she going to lose Ray? How could she *bear* it if he stayed with his wife? But she had forced the issue, asked the impossible, hadn't she? She deserved all she got, she was a selfish cow! Oh, Ray, she mourned, I want you any way I can have you. If we could put things back as they were I'd just take what I could and be grateful. I wouldn't make any more demands.

'Penny for them,' said Phyllis.

Queenie looked up, the glimmer of tears in her eyes. 'I was just thinking what a bloody awful orchestra this is. They're murdering this tune.'

They travelled back to Felixstowe in early January snow. The train was late, the children grizzly, the flat cold and dreary. Queenie put the gas-fire full on in the living room, lit the oven in the kitchen and put hot-water bottles in their beds.

Was Ray out on patrol on this bitter night? Life was bad enough for poor sailors, soldiers and airmen, without them having to operate under these freezing conditions.

*Would* he come?

She arranged for Peggy to have Emma and Hannah after school the following afternoon – just in case. But waited in vain. Queenie felt almost suicidal. He was not coming. He had chosen to stay with his wife. That would be the right decision, she knew, but it hurt so much.

When the doorbell rang on the third day after her return, she flew to open it.

Ray stood there, enormous in his snow-dusted greatcoat and cap. His nose was red, his eyes wary. 'Hello, girl . . .'

'Ray! Oh, Ray, I shouldn't have – '

'It's all right. Everything's all right.'

Queenie's eyes widened. 'It is? How did she . . .? Come in, come in.' He entered and she shut the door behind him. They stood looking at each other cautiously. She was the first to speak.

'Ray, I've been so unhappy, so worried. I thought about us a lot while I been away and I realised it was selfish, wicked of me to put you in that position. It doesn't matter any more. I just want to be with you.'

A smile glowed in his dark eyes. 'I thought about you all the time, girl, and I knew that whatever it took, I had to be with you. But . . . I can't rush things. Do you understand? If you can be patient, it'll all come right in the end.'

'I can wait, Ray,' she said breathlessly, her hands clasped together at throat level, her eyes shining a beacon of joy. She hardly dare believe what he was saying – that one day they might be together. 'I can wait, darling.'

'I love you.'

She launched herself at him and was enclosed in his wet coat, kissed by his cold lips. She laughingly brushed some drops of melted snow from his beard. Then he put her from him. 'I'd better get this off.'

Taking the heavy coat from him, she shrugged it around her, enjoying his warmth, burying her nose in its masculine smell. 'I got the living room nice and warm for us – just in case.' She hung the coat up and took his cap.

'You *knew* I'd come?'

'I hoped, oh, I hoped you would.' She threw him an inviting look over her shoulder as she led him along the hall to the front room, where she had made a little nest of blankets and pillows in front of the fire.

'What's all this then?' he laughed.

'To welcome you back.' Her eyes shimmered with love and desire. 'The bedroom is so cold.' Her hands went to the bottom of his jersey.

Gathering her up against him, Ray kissed her hair, her eyelids, her cheeks and her lips. No more words were necessary as they quickly divested themselves of their clothes and sank down into the warm nest Queenie had lovingly made for them.

They abandoned themselves to passion as never before, the fire lending warm shadows and rosy tints to their twisting limbs in the dull light of the winter afternoon.

Later, sitting astride him, flushed with love-making, Queenie bent towards Ray's face, enclosing them both in the fragrant curtain of her hair. He reached up to cup her head in his big hands and they gazed into each other's bemused eyes.

'I never knew it could be like this,' he murmured with awe.

'I wish I could find words to tell you what I feel, but I can't. I love you, that's all. You are my ray of sunshine,' she giggled. 'I'm not a poet like you. All that stuff about gold and diamonds.'

'I'm no poet, either. But *you* make me feel – everything is possible.'

She put her cheek against his, murmuring shyly, 'You are my lover, my father and my friend. We're the luckiest people alive, aren't we?'

Snuggling down between Ray and the fire, Queenie asked what she knew was better not asked. 'Did you and Marjory – you know?'

'What d'you think?' he murmured against her neck. 'Look, I don't want to talk about Marjory. It was . . . difficult, you know? And it's between her and me, isn't it? You wouldn't like it, would you, if I discussed you with her?'

Queenie had to be content with that. She was not going to put any more pressure on him. It was enough, after all, to know that he had told his wife about her, and that he might leave her – eventually. She didn't want to think about that – it was his decision to make, wasn't it? That's what he had told her in the beginning. Perhaps his wife would throw *him* out, then neither of them need feel so guilty.

They were so much in love that for months Queenie thought she was the luckiest girl in the world. Until, in June, her luck ran out.

# · *Twenty-nine* ·

Peggy came with her husband Geoff to tell Queenie that Ray had been seriously wounded.

Queenie rushed to the kitchen to be sick in the sink. Peggy sat her down. 'Wounded, Queenie, not dead.' Ashen-faced, Queenie asked Geoff what had happened.

'There was a scrap off Cap Gris Nez last night, apparently. Ray was hit in the chest and stomach. He isn't dying but it's pretty serious. He was taken into Dover with several others. His boat has just returned.'

Queenie, dazed, got to her feet. 'I must go to him.'

'Is that wise?' Peggy asked, her pleasant face creased with concern. 'I hate to remind you, Queenie, but whatever Ray's intentions are, *you* are not his next-of-kin.'

Queenie's eyes were desolate. 'I know that only too well, but he loves me. I love him. I've got to go to him – to tell him.'

Peggy shook her head. 'But his wife – '

'If I go at once, I'll get there before her. I mean, it'll take a while for a telegram to reach her and then she's got to get up from Devon.'

'But what good will it do, Queenie? He'll be sent home to *her* when he's fit enough, you know that's how it's got to be.'

Queenie buried her face in her hands and sobbed. 'I g'got to see him. And he'll want to see me, I know he will.'

Peggy and Geoff exchanged a worried look. 'Well, if you really must go, you know we'll have the kids.'

'Thanks Peg, you're a real pal.' Queenie raised her ravaged face. 'You do understand, don't you? If Ray dies and I haven't told him that I'll always be waiting for him, I'll never forgive myself.'

Getting off the train at Dover brought back painful memories to Queenie of her visit of fifteen months earlier. Then, spring flowers were just coming into in bud; now, in spite of the war, summer was in its first tender blossoming. Then, she had come to bury her husband; now, she had come to see her wounded lover. Grief, guilt and tremulous hope were Queenie's companions as she made her way to the hospital.

The elderly receptionist directed her to Ward Ten, and walking down the corridor smelling of distinfectant, Queenie found herself praying that Ray's wounds would not be too serious, yet bad enough to keep him out of the rest of the war.

'We're run off our feet,' a harassed nurse told her. 'You're between visiting hours – '

'But I've come a long way.'

'Don't worry, we're letting relatives in to see our brave heroes. Matron's just doing her rounds. Take a seat for a minute, dear.'

There were a few other people waiting in the corridor. Queenie took a seat beside an elderly couple – some poor lad's parents. A young girl was crying and being comforted by an older woman. 'Come on, duckie, you don't want him to see you like this.'

Most of the Coastal Force's crews were such young boys; like the Airforce and young Jimmy Mallory. Queenie took off Peggy's fur coat, which she had borrowed for her previous visit to Dover, and sat nervously clutching a bag which held some apples, two past copies of *Picture Post* that Peggy's husband had given her and a pair of navy socks she had knitted for Ray.

She had looked at the magazines on the train. One was the March issue and was all about *The Beveridge Report*.

There was a lot of argument about it, and she didn't understand it all, but some old bloke, Sir William Beveridge, wanted to do great things for the poor. Social security it was called. Pensions, a National Health Service, unemployment pay. About bloody time too. When she thought of the hardships poor old Ma had gone through . . .

'Your husband is it, dear?' the woman next to her was asking.

'What? Oh, yes. I don't know how serious it is yet.'

The woman shook her head. 'My boy has lost a leg. It's terrible, but you know I'm almost glad. He'll be able to come home now, won't he?'

'I was thinking the same thing,' said Queenie. But they would send Ray home to his wife – to Marjory. Jealousy knifed through her. Well, painful as it was, she had to accept that. Meanwhile she had come to let him know that, whatever happened, whatever he decided, she loved him. If she never saw him again, at least he would know that.

A nurse came to tell them that they had an hour with the patients, but only two at a bedside please, and that Sister was at the desk to answer questions.

On legs like jelly, Queenie walked down the ward, surveying the two rows of beds holding injured men, some with visible bandages, some lying still and deathly pale. Please God – don't let him be too badly hurt. Some patients already had visitors at their bedsides, others watched the doorway hopefully. One lad gave her a lecherous wink.

Then she saw Ray.

But he was not alone. Queenie froze. Two women were at his bedside. An elderly woman on the far side and a fair-haired woman with her back to Queenie – Marjory. Ray lay on his back looking towards the older woman, presumably his mother, the bandages stark against his hairy torso.

Queenie hovered uncertainly, her heart beating like a tom-tom. She could go forward and introduce herself;

bring it all to a head. After all, Marjory knew about her. But should she? It would be embarrassing and she didn't want to upset Ray when he was ill. She did not know what to do.

Marjory stood up and went to the foot of the bed to rummage in a bag and with a jolt Queenie registered her thickened girth. She was pregnant. Looked about six months.

Conceived when he went home at Christmas. '*Did you and Marjory . . . you know?*' she had asked. 'What do you think?' he had answered. Not a direct lie but –

Queenie felt a scream building up inside her and the shopping bag dropped from her nerveless fingers, spilling its contents on the floor. Ray looked in her direction and shock immobilised his features, his eyes widening with dread, his mouth slack. He shook his head and she knew at that moment that he had not told Marjory about her.

'Who is it you're looking for, dear?' A middle-aged nurse approached her from the other end of the war. 'Oh, look, you've lost your apples.' She reached out to Queenie. 'Are you all right?'

Queenie tore her eyes away from Ray's beseeching gaze, crouched as his wife turned to see what her husband was looking at, and scrabbled for the contents of her bag. The nurse bent down too. 'Is something wrong, dear?' she asked.

Queenie nodded and the woman helped her to her feet. 'Come to the desk. We'll see if we can sort it out.'

Without a backward glance, Queenie walked out of Ray's life.

They gave her a cup of tea at the ward desk which she raised to her lips with a shaking hand. She could not give them any answers to their questions, her throat was tight with grief. A nurse brought her a couple of aspirins and some water. Eventually she managed to thank them and assure them that she would be all right. On shaky legs Queenie found her way out of the hospital and to a bus stop. She had a visit to make.

'St James's Cemetery, please.'

She walked along the paths between the old gravestones and tombs, to the current war graves. There were several more rows occupied now. She couldn't remember which row her husband's grave was in and, distressed, wandered up and down between the wooden crosses. Eventually she found it between that of a soldier with a foreign name and another sailor – the one he had been buried with.

The graves had grassed over. Someone had planted some flowers on the plots, she didn't know what they were. Keith's name on the cross swam before her eyes and the tears spilled over, the painful knot in her throat threatening to choke her.

She sank down on her knees. Where are you, my love? She cried in silent anguish. Have you been watching me making a fool of myself? A stupid, wicked fool. Forgive me. Please forgive me. I was so lonely, you see. Ray told me it was all over between him and Marjory and that we'd be together one day. At least I think he did. I wanted to believe him. But she's six months pregnant with their fourth child. He'll never leave her now. *He never was going to*. How could I have been so bloody stupid?

Slowly the lump in her throat dissolved and the tears flowed fast. She told Keith how Hannah and Emma were growing up and still asked after him. About her misery and her fears for the future. A light rain started falling, drops standing on the fur of her coat. The late afternoon was cool. The old castle on top of the hill stood sentinel. Shivering, she got to her feet to find her knees damp and muddy.

'Goodbye, my love.'

Somehow she walked down the hill to the railway station, munching an apple on the way. She had not eaten since breakfast.

Well, she told herself bitterly, *that* little episode was over and done with – she had been taken for a bloody fool. She had believed Ray. Bitterness gave way to common sense. He was a good man. She knew he had not intended to hurt her, and a little voice inside her murmured that she might have done the same thing if she'd wanted something badly enough and that was the only way to get it.

But she wasn't going to waste any more time over it. She had her kids to think of – and survival. Felixstowe had nothing to offer her now, even it it was safer. There she had lost Keith, Jimmy and Ray. She would pack up and go home to Pompey. Longing for her battered birthplace swept over her. She even longed for Ma – that was a turn-up for the book.

Yes. Hannah and Emma could go down to their grandparents in Cornwall. She wouldn't have to worry about them there. She would enrol for some war-work, they needed every woman they could get now.

She felt bruised, cynical – but determined. She would never, ever, allow herself to trust another man in her life.

But the children were not sent to Cornwall because when Queenie reached home, a letter was waiting on her doormat from Bernard Jackson.

Michael's ship had been blown up. They had received a letter from the War Ministry saying that her brother-in-law was 'missing' at sea. But a friend of his had been in the same convoy and witnessed the whole thing. He had written, telling them not to cling to false hope – there could have been no survivors.

Queenie's heart bled for the Jacksons and she was numb with shock and sorrow as she tried to write a few words of condolence. She could not take any more grief – the only way she was going to survive was to erect an impenetrable wall around herself.

# · Thirty ·

Vera Lynne sang 'We'll Meet Again' on *Force's Favourites* while Queenie pulled her hair back from her face and tucked it all round into a padded ring of material. Looking critically at herself in the mirror of the dressing table, she asked, 'There. Latest fashion. How does that look?'

'Like a black sausage,' said Phyllis watching from her lounging position on the bed. 'It's too tight. Loosen it a bit over your forehead.' She yawned. 'I don't know why you bother. Thought you was off men.'

'I am,' agreed Queenie, teasing the front hair out into a wave. 'Can't trust them further than you can throw 'em – rotten sods.'

'They're not all like that. Johnny weren't.'

'You weren't married long enough to find out.' Then seeing Phyllis's stricken face in the mirror, 'Oh, I'm sorry. I didn't mean that. John and Eddy take after our Dad. Honest and reliable. Suppose I've had bad luck with my men. But that doesn't mean I'm giving up on life – like you have.'

Queenie swivelled round to face her friend. 'Listen Phyll. Going back from Dover on that train I made a few decisions. Life's been pretty rotten to me, one way or the other. A lot of it's because of the war, I know. Everyone is suffering. But we've only got one life, for Christ's sake, and I'm not going to mope around and let it pass me by.'

'Oh, what you going to do about it then?' Phyllis tossed the challenge at her half-heartedly.

'I'm going to enjoy it as much as I can, while I can. I

might be blown up by a bleedin' bomb tomorrow. So – I'm going dancing, and to the pictures and out to the pubs. I'm not going to get involved with anyone, but I'm going to give a few chaps a run for their money. See if I don't.'

Phyllis looked shocked. 'You'll get yourself into trouble, Queenie.'

'So what! It's better than shrivelling up like you.' She looked despairingly at the girl who lolled in front of her with no make-up on her thin face and her fair hair hanging straight and lifeless.

Continuing with determination, she said, 'Our John was the best there was, but he's gone, Phyll, and you've got to face up to it. You're still a girl. Come on, live a little. We'll go to Kimbells in Osborne Road tomorrow night with my friend Sally from work. She says all the young officers hang out there – how about a bit of class for a change, eh? Come on. It'll be fun. I only came back to Portsmouth to cheer you up, you know.'

Phyllis shrugged. 'I don't know how you do it. Queen – straight I don't – but you always manage to get the better of things. I mean, you seem to have got over Ray – '

'Like hell I have! It's just what I said, I am *not* going to let it get me down.'

'What about the kids. Aren't you missing the kids?'

Queenie's face clouded. ''Course I am, but they'll be better off at Shamley Green, away from the bombs. Mrs Walker was ever so nice. Her kids are grown up, "flown the nest" she said. And she said she was pleased to have such nice little girls to look after.'

She had hated leaving them there though, just outside Guildford. The evacuation lady had assured her that Mrs Walker was a kind and responsible woman whose earlier evacuees had returned to their homes. It was a clean, semi-detached house in a village with a nice little school nearby for Hannah, which Emma could attend in the mornings. It seemed the best thing all round. But Emma had cried when she left, and Hannah had looked stony-faced, accusing.

Well, they couldn't go to Cornwall, with all the grief going on there, so what else could she do?

'What about your job at Airspeed?' Phyllis asked. 'You enjoying it?'

'Got a transfer to the Embodiment Loan Store – '

'What's that for Chris'sake?'

'It's where all the plugs, sockets and components – bits and pieces to you – are stored. I have to check them, shelf them, and then issue them for various jobs. I got sick of the noise on the factory floor, with the machines going and *Worker's Playtime* blaring out. It was boring too, standing there pulling levers down on a milling machine, making bracing-tube sockets correct to a thousandth of an inch, or sitting at a bench and checking hundreds of nuts and bolts. So I sort of – ' she grinned ' – gave the foreman the eye, and he asked if I'd like a nice little job.'

Phyllis shook her head in wonderment. 'Don't know how you do it.'

'If you've got it, don't waste it, I say. Mind you, he's becoming a bit of a pest, keeps coming in for a grope. I'm finding it a bit difficult to sort of discourage him without offending him. Still, it's probably better than greasing and repairing old railway engines. Look at your nails.'

'I love my old locomotives. Wouldn't change my job for anything. And why should I give a damn about my nails?'

'Because, like I say, you shouldn't give up. Why don't we get a flat together, Phyll?' Queenie's face was animated. 'You must be fed up living with your fam'ly and I don't think it's fair, me pushing poor Josh out his bedroom and him sleeping on the settee. Besides,' she groaned, 'having had my freedom, I don't think I can stand being with Ma for much longer.'

'I'll think about it.'

'I . . . er,' Queenie's face coloured, 'had a letter from Ray. Redirected . . .'

Phyllis sat up. 'Bloody cheek! What did *he* want after giving you all that grief?'

Queenie shrugged. 'Said he was sorry.' Her lips were tight. 'He never meant to hurt me but when it came to it he just couldn't tell his wife about me. He'd thought it would all work out in the end.' She turned back to the mirror. 'Oh, this bloody hairstyle doesn't suit me.' She started pulling the pins out angrily, ripping the padded ring from her head. 'I suppose he thought he'd be killed and Marjory and me'd be left grieving, both of us thinking he was ours . . .'

'I'm so sorry, Queen.' Phyllis wiped her eyes.

Queenie looked at herself in the mirror, unseeing, recalling the other things he had written. He had loved them both – in different ways. Gold and diamonds. But his duty was to his family. And he didn't know how much use he'd be to them now. Poor sod.

But she was no saint. She felt betrayed and bitter. And, as she had told Phyllis, she was going to go out and enjoy herself as if nothing mattered. It was her way of coping.

Picking up her brush, she began brushing her hair vigorously. 'So you see, I've just got to pick meself up and get on with me life, and that's what you've got to do, Phyll.'

Phyllis got off the bed, bent and hugged her sister-in-law, looking over her shoulder into the mirror. How pinched and pale she looked in comparison with Queenie, in spite of the latter's recent suffering. Her friend was a survivor, but *she* had let herself be crushed by sorrow. 'You're right, Queen. I don't half look a mess. Come on, wash me hair and curl it for me. We'll go to that dance tomorrow. Yes, and perhaps we'll see if we can find a flat.'

Phyllis turned up at Beatie's flat the next night looking vastly improved, with shiny hair curling under at the ends and a cheerful expression on her pretty face. She was wearing a blue blouse and navy skirt under her coat.

Queenie looked stunning in a red and white gingham

dress with a rounded neckline. 'Like me Rita Hayworth hairstyle?' Her hair, with side parting, fell in luxuriant waves to her shoulders.

'She looks lovely, don't she, Ma?' Phyllis asked of Beatie who sat by the gas fire.

'She's all right. But you two behave yourselves, do you hear me?'

Queenie grimaced. 'Not if I can help it.'

Beatie shook her head.

'Stockings? *Where* did you get them?' asked Phyllis in envy?'

'Leg paint,' laughed Queenie, twirling round. 'Look's all right if you don't get too close. Come into the bedroom and we'll do yours. I didn't trust Ma to draw a seam up the back with me eyebrow pencil. Zig-zags aren't in fashion.'

The two girls disappeared, giggling, into Josh's bedroom. 'Ooh, it's bloody cold,' complained Phyllis as Queenie painted her legs with the brown dye on a wad of cotton wool. 'It's made me legs go all goose-pimply.'

They drew seams up the backs of each other's legs and then Queenie insisted on Phyllis putting on some make-up. 'Only powder and lipstick,' she protested.

They came out of the bedroom, coats over their arms, to find Eddy standing in front of the fireplace. He looked them up and down critically. 'Where you two off to then?'

'Dancing at Kimbells,' Queenie challenged him, noticing how his jaw was working as he regarded Phyllis.

'Are you going to let them go out looking like this, Ma?' he asked with lowered brow.

'Like what?' asked Queenie defiantly.

'It ain't nothing to do with me,' complained Beatie. 'They're adults.'

'You look like . . . a couple of tarts,' said Eddy angrily. 'I don't like it.'

'Thank *you*,' answered Queenie. 'A little bit of make-up is no sin. Don't be such a stick-in-the-mud, Edward dear.

Look, why don't you come with us? Be our escort. You can make sure we behave ourselves.'

'You know I don't dance,' he grumbled. 'And I'd be bored stiff watching you two making fools of yourself. You don't want me with you, cramping your style,' he said bitterly, giving his sister-in-law an imploring look. 'Don't let Queenie lead you astray, Phyllis – '

'Get him!' exclaimed his sister angrily.

'It ain't right, Queen. You're both widows.'

Phyllis coloured with embarrassment.

'Yes, and it's about time we become "merry" ones an' all,' stated Queenie. 'There's enough doom and gloom around with out you trying to make us feel guilty.'

'We're only going to have a little bit of fun, Eddy,' said Phyllis placatingly.

'And it's none of your damn business, brother dear.' Queenie grabbed her sister-in-law's arm. 'Come on, Phyll, or it'll all be over by the time we get there.'

'You watch out for those bloody Yanks,' shouted Eddy after them.

'Oh we will, don't worry. We'll grab a couple of them double-quick,' laughed Queenie, excited by the prospect of something new. American soldiers billeted at Hilsea Barracks.

'"Over-paid, over-sexed and over here", that's what they're saying about the Yanks,' Phyllis informed her as they walked briskly down the Square to the bus stop.

'Our chaps are just jealous – '

'Yes, but you can't blame them. Those Americans have lovely uniforms and they look very smart and . . . clean-cut. I've heard their shop is stuffed with chocolate and cigarettes, and things we can't get. The kids run after them all the time begging for gum. They seem nice and friendly.'

On the top deck of the trolleybus, trams now being obsolete in Portsmouth, Queenie lit a cigarette.

Phyllis refused one. 'Eddy hates to see women smoking.'

Queenie gave her a narrowed look. 'Since when does it worry you what Eddy thinks?'

'I don't really, but in fact I don't like smoking.'

'You know,' Queenie said thoughtfully, 'I got the distinct impression that Eddy was more annoyed with me "leading you astray" tonight than he cared about what I was going to get up to.'

'I suppose he does keep an eye on me, come to think of it.'

'I wonder why?' asked Queenie with sly suggestiveness.

Phyllis frowned slightly and then blushed bright red.

'You don't think . . .?' pressed Queenie.

''Course not!' Phyllis's denial was a shade too emphatic. 'He's me brother-in-law.'

'That doesn't mean anything. Phyll, I do believe our Eddy's sweet on you.' She dug her side with her elbow and gave a delighted smile. 'Oh, it would really please me and Ma – '

'Don't be daft!'

'My lips are sealed.'

They enjoyed their evening out and danced with some nice young officers, but the Yanks had not yet discovered Kimbells.

A few days later, having embarked on her new life-style, that of having fun, Queenie let herself into her mother's flat at seven in the morning as quietly as possible. Biting her lower lip she pressed the door closed and stood listening. All was quiet. Ma must still be asleep. Breathing a sigh of relief, she tiptoed the few steps to her bedroom. Pulling off her clothes she slipped into her nightdress. Oh, she felt awful – bitterly ashamed and talk about hangover! Her head was throbbing and she felt sick at what she had done. She needed a hot bath and a cup of tea.

She crept along to the kitchen to put the kettle on and light the geyser – and nearly jumped out of her skin. Beatie was sitting at the little kitchen table.

'Oh, hallo, Ma,' she said cheerfully, feeling flustered, 'You gave me a fright. I'm dying for a cuppa. What gets you up so early?'

She knew the answer before her mother spoke, from the expression of outrage on her face. Beatie stood up, pulling the tattered dressing gown closed across her chest, her hair, now rusty grey, in its customary night-time plait. 'Where've you bin?' she hissed with narrowed eyes.

'I . . . what d'you mean?' But she knew the game was up and couldn't meet her mother's eyes.

'I bin up most of the night, worrying about you. That's what I mean. Where've you bin?'

Queenie coloured. 'Oh, you shouldn't have worried. I mean, I'm a big girl now.'

'I know you wasn't with Phyllis. Eddy called in on his way home and said she had a cold and you went off somewhere else.'

'I met up with some mates from work. Went for a drink. Had a bit too much,' she forced a laugh, 'so I went home with Sally.'

'Pull the other one!'

'What?'

'I don't believe you.'

Queenie shrugged, feigning indifference, took the kettle off the gas-stove and and went to the sink. 'Believe what you like, I'm free, white and over twenty-one. Sorry you had a sleepless night, though.'

Beatie grabbed her by the shoulder, swung her round and slapped her hard across the face. 'Liar! Slut.' Water slopped out of the kettle in her daughter's hand.

Queenie's eyes blazed along with her stricken cheek. For a moment she was tempted to slap her mother back. 'Don't you *ever* hit me again, Ma,' she said through clenched teeth. 'Do you hear me? It's none of your business what I do. And if you don't like it, I'll move out. Phyllis and me are thinking of getting a flat together anyway.'

Beatie's cheeks were scarlet with anger. 'Make it all the

easier for you, won't it? You keep away from that girl, d'you hear? She's decent.'

'Meaning I'm not?'

'Meaning you've always been trouble. I thought getting pregnant at sixteen was bad enough. But your poor husband's no sooner in his grave that you pick up with a married man – '

'I *told* you Ray was going to leave his wife. We fell in love – '

'Love! You didn't care about his family, did you? As long as you got what you wanted.'

'That's just not fair. You don't know the half of it.'

'And I don't want to. But I can guess what you were up to last night. If your poor father was alive . . . he'd disown you.'

Queenie stared at her mother, her eyes filling with tears. She turned and walked out of the kitchen. In her bedroom she flung herself on the bed and wept. *Oh, Dad, I didn't meant to do it. I'm so sorry.*

She was sorry now that she had, in a moment of weakness, told her mother about Ray. She might have known that she wouldn't understand, wouldn't have any sympathy for her lonely, battered daughter when what she needed most was a hug and a kind word.

But she deserved her mother's scorn and disgust for this latest escapade. She couldn't believe it this morning when she had woken up in a strange bed, beside a strange man. She had looked, appalled, at the ginger head resting on the next pillow. The mouth slack in sleep, ragged snores issuing from a broad nose. A quick glance around the room showed his bell-bottomed trousers flung over a chair with her dress. She had no recollection of how she had got there, or of undressing. Or anything else.

It had come back to her with a sickening rush. She slid out of bed so as not to wake the man and pulled on her clothes, her one desire to get out of Totterdell's Hotel as quickly and unobtrusively as possible. Creeping down the stairs she saw no-one as it was before seven, and once in the street, ran down St George's Square as one pursued.

Slowing down with a stitch in her side, she had recalled the events of the previous night when she had called for Phyllis to go the pictures and found her sister-in-law with a cold and not wanting to go out. Walking back from the house Phyllis shared with her parents, Queenie had been fed-up and bored with the prospect of an evening at home with her mother. On impulse she had popped round to Victory Road, past the little house she had shared with Keith and into the Victory for a quick port and lemon. No harm in that, or so she thought.

The pub was full of sailors – liberty men – a lot of them with girls. She had been amused to see 'Pompey Nell and 'Big Joan' getting off with a few customers. As a child she had not understood what their trade was but had been warned to give them a wide berth. Ma didn't know that she had sometimes earned a penny or two doing their shopping for them, but she had never been into their house.

Well, it was inevitable really that Queenie had soon attracted the attention of a group of Jacks. They came over to her and plied her with drinks. She kept saying she had to go, but they didn't want her to, and she felt sorry for them. Some of them were only boys, away from home for the first time and fighting a bloody war.

Besides, they were from *Hornet*, the Coastal Force's base over at Gosport. On torpedo and gun boats. She felt a bond with them and was proud to tâlk about Keith, HMS *Beehive* at Felixstowe, and how she was a widow.

She knew she was drinking too much and kept saying she had to get home. Eventually one of them got up, took her arm, and said he'd see her safely home. There was a bit of argument between the sailors and some suggestive remarks. A coin was tossed.

'What d'you think I am?' she had laughed. 'The bleedin' prize?' The ginger-haired one won the toss.

'I'll be all right.' She tried to resist but knew she was unsteady on her feet. What had happened after that? The sailor got her outside and she told him which direction she lived in, but she had no recollection of anything else till she had woken up in Totterdell's Hotel. She *had* been the prize.

Now, crying on her bed, she hated herself. She felt soiled, and appalled that she could be taken advantage of so easily. That she was lonely and had been bitterly hurt, and her life made no sense any more, was no excuse for behaving like a whore. Ma was right to be disgusted with her. She was the lowest of the low.

An uneasy truce was established by degrees between mother and daughter over the next few days. Queenie apologised to Beatie and attempted to vindicate herself. Beatie was stony-faced and unyielding but the incident was not spoken of again.

There was no more talk of finding a flat with Phyllis either. Queenie thought she would be safer under her mother's eagle eye, though she realised it could not go on indefinitely. She wondered what she was going to do with her life. She missed her children.

Mrs Walker was kind to her little evacuees, and her husband took little notice of them, so the children were reasonably happy at first. They had each other.

Hannah liked school and had fallen in love with one of the big boys. She told Emma she was going to marry him when she grew up. Emma sometimes cried for her Mummy, and Hannah did her best to comfort her little sister.

Then two more children arrived from London and things took a turn for the worst. Frank and Betty Love were quite unlovable, being dirty, rough and rude. Added to which, Betty told lies and often got the younger children blamed for misdemeanours.

Mrs Walker, tried beyond patience, took to scolding all the children and her husband went around with a scowl on his face.

Emma started to wet the bed, and by the end of the week, Hannah and Emma had caught lice from the Cockneys. Exasperated, Mrs Walker got advice from the Welfare people and was given a special potion along with rubber hats. All four heads were thoroughly treated and the children put to bed with rubber hats on.

Hannah could not sleep, it burned so. After some hours of trying to be brave, she swung down from the top bunk, careful not to wake Emma in the lower one, or the unlovely Loves in the other bunk beds. She crept down to the kitchen.

Poking her rubber-hatted head fearfully round the door, she saw Mrs Walker sitting at the table darning socks as she listened to the wireless. Hannah dared a piteous 'Aunty'.

The woman looked up with an annoyed expression on her face. 'What is it now?'

'It stings.' Hannah burst into tears.

Mrs Walker's tutted. 'Come here, then.' Hannah looked up into the woman's stern face which softened slightly. 'You've got to keep it on, to get rid of those horrid nits. Tell you what, I'll make us a nice cup of cocoa, shall I?'

Hannah nodded and listened to Mrs Walker's grumbles as she made the hot drinks; about wanting to do her bit, but how unfair it was that they expected her to cope with more than her fair share, and those dreadful London children. Hannah's head still stung, but 'Aunty' gave her a little cuddle after the cocoa and the bit of sympathy went a long way to helping her discomfort.

'Come on, now, time for bed. Go and spend a penny, You'll be all right now, won't you?'

Hannah did not really think she would be, but nodded obediently. Mrs Walker took her upstairs by the hand and whispered in the bedroom, 'There, look at your little sister. Sleeping like an angel. She's not making a fuss.'

However, shortly after this, Emma, now immaculate in head, caught German measles at school and was so poorly that she had to go to hospital. Hannah was desperately unhappy without her and could only guess at what her little sister was feeling, all alone and ill in a strange place. And Mrs Walker, at the end of her tether, told the Evacuation Committee that she could not be expected to cope with four children, particularly one that wet the bed, so little Emma was discharged to a local children's home.

Hannah was allowed to visit on Sunday afternoons. They had fun on the swings and slide in the garden, and they could have either butter or jam on their bread at tea-time but Emma cried when the time came for her sister to leave. 'Be a good girl, now. I'll come next week,' Hannah told her, but Emma went on crying and Hannah hurt inside, knowing it was all wrong but not knowing what to do about it.

Then Mummy came and Hannah could see she was very angry with Mrs Walker. She was sent into the garden but she could hear their screaming voices coming from the kitchen. Mummy came out with her bags and told her that they were collecting Emma from the home and she was taking them down to Cornwall to stay with their Granny and Grandpa.

'And you'll have to be very good and do as you're told. Granny isn't feeling very well since Uncle Michael's . . . been lost at sea.'

Hannah was very sad for nice Uncle Michael whom she had met once or twice. 'The sea is such a big place to get lost in, isn't it, Mummy? I hope Uncle Michael can walk on the water like Jesus did, then he can find his way home again.'

# · Thirty-one ·

'I was so angry I could have knocked that woman's block off,' Queenie told her mother and Phyllis. 'Fancy them putting little Emma into that home and no-one telling me for weeks – bloody authorities!'

Beatie wiped her eyes and sniffed. 'Poor little sods, having to be away from their families. Still they'll be all right with the Jacksons, won't they? And please God this latest bombing won't go on for much longer and they'll be able to come home. How was your mother-in-law?'

'Crushed. They looked so old and haggard. Both their sons! But having the kids will give them something to think about.' She blew her nose. 'Oh, I do miss them, Ma.'

'A letter's come for you. Official, from the Admiralty.'

The envelope contained a 'Certificate Of The Inspector Of Seamen's Wills' in respect of the effects of her late husband, and a postal draft. Queenie read it aloud with furrowed brow. 'Residue of wages; two pounds, eighteen shillings and sixpence. Cash found; one pound, thirteen shillings. Post War Credit; one pound, eleven and six. War Gratuity; fifteen pounds, and Naval Prize Money; four guineas. That adds up to a grand total of – ' she looked at the postal draft ' – twenty-five pounds and seven shillings.'

The three women looked at each, shocked. 'What price a life?' asked Queenie bitterly.

*

Queenie, Phyllis and Sally had an occasional night out and it took their minds off their problems.

Kimbells was posher and more intimate than South Parade Pier Ballroom, which Queenie and Phyllis used to frequent before the war, and which was now closed to the public. Chandeliers, little tables, a dance band and lots of girl-hungry young officers; among them a group of American Army officers in smooth beige uniforms, hogging the bar.

The three girls, feeling rather conspicuous, ordered lemonade shandies and occupied one of the tables, Queenie and Sally hiding their awkwardness with jokes and laughs, but Phyllis looked uncomfortable. She had been reluctant to come. Queenie was glad she had though – safety in numbers and all that. She was never going out on her own again.

A tall American loped over and asked Queenie to dance. He was a 'loo-tenant' he told her, from Vermont. 'You sure are lovely, honey,' he murmured, holding her too close. But he wasn't John Wayne or Clark Gable, and after a couple of dances the novelty of the uniform, the accent and the gum-chewing wore off.

Queenie looked over to where a group of English officers stood in their familiar dark uniforms. Catching the eye of the most gorgeous one, she winked at him, hoping he would come and rescue her.

The American had her in a tight clinch now. 'How about it, honey?'

'How about what?' As if she didn't know.

'Some action. You know what I mean. Bet you'd like some nylon stockings, eh?'

Wouldn't she just? But not at that price. 'No thanks. Leg paint is much cooler.'

He chuckled. 'You don't have to worry none. There's no lead in my pencil.'

What exactly did that mean? Not that it mattered. 'I'm not that sort of girl,' she told him frostily, looking up into his lust-glazed eyes and suggestive smirk. His sweaty hand was burning into her back and his swollen crotch was thrusting against her belly.

'Get lost!' Disgusted, she was trying to break away when the fair-haired officer appeared at her side.

'I think you've monopolised this English Rose long enough – *buddy*. May I have the pleasure of this dance, young lady?'

'The pleasure is all mine,' Queenie told him twisting out of the American's grasp.

'Now see here – ' said the latter, but she was already gliding away in the other man's arms, laughing over her shoulder at the American.

'I only go with English blokes,' she called. 'I'm patriotic, see?' She smiled up at her rescuer, pleased with herself that she had the power to bring him to her side. 'Whew, thanks.'

'Thought he was coming on a bit heavy. Arrogant bastards, these Yanks. You're a good dancer, and very pretty with it.' He smiled down at her.

'Thank you, kind sir,' she sparkled up at him as they foxtrotted round the floor. He really was *something*. 'I wonder why English compliments sound so much nicer than Yankee ones?'

They exchanged names, then nodding his head towards a group of young officers standing near the bar, he said, 'My friend over there wants to meet you. The tall, dark one.'

Queenie's glance locked with that of a slim young man who was watching her. She raised an eyebrow and looked up at her partner. 'What's the matter with him, then? Why can't he come and introduce himself? Lost his tongue, has he?'

Bill pursed his lips. 'He's a bit shy. Hasn't had a lot to do with girls. Hasn't had much time, you see. Straight out of nappies these days and into training.'

'Oh? What about you, then, Lieutenant?' she flirted. 'You're not shy.'

'I'm older. Got a bit of experience in before this shower started. I'm getting married next leave, actually.'

Queenie was disappointed. 'So, you're just a messenger boy, then? And I thought you were after me.'

'Oh, I would be – if I wasn't spoken for.' He grinned. 'Come and be nice to the poor lad.'

Reluctantly, Queenie allowed herself to be led to the bar. The young officer who smiled uncertainly at her approach was quite good-looking, with straight dark hair, a thin, bony face and a Roman nose. Big, clear, grey eyes. Thoroughly decent-looking. She preferred Bill.

'Let me introduce Sub-Lieutenant Paul Knight, a respectable and promising chap. This delightful young lady is Queenie Jackson.'

Paul Knight smiled nervously, revealing large, white teeth. 'How do you do?'

'All right, thank you.' Queenie gave him a saucy grin. 'Mine's a port and lemon, please.'

'Oh, oh certainly.' He tore his eyes away from her and ordered two drinks from the bar. Queenie was rather cross when Bill excused himself, leaving her alone with Paul Knight. She looked around for Phyllis, but she was dancing with another naval chap and looking quite animated. She had really perked up since Queenie took her in hand. 'Shall we find a table?' asked Paul Knight, turning from the bar with her drink in one hand and a gin and tonic in the other.

'All right,' she answered with little enthusiasm, leading the way to an unoccupied one. She was only here for a bit of light-hearted fun, but she sensed this chap was going to be heavy-going. She sat down and he put her drink in front of her. 'So Queenie,' he sat beside her, a keen expression on his face, 'have you always lived in Portsmouth?'

'All my life. I come from a naval family and I'm proud of it.' She was also proud of the way she spoke, hardly made a slip these days when she made the effort. 'My father – he was in submarines in the last war – said I've got sea-water in my veins.' She gave him the full benefit of her most seductive smile and was gratified to see the bony Adam's apple in his throat go up and down in a nervous swallow. It would be fun to lead him on a bit. She fluttered her eyelashes as she told him a bit more about her Dad. 'What about you, Paul? Where were you born?'

'Near Faversham, in Kent. Not far from Canterbury. Do you know it?' She shook her head. 'Lovely sailing area. The Swale and the Thames Estuary. I've sailed since I was a tiny lad.'

He didn't half sound posh. 'But now you're a real sailor, on a real ship.'

He nodded. 'Motor gun boat.'

'Really?' This was more interesting. 'I'm always meeting chaps – '*though I wish I'd never met that ginger-haired one* ' – from the "Costly Farces".'

He laughed at the old joke. 'Coastal Forces are proving their worth now. Got the Jerries worried, for all their superiority in numbers and armaments. I've done my time as midshipman. Recent commission and I've been down at HMS *Bee*, working-up with the crew in my new steam gun boat, *Grey Ghost*. Superb little ship.'

'Ooh, that's a funny name. Anyway I thought naval boats only had numbers? My Dad's submarine was the *E1*.'

'Normally, yes, but we are just within the limits of length that entitles us to have a name and it gives the boat more personality somehow. So we decided on *Grey Ghost*, *Grey Phantom*, *Spectre*, *Waith* and *Demon*.'

She gave him an arch look. 'Should you be telling me all this? "Careless talk . . ." and all that.'

'You don't look like a spy. I'm sure the Germans don't have such pretty ones.' He grinned, pleased with his compliment. 'I can't wait for a bit of excitement in her – the real thing. Only been on trials so far. Not for nothing are gunboats called "The Spitfires of the Sea". Shooting down aircraft is our speciality.'

His face was alight and in his enthusiasm he had lost his bashfulness. Queenie's eyes sparkled at him. She was thinking she would quite like to kiss him on his well-bred mouth. He was nice, and a man with such clear eyes could only be honest and trustworthy. Far too good for the likes of her. 'But here I am going on and on about myself,' he was saying. 'What do *you* do, Queenie?'

'I'm in airplanes. You know the airspeed factory on Eastern Road?' He shook his head. 'Well, I'm in the Embodiment Loan Store. Sounds ever so important, doesn't it. I check parts and issue them for jobs. But, coming from a naval family, I'd like to have joined the Wrens, really.'

'What's stopping you?'

'My kids.' Amused, she watched the smile leave his face and his eyes slide to her left hand and her wedding ring.

'Oh. How many have you got?'

'Two girls. Hannah's nearly seven and Emma's five.'

'I see.' He was finding it difficult to hide his disappointment. 'And your husband?'

She took pity on him then and told him she was widowed.

His cheeks reddened with embarrassment. 'I'm so awfully sorry. Things must be hellishly difficult for you.'

'Yes, but the kids are away with their grandparents at the moment. Safe and sound. I hope it won't be too long before they can come home again.' To change the subject from one she found depressing, she commented, looking at the wavy stripe on his sleeve, 'You're not a regular then. What were you doing before the war?'

'I had just started at university, studying Law.'

'Ooh. I'm impressed.' He would soon get bored with an ignoramus like *her*, but no doubt, like all the men she met, he was just after a bit of 'the other', if he ever plucked up the courage to suggest it. And if he did, he was going to be even more disappointed. 'Shall we dance?'

'If you like. I'm not awfully good at it, I'm afraid.'

'Don't worry, I'll show you.' She gave a twirl and put her hand in his. He held her loosely as if afraid to get too close, and the hand holding hers was slightly damp. Strange that a lad who was anxious to get out and fight the enemy, risking life and limb, should be so nervous with a girl. She guessed he was a few years younger than she was, and, like Jimmy, had not yet had the chance to prove himself a man in *that* way. 'Relax. I promise I won't stamp on your toes.'

'I'm afraid I might step on yours, though. This is a waltz, isn't it? I'm not too bad at this. One-two-three, one-two-three . . .'

They progressed reasonably well around the floor until the tempo changed to a tango. Oh he'd be hopeless at that. 'There, that wasn't too painful, was it?' Queenie pulled him by the hand to the table where Phyllis and Sally were sitting, flanked by Bill and another young officer.

Her sister-in-law was obviously relieved to see her. Introductions were made, the third man being Dutch, by the name of Keyes. The three young officers talked excitedly about the surrender of Italy.

'It is er, a turning point,' said Keyes in his heavy accent, though his English was good.

'"A toehold in Europe", old boy,' Paul quoted enthusiastically.

'The Hun is on his own in Europe now!' Bill grinned.

'Oh, do you really think it's the turning point? Wouldn't that be bl-, er, wouldn't that be marvellous?' Queenie's eyes sparkled up at Paul and he reached over and squeezed her hand, blushing a little as he did so. In spite of her determination to be aloof, she felt a familiar little tingle at the contact. He was so like Jimmy – a sweet boy. *Watch it, girl!* she told herself, gently disengaging her hand.

Bill asked Queenie to dance which caused Paul Knight

to look annoyed and Queenie to smile to herself. She wasn't his property and, whatever he thought, she had no intention of becoming so.

When next Paul danced with her, he asked her to go to the cinema with him the next night. 'We're on a shore leave until twenty-three hundred hours. Then a patrol in the Channel.'

'Won't you need some sleep before that?'

He smiled disarmingly. 'I'd rather go to the flicks with you. I'll lie in the next morning.'

Queenie shrugged. 'If you like. We live quite near the harbour. Do you know the Queen's Cinema in Queen Street? It'll be the nearest for you.' He said he'd find it. 'There's that good film on this week, *Casablanca*. Phyll and I were going to see it anyway.'

'Sounds fine, but er, any chance of you coming on your own?'

'I can't let Phyll down, can I? Look, you bring a mate too.' His face clouded. 'Look, Paul, it's only fair to tell you now that I don't want to get involved with anyone. Not till this bl- rotten war is over at any rate. I've had enough grief to last a lifetime.' *That way I can't be hurt again.* 'Let's just have a bit of fun.'

He nodded. 'Fine.'

'Time we went,' Phyllis stood up as they went back to the table, 'or we'll miss the last bus.'

'Let me see you to the bus-stop,' Paul Knight offered, looking at his watch. 'I've got twenty minutes or so before my transport comes.'

'We'll all come,' said Bill.

Queenie raised an eyebrow at the other girls. 'All right – if you want.' Paul tucked his arm possessively through hers and Queenie found herself thinking again that, although he wasn't her type, he was a nice lad. Bill and Keyes larked around on the way to the bus-stop and they all had a good laugh. Sally's bus came first and they sent her noisily on her way.

'Tomorrow. Seven o'clock outside the Queen's. If we don't turn up, you'll know why. Don't wait,' Paul said as the next bus came along.

Queenie wiggled her fingers at him as they boarded. The girls went upstairs and looked down at the young men grinning up at them from the pavement, standing to attention and saluting as the bus pulled away. Queenie blew them a kiss. 'That Paul's a bit soppy,' Queenie told Phyllis, 'but nice with it. It'll be fun to go to the flicks tomorrow night with him and his mates. Sally's got something else on, though.'

'I don't know about all this . . . gallivantin',' said Phyllis uncertainly. 'I feel sort of awkward with these blokes. They're a bit posh for me.'

'Oh, come on, you only live once. Anyway, just 'cos we don't speak posh, doesn't mean we're not as good as they are – in things that matter.'

'What things?'

'Well, we were brought up proper, weren't we? We obey the ten commandments – well, you do.' She looked out of the window, wishing it were true of herself. Perhaps if she was an atheist like Keith it wouldn't worry her so much, being a sinner.

She'd been a toe-rag of a kid, hadn't she? Disobedient, back-chatting, always in trouble with Ma. A bit of thieving, but only coal and the odd thing off a market stall. Well, all the kids round her way had done that. It was a necessity of life.

But as she grew old enough to know better, she had committed real sins. She had lied. Got herself pregnant outside marriage – was that one of the ten commandments? She had committed adultery with Ray knowing that was a sin, even if it didn't feel like it at the time.

Lust, and 'coveting thy neighbour's wife' – husband in this case – two of the Seven Deadly Sins. She couldn't remember the other five but was willing to bet that she'd committed them all at some time or other. 'Thou shalt not kill' – she hadn't murdered anyone yet.

'Here, Phyll,' she asked. 'If it's a sin to commit murder, do you reckon it's a sin to kill in battle?'

'Dunno.'

'If it is, half the world's population are guilty. Hell will be bursting at the seams. Won't be room for me down there.' Perhaps her night with that sailor wouldn't seem so very terrible after all! But bad enough. Even if she had not really known what she was doing at the time, she could never forgive herself for doing it. She had really thought she was on the slippery slope to damnation after that.

Going up the cemetery to ask Dad's forgiveness the next day had not helped, because when she found that weedy mound of earth and remembered how she had spent the money for his headstone, she had really cried. She had started a new fund the next day. It would take a long time, but by staying on with Ma she could could put a few pennies aside each week.

The next evening's assignation did not turn out quite as planned even though Paul, Bill and Keyes turned up as arranged.

Queenie was pleasantly surprised anew at the clear-cut, good looks of Paul Knight, and it was a giggle to be going into the scruffy old Queen's – 'the flea-pit' the locals called it – with three young officers.

They had a good laugh at the 'B' film, a Laurel and Hardy, even though Queenie was aware that Paul was paying her as much attention as he was the screen. She remembered her first date at the flicks with Keith. That had been so exciting. She had thought he was the answer to her prayers. Poor darling.

The Pathé Pictorial News was, to the delight of the young men, all about the surrender of Italy. After a bit of noisy chatter an elderly man turned round to shush them and got the standard reply from Bill, 'Don't you know there's a war on, mate?' They settled down to the main film amid good-humoured laughter from the people around them. 'These are some of our fighting boys, you ungrateful git,' one of them informed the complainer.

Humphrey Bogart – ooh he was gorgeous – was looking suitably tough and laconic in a topical tale of heroism against a background of turmoil and treachery, and Ingrid Bergman as appealing as ever, when suddenly an announcement flashed onto the screen: *ALL OFFICERS AND CREWS OF BOATS REPORT TO BASE AS SOON AS POSSIBLE.*

'Oh, bloody hell!' Queenie exclaimed before she could stop herself.

Paul grinned at her and she could see that excitement was overcoming his disappointment at having to leave her. 'It's my first official run in *Grey Ghost* – what we've been waiting for. Should be fun, what? Look, I haven't got your address – '

Thank God for that she thought. Imagine a meeting between him and Ma. 'Phyllis and me'll go to Kimbells next Saturday – '

'I'll be there – if I possibly can.' He reached over and gave her a quick kiss on the cheek, looking bashful as he stood up.

'On your way, boys', and 'Good luck, lads', and 'We'll pray for you', came from members of the audience as the young men made their way up the aisle.

Queenie's eyes misted. 'Keep those brave boys safe, please God,' she murmured to Phyllis, who answered, 'Hear, hear,' before they settled down to enjoy Bogey's rugged charms on the screen.

The three young officers loped up the road to the dockyard, arriving breathless, to be picked up with a number of other personnel and taken to the jetty where a launch awaited to take them across to *Hornet*. They settled themselves inside the cabin.

'Good to be back in action,' said Bill.

'Pity to have to leave those girls, though,' said Paul.

'You rather fancy Queenie, don't you, old boy?'

'Never met a girl like her. Full of life, isn't she? She's had a jolly hard time too, widowed so young and left with two children.'

'A lovely girl,' agreed Keyes. 'The other one also is pretty but very quiet.'

'Did you know that Phyllis has lost her husband, too?' Paul informed the Dutchman. 'He was Queenie's brother. And her father going through such a rotten time in the last war and dying so young. How that poor girl has suffered – '

'Just be careful, or you'll get your fingers burned there, I reckon,' said Bill. 'She's got a reckless look about her, that one. All right for a quick fling, I suppose.'

'I don't go in for casual affairs,' Paul shot back, a look of distaste on his thin face. 'And I'm sure she's not like that. She needs someone to look after her – '

'What? That sort is quite capable of looking after themselves, believe me.'

'What *sort*?' Paul spat at him, his mouth tightening with anger.

'Working-class. She's tougher than she looks, believe you me. And she's older and more experienced than you. Just be careful, is all I'm saying.'

'I'm not a fool. I'm aware that we have different backgrounds, and that means that she would benefit greatly from . . . what I could offer her – '

'My God, you've really got it bad, haven't you?'

'Love at first sight, eh?' asked Keyes with a grin.

'I suppose you're all so bloody level-headed in Holland? And you're jaded before your time, Bill. Let's change the subject, shall we? Wonder where we're going tonight?'

Alighting at the jetty at *Hornet*, they shook hands,

wished each other luck, and made for their respective boats. The five gun boats – two of them with Dutch crews – were moored two abreast behind a flotilla of MTBS: the 'Spitfires and Bombers of the Sea'.

Proudly, Paul boarded *Grey Ghost* and made his way to the charthouse, forward of the bridge. Lieutenant Wilkes, 'Wilkie', looked up from the chart-table, his dividers in his hand. His rugged face creased into a smile. 'Sorry to have interrupted your night out, Paul. I was only in a Gosport pub, so was able to be fetched back in a matter of minutes.' Only a few years older than his junior officer, Gordon Wilkes had nevertheless seen a lot more action.

Paul grinned. 'Had to leave a gorgeous girl in a Pompey cinema but that's war for you. What's on?'

'German Convoy in the Channel, close to the Normandy shore. Couple of supply ships with a heavy escort. Take us a couple of hours to get to interception. Most of the chaps are back. You get yourself togged up and check the crew. Then we'll warm up the engines and make ready.'

Paul swung down into the wardroom which doubled as the officers' sleeping cabin, with seat-bunks on either side of collapsible tables, and with a small serving-hatch through from the galley.

Hardly room to swing a cat, thought Paul as he struggled into his white jersey and sea-boots. But it had become home to him over the weeks of working-up, and was a vast improvement on the older wooden boats.

A little later, to the accompaniment of the loud roaring of the engines, having checked the men at their posts, Paul went up to the bridge to report to 'Wilkie'. 'Able-Seaman Barnes has not been located, sir. I've sent for spare crew.'

'Probably getting his end away. He'll be sick as a parrot to miss the maiden sortie.' He looked at the other boats. 'Right, we'll make ready.'

Leaning over the bridge, Paul called, 'Clear away springs. Uncover guns. Chop-chop.' The crew scurried round the decks. 'Fore and aft – let go,' shouted Paul and

*Grey Ghost* slipped her mooring. Soon they were on their way out of the narrow entrance of the harbour, with Dolphin Naval Base to starboard and old Sally Port opposite. Paul briefly thought of Queenie, who had told him she used to swim there before the war. Oh, there was so much he wanted to learn about Queenie.

It was a moonlit night. Beautiful, Paul thought, as they opened up the engines to take station on the port quarter of the lead boat. The boats lifted onto the plane, the bow waves sheering away and leaving phosphorescent wakes streaming behind.

To port was the silhouette of one of the old, round Napoleon forts, and ahead the dark shape of the Isle of Wight. Then, past the Nab Tower and out into the open Channel, heading towards France.

Paul's stomach churned with excitement as he muttered his usual prayer, 'Please God, watch over Mother.' He saw his mother's pale, oval face; the clear grey eyes that he had inherited. She was the sweetest person in his universe. Or had been – until he met Queenie.

'Keep Father safe.' The father he tried so hard to love, to please, but only ever seemed to disappoint. He had never come up to expectations, academically, sportswise or ambition. The only thing he and his father had in common was a love of sailing, and in this, his father had been a harsh teacher, driving the young boy to pit himself against the elements.

'You are too hard,' his gentle mother had once remonstrated.

'Nonsense. It's character-building stuff. Make a man of him.'

His commission in the Navy had been met with conditional approval. He had suggested going in as a seaman as he thought it right to work his way up, learn the trade, so to speak. But Frederick Knight had thrown back his leonine head and roared, 'You weren't reared a gentleman and sent to an expensive school to join the ranks.' Very important to his father that – being a gentleman, having started from humble beginnings and clawed his way up the social ladder.

'Please, God, give us success tonight, and grant us eventual victory in this war against the wicked Hun.'

And tonight there was an extra plea. 'Le me come back safely to Queenie.'

## · Thirty-two ·

Queenie and Phyllis, arm-in-arm in the moonlight, took a nostalgic walk home through Baker Street. Number Twelve's doorstep was dirty these days, the white-painted edge almost obliterated by the tread of feet, and the door paint peeling off.

'Wonder who lives there now?' Queenie mused. 'Bet old Lil doesn't like having a load of dossers next door. They were hard times, but there were always plenty of laughs, weren't there, Phyll?'

Phyllis squeezed her arm. 'Yes. Your family was a lot worse off than mine, but I'll never forget those great family get-togethers of a Sunday.'

Queenie snorted. 'Yes, all the uncles and aunts and snotty-nosed little cousins. Uncle Arthur's at sea somewhere – hope he comes back safe. Uncle Danny with his funny eyes and dirty jokes. Uncle Bert with his secret bit-on-the-side. I was glad that he married that poor cow after dear old Aunty Ethel passed on last year.'

'What a shock that was. Not a sign until it was too late. Here, but what about the day that your Keith came back. That was a turn-up for the book.'

The familiar wrench of her insides when his name was mentioned. 'Mmm. He looked so gorgeous with that beard, I hardly recognised him on the door-step. I never expected to see him again, you know. I really didn't. But as soon as I saw how he was with Hannah, I knew everything was going to be all right, and I forgave him on the spot for all the trouble he'd caused me.'

'Forgiving nature, that's what you've got, Queen.'

'I don't know about that.' Had she forgiven Keith for his subsequent womanising? She wasn't sure. But the poor love was dead, so what was the point in agonising about it now. And those last few days with him had wiped out all the bitterness. She was glad they'd had that together.

Forgiving? She certainly had not forgiven Ray for taking her love and deceiving her. She had needed him at the time so perhaps that made it all right, but it would take time for those scars to heal.

The scar that would never heal was the lack of childhood love from Ma. Queenie would never be able to forgive her for that. She had never understood what it was about her that made Ma withhold that love, unless it was jealousy over Joshua's favouritism?

She and Ma had come closer together in her adult years, but that business over the ginger-haired sailor had opened up old wounds. Bashing her like that and calling her a slut. Not even trying to understand. But at least the old girl had kept 'that' to herself – apart from telling Eddy, and that had hurt more than any physical blow. Oh yes, she'd been too ashamed of her daughter to want anyone, even Lil, to know what a tart she was becoming.

But it wasn't true, thought Queenie vehemently. Just a mistake. Everyone must be excused a mistake or two in life. And she was going to be *really* careful never to make another. Paul Knight was all right. At least officers were gentlemen – she hoped.

'You going to meet that Paul again?' asked Phyllis, almost as though she had read her friend's thoughts.

'I said we'd go to Kimbells next Saturday, and he said he'd try to be there.'

'Oh, I don't really want to go . . .'

'Come on, be a sport. Just this once. I can't go on me own, can I?'

'And suppose he isn't there?'

'We'll go the next week.'

'You really want to get to know him then?'

''Spose I do,' Queenie shrugged, surprising herself with the knowledge. Paul was so fresh and open, like young Jimmy. Perhaps some of that goodness would rub off on her. And there was no doubt that he was smitten, poor lad. Well, she'd be kind to him – there was a war on. Just a bit of fun though, she wasn't going to give him any of 'the other'.

The house opposite the bakery on the corner was just a pile of rubble. 'Poor sods,' mourned Queenie, who had played with the kids as a child.

'Yeah, but the Greens was all down the shelter, thank goodness.'

They crossed over into Butcher Street. Two houses burned out by incendiary bombs, but again no casualties, Phyllis informed her. Eddy had helped put the fires out.

'I'm glad the old church hasn't been hit. It's a sort of symbol – of life,' Queenie said, averting her eyes from Totterdell's Hotel opposite and her night of shame.

Thank God she'd had the curse since, so that bleeding sailor must have had the sense to use a French letter. Well, Jacks were issued with them as a matter of course, weren't they? But – a cheering thought struck her – perhaps he'd been too drunk to do anything after all.

They passed the air-raid shelter, the entrance to which had been bombed the previous year and two people had been killed. Beatie and Lil, who had been inside at the time, said their nerves had been shot to pieces by the explosion. 'Poor Ma,' Queenie was overcome with remorse at her previous hard thoughts. 'She's been through so much, and she does look old these days. I must be kinder to her, Phyll. I'm a selfish cow – only think about my own problems.'

'Don't be hard on yourself, Queen. You've had a rotten time, too.'

'And you.' They turned and embraced each other outside Phyllis' home in Dean Street.

'Come in for a cuppa.' Phyllis sniffed.

'Just a quick one, then.' Queenie wiped her eyes on her sleeves. 'I don't want be too late home. Ma will be worried.'

'Oh, here's the girl who always cheers us up.' Jean Banks welcomed Queenie with a kiss. Nice people, the Banks. A bit better off than the Ellis family, Mr Banks being a docker. 'Come and tell us all your news, love.'

Queenie soon had them laughing over her tales of what went on at work. About half an hour later there was a knock on the door. She rose from her chair as Phyllis got up to answer it. 'I'll be on my way.'

'It'll only be your Eddy, I expect,' said Jean.

'Oh?' Queenie had noticed that Phyllis looked a bit flustered as she left the room.

'He often pops in as he's passing, just to see we're all right. Nice young man.'

Why would he be 'passing' through Dean Street, Queenie wondered, when it was out of his way to St George's Square? She thought she knew the answer.

Her brother followed Phyllis into the kitchen. 'Evening, Mrs Banks. Oh – hello, Queen,' his voice cool in spite of his furiously flushing face. He had not spoken to her since that awful night-out business.

But she had him at a disadvantage now all right. 'What you doing here then, Ed?' she asked with a saucy grin.

With a challenging look in spite of his obvious embarrassment, he said, 'I often pop in. But I had a special reason tonight actually, if you must know. I came to ask Phyllis to go to the flicks with me.'

Their sister-in-law turned brick-red. Or was she now their ex-sister-in-law? Queenie wondered, hiding her delight, not wanting to cause them any more embarrassment. This was a delicate situation.

Eddy turned to Phyllis. 'Humphrey Bogart's on at the flea-pit if you fancy it.'

'Thanks, Eddy, I would've an' all . . . but we've just been. It was ever so good.'

He looked deflated. Having obviously plucked up a lot of courage to ask her, it appeared he was not sure if he had just been rebuffed. It was on the tip of Queenie's tongue to say they'd been with three nice young officers, just to stir him up – if such a thing was possible – but it was up to Phyllis to admit that if she wanted to.

Phyllis obviously didn't. 'I'll go with you on Thursday if you like. What was the new programme, Queenie?'

'*Desert Victory*, wasn't it?'

'Right.' Eddy grinned his pleasure. 'I'll pick you up at six-thirty – '

'Oh good, I'm free on Thursday,' said Queenie, then seeing his face fall, 'only teasing.'

Eddy sighed with relief. 'We'll get some of Fred's fish and chips afterwards if he's got any fat to fry them in.'

Queenie laughed. 'Dear old Fred – give him my love. Oh, I enjoyed working there. All those lovely sailors coming in. That's where I met my Keith, if you remember?'

Eddy nodded. 'Come on then, Queen, I'll walk you home.'

'Oh, I don't want to drag you away, Ed.' She smiled coyly. 'I won't come to any harm walking those few steps.'

'I was going to look in on Ma. See you Thursday, Phyllis,' giving her a shy smile. 'Goodnight, Mrs Banks.'

Out on the pavement, Queenie dared to link her arm through her brother's. 'Oh, Ed, I'm ever so pleased.'

'About what?' he asked gruffly.

'About you and Phyllis, you silly sod.'

'Watch the kerb,' he said as they crossed the road. 'Look, don't go reading anything into it. I've only asked her to the pictures. And keep your big mouth shut, I don't want anyone else to know. I don't suppose it – she won't want it to go any further. I just like Phyllis, that's all. I feel sorry for her.'

'Don't make excuses, Ed. I know she likes *you*. And

don't sell yourself short, neither. You're a good bloke and Phyllis knows it.'

'Do you think so?' she could hear the smile in his voice.

'I know it. And Ed,' she squeezed his arm, 'can we be friends again? I know you were shocked about what happened the other night, and I don't blame you. There was no one more disgusted than me, I can tell you. I'm never going to put myself in that position again.'

'You're too attractive for your own good, girl. And you do like attention from the blokes – you know you lead them on.'

'I know, I can't help it, but I shall be a perfect lady from now on. I promise.'

'That'll be the day.' He laughed, putting an arm around her waist.

She was so happy that she told him about her plan to save for a headstone for their father.

'Good idea. I'll contribute.'

'Will you? I never thought of asking. Perhaps Billy will too when he comes home on leave. Here, suppose I was to put a box with a hole in the lid on the mantelpiece? Then anyone who wanted could put a few spare coppers in and it would mount up lovely. Whatcha think?' Eddy agreed. 'Coo, this'll cheer old Ma up.'

Queenie was aware of a keen sense of disappointment. Paul Knight wasn't coming after all. Either he'd gone off on a mission, or he'd had second thoughts about becoming entangled with a girl like her.

And here she was, looking absolutely gorgeous in a new dress, bought this morning from Handley's with coupons purchased from Mrs Kelly. A wicked extravagance but you had to do something to cheer yourself up sometimes, didn't you? Anyway it had been a real bargain. Pre-war, she reckoned, with all that material in the full skirt. Wine-red grosgrain with little diamanté buttons down the bodice.

She was wearing her swallow brooch and had borrowed the marcasite earrings that Ma had inherited from *her* mother. Beatie's family had been worth a few bob in their day; pony and trap, nice home and furniture. But when Beatie's parents had died, they had been pretty near destitute, and their daughter had been forced to sell almost everything of value to bring up the younger children. A crying shame. Yes, Ma had lived a hard life, Queenie mused, but she would have liked to have known her grandparents.

She hoped she would live long enough to see her girls grown up and married – and her grandchildren. She was missing the kids. Perhaps they'd be able to come home soon, now that things had quietened down so much.

She and Phyllis had been sitting at the table for over an hour. They'd had a few dances, but Queenie realised that she'd been looking forward to seeing Paul again.

'That's a pretty brooch that your Eddy gave you,' Phyllis commented.

Queenie pulled her eyes away from the doorway and fingered it. 'Yes, it's one of my favourite things. Here,' she said, her eyes brightening, 'perhaps he'll give *you* something like it one day.'

Phyllis blushed. 'Don't be daft.'

'How did you get on at the pictures the other night?'

'All right. Why shouldn't we, you silly cow? We've known each other for years, after all.'

Queenie gave her a knowing look. Phyllis was definitely looking much livelier these days. 'Sometimes people don't see what's under their noses. I reckon Eddy's just right for you, Phyll.'

The girl looked down, her face peony-red. 'I like him a lot, Queenie, but that's all there is to it. Besides it's much too soon after . . . Don't you dare go saying things, p-l-ease. I don't want to embarrass him.'

'Scare him off, you mean? He's ever so shy, ain't he? All on account of his silly old foot.'

'I wish he could see that it's not important.'

'You might have to tell him.'

Phyllis looked at her thoughtfully.

'Would you care to dance?' A young officer bowed towards Queenie with outstretched hand.

'Don't mind if I do,' she twinkled up at him, getting to her feet. 'Oh, it's a jive.' Swinging out from one of his hands, she swivelled her hips, throwing her other hand up and wiggling it. It was fun. She threw back her head and laughed.

That was how Paul saw her as he entered Kimbells and that was how he would always remember her on cold night-runs in future. A vivid, laughing girl, dark hair flying, wine-red skirt whirling and showing her shapely legs, her full figure narrowing to a tiny waist.

Jealousy knifed through him, seeing how she was enjoying herself with another man – exhibiting herself. He wanted her so much, but what chance did a dull chap like himself have of capturing such an exotic butterfly? And if he did, he would want to keep her all to himself and he sensed she would not take kindly to being imprisoned.

When the dance ended, he moved quickly to her side, his heart knocking in his chest. 'Hello, Queenie.'

'Oh,' she smiled up at him. 'I thought you weren't coming.'

Her eyes were incredible. Sapphires? No, too dark, but they sparkled like jewels. He swallowed. 'We were on five-minute standby, but it turned out to be a false alarm. How are you?'

'All right, thanks. It's a waltz. Want to dance?'

She moved into his arms. He wiped his damp hand on his trousers before taking her hand. God, why did he have to be nervous? Her forehead was slightly sheened with moisture from her exertions, and mingled with her perfume was a faint odour of womanly perspiration.

'I've been thinking about you,' he murmured. 'Wanting to see you.' *Wanting you.*

She flirted her eyes at him. 'You should keep your mind on your work. It don't do to think of girls when you're firing at old Fritz. Give him one from me, did you, the other night?'

He grinned. 'We got a couple of them, with hardly a scratch to show for it.'

'Keith used to say that in spite of them having bigger guns, they weren't so keen to fight. He reckoned they had orders not to attack anything smaller than themselves unless they was attacked first.'

Paul did not want to hear what Queenie's former husband had to say. He wished he had not existed. Nevertheless he smiled. 'Could be. I have a theory that the Germans, not being a sea-faring nation like us, lack confidence in themselves when it comes to sea-warfare. They never seem to expect us to go straight at them – whatever the odds. The Teutonic nature is to weigh things up carefully, so usually we have the element of surprise.'

What the hell did *Teutonic* mean? 'You boys are so brave. I'd run a mile.'

'You wouldn't. You couldn't. When you're there, you've just got to get on with it. Life or death, and I'm never more alive than in action. Everything is crystal clear. It's funny how you notice every little detail. The flash of the star-shells and the tracers are terrifyingly beautiful. You hear the excitement in men's voices, feel the comradeship, see the determination in their eyes. It's fearfully – ' He was overcome with emotion and embarrassment.

Queenie's eyes were sympathetic. Sad. She moved closer to him, linked her arms around his neck. He could feel her breasts against his chest, her hair tickling his chin. He trembled and his body responded in an embarrassing manner.

'Do you pray?' she asked softly.

'Yes, all the time.'

'Keith was an atheist.'

*Keith again.* 'It's a great comfort to have someone to pray to. But let's not talk about the war.' He hesitated, then bravely murmured what he wanted to say. 'Queenie, I think about you all the time. You are the most wonderful girl I have ever met.'

She threw back her head and laughed, revealing even teeth. 'Go on! You can't have met many then.'

'I suppose I haven't had much to do with girls. I was just getting to know some at university. But I'm a chap who makes up his mind about things quickly. And with you, I knew straight away. I'm in love with you.' He went bright red as she stared up at him, but his clear eyes held hers unwaveringly.

She shook her head. 'It's the war talking, Paul. Everything seems urgent. Look, don't get serious. Let's just have some fun. I did tell you, didn't I?'

He looked miserable. 'But I can't help – '

'Bet your family are real toffs.'

'Not really. Anyway, does it matter?'

'Yes, it does, I can tell you. It matters to me. I had a lot of trouble with Keith's parents. They didn't think I was good enough for their son.'

'What a bloody cheek!' His mouth tightened with anger. 'You're good enough for anyone. Far too good – '

'Look, what are we going on about?' He only wanted an affair, after all. He couldn't possibly be serious about her. Well, she had her pride – a bit dented since Ray – but she wasn't about to squander herself on anyone ever again. Forget about that bloody sailor! Any future relationship would be on her terms. And there was certainly no future with Paul Knight. 'I don't want to get involved with anyone. I told you.'

'I can't help being involved – '

'Go on, then, tell me about your family.'

He shrugged. 'Father's in the War Office.'

'Sounds ever so important. And you live in a great big house, and your mother's never had to go out to work. I'll bet she doesn't even have to do her own cleaning!'

'We have a living-in maid, it's true, but so do lots of people.'

'Not people like me. And a gardener?'

'Well, yes, and a chauffeur, but so what? It's not important, is it? It's what people are that matters.'

'Oh, yeah? Bet you had a nanny when you were a kid.'

He nodded.

'There you are then. I was *dragged* up in the streets of Pompey. We never had a spare penny to bless ourselves with after my Dad was invalided out of the Navy. So – you might as well be the Prince of Wales as far as I'm concerned.'

'We haven't got one,' he laughed. 'But in any case, the former one married a Commoner.'

'Well they don't come much commoner than me, I can tell you.' Queenie's eyes flashed. 'Not that I'm ashamed of my background. Oh no. My Dad could hold up his head with the best of them.'

The music had stopped and Paul realised that they were standing alone on the dance floor, facing each other tensely. He reddened with embarrassment. 'For heaven's sake, what are we arguing about, Queenie? I've only told you that I . . . like you. Everyone's looking at us. Come on, let's sit down.'

Queenie shrugged off his hand, unaccountably angry. There was no justice in this world. Why did some people have it all, and not even appreciate their good fortune, while others had such a bloody difficult life? She flounced to the table.

'Lovers' tiff?' smirked Bill.

'Put a sock in it,' said Queenie furiously.

'Oops, care to dance, Phyllis?' Her sister-in-law threw her a worried look as she went on the floor with Bill.

Paul leaned over and touched her hand. 'I'm sorry, Queenie, I don't understand what I've said to annoy you . . .'

'Want to dance, Keyes?' she asked, ignoring his plea, the hurt in his eyes.

'You know, you should treat that young man kind. He loves you,' the blond Dutchman told her.

'He's only known me five minutes.'

He shrugged. 'Long enough sometimes. Destiny.'

She looked over to where Paul sat looking gloomily into his glass. 'You're right. I mustn't be unkind to one of our brave boys. But I'm not going to do nothing to encourage him, neither.'

'Fair enough.'

She looked up at her partner sympathetically. 'All this fuss about nothing, and here's you, fighting in a foreign country, wondering what's happening at home. I used to look across from Felixstowe to where Holland was. What's it like?'

Keyes talked to her animatedly about his family and his country and she returned to the table in bubbling good spirits again, dividing her time equally between the three young men for the rest of the evening. Paul began to feel desperate. He must make her understand how important she was to him.

'Can I see you home?' he asked.

'Gawd, no!' Paul Knight and Ma – she laughed. But he looked so disappointed that she added, 'Let's go to the flicks tomorrow if you can get off – just the two of us.'

Paul's eyes lit up. It occurred to Queenie that probably the surest, quickest way of ridding herself of this young man's attentions would be to let him meet Ma. Then he'd see how impossible the situation was. But she wasn't *quite* ready to say goodbye to Paul Knight yet.

# · Thirty-three ·

Queenie let herself into the flat, feeling tired and cross. She was really getting fed-up with her job and the advances of that pig of a supervisor, who was hinting that if she wasn't 'nice' to him soon, she'd find herself back on the factory floor. It was blackmail, and it wasn't right that men had such power over the females in their employ. They needed women all right when there was a war on, didn't they? And those women had proved that they were every bit as capable as men when they were given the chance. Things had better change after the war or women would have to rise up and demand their rights, and she'd be up there at the front, waving the banner. She opened the living-room door and got an awful shock.

Paul Knight was sitting at the table between Ma and Lil, an empty tea-cup on the table in front of him. He smiled at her, looking very pleased with himself. 'Hello, Queenie.'

'What you doing here?' she asked ungraciously, her face red with embarrassment. She could imagine the tales those two had been telling him – their language. And after she'd been trying to give him a good impression of herself and her background.

His face fell. 'I had some time off, so I came looking for you. Phyllis said you both lived near St George's Square, and as luck would have it, I bumped into the vicar.'

'I'll kill Phyllis. And the vicar. You've no right to turn up like this. If I'd wanted you to call, I'd have given you the address, wouldn't I?'

'Get her!' said Lil, goggle-eyed. 'The girl who was

always too good for the likes of us. Always wanted to get ahead.'

Queenie rounded on her furiously. 'Mind your own bloody business, Lil.' Paul blinked in surprise.

'Now, there's no need to be rude, Queen,' remonstrated Beatie. 'There's a cuppa tea in the pot. I've invited your friend to stay for supper. It's only "Woolton Surprise Pie".' She cackled with laughter. 'You'll be surprised if you find a scrap of meat in it, but you're welcome.'

Queenie's expression was incredulous, her mouth tight with anger.

'Very kind,' murmured Paul, looking from one to the other. 'But if you'd rather I didn't, Queenie?'

'I'd rather you didn't.'

He stood up, picking his hat up from the table. 'Then I'd better be off. Thank you for your hospitality, Mrs Ellis.'

Beatie opened her mouth to press her invitation but Queenie forestalled her. 'I'll see you to the door,' she offered, icy cold.

'Look, I'm awfully sorry if I've annoyed you,' Paul said in the hall. 'It was presumptuous of me, I suppose – '

'If that means a bloody cheek – I agree,' she hissed. 'I told you I wanted to keep it casual.'

'I was getting on so well with your mother. She's a splendid little woman, salt of the earth, and what a hard life she's had. I'd no idea. But now, I suppose, I've ruined my chances.'

'Chances of *what*?'

'I had hoped . . .' his voice dropped to a whisper. 'I was going to ask you to marry me.'

Queenie's eyes flashed in the gloom of the hall. 'You must be mad. And I'd have thought that meeting Ma and Lil would have made you realise it.' She opened the door.

'It's *you* I love,' he said desperately as she attempted to propel him over the threshold. 'I mean it, Queenie. I don't go around proposing to every girl I meet, you know. I could give you a better life. Look after you and the little girls – '

'What d'you think I am? A bleeding charity case?'

'Oh, God, no! I didn't mean it like that. I could make you happy. Cherish you.'

'Well, I'm not so sure you could make me happy and I don't want cherishing, thank you. My husband promised to cherish me and it didn't do me much good along the way – '

'What happened?' He was obviously eager to hear that her first marriage had flaws.

'I don't wish to discuss my marriage with you,' she answered haughtily. 'One thing I did learn was that I'll be happier if I stick to my own kind. I've had enough of snooty mothers-in-law.'

'My mother is the sweetest woman.' His young face was so earnest.

Queenie sighed. 'I'm sorry, Paul. I'm an ungrateful cow. I suppose I should feel honoured, but it wouldn't work, you know. Oh, it'd be all right for a while, I expect. But when the war's over you'd soon realise that we weren't suited. I'd hold you back.' He opened his mouth to protest. 'No. You're too young, Paul. When you come to your senses you'll be glad you're not saddled with another man's kids.'

He shook his head. 'Queenie – '

She stood on her toes and kissed his cheek. 'Goodbye, Paul.'

'Are you saying I can't see you again?'

'Better not. You go to Kimbells next Saturday and meet a nice young girl.'

'You won't be there?'

She shook her head.

His mouth set in a determined line. 'I won't give up, you know. I'll make you change your mind.'

'Goodbye, Paul.' She watched him walk away, his shoulders drooping with disappointment.

'He was a nice young man,' said Beatie indignantly when she returned to the living-room. 'What you want to send 'im off with a flea in his ear for?'

'You could do a lot worse,' nodded Lil sagely.

'I told him all about your Dad and the submarines, and what a little devil you was, always in trouble. Made him laugh, that did.'

Queenie groaned.

'Coo, the airs and graces you used to put on,' Lil reminisced. 'Thought you was above us lot, din't you? Well, 'ere's your chance to prove it. Go on, run after him before it's too late.'

'No.' Queenie flung herself down in a fireside chair. 'It wouldn't work. Look at the trouble I had with Violet Jackson.'

'She was a stuck-up cow,' chuckled Lil. 'Remember that day we went up to Porchester, Beatie? She wanted to wipe the floor with us.'

Beatie laughed. 'She were a different person once she'd got a few drinks in her, though. Remember her singing at the weddin'?'

'Ooh – "Stormy Weather".' Lil sang a few lines rolling her eyes and vast hips. 'Reckon old Bernard had a treat that night.' The two women laughed suggestively and Queenie, knowing more than they did, grinned.

'Anyway, our Queenie,' went on Beatie, 'Old Violet was all right when you got to know her, weren't she? And she's a good grandmother. As for Keith, well, he might have had a better ejucation and all that, but you got on really well together, didn't you? He was lovely, was our Keith.'

Queenie nodded. 'The thing about Keith was that he was so easy going. He didn't care about nothing really, as long as he got no bother. Anyway, he *had* to marry me didn't he? But Paul, well, he's sort of top drawer, isn't he? Real posh. God knows what he sees in me. And I bet his mother is all . . . lavender and lace.'

'I should think about it, girl,' her mother advised her.

'This old world is going to be in a hell of a mess when this war is over and times is going to be hard. If you can do a bit better for yourself, you do it. For the kids' sake. And anyway, there ain't going to be no more "class" when all this lot's sorted out, so they tell us. This war has made us all equal.'

Lil snorted. 'If you believe that, girl, you'll believe anything. But in any case, *I'm* not ashamed of being working class. I mean – hallelujah – it's the likes of us what keeps this bleedin' country going.'

'Oh, I agree, I agree. All I'm sayin' is – '

'Well, don't,' interrupted Queenie, rising to her feet, ''cos I'm not having any more to do with Paul Knight.' He had said he wouldn't give up. 'I'm not going to Kimbells again, and if he dares to show up at the door again, Ma, you tell him to get lost.' She went to the door. 'In any case,' she turned around and informed them indignantly, 'how could I possibly marry him? I'm not in love with him.'

Queenie was bored and lonely. She couldn't go dancing at Kimbells any more. Phyllis was going out more frequently with Eddy, and though they sometimes invited her, she didn't want to play gooseberry.

Sally from work was dating an American soldier, chewing gum, and saying she wanted to go to the 'US of A' after the war. In desperation, Queenie looked up Pearl from Fred's fish and chip shop, but she had married a sailor and grown fat and blowsy in pregnancy.

And to cap it all, Queenie was given the sack at work. The supervisor had tried it on too ardently, pressing her up against the bench and putting his hand up her jumper and she had slapped his face.

'I love women with spirit,' he grinned as she glared, red-cheeked, at him. He came at her again and tried to grab her in a more intimate place.

'You filthy pig!' she cried, and kneed him in the groin.

'That's it, you teasing bitch,' he had gasped, his eyes watering with pain. 'You'll get your cards tomorrow.'

She had stormed into the manager's office demanding justice. He called in the offender, who accused her of being a trouble-maker and stirring up the men.

'Men?' she had shrieked. 'The only men here are grandads, apart from rotten scivers like you two who've found some excuse not to get out and fight for their country. Call yourselves men?'

Her accuser put on an injured air. 'See what I mean?'

The manager, offended at her aspersions of cowardice when he had a legitimate reason for not fighting and a responsible war-job, sided with his supervisor. She was dismissed.

What chance did a woman have? Queenie raged. Well, she wasn't sorry to give up that boring job, she could easily find something more interesting.

And she did. As a Clippie on the buses. Starting on the dockyard to North End route. She was fitted out with a smart navy uniform; collar and tie, trousers, a battle-dress style jacket, and a jaunty peaked cap. Almost as good as the Wrens.

'It's just up my alley, Ma,' she said enthusiastically after her first day's work. 'I love it. You can have a chat and a joke with the passengers.'

Beatie laughed. 'And we all know how much you love the sound of your own voice.'

'Huh! I got a bit muddled on me ticket machine a couple of times and gave some of them the wrong change, but they were ever so good-natured about it.'

Her mother looked at her glowing face. 'Well, our Queen, we all know you can charm the birds off the trees when you want to.'

Queenie was happy again, wearing her cap at a jaunty angle, swinging along the aisle of the bus or up the stairs, pinging on the bell for a request stop, singing the popular songs, helping old ladies up and down from the platform. She had a cheerful comment for everyone and frequently a cheeky one.

After a few weeks she was transferrd to the service which ran from the dockyard to Southsea, via Guildhall Square. She liked this route, but was always sad to pass the great gaping bomb craters that had once been smart shops and businesses.

She was on the evening shift one night in January when a group of noisy young naval officers got on at the dockyard and went clattering up the stairs. 'Come on now, let's be having you,' she grinned as she swung with the rhythm of the bus towards them. 'Of course, if it was up to me I'd let all you lovely boys go free, but I'd get the sack if I did.'

The first two proferred their fares with suggestive remarks about what they could do with a girl like her on board ship. 'Would really raise our morale,' said one. 'And that's not all it would raise,' laughed his seat-partner.

'I'm sure I don't know *what* you mean, cheeky sods,' she informed them with a toss of her curls and a saucy grin as she passed on to the next pair.

'Hello, Queenie.' She found herself looking down into Paul Knight's unsmiling grey eyes. Her own smile vanished. He courteously took off his cap and his thin face was stiff, either with embarrassment or displeasure over the previous remarks. 'Enjoying the job?'

She nodded. 'Yes, I am, thanks. How you been keeping?'

'Not too bad. Hitler's boys have kept us busy lately. Two returns to Osborne Road, please.' He gave her a shilling.

'Going to Kimbells?' she asked, pressing buttons and rolling out the tickets.

'Yes. Are you missing it?'

'No,' she lied, avoiding his eyes as she gave him his change. 'There are plenty of other places to go.'

The other chaps were nudging each other, regarding

them curiously. Queenie ran her eyes over them. 'Bill and Keyes not with you tonight, then?'

Paul shook his head. 'Bill is on leave, getting married. Keyes is – ' his jaw clenched ' – not with us any more.'

'You don't mean . . .?'

He nodded and her eyes filled with tears. 'I'm sorry,' she mumbled and she passed on to the next seat. Standing downstairs on the draughty platform, she felt pretty miserable. That lovely Dutch boy would never go home to his country and family again. It was so cruel.

Paul was looking strained; shadows under his eyes, deep lines from nose to mouth. He needn't have spoken to her after the way she had treated him. She wouldn't have blamed him, but he was decent and polite. And he looked so sad.

The group clattered down the stairs as the bus neared Osborne Road. Paul came last and stood looking down at her. 'Take care of yourself, Queenie.'

She nodded, unable to speak. They alighted at the stop and as the bus started up again, Paul raised his hand to her. She waved back. 'You take care an' all, Paul Knight,' she called, hanging out from the platform rail as the bus drew away. 'I'll never *forgive you* if you go and get yourself killed.' He blew her a kiss which she did not return.

She felt curiously deflated for a few days after the meeting with Paul. She couldn't understand why, really, when it was she who had ended their relationship. That was the trouble, of course. He had wanted a relationship, while she only wanted a friend. Why did life have to be so complicated? But she had to admit that she missed him.

Phyllis and Eddy walked through Pembroke Gardens on a blustery Sunday afternoon. He was wearing an old mac and her threadbare coat was too thin. The trees were bare.

'This used to be so pretty,' mourned Phyllis looking at

the fenced-off areas now growing winter cabbage and root vegetables.

'Some things have stayed pretty in spite of the war,' Eddy told her with a twinkle in his dark eyes.

Phyllis glanced at him. His straight black hair had blown up into a crest. She giggled. 'You look like a cockerel.' He crowed. She laughed and he took her hand. She did not withdraw it but looked away, blushing. 'Queenie's up and down these days, isn't she?'

'Missing the kids. Poor little devils won't know us when they get back.'

'Oh, Ed, it's awful, isn't it? Families split up, fathers being killed. Husbands . . .'

'How long has it been since John . . .?'

'Fifteen months.'

'Is it . . . just as bad?'

She scuffed the path with her toes, stirring up damp, dead leaves, considering her reply. She sensed it was important. 'I think about him just as much, but it's not quite so painful. We had such plans, you know. A little house, three kids. We didn't ask for much, we didn't want anything out of the ordinary. But we wasn't given a chance. That's what hurts. He was so young.'

She noticed that Eddy was dragging his crippled foot. It had been a long walk from Portsea. 'Whew, I'm tired,' she said, 'shall we sit down for a bit?'

They sat on a park bench and the wind whistled round them. Phyllis shivered. 'Not the most comfortable place on a winter afternoon,' said Eddy, taking the opportunity to put his arm round her. She huddled gratefully against him.

'Your hair is tickling me,' he laughed. Some strands had pulled out of the mauve scarf tied under her chin. She turned to laugh up at him and found that their faces were very close together. They stared into each other's eyes and Phyllis was sure that his heart was thudding every bit as hard as hers. He blinked, ran his tongue nervously over his lower lip.

They had been at this juncture many times, but Phyllis knew he was too afraid of rejection to say what she knew he wanted to say. What she wanted to hear. She would have to help him or they would be middle-aged before he found the courage. 'Ed. You've been a great help to me, you know. Over John and all that.'

'I'm glad, Phyll. I'd do anything for you – you know that.'

'Would you, Eddy? Why?' she asked softly, her words scarcely audible above the wind. Her blue eyes looked artlessly into his, her lips puckered softly.

Eddy cleared his throat. 'I – you're a sweet girl, Phyllis and . . .'

'And? Say it, Ed.' She smiled her encouragement.

'Oh, Phyll,' his arm tightened around her. 'I've no right to ask. What would you want with a . . . with someone like me? You could have any man you wanted.'

She laughed. 'I doubt that very much, Eddy. It might be true of your sister, but not me. In fact I'm finding it quite difficult – to get the man I want.' He looked at her questioningly. 'You don't realise it, but we're very similar.'

'Are we? How?'

'Both shy, just want a quiet life. Someone to love.'

Hope shone out of his eyes. 'Are you saying . . .? Phyllis, I think you know that I love you, but – '

'And I love you.'

The hope was replaced by joy. 'You do? Really?'

Phyllis reached up, pulled his head down and kissed him soundly on the mouth. Galvanised into action, Eddy clasped her to him and kissed her passionately. After a few minutes they drew breathlessly apart. Phyllis laughed. 'I knew you'd be all right once you got going, Edward Ellis.'

'You're the first girl I've kissed and the only one I've ever really wanted to.' He kissed her again.

'Is there anything else you want to do with me?' she prompted.

'Well yes,' he grinned, 'but perhaps there's something we'd better sort out first.'

Phyllis smiled her delight as he slewed round and dropped on one knee in front of her. 'Phyllis, will you marry me?'

'You should know the answer to that, you chump. Eddy, I'd feel . . . honoured to be your wife. It's funny though, I've thought about it and I'll still be Mrs Ellis.'

'It's an honourable name,' said Eddy, taking her hands and kissing them.

'It is.' She cupped his face in her hands. His dear, gentle face that she had loved long before she realised it. Queenie had made her see what he meant to her. 'I'm never going to forget John. You know that, Eddy. I'll always love him, love what he was to me. But you and me – we're a different story. We've got a future.'

They kissed lingeringly and she helped him to his feet. The cold suddenly clenched her bones and she shuddered. 'Let's go and catch a bus home. Queenie's on this route this week. Wouldn't it be a laugh if we got her bus and told her our news.'

'Think she'll be pleased?' Eddy asked unnecessarily, tucking her arm through his.

'She'll be dead chuffed,' laughed Phyllis.

## · Thirty-four ·

As if the British people had not got enough on their plates with the anxieties and stringencies of war, the winters added to their discomfort, and that of 1943–4 was no exception. Fuel was rationed and difficult to come by and it was snowing hard.

Queenie struggled home down St George's Square in wellington boots, with a mac over her uniform and a scarf tied around her cap. Her toes were frozen and her fingers were welded to the string bags that were hanging heavily from them. She'd had several really miserable days at work, with the buses freezing cold and having difficulty getting anywhere on time. She had almost wished she was back at the factory on occasions.

She yearned for her children. There had been a lull in the bombing for some time, but what was the point in bringing them back to this dreadful weather when it was milder down there and Violet would be looking after them well?

Now Queenie hunched against swirling snow which lessened visibility to a few yards and deadened the world to eerie silence. It was all right on Christmas cards, but no fun when you had to get to work early in the morning and do your shopping. She had called at Valerio's and Cole's in Butcher Street for the week's rations, having forbidden Beatie to set foot out of doors.

A few rashers of bacon, six ounces of cheese, four ounces of tea, a quarter of butter, half a pound of margarine, a packet of dried egg and cooking fat. Sixteen points for a tin of sardines and the same for a tin of Spam. A couple of bobs' worth of pork and some liver. Not much there for two people to keep body and soul together on for the week. *Roll on peace and plenty.* Surely now . . . with the Russians defeating the Germans and Italy siding with us?

Valerio's shop, not many degrees above the outside temperature, had seemed relatively warm and inviting. The proprietor's wife, bundled up in many layers of clothing, woolly hat and fingerless gloves, was saying that she wished she was in Italy, which she had never seen, but was sure was a lot warmer. Women customers were standing around, stamping their feet and blowing on their fingers but unable to forego the pleasure of a gossip. One of them was Lil.

'Hello, Queen, girl.' She kissed Queenie's cheek. 'Gawd, you're like a block of ice. Here, ain't it good news about your Eddy and Phyllis? We need somethink cheerful to buck us up. It's not likely to be much warmer for the wedding in two weeks' time, though, is it? Still, as the saying goes – they've got their love to keep them warm.'

Queenie agreed, feeling envious and thrilled for them at the same time. Eddy and Phyll were so well suited and ecstatically happy. It was to be a very quiet wedding and they were to share Eddy's tiny flat afterwards.

Queenie carried Lil's shopping home to Baker Street for her, arranging to pick hers up on the way back from calling into the butcher's. Lil clung to her arm, Queenie hoping the big woman wouldn't slip and pull them both down. The bombs had spared her so far and she didn't fancy being crushed to death by any other means.

'Give my love to Beat.' Lil embraced her at her door having popped in to get her four eggs. The Ellis's old home next door had an air of desolation and neglect about it. 'Gawd knows when I'll see her again if this keeps up.'

'Gawd knows how I'll survive many more of these days at work,' Queenie muttered to herself now as she reached the block of flats and pushed backwards through the entrance door. As she turned, a large, dark figure moved menacingly towards her in the gloom. She screamed.

'It's only me, Queenie,' uttered a cultured voice.

She gasped. 'Paul Knight! What the hell are you doin' here? Lurking around and frightening people to death.'

'Had to come to see you. Couldn't keep away any longer. I've been here for absolutely hours. The blood is freezing in my veins.'

'Idiot! Why didn't you go up and sit with Ma?' Then she remembered her instructions. 'Oh, she didn't tell you to get lost, did she? No, she wouldn't turn a dog away in weather like this.'

'Thanks for the compliment. Actually, I thought I'd better not go up after your reactions the time before. Didn't want to put my foot in it again. But I was just beginning to get worried that you weren't coming. If you'd been on night shift you'd have returned to find my frozen corpse grinning at you at the bottom of the stairs.'

'You twerp. I suppose you'd better come up, now you're here.'

'Let me take those.' He took her laden bags from nerveless fingers.

Beatie was sitting huddled over a low gas-flame in the fireplace, knitting and listening to the Forces programme on the wireless. The room felt deliciously warm. 'I was gettin' worried about you, Queen,' she said, turning in her chair. 'Who've you got with you?'

'Paul Knight, a refugee from the blizzard, I'm afraid, Mrs Ellis. Hope I'm not intruding.' He bent and took off his boots in the hall.

'I found Paul frozen at the bottom of the stairs, Ma.' Queenie removed her wet mac and hung it on a peg.

Beatie got up, smiling. 'Come and sit by the fire. I'll go and make a nice, hot cup of tea. Good, you got the shopping.' She pulled an old shawl over her shoulders. 'It's freezing in that kitchen.'

Paul took off his heavy greatcoat and Queenie held out her arms for it, hugging the warm interior to her before hanging it up, recalling how Ray had returned to her in the snow last year after his Christmas leave. Ray was probably still at home with his family in a warm farmhouse. How well had he recovered from his injuries? she wondered. She had made a cosy nest for them in front of the fire and they had made wonderful love. She had believed he was hers. But, she realised with surprise, she felt little bitterness any more.

She only knew she was lonely. Would she like to do the same with Paul Knight? Make love to him in front of the fire? He came to her in the hall and bent to pull off her boots, massaging her frozen feet. 'Oh,' she moaned as he helped her into the warm living-room.

'Don't get too close to the fire,' he advised.

'Coo, it's agony when you thaw out.'

'Oh, Queenie, I wish you didn't have to go out in this weather and do that frightful job.'

'The job's all right. Anyway, we got to eat.'

He knelt beside her, chafing her cold fingers in hands kept warm in the depths of his deep pockets. He was quite sweet, really, she thought. 'There is an alternative, you know,' he said, looking at her earnestly. 'You don't have to go out to work.'

'Don't, Paul,' Queenie warned. 'I must look an awful mess,' she cried, jumping up to look at herself in the mirror above the fireplace and pushing at her hair which had been flattened by her cap. Her nose was red. 'Ooh, me chillblains!' She hopped from one foot to the other as her feet began painfully to thaw.

Paul scrambled to his feet and stood behind her, smiling ruefully. 'You couldn't look a mess if you tried.' He raised a hand and smoothed her hair back from her cheek in a tender gesture.

Their eyes held. His, once so clear and innocent, were now shadowed with the danger, the fear, and the carnage they had witnessed. Queenie's heart went out to him. No one so young should have to experience those things. 'You look tired. Having a hard time?'

He nodded. 'Bloody'.

She felt so sorry for him. She wanted to turn and hug him – promise him anything – to give him hope, the strength to go on.

'You didn't mind me coming?'

She shook her head.

'You were so angry the last time I turned up.'

'I was embarrassed. Didn't want you to see how I lived when you – '

'But it doesn't matter, does it, Queenie?' He turned her towards him. 'Not really?'

Last time he had some leave he went home to gracious living in Faversham and compared it to Queenie's spartan existence. He began to understand the difficulties that she would have, fitting in with his family and their way of life. It made him sad, but even more determined to share his good fortune with her. He could do so much for her. 'I love you,' he murmured, his hands gently kneading her shoulders.

Queenie bit on her lip. She didn't want him to love her, yet was flattered that he did. She did not love him, though she wished she could. She knew she should discourage him, but was reluctant to hurt him. It could never work out between them, could it? He was even posher than Keith. She was thoroughly confused, and glad when Beatie reappeared with a tray of tea and some bread and jam.

Conversation was a bit strained. Queenie, unusually subdued, talked about her job. Ma talked about rationing and the forthcoming wedding of Phyllis and Eddy. Paul told them a little bit about his missions. And as he unburdened himself to them, Queenie found herself liking him a lot.

'You can be coming back at dawn exhausted from a night out, having not even seen the enemy. Or limping home after a nasty skirmish, with damage to the boats and some men wounded or dying – hating the bloody Bosche – when suddenly dawn lights the sky and a school of porpoises leaps alongside you, and life seems beautiful again. Another night or morning you can be fishing German survivors out of the sea, after you or some other British boat has pitched them there. And you look at the enemy you loathe and realise – ' he swallowed painfully ' – that they're just frightened young chaps like yourself.'

Beatie sniffed and Queenie's eyes filled with tears. Keith had said the same thing. 'Everything's topsy-turvy,' she murmured. 'Will it ever be normal again?'

'I'm being made up to lieutenant.'

'Congratulations. You'll be given more responsibility then?'

'I'll be earning more,' he said, giving her a meaningful look.

Everyone shivered through the Christmas wedding service when Eddy and Phyllis got married. St George's Church had no heating and was dark and drear as a nearby bomb had blasted out the stained-glass windows and most of them were boarded up, only those behind the altar having been replaced by plain glass.

Nothing, however, could diminish the young couple's joy in each other. Eddy, in his shiny old suit, shone; proud for once to be the centre of attention. Phyllis, in one of Vera's cast-off coats, bloomed like a winter rose. She and Queenie had fashioned a little hat for her with a couple of artificial flowers and a piece of stiff net fastened to an Alice band.

Mrs Banks, in spite of rationing, had got together a nice little reception in her front room and everyone was very merry. A wedding, always a happy occasion, was a particularly welcome one in the midst of a war-time winter.

Queenie, watching Phyllis and Eddy exchange loving

glances as they sat with hands glued together, shed a glad tear for them and wondered if she would ever again find happiness like theirs.

Paul Knight took to dropping in occasionally. Beatie did not mind, and Queenie, sensing his loneliness, did not discourage him. He sometimes brought a little gift – a bar of soap, a bunch of snowdrops. She found herself studying him carefully and when she asked herself why, realised with surprise that she was beginning to consider his offer of marriage.

'Well, where's being in love ever got me?' she asked Phyllis, the radiant bride of a few weeks. 'I was in love with Keith when we got married but that didn't stop us having lots of problems. I was blinded by love with Ray and he took advantage of me. Perhaps you should go into marriage with a clear head. You know, weigh up all the pros and cons.'

'Sounds ever so cold-hearted,' said Phyllis. 'I couldn't do it.'

'You'll be all right with our Eddy.'

'But you want somethink better, don't you, Queen? You want to get out of this rut. That's why you're thinking about Paul. He's got a lot to offer.'

'I was ambitious when I was young, wasn't I? Couldn't wait to get away from all this and do well for meself. Then things sort of got out of control and life's picked me up and dumped me so often. All I'm doing now is stagnating. And as you say, Paul has got a lot to offer . . .'

'He's young – '

'Too young.'

'Good-looking – '

'Not important.'

'He'll go places, he's well-educated – '

'Too well-educated. He doesn't seem to realise what an

ignorant sod I am. In all sorts of ways. What would his family think of me?'

Phyllis shrugged. 'You've always said the Ellises were as good as anybody.'

'My Dad was better than most.'

'Well then. He'd have wanted you to get on, wouldn't he? Paul's got good prospects. He's honest – '

'He's too bloody perfect, if you ask me. How can I match up? A marriage has got to be give and take – I learned that with Keith. What have I got to offer Mr Perfect? What does he see in me?'

Phyllis studied her, considering. 'You're very attractive.'

'I know but – '

'And vain with it,' laughed Phyllis.

'True. I'm also selfish, stubborn, impulsive, tactless, crude – '

'Here, don't be too hard on yourself, you must have some good points.' They wrinkled their brows in thought, then burst into laughter.

'Can't think of a bloody thing,' spluttered Queenie.

'Go on! You've got a sense of humour and that's important. You don't let things get you down. You're one of the bravest people I know.'

'Thanks,' said Queenie, pleased. 'You know, if I did something like this, I'd be loyal, Phyll, and I'd make a good home. I'm not a bad cook, thanks to Ma. It would be a sort of bargain, wouldn't it?' She jumped up and took an excited turn around the room. 'Think it would work?'

'Well, some of these foreigners, Indians and what not, have arranged marriages, don't they? They don't marry for love. Their parents decide for them.'

'Oh yeah, but that's all to do with a dowry, isn't it? The bride's supposed to bring money and a few pigs and that. I couldn't even rustle up a couple of scrawny chickens.' They laughed, then Queenie looked thoughtful. 'I've got a couple of kids, though.'

'Mmm. Think he'll be a good father to them? That's important.'

'I think he'd be fair, but he might expect a lot. He's very stiff and proper, you know. He says he can't please his own father, and even if you don't mean to, you do sort of copy your parents, don't you? Not that I'd ever copy Ma!'

'What about . . . you know?' Phyllis went pink.

'Sex, you mean?' asked Queenie with an expression of mock-horror on her face. 'Oh, Gawd! Well, I suppose I'd have to give him a bit now and then in exchange for housekeeping money, wouldn't I? Fair's fair, Phyllis.'

They dissolved into giggles again, but by the time Queenie got home, the seed that Paul had sown had begun to germinate.

When the weather improved Queenie and Paul went to the cinema or dancing at Kimbells. He became easier with her, she got to know him better and to like him more.

Under her tuition, his dancing improved too. They were executing a very passable foxtrot round the dance-floor one evening when out of the blue he said, with deadpan expression, 'When are you going to marry me then?'

And to his enormous surprise, she answered, 'In six months – if you still feel the same.'

His mouth fell open, his eyes lit up and he gave a great whoop of delight. They stopped and smiled at each other, her smile a little uncertain as she had not planned to say the fateful words that she had just uttered. 'Darling, darling, darling,' he enthused. 'Why wait so long? You know how I feel about you.'

'Let's sit down, Paul. I want to explain something to you.' Queenie led the way to their table and took a large swig of gin and tonic for courage. He held her hand and leaned towards her with shining eyes. She bit her lower lip, then blurted it out. 'I want you to be quite, quite sure about this, Paul. Taking on an older woman and two kids. You've had nothing to do with children, have you? Suppose you don't get on with them?'

'They're yours. I shall adore them.'

She shook her head. 'You've got to meet my children and I've got to meet your parents, before we really commit ourselves.'

He grinned. 'You're such a sensible girl. One of the things I love about you.' His brow puckered. 'Could we compromise and make it four months, though, because apart from the fact that I'm crazy about you and will probably have died from longing by June, there's something very, very big and important coming up about then. I can't tell you about it, it's all very hush-hush and I don't know the details myself, but it won't leave time for any personal life. It's . . . well, really it's going to be a life or death situation. I mean, win or lose – finally.'

A shudder ran down Queenie's spine. 'That's what all the extra activity's been about, isn't it? All along the coast, I hear. Ships and troops pouring in, barricades to keep the public out of areas. Eddy says there's camouflaged lorries in all the country lanes.'

He nodded. She studied his bony, young face. The face she was becoming very fond of. He might not survive this venture. 'End of April, then,' she said slowly. 'If you still feel the same.'

'My darling,' he took her hand and pressed fervent kisses upon it. 'I shall still feel the same. I'd gladly *die* for you.'

'Don't say that,' she implored, suddenly afraid.

A couple of weeks later, Queenie was becoming quite happy at the prospect of marriage. Paul, in the highest of spirits, called to tell her that if she would like to see over his boat, which was in the dockyard having some repair work done on it, he had obtained permission to take her aboard. They arranged to go on the Saturday afternoon.

They walked to the dockyard in the thin winter sunlight, Queenie hanging on his arm as the pavements were still treacherous with ice in places. She felt proud to be walking alongside the handsome officer in his long greatcoat. She was wearing a half-decent winter coat in mulberry wool with a fur collar, which she had bought from her sister-in-law, Vera, who could afford better now that Billy was an Army captain. The family were so proud of him.

Queenie was impressed as they went up the gangplank of *Grey Ghost* and were whistled aboard by the bosun. She gave a nervous giggle; fancy her being shown round a ship by an officer when all the sailors she had ever known had been in the ranks. Would her Dad have been proud of her?

'It's bigger than Keith's MTB.' She wished she hadn't said that as she watched his mouth tighten. She had come to know that he was very possessive – something she would have to watch out for.

'She's a hundred feet in length,' he told her and took her along the deck to show her the guns and the bridge, which he called 'the dustbin'.

Looking forward from the bridge, Queenie saw two MTBs docked ahead of the gunboat. She felt a wrench she had not experienced for some time as she thought of how her husband had met his death on a similar craft. And now she was contemplating marrying again. Fighting the feeling of guilt, she turned away and asked a question about the speed of the boat.

They went below deck and she was interested in what he showed her. They ended up sitting at the table in the wardroom with a cup of tea that was passed through the hatch by a steward seaman. Queenie secreted a few sachets of sugar into her bag when Paul's attention was elsewhere. 'I'm glad I came,' she said, 'to see how you live when you're on board. A bit cramped though, isn't it? But not half as bad as being in a submarine, like my Dad was.'

She was introduced as 'my fiancée' to another young officer who came into the wardroom. She could hardly believe it. She had resisted the buying of a ring. 'Not till the end of April,' she had insisted, 'and then, *if we go ahead*, I only want a wedding ring. We won't have money to waste.'

They took another turn round the deck, Queenie feeling very grand, commenting on Nelson's flagship HMS *Victory* nearby, which had pride of place as a museum in the dockyard. 'My Uncle Arthur took us aboard when we were little. The ceilings were so low; men must have much smaller in those days.'

'Don't know about that, Captain Hardy was a tall chap. I think it was that they had to keep the superstructure as low as possible for stability.'

'Nelson asked Hardy to kiss him when he was dying.'

'There's some debate about that. He may have said "Kismet" which is Arabic for fate.'

Queenie grinned up at him. 'You're educated, you are.'

Paul stopped at the top of the gangplank to speak to a rating and she continued to the bottom. A group of sailors were going past and she encompassed them with a bright smile, for hadn't she always loved bell-bottoms?

'Queenie,' a voice boomed and the group stopped.

She turned startled eyes to an unfamiliar face, though there was something . . . She wrinkled her brow. 'I don't think I know . . .?'

'Course you do, girl. Now how could you ferget that night in Totterdell's Hotel!' the rating laughed coarsely, and as the meaning of his words sank into her shocked brain, she registered his ginger hair.

# · *Thirty-five* ·

Paul's hand came from behind and grasped Queenie's upper arm and she was steered, face on fire, through the group of saluting ratings.

'Going up in the world,' she heard one say.

A guffaw. 'There's more to the Wavy Navy than meets the eye.'

'Too good for the likes of you now, Ginger.'

Paul turned and quelled them with a glare and his fingers bit cruelly into Queenie's flesh as he marched her towards the dockyard gates. She took a quick, frightened glance at his thunderous face. This was a facet of his character she had not before witnessed.

'That Jack must have mistaken me for somebody else,' she ventured.

'Don't give me that,' he snarled. 'He called you by your name, didn't he? God, the humiliation. Sniggering away behind my back, the lot of them.'

'Well, I might have had a drink with him once . . .'

'At Totterdell's Hotel!' He dropped her arm in a gesture of disgust. 'Sailors only go to hotels for one thing – God!'

Queenie, feeling sick with shame and self-loathing, compressed her lips and her nostrils whitened. 'Your sins will find you out,' her mother used to say, and they always had. No excuse would suffice for this sordid episode but she wasn't one to grovel. 'Believe what you like then,' she flung at him defiantly.

They glared at each other and bristling, like a pair of

dogs with raised hackles, they passed through the gates, Paul stiffly acknowledging the guard's salute.

Once outside they faced each other, Queenie flinching from the disgust in Paul's face. 'I imagine this is where we say goodbye,' she remarked.

'What are you known as round here? Matelot's Moll?' he snarled.

She gasped and her eyes widened in pain before she turned away, and seeing how he had wounded her, Paul said, 'I'm sorry. I shouldn't have said that.'

'No, you shouldn't,' she answered in a small voice. 'Goodbye, Paul.'

He caught her arm as she stepped away. 'For God's sake, let's at least discuss it. Can't you understand how I feel? I can just about accept that you were married before, but this!'

'That's mighty big of you,' she flared, shaking off his arm. 'But you don't like any mention of Keith, do you? I've noticed how you always change the subject when I say his name. Well, he was the most important person in my life for about seven years, the father of my children, and he died fighting for his country, so I'm not going to . . . to bury his memory just 'cos you're jealous.'

'Of course, of course, but I need to know,' he said intensely, 'how many others there have been since?'

For a moment Queenie was tempted to tell him about her infatuation with Ray and explain her mistake over 'Ginger'. Only two, after all. But would he believe her? Of course he wouldn't. She had always known it wouldn't work between them, so why try to explain? 'Believe what you like,' she said again with a careless shrug.

He took her by the shoulders. 'Queenie, don't,' he implored. 'You wouldn't speak like that if you loved me.' She continued to look at him coolly. 'So you don't love me?'

'I never said I did. You asked me to marry you and I told you we weren't suited. You begged me and I said I'd consider it.' His poor, young face was stricken and she was sorry, but she was hurt too. 'You don't trust me, so I reckon that's that, don't you?' She turned away but he held on to her.

'Let me go. Oh, can't you see it's hopeless, Paul? You're a decent bloke, hardly had time to find out what life is all about. I might be only a few years older than you, but I'm a bloody sight older in experience. I've *lived*, Paul, and whatever way we look at it, whatever excuses I make, I know now that my past would come between us. You'd never be certain. And I know what I'm talking about – I've had some of that!'

'Oh? With . . . Keith? It needn't be like that with us if we're honest with each other.'

'It would be. I'm sorry, truly I am. But you'll get over it, you'll meet the right girl one day, and then you'll be glad that you didn't get stuck with me. Good luck.'

She walked quickly away from him, slithering in the slush, and was surprised to find tears on her cheeks. Well, that's that, she told herself as she crossed over the road to cut through Baker Street. It had seemed a good idea while it lasted, but when it came down to it, she had just made a fool of herself again.

She glanced back and saw that Paul was following her at a distance. 'Go away,' she called, but he came on. She quickened her footsteps, arms held out from her body to keep her footing on the treacherous pavement. She didn't want him following her home and continuing the discussion there. God knows how it would end if Ma put her penn'orth in. There'd be plenty of mud-slinging then. And if Lil was there, having a chin-wag – hallelujah! Even Paul Knight shouldn't be put through that.

On impulse she stopped outside number twelve and watched him come up to her with an apologetic expression on his face. 'Take a good look.' She was grimly satisfied to see the distaste on his face, the curling of his fastidious lips, as he regarded the rotting door, the grimy step, the dingy nets drooping from a sagging curtain-wire.

She did not tell him that it had not looked like that when the Ellis family had lived there, that they could have eaten off the lino that they kept so clean. How the step had gleamed red from her elbow-grease, how the polished brass bands had held the velvet curtains away from Ma's prize aspidistra in the weekly washed window. She didn't tell him about the fun they used to have, the family quarrels and the making-up.

'Not a pretty sight, is it? We had a lav at the bottom of the yard and we used to bring in the tin bath of a Friday night and the kids went into the water one after the other. We never could get rid of the cockroaches in the scullery, and every so often we'd get an outbreak of bed-bugs.'

Visibly shocked, Paul lowered his eyes to the pavement.

'Ma birthed nine babies in that house and three of them died. After my Dad's death we used to go to school with cardboard in our shoes to try to keep the wet out of the holes in the bottom. Ma used to pawn her wedding ring when she had nothing else to pop, just to keep some food on the table till her next wage come in. And there were thousands worse off than us.' She flung her final words at him. '*That's* where I come from. Still want to marry me?'

She had her answer from the appalled expression on his face. When she walked away, he did not follow.

Paul walked disconsolately back to the harbour. He had realised that the Ellis family were poor, inadequately educated, and had not had an easy life, but the things Queenie had just revealed were beyond belief. Who would believe, with her natural style and good humour that she had lived such a deprived childhood? He was shocked, never having bothered to give much thought to those less fortunate than himself.

It wasn't right, the great divide between rich and poor.

The Victorian adage of God ordering 'man's estate', with 'the rich man in his castle and the poor man at his gate' was absolute hypocrisy in its lack of Christianity. He hoped the government would act on the recommendations of the Beveridge Report, which he would study again with more care.

He stood gazing out over Portsmouth Harbour, watching a ferry leave the pontoon for Gosport on the other side, thinking back over what he now perceived as his own privileged childhood.

He had wanted for nothing in the material sense, yet he could not say he had been happy. He had been a nervous, shrinking boy, terrified of his demanding father, and sad for his beautiful, gentle mother in whom he sensed similar feelings to his own. His parents' marriage was sterile. He never saw any evidence of affection or otherwise between them.

He was sent to boarding school at an early age. The only times he and his father connected in any way was when they sailed together after years of hard schooling in seamanship. He could see his father's fierce countenance now, hair tousled and teeth bared against a stiff wind.

'Come on, boy, pull that sheet in. Put some muscle into it.' Paul straining against the taut ropes, his fingers sore from the rough fibre. Fear gripping his vitals when a sudden squall made the boat heel over at an alarming angle, and his father merely laughing at the challenge. Never daring to show his fear, never receiving any praise for his efforts. Only in later years when he had mastered the skills of sailing did Paul ever feel the equal of his father, and only in their sailing boat was he shown any respect from him.

Paul seethed with pent-up passions for which he thought, in Queenie, he had found an outlet. He ached for her physically, adored her completely, admired her carefree spirit and courage, and wanted to possess her absolutely. He asked nothing in return except to be given the opportunity to cherish her and her children and raise them up, making up for all the things he had taken for granted but that they had lacked.

No, who was he kidding? To be honest he knew that wasn't all he asked. He *needed* Queenie. As much, or more than, she needed him. Her ordinariness, her sane grasp on life would keep him anchored firmly to the ground. Because sometimes he sensed in himself a wildness, an uncertainty, a desire to break free from constraints, and he was afraid of where it might lead him. There appeared to be two sides to his character, forever warring for supremacy: light and positive against dark and depressive.

In Queenie he had thought he had found his salvation. Now the rock on which he wished to build his life had crumbled into shifting sand.

Queenie answered the door to Lieutenant William Saunders. 'Oh, hello, Bill,' she stuttered.

'Hello, Queenie. Hope you don't mind me turning up like this. It's Paul, you see . . .'

'Paul? You better come in.' She stepped aside and ushered him into the living room, feeling embarrassed at the humbleness of her home. She was glad that Ma was round at Lil's. 'What about Paul?'

'He's in hospital – '

'Oh no!' Horror shuddered through her and she felt faint. Not again! Keith, Jimmy, John, Ray – now Paul.

'It's nothing to worry about,' Bill assured her, taking off his hat and holding it to his chest. 'Shrapnel wounds to the arm and shoulder. But – he's awfully depressed. I'm worried about his mental state. I gather you and he have had a bust up?'

'You can say that again.'

'He er, he loves you, you know.'

'He's got a funny way of showing it.'

'Mmm. He's a strange cove in some ways, but from

what he said to me last night, I gather he adores you and is devastated at losing you. It's none of my business, of course, but I thought I'd try to play Cupid and bring two lovers together again.'

Queenie shrugged. '*That* we never were. I don't know what I feel for him, and he seems to be in love with his idea of me. But he couldn't take it when he thought he'd found out what I was really like. He was ready to believe the worst of me. Be honest, Bill, you never approved, did you?'

He gave her a wry grin. 'I did wonder if you were taking advantage of him, if you don't mind me saying so. He's such a baby where women are concerned.'

'He chased *me*, you know. I wasn't all that keen. But then I got to like him and to think it might work out between us. Till we had that row. What do you want me to do now?'

'I thought you might go and see him. Cheer him up a bit.'

'Here, did he send you?'

'He did not. Scout's honour. Come on, do come. I've got a pass for you. Had to say you were his fiancée, but that doesn't matter. You can come across with me in the launch if you come now.'

She hesitated for a moment. Wouldn't it be better to leave things as they were? 'I don't know. He was pretty disgusted with me, and I don't have to take that from anyone.'

'I'm sure, from what he told me last night, that he's very sorry.'

'I don't know if I want to get involved with him again.'

'Come on, Queenie, be a sport. Just to cheer him up a bit. I'm sure he'd like to apologise at least.'

'Oh, all right. Give me five minutes to tidy meself up.' She was sure it was a mistake, but she felt a responsibility. That's what people did to you – got under your defences and made you feel you owed them something.

*

Paul was laying against the pillows, white-faced and with mauve shadows under his closed eyes. His hair, usually so immaculate, was ruffled. He looked very young and vulnerable.

Queenie's shadow fell across him and he opened his eyes. Clear grey-blue, with not a hint of duplicity in their depths.

'Queenie,' he cried with delight, sitting up suddenly and falling back with a groan.

'Are you in a lot of pain?' she asked with furrowed brow.

'Only when I move.' He smiled, his teeth looking too big in the thin face. 'This is wonderful. How did you know? Why have you come after . . . the way I behaved?'

'Bill came to see me.'

'Good old Bill.'

'I just wanted to see if you were all right. After all, we were friends.'

'More than friends, I hope. Oh, Queenie. Lovely, warm-hearted Queenie.' Reaching out, he grasped her hand, his expression intense. They both watched his thumb massaging the back of her hand.

'Oh well,' she said perkily, 'Look on the bright side. You're in here, having a nice rest instead of going out on those nasty night patrols.'

'Sit on the bed.' He told her how he had been wounded by enemy aircraft fire. 'We got the blighter, though. One of the seamen was killed. Makes you feel glad to be alive and guilty at the same time.'

She smiled. 'I'm glad you're alive.'

He looked at her solemnly. 'I don't know why, after the way I've treated you. I'm so sorry – I don't know what got into me.'

'We all get angry and disappointed at times, it's only human. Trouble with me is that I'm more human than most. Made lots of mistakes, done lots of stupid things.'

'I think you've come through it all marvellously. You're a wonderful girl.'

She shook her head. 'That's the mistake you made before, Paul. You have to accept people as they really are. I can't undo all the bad things I've done in my life.'

'I'm sure you haven't done anything really bad – '

'I don't want to talk about it. How long are they keeping you in? Will you get some sick leave?'

'Time enough.'

She raised an enquiring eyebrow.

'To get married.'

Her eyes opened wide. 'Here, you don't mean what I think you mean, do you? I've told you – '

He sat up and again sank back with a groan. 'Queenie, marry me. What are we waiting for? We may not have time to waste. I've had nothing to do but lie here and think. Take stock of what I want out of life. The thing that kept coming to me was that I want you – I can't envisage any sort of life without you – '

'Paul – '

'Let me finish. Can you try to forgive me? I've been a narrow-minded prat. It's just an accident of birth if someone is born in a castle and someone else is born in – '

'A slum?'

'Whatever. Your background has made you strong. Bill told me that, I remember. We both have things to give each other. You are a coper, a survivor. You can give me your strength, your humour, your good commonsense. And I can give you a better standard of life. You deserve it. The only question is, do *I* deserve you?'

'Don't be daft. You deserve better. Not that there's anything wrong with the Ellises mind, but – '

'Marry me! As soon as we can, by special licence.'

Queen bit on her lip. 'I said your parents had to meet me first and you had to meet my children.'

He grinned. 'There you are, you see, ever practical and sensible. Don't be, this time. Let your heart rule your head. It's *us* that counts. It's *our* life, our marriage. The others will have to fit in.'

Queenie laughed. 'I don't know where you get the idea I'm practical and sensible, I've always acted on impulse, and that's what's got me into all sorts of trouble.'

'Then let this be no exception. Let's be impulsive together. Oh, Queenie, my darling, there's so much misery in the world. Let's find some happiness together – while we can.'

Queenie studied his eager face. Was it a possibility after all? He was keen enough for both of them. Would it be wrong to fulfil her early ambitions in life, to snatch at a chance to better herself? After all, he had said she had a lot to offer him too. She had done some stupid things in her life, but surely marrying a fine young man like Paul wouldn't be one of them?

She walked to the window, looked out over the sparkling sea. It was cold but a lovely sunny day. She remembered the day at Sally Port when she had looked at a sea like this and yearned to marry Keith Jackson. She had wanted love, but thought he could give her a better life too. She still wanted those things. Was it wrong? Life was too short . . .

She came back to the pale young man in the bandages, bent and kissed his cheek.

'All right. You're on. But don't ever say I didn't warn you.'

# · Thirty-six ·

On a January morning in 1944, Frederick Knight, now occupied in the War Office, padded barefoot to the phone in his Kensington apartment in his Paisley-patterned pyjamas. 'Yes!' he barked into the handset.

His wife's near-hysterical voice vibrated in his ear. Something about 'Paul . . . today . . . you must put a stop to it at once!'

It must be something really serious; Olivia was normally so cool. Too damned cool. Cutting in on her cultured voice, he insisted, 'Calm down, dear, calm down. Now start at the beginning.' His heavy-jowled but still handsome face was set in lines of exasperation.

'Then *listen* to me, dear. I've had a telegram from Paul. He says he is getting married today, in a Portsmouth *Register Office* by *special licence* of all things and – '

'What's the hurry?'

'I'll tell you what the hurry is. He is marrying a *widow* with two children! And he's left it till the last minute to tell us because he knows we'll disapprove. He's only just twenty-one for heaven's sake.'

'Young fool!' Frederick ran his fingers through springy hair, that though greying, was as full of vitality as everything else about him. Upright, impatient, eagle-eyed, he met life head on at full tilt. 'Well, we may not approve, my dear, but there's precious little we can do about it now. We think of him as a boy, but by law he's a man, old enough to marry, to fight for King and Country and lay down his life for them if necessary – '

'Frederick! Don't even *think* things like that,' Olivia wept.

'We've got to face facts, my dear. His life may well be a short one, so let's wish him a merry one while he can enjoy it.'

'How can you say things like that so calmly? And what sort of woman can she be?' his wife wailed piteously. 'She must be years older than him to have two children.'

'Do him good to have some responsibilities.'

'Don't you think he's got enough already being first officer on a fighting boat,' she asked sharply. 'He's only a boy – '

'He's obviously growing up faster than we realise, my dear,' Frederick chuckled. 'Now, I must get off. See you tonight – '

'But Frederick, why hasn't he given us a chance to go to his wedding? It's *very* suspicious.'

'He must have his reasons. Perhaps he's being posted.'

'But Frederick – '

'Leave it, Olivia. There are far more important things to think about, after all. Have you seen the papers this morning? No? Well, go and read about the Americans defeating the Japanese in the Solomons. That should cheer you up. Now the Allies just need to finalise a second front in Europe and we'll squeeze that Fascist Hitler out of existence.'

'Frederick, we must stop Paul – '

'There's nothing to be done. You send them a telegram wishing them good luck, d'you hear?'

'Women!' he stormed, slamming the handset down. Why ever did they give them the vote? – unreliable, irrational creatures.

No-one, witnessing Olivia Knight's stillness and the calm expression on her oval, madonna-like face, would guess at the turmoil raging within. Her prematurely white hair was plaited around her head like a coronet, and her large, clear-grey eyes appeared untroubled as she sat at the lead-paned window overlooking the Knot Garden.

Olivia wished that, just occasionally, her husband would be sympathetic to *her* viewpoint, would take notice of her distress. But he was always absorbed in his own interests, his own importance. To him she was merely the mother of his son, châtelaine of his Tudor house, occasional hostess and a necessary appendage in public.

*Now if she was Alice . . .*

But Frederick should have tried to do something about this latest business. She was so worried that Paul was going to ruin his life over an unsuitable woman. 'Marry in haste and repent at leisure.' She believed in that proverb, because hadn't she . . .? Well she had certainly married in haste, given it scarcely a thought, she had wanted the charismatic Frederick so much.

She recalled the night that her father had brought his young protegé home to dinner. Frederick Knight's bold, golden eyes had raked her from head to toe and everything in her leapt in startled response before subsiding, trembling, beneath her usual modest demeanour.

All through dinner, while he talked to her father, and complimented her mother, she was tremulously aware of him; his height and breadth, the dark hair springing in vibrant curls from his brow, the large Roman nose and sensuous mouth. And above all, the piercing gaze of those tawny eyes. *A hawk*. When he addressed her, she stuttered her answers foolishly, with downcast eyes.

With the blessings of her parents, she was carried along in fearful delight on the swift tide of his courtship. Terrified of his power but unwilling and unable to resist.

Alice came back from Paris for the wedding.

'The lovely Latimer girls,' they were known as in London society, but Olivia was under no illusion. Alice, her identical twin, febrile and passionate, was the substance; *she*, the pale shadow. It had always been so. Where Alice soared through life, Olivia was pedestrian. Where Alice brightly shone, Olivia merely glowed.

It was a Society wedding. Alice, in old gold satin, had

played the bridesmaid with an angry, troubled beauty that far outshone the outward serenity of the bride. While Olivia's hair was dark, Alice's was ebony. Olivia's grey-blue eyes shone, but Alice's were turbulent. Olivia's complexion was pearly pale, Alice's was peachy bloom. Olivia was tall and stately while Alice swayed like a supple willow. But Olivia was oblivious to comparisons on that occasion – she had eyes only for her bridegroom.

Alice had flung off to Europe while Olivia and Frederick honeymooned in Scotland. She married a count and divorced him a year later and had been in trouble of one sort or another with undesirable men ever since. She flitted in and out of their lives from time to time, like a migratory swallow; Olivia sensing the undercurrents of excitement in Frederick at her presence, the arc of attraction that joined them with an invisible yet palpable thread.

Olivia shuddered, and not from cold because it was a surprisingly mild day. It was the certainty of her sister's mental instability that upset her. Alice wrecked everything and everybody she came into contact with, and seemed set on a course of self-destruction. What eventually would become of her?

Sighing, Olivia rang the bell for coffee, wondering as she did so what sort of woman her son had got mixed up with. Of course people did all sorts of reckless things in these uncertain times. She heard so often lately about sons and daughters of villagers meeting someone in the Forces and marrying a few days later. She imagined that divorce would become very fashionable after the war – if it ever ended – and if there were any young men left to divorce.

What would Paul's bride be wearing this morning? White would be inappropriate so it would probably be a utility costume with a tight, short skirt and a flower pinned to her lapel. How sad that it would not be the society wedding in Faversham church, with lots of guests and the three-tiered cake, that she had always expected for her only son. This war had a lot to answer for, all the old values disappearing. Olivia took out a lace-edged handkerchief to wipe the tears from her cheeks, inhaling from it the scent of lavender culled from her own garden.

What sort of girl was Paul marrying? Pretty? Kind? Would she like her new mother-in-law? Was Paul fond of the children he was going to be father to? The best that Olivia could hope for was that his bride wasn't some scheming, money-grabbing little madam, bent on social advancement. But Paul would have the sense to see through a girl like that.

Frederick Knight usually went home to Faversham on Wednesday nights, spending four nights a week in London. Pressure of work became a useful excuse for sometimes staying up in the city on the Wednesday as well.

Frederick had no difficulty in organising his life into neat compartments. There was his gracious weekend life in the country, regular holidays with his wife and family, his working life in London and an exciting, secret compartment, opened only occasionally, and known only to him and one other.

He was waiting for that 'other' to arrive at any moment on this particular Wednesday evening. The apartment was cosy. There were candles and flowers, chilled wine and edible delicacies – such as wartime would allow – under cover.

Frederick was bathed, shaved, and, in his mulberry smoking-jacket and cravat, relaxing with a cigar. Or trying to relax, because these occasions were so fraught with delicious anticipation, that he found calm difficult. When the doorbell rang, he laid down the cigar, sprang to his feet, examining himself quickly in the mirror over the mantelpiece, before going to answer it.

'My darling,' he murmured to the apparition who waited on his threshold, and gathered her into his arms.

## · *Thirty-seven* ·

Queenie's second wedding was a quick and spartan affair. No aunts, uncles or cousins. No neighbours from Baker Street to wish her well. No singing and dancing in the church hall afterwards. No in-laws – for which lack she was profoundly grateful.

She wore her wine-red grosgrain dress under her mulberry coat to the Register Office, with a corsage of snowdrops pinned to it with the bird brooch. The only witnesses and guests on her side were Ma, Phyllis and Eddy. On the other side, Paul and Bill, his best man, looked handsome in their uniforms, if you could ignore that Paul had to wear his draped over the arm in the sling.

Paul had managed to obtain a utility gold ring as he wanted his bride to wear *his* marriage token, so Queenie had sold her first, better-quality wedding ring to buy some things they needed for the flat and to complete the fund for her father's headstone.

Paul had accompanied the Ellis family the week before, in bitterly cold weather, to see the headstone installed at last in Kingston Cemetery. A plain, round-topped stone bearing the inscription

Joshua Ellis<br>1888–1929<br>Beloved husband and father<br>R.I.P.

Paul stood a respectful distance from the family group, watching the dignified little ceremony.

Queenie placed a wreath of chrysanthemums against the stone, and she and Beatie, arms linked, cried and murmured together. Phyllis reached out for Eddy's hand and he linked his fingers with hers. Billy was in Sicily, Jimmy was away at sea, so the only other family member was Josh, now a tall, seventeen-year-old in sailor's uniform. He looked a bit embarrassed, obviously wondering what all the fuss was about, having been only three when his father died.

Queenie turned to Paul, eyes pink-rimmed from tears and nose red from cold, with a sweet smile on her face. He went to her side and she threaded her other arm through his. 'I feel so happy this has been done at last,' she said to him. 'And I like that little border of stone – it keeps him private, like.' She turned to Beatie and said, 'Now darling Dad can rest in peace, Ma.'

Beatie blew her nose. 'He was a lovely man. One of the best. And don't you ever forget, our Queenie, that you was his favourite.'

Queenie walked away down the path on Paul's arm, radiant as the bride she was today, and his heart had swelled with love for her.

They had a small wedding reception at Kimbells and joined in the tea-dance. A few of Paul's shipmates turned up and a few more of the Ellises and Lil, of course. The cake was a small, soya-marzipanned affair, overlaid with a white satin cover and a spray of artificial white roses in place of icing. They were all very happy with it.

Then the bride and groom left to walk down Osborne Road to the Queen's Hotel on Southsea Common where they were to spend an extravagant honeymoon night at Paul's insistence. He had seventy-two hours left of his sick-leave and tomorrow they would walk down Western

Parade, alongside the Common, to Castle Road and their first home – a flat above a shop.

The Queen's Hotel was like something out of a film for Queenie. They walked up red-carpeted stairs to an elegant room with a view of the sea. There they stood looking out of the window, Paul clasping his good arm around his bride's middle, his chin resting on her hair. Her hands rested on his.

'Won't it be lovely when those barricades can come down and we can go swimming again,' Queenie said. 'Do you think this war will ever end?'

'Yes, darling, and we're going to win it. It will drag on in the Pacific, of course, but with Operation Overlord being mounted soon – '

'I keep hearing about that, but what is it?'

'Can't say any more, I'm afraid. But, if it's successful, *and it must be*, it could be the beginning of the end.'

'Oh, wouldn't it be wonderful? But what will we do when the war is over? It's become a way of life, hasn't it? Will you stay in the Navy?'

'I doubt it. I'll probably do what I always intended, become a lawyer or a solicitor. My father quite approves of that idea, though he'd like me eventually to go into politics.'

Queenie broke away and twisted round to look at him, horrified. 'Oh, Gawd, I could never be a politician's wife, Paul, I'm pig-ignorant about things like that. I wouldn't know what to say to people, how to behave.'

'I've never known you lost for words, my darling. But let's not worry tonight about things that might never happen.'

'But we should have discussed all this before we tied the knot. I should have thought – I should have realised. I mean, being married to a chap in the Navy is one thing, but I'll let you down, won't I? I warned you we weren't suited – '

'Darling, darling.' Paul embraced her with his good arm.

'Don't upset yourself. If there's one thing I'm sure of, it's that you have the courage to rise to any occasion. Whatever we do, we'll do together – you won't have to face any ordeal on your own.'

She looked doubtful, then laid her head against his shoulders. 'But one thing that I have got to face is meeting your parents. You won't be able to help me much there. I'm terrified – suppose they don't like me?'

'How could they possibly resist you, my darling? I couldn't. But suppose your little girls don't like me? That's far more important.'

'They'll love you – love having a new daddy.' She hoped they would. Hannah might be difficult. Guilt swept over Queenie as she thought of Keith. How would he feel about her marrying again so soon? Just under two years. In her mind's eye he came to her, that wry smile on his face. 'Go on, be happy, Queen of the May,' he might say. 'Life isn't a dress rehearsal, you know. You only get one chance.' No, she wouldn't spoil her wedding day with feelings of guilt. It wasn't fair on Paul.

Paul was now whispering in her ear, causing a shudder to go through her, 'And what about you, Mrs Knight? Do you love your children's new daddy?'

Queenie turned in his arm and reached up to link hers around his neck. 'Well – 'course I do,' she said a little hesitantly but kissed him lingeringly. He pressed her to him urgently, quickly becoming aroused.

She wanted to make his first time wonderful for him – it was one thing *she* could do for *him*, so she whispered. 'Don't let's hurry it. It'll spoil it for you. Let's go down and have supper – ooh, I hope there's something nice on the menu – then we'll come up here and . . .' kiss, kiss, kiss, 'we'll take it nice and slow.' She began to get excited herself so broke away with a laugh. 'I better put some more lipstick on.'

Paul reclined on the bed, watching with a smile of wonderment on his face as she brushed her hair and leant towards the mirror to carefully outline her lips with wine-red lipstick and rub them together to coat the lower lip before applying more to the top one. A dab of perfume he had bought her as a wedding present and she was ready. 'How's that?' She twirled round with a swirl of her skirt.

'Mysterious woman. I'm the luckiest man alive,' he smiled.

The main dish on the menu was Coq au vin which, to Queenie, sounded very exotic. She cut Paul's portion up for him to eat off his fork. After a few mouthfuls, Paul removed a bone from his mouth and examined it. 'I believe this is rabbit masquerading as chicken,' he said in disgust.

'Don't you know there's a war on, mate?' laughed his bride. 'I've never tasted anything so nice.' The manager found a bottle of red wine for them as they were 'honey-mooners' and they gazed into each other's eyes and held hands across the table.

'I love you, Mrs Knight.'

Queenie examined his thin young face with the nose that was just a little too big for it. She loved him – of course she did – but she was not *in love* with him. Did that matter? It would come in time, wouldn't it? Gazing into the depths of his clear-grey eyes, she was suddenly afraid of her impulsiveness. How had she come to marry this stranger. She knew virtually nothing about him. But she had struck a bargain with him and with herself and she was going to honour it.

'Paul Knight,' she said softly. 'I am going to be a good wife to you. I'm going to try to make you very happy.'

'Amen to that. Finished? Shall we go upstasirs, my love?' His eyes were adoring.

They climbed the lushly carpeted stairs again, hand-in-hand. ' I bet Buckingham Palace isn't no better than this,' Queenie observed, looking up at the chandeliers.

'I'm not sure I can carry you across the threshold,' he said as they reached their room.

'Never mind.' She opened the door, drew him in and

closed it behind them. Threading her arms around his neck, she purred. 'You'd better save your strength for something more important.'

'But how are we going to manage with this arm of mine?' asked Paul desperately.

'Don't worry, we will. Here, let me.' She removed his uniform jacket, unlooped his tie, and with tantalising slowness and smouldering glances she undid his shirt buttons and eased it off his injured arm. They both giggled with nervousness when she got to the trousers, and she left him sitting on the bed in his underpants and in a state of arousal while she slowly unpinned the brooch and corsage from her dress. With the tip of her tongue protruding saucily between her teeth, she unfastened her diamanté buttons and lifted the full-skirted dress above her head.

'You are so lovely,' Paul gasped as he gazed at her in her white satin French knickers, camisole and suspenders. Enjoying the effect she was having on him, Queenie stepped out of her new shoes – coupons courtesy of Ma – lifted one foot onto a chair, undid the suspenders and rolled one nylon stocking slowly down her leg. She felt deliciously decadent in the sheer nylons given to her by Sally's Yank.

'You wicked girl,' murmured Paul throatily. 'For God's sake hurry up.'

Laughing merrily, Queenie divested herself quickly of her underwear and walked towards him clothed in nothing but blushes and a new wedding ring.

'Oh my darling,' Paul murmured against her breasts, holding her tightly to him with his good arm.

Queenie was used to following where men led in love-making, but tonight, with an injured and uninitiated bridegroom, she knew she must take the lead. Tenderly, putting aside her shyness, Queenie led her young bride-groom through the mysteries of love to manhood.

*

The first day of married life for Mr and Mrs Paul Knight in the Honeymoon Suite of the Queen's Hotel dawned crisp and clear. A chambermaid brought them morning tea, and at their request pulled back the curtains. In the warmth of the soft bed they turned to each other and smiled. Paul leant on his good arm and kissed his bride. 'I love you.'

'I know you do.'

'You made me so happy last night.'

Queenie pushed his hair from his forehead. 'I'm glad. You deserve it.'

'How do you mean? For being a good boy? My reward for services rendered to my country?'

'No, I mean for marrying me. You don't know what you've let yourself in for.'

He grinned. 'After last night I've a pretty good idea.'

'There are other things to marriage, you know,' Queenie said, sitting up and revealing her tip-tilted breasts as she reached for her cup of tea. She took a long drink then turned to him as he lay adoring her with his eyes. 'I hope you won't ever regret it, Paul.'

There was an expression on her face that made him ask. 'Not having second thoughts, are you?'

''Course not. I'm going to have a lovely bath in that luxurious bathroom, then I'm going to put a new dressing on your arm. After that we'll have breakfast and a brisk walk along the sea-front before we go home.'

'But before all that . . .' he said, reaching out to her, his eyes warm with desire.

'Oh, yes, before all that – ' She enveloped him in her warm flesh and tickled him with her hair.

Paul dozed while Queenie warbled in the bath. Beneath the haze of euphoria in which he was wallowing, lurked the uneasy knowledge that he still had to face the music as far as his parents were concerned. He would rather face a flotilla of E-boats any day. He knew that if he had taken Queenie home to meet them first, he might well have been bullied against it by his father, and tearfully dissuaded by his mother. This way there was nothing they could do about it, but he hoped they would be kind to their daughter-in-law.

Queenie's voice cracked on a high note and he smiled in delight. His new wife could not sing, but she did not let that stop her. He had so many discoveries to make about her. His wedding night had been all he had hoped for in spite of the impediment of his injured arm. Perfect. Of course it would have been less so if Queenie had been as inexperienced as he.

He was grateful for her initiation that gave him such unimaginable pleasure . . . yet, unreasonably, in the cold light of morning he bitterly resented it. She had belonged to others – learnt from other men. How many? He wanted to know every detail of her past yet knew he would not be able to bear the knowledge.

She would never be solely and entirely his. He thumped his clenched fist against the mattress. He must not allow thoughts of this nature to intrude on his happiness. He *must* put it out of his mind.

After a bracing walk along the sea-front, the newly-weds walked past the Queen's Hotel into Western Parade, towards Castle Road. This was a narrow little commercial street of shops and businesses and their first home was to be over an antique shop.

Paul managed with some difficulty to lift his bride over the threshold of the cold and cheerless two-bedroomed flat. They exchanged a lingering kiss.

'We'll soon have this place feeling like home,' trilled Queenie, skipping from room to room. 'First thing is to put these snowdrops into water.' She rummaged in a cupboard and found a glass. 'You light the gas-fire in the front room, then we'll unpack our boxes before we go out to buy some food. I'm looking forward to seeing what the shops are like round here. It's ever so much posher than Portsea. And we've got that little view of the sea from the bay window.'

Apart from his clothes, Paul had little more than a few books and a couple of photos to contribute until he could bring some of his belongings from the family home. But once Queenie had unpacked her ornaments, the lamps that were a wedding present from her mother, and bits and pieces, the place began to feel cosy. She put a hot-water bottle in the bed that they were keen to get into, and had just made a pot of tea when the doorbell rang. Queenie groaned. 'Hope it's not Ma, come to see how we're settling in.'

But it was a couple of telegrams. 'From my parents,' said Paul with a strained smile, opening the first one. He gave a sigh of relief; 'Wishing us happiness.'

'That's nice.' Queenie smiled at the telegram boy. 'No answer to that one, anyway. Who else would be sending us one?'

Paul read the message with a puzzled frown: VIOLET ILL. MEET CHILDREN HARBOUR STATION 6 p.m. TRAVELLING WITH FRIENDS. B. JACKSON.

Oh, my Gawd,' shrieked Queenie, hand to mouth, 'What a wedding present. The kids are coming home.' She laughed and laughed, and the messenger boy hopped from foot to foot waiting for an answer or a tip.

'Oh, sorry, Paul,' she put her arms around him after they closed the door. 'A honeymoon for four. Still, you'll love them – I hope.'

Paul gave a wry smile. His few precious days with his new bride were threatened with ruin, but seeing Queenie's excitement, he was happy for her.

They called on Beatie before they went to the station to tell her the news. 'Some honeymoon!' she cackled, wiping tears from her eyes. 'But it'll be lovely to have them back, poor little sods.'

Amongst all the other travellers, two little girls, accompanied by a strange woman, alighted from the train. The tallest of the two wore her hair in pigtails and her thin legs were exposed between knee-length socks and an outgrown camel coat. Mournful eyes in a white face revealed that Hannah had not outgrown travel-sickness. Those hazel eyes in shadowed sockets and the cleft chin made Queenie's breath catch in her throat. She was so like her father.

The smaller child was encased in plum red from head to foot, from the bonnet over the elastic of which her plump little cheeks bulged, and the velvet-collared coat, to the leggings buttoned at the ankle and overlapping her red shoes. Emma had left her babyhood behind and bore a distinct and self-possessed resemblance to her grandmother, Violet Jackson. How they had changed in the space of a few months.

'Mummy!'

With a lump in his throat, Paul watched as Queenie went down on her haunches and hugged and kissed her youngest daughter. The child responded, clinging to her mother's neck like a limpet. 'Hannah?' The other child was unresponsive as her mother embraced her.

Wiping away tears, Queenie stood up and thanked the pleasant-faced woman and her husband, who said, 'We're so glad you got the telegram or we'd have been chasing round Portsmouth trying to find you. It was fortunate that we were coming up this way, wasn't it? We're on our way to London. Bernard would have brought them but he could hardly leave poor Violet in the state she is in. Complete breakdown, you know. Still it's hardly surprising . . .' She rummaged in her bag. 'I've got a letter from him.'

Paul offered the couple refreshment in the station bar, but they declined as they had only fifteen minutes to make their London connection. They took their leave with a fond hug of the children and a last curious glance at the young couple.

Paul and Queenie looked down at the children and then at each other with slightly dazed expressions. Queenie took her children each by a hand and the newly-formed little family walked up the platform. Emma was skipping and clinging to her mother's hand as she looked up at her, wreathed in smiles. Suddenly she stopped in her tracks. 'Where's my case?' she demanded.

'Daddy's got it,' her mother informed her.

A little frown creased Emma's brow. 'I haven't got a daddy.'

'Yes you have.' Queenie drew Paul forward. 'Emma, Hannah, this is your new Daddy.'

The children's surprised gazed travelled up the navy-blue length of the stranger at their mother's side. Up, up and up. Two pairs of eyes, both hazel but quite different in shape and expression, slowly appraised the anxiously-smiling face. 'Do you think you'll like that?' the mouth with big teeth asked.

There was a long pause while the adults wondered what thoughts were going through the little heads. Were they comparing the new Daddy with the old? Suppose they burst into tears? Suddenly realising how alarming his height must be, Paul went down on one knee. The children solemnly studied his peaked cap, his candid eyes, the Roman nose, the anxiously-smiling mouth. Hannah's eyes were suspicious under lowered brows, Emma's curious.

'Yes,' Emma said eventually, 'I think I'll like that very much,' and threw her arms around his neck. Hannah studied her shoes.

With Emma's plump little cheek pressed against his, Paul's heart swelled with emotion, and his eyes with tears. He had no experience of young children and he was humbled by this little scrap of humanity putting her trust in him. He hoped he would be worthy and he hoped he would win her sister over. He lifted his youngest stepdaughter with his good arm, smiling into her sweet little face, and Queenie followed behind with the cases and Hannah.

# · *Thirty-eight* ·

It was wonderful to have her babies home again, mused Queenie. And to have her own home and a passionate new husband. So why was she feeling so irritable? Well for one thing, she and Paul hadn't had the quiet few days they had expected in which to get to know each other better. And the children were each proving rather difficult in different ways. It wasn't surprising after the insecurity of the last few years, but there were thousands of kids worse off.

Emma woke most nights and screamed out in fear, Hannah crying in sympathy, and then Queenie had to go to her with reassurance that she was home to stay with her Mummy and new Daddy. This would sometimes interfere with their lovemaking, as did the child's early morning visits. Often Paul's mouth would tighten ominously and his eyes reveal his frustration, but so far he had kept his temper.

But Emma was such an affectionate and quaint little girl when she was in a good mood and often had them in fits of laughter. Like the time she was explaining how someone 'frew' something away.

'*Thr*ew,' prompted Paul with exaggerated tongue and cheek action.

She tried, poking out her little pink tongue, but it still came out 'frew.'

'*Thr*ew.'

'Fr – Oh well, he *chucked* it away.'

Her parents laughed. 'Have to teach you to speak

properly before you meet your new Grandma and Grandpa,' said Paul.

Queenie felt a thrill of unease. 'She's only just coming up to five, Paul.'

'Oh. Well of course I don't know much about child development, but I suppose we need to correct her or she won't learn, will she? Hannah speaks very nicely having been with the Jacksons so much longer – when she speaks, that is.'

Hannah was an introverted, moody child, given to colouring painting-books meticulously in quiet corners. Only in play with Emma did she reveal any spontaneity, and Queenie found her very aggravating. She resented Paul's reference to the Jacksons' good influence on Hannah.

'Well, it isn't my fault that the poor little sods have been pushed around and haven't had an easy time over the last few years, is it? It hasn't been a piece of cake for me either, you know.'

Paul's brows drew down. 'I know it hasn't, darling, but it would help, you know, if you didn't use that sort of language in front of them.'

Queenie stared at him, puzzled for a moment. Did he mean 'sods'? She decided to laugh. 'Gawd, they've been brought up with it. In case you hadn't noticed, it's the way the Ellis family speak.'

'I had noticed, and I appreciate that when you're with them – naturally – you want to be like them. And I've also noticed that you *do* make an effort when you're not with them. So I was hoping that now we're married we could put that sort of language behind us.'

Queenie's eyes flashed but she said carelessly, 'Oh girls, we're going to have to watch our Ps and Qs. Soon the Ellis family won't be good enough for the likes of us.'

'Hrmm. Sorry if I've offended you, my sweet.' Paul reached out a hand to stroke her hair but she tossed her head away from his hand.

Thinking about her reasons for feeling less than ecstastic in the first days of her new marriage, Queenie acknowledged to herself that she was bored, stuck in the little flat for large parts of the day now that Emma and Hannah had just started at St Jude's school. It was frustrating waiting for Paul to turn up when he could, now that he was back in commission. He was away most nights too, and life was very erratic.

If she wasn't expecting Paul home, Queenie would go shopping for something to do and invariably found herself buying things to make the flat more attractive, incurring Paul's thin-lipped disapproval when she told him she had spent her houskeeping allowance by Wednesday. 'We'll have to cut down on luxuries, darling, we can't afford this sort of thing on my pay.'

'Thought a lieutenant's pay was good,' she answered truculently.

'Not all that marvellous with a rent to pay and four people to feed.'

Some days she would catch a bus to Portsea to see Ma. If she was late back or Paul was home unexpectedly early, he would be clearly annoyed.

'Well, I got to do something to keep myself from going round the bend,' she told him crossly on one occasion.

'I don't understand it. My mother has never minded being at home . . . but then I suppose your situations are quite different.'

You can say that again. Look Paul, I had a talk with Ma and she's quite happy to come up and take care of the kids for an hour or two after school, so I could get a job. We could do with the money and I'd like – '

'No! We've discussed this. I won't have a wife of mine working. I married you to take you away from all that. And in any case, I'd prefer that Emma and Hannah do not spend too much time with your mother.'

'Why not?' asked Queenie with a dangerous glint in her eye.

'Well,' he hesitated, the colour rising in his cheeks. 'As you know, I think Mrs Ellis is an admirable little woman but – '

'But?'

'It's just that, well, we want the best for our little girls. We both want that, don't we? And I don't think . . . I'm not sure that your mother is a good influence.'

'She brought me up, didn't she?' Queenie gave an angry laugh, her hands on her hips. 'If you don't like the way I've turned out why did you marry me?'

'Oh darling, darling, need you ask?' He came to her and took her in his arms. She was stiff at first but then allowed him to kiss away her bad humour. 'Try to be patient with me, my love. I know I can be an awful prig.'

'And a bleeding – oops, sorry! A real snob.'

They laughed together but both knew that a quarrel had been narrowly averted.

Yet Paul could be very sweet, Queenie thought, and now that his arm had more or less healed, he was a very ardent lover – when they got the chance. She knew that he adored her. And of course, she loved him – in a way.

Queenie discovered she was pregnant. And was absolutely devastated. So was Paul.

'Christ! That's all we need,' he stormed at her. 'I've only been married to you five minutes and we're already sharing our home with your two difficult children and now another one on the way. Am I ever going to get you to myself?'

'I don't want it any more than you,' she cried. 'I've got me hands full as it is. And how dare you talk about my chidlren like that.'

'How could it have happened, for Christ's sake?'

'Haven't you learned the facts of life yet?'

'I mean, we've been taking precautions.'

'Sometimes you get a bit over-enthusiastic – if I may

remind you. There have been occasions when precautions haven't been taken.'

Paul sat down, burying his head in his hands. Queenie looked out of the window, bitter-faced. 'I warned you, didn't I? I said you'd regret marrying me.'

After a few minutes he went to her, winding his arms around her midriff, resting his chin on her head. 'Forgive me, darling. I'm so sorry I said those things. I love you, and I love the little girls. It's just, as I said, I'd like to have you to myself. And I'm under a bit of strain with this Overlord coming along. It's so damned important.'

'I know.' They rocked gently together. 'You're just a boy, and you've got too much responsibility.'

'I'm such a lucky boy, though.' He nuzzled her ear, making her squirm. 'Hey, I've just had a thought. It might be a son. I'd love a son.'

'Would you really?' Queenie turned in his arms and wound hers around his neck. They smiled tenderly at each other.

'We'll call him Christopher.'

'We'll call him whatever you like, darling. The girls will be excited to have a little brother.'

'I love you, you fecund little earth mother. You're wonderful.'

'You're not so bad, yourself, when you're not calling me rude names.'

'That wasn't rude, I was merely paying tribute to your fruitfulness, you fruity morsel. I could eat you.' He kissed her lingeringly. 'You know what this means, don't you? We'd better get on with this visit to my parents.'

'You're just as worried as I am about that, don't try to kid me. Oh, I know they won't think I'm good enough for you.'

'The mother of their grandson? They'll love you. Just as I do.'

*

Paul's announcement that he was an expectant father was as good an excuse as any for a fog-bound Saturday night celebration on board *Grey Ghost*. The junior officers asked the cook if he could stretch the rations and come up with something special. They invited a couple of friends from one of the other boats.

One of them had typed out the menu and Paul read it aloud.

'*Potage de pomme de terre* – spud soup,
*Poisson rouge garné de lettuce* – tinned salmon,
*Ham Americaine et pommes frites* – spam and chips.
Cheese and Biscuits.

'God Almighty – a gourmet's delight. You'd never think there was a war on, would you? Sherry Amontillado, three and six a glass; Port, very superior, five bob a glass; Rum, Stripey's delight, seven shillings a glass; Lemon à la Grey Ghost, a tanner a glass. But water's on me, and thank God no one's drinking any.'

By the time the half-dozen young men had reached the cheese and biscuits, having washed the previous courses down with considerable amounts of the above beverages, they were very merry.

'Have another drink, Paul, old chap. Or d'you think we'd better not? We'll be in a pickle if this pea-souper clears suddenly and we have to go out and chase the Krauts,' observed 'Lanky Len' with a hiccup.

'No chance. The whole of the English Channel is as silent as the grave. Not a soul is stirring out of port tonight,' Paul assured them with owlish intensity, having been plied with several congratulatory drinks. 'Hey. Save some of that bloody mousetrap fodder for this end.'

'We'll really know the war's over when we can sink our teeth into a good T-bone steak.' Bill, Paul's best man, waved his arms about. 'God, am I sick of bloody *spam*. Spiced ham! What's in it, I'd like to know? Animal, vegetable or old socks? We'll be a race of pale pink zombies if we have to eat much more of it.'

'Unlike the child who was born – who was born as a result of an affair between . . . er, between Miss Starkey and a darkie,' offered Tod confidentially.

'What was the result of the affair between . . . those two people?'

'The offspring turned out khaki.' Groans all round.

'Twinkle, twinkle, little shtar,' began Paul.

'Shut up, Knight – you're tight.'

'Pissed as a newt in a brothel,' agreed Ted, which he followed by a rather garbled limerick about a young blade from St Paul who wore a newspaper kilt to a ball, which then 'caught on fire and burnt his entire – front page, sports section and All.'

'Twarkle, twarkle little stink,' chuckled Paul.

'Shut up Knight. This is Virgins Only night.'

'Who the hell are you, you think?' asked Paul.

'Bill, the most sober, raised his glass. 'I give you a toast. To Lieutenant Paul Knight, our comrade-in-arms, who has undertaken single-handed to . . . to what? What has he undertaken to do single-handed?'

'To proliferate,' Jim supplied, waving his glass in the air. 'But I don't think it had much to do with hands.'

'To Paul and his lovely bride.' They drank.

'Defeat to the Hun!' shouted Paul, jumping to attention with raised glass but swaying where he stood.

'Defeat to the Hun,' they repeated, someone squirting him with a soda-water syphon. He slumped to his seat spluttering and dripping.

'What was that word, Jim?' asked Ted. 'Proliferate? Sounds painful – like piles.'

'It means to re-pro-duce. The best of British luck to the happy couple – soon to be a trio.'

'Or a quartet – '

'Or a quintet.'

'No, make it a sextet. Nice round number.'

'Too much sex already.'

'There can never be too much sex,' slurred Paul.

'I agree,' said Len, 'but if your lovely wife could see you now, she'd never let you into her bed again. Pass the port to the exshpectant daddy. Speech, speech.'

Paul struggled to force the glass to make contact with the decanter, and with much clinking eventually managed it. He grinned and took a large swallow. 'I'm not so much under the affluence of incohol . . . as some people think I am,' he said with aplomb before passing out.

# · Thirty-nine ·

Paul hired a car to take his new family to Kent for the day to meet his parents. 'This will be my last leave before . . . you know what.'

'Operation Overlord – whatever that is.'

'Well, I can tell you this much, darling,' Paul told Queenie enthusiastically. 'It's going to be one of the biggest and most exciting military undertakings ever.'

'All those ships in the Solent and all down the south and east coast, Eddy says, must mean invasion of France. And you can't tell us that Hitler's spies haven't found out what's going on.'

'Obviously they know, but they don't know what the men at Portsmouth Combined Headquarters know, plotting deep in their hillside. And a lot of false information is being fed them as to where it will be. We'll give them the biggest surprise – '

'Just hope you live to tell the tale, that's all,' Queenie flung at him. 'You stand there all shiny-eyed and excited like a big kid. What's going to happen to us, I'd like to know, if you get yourself killed? And with another baby on the way – how am I supposed to cope?'

Paul gave an exaggerated sigh. 'I know, darling. Men have all the fun – ' chuckling at the absurdity of that statement ' – and women have a hard time of it, waiting and worrying.'

'And picking up the pieces. I just wish we wasn't having this baby, Paul. We should have been more careful until the war was over.'

'It was bad luck. That's why I want my parents to meet you now. If anything happens to me, they'll take care of you.'

'Will they? They won't like me.'

'They'll love you – just like I do.' He kissed her frowns away. 'Darling . . . you do love me, just a little bit, don't you?'

She pushed him away. ''Course I do, you daft bugger.'

'Uh uh, language!' he admonished with an anxious smile.

Remembering another row between her and Paul a couple of days previously, Queenie found it difficult to maintain a nonchalant attitude to the visit.

'There is one tiny thing you could do, to make things a little more . . . acceptable to my parents, darling.'

'Anything,' she said rashly.

'In that case,' he said, pleased, 'perhaps we could do something about . . . I haven't actually told them your name. Queenie is rather quaint, but – '

'You want me to change my name?' she had asked with raised eyebrows, hardly believing it.

'I've always rather liked Janet – '

Her eyes flashed. 'Then you should bloody well have married a Janet, shouldn't you? Bleeding nerve.' Her voice rose. 'My Dad called me Queenie and if it was good enough for him, it's more than good enough for me. I don't know how you've got the cheek – '

Paul raised his hands placatingly. A serious error of judgement. 'Of course, you're right. I'm sorry, darling. Of all the crass, stupid things to suggest.'

She stood glowering at him with her hands on her hips. 'How would you feel if I asked you to call yourself Charlie or somethink? You wouldn't feel you were *you* any more, would you? I grew up as Queenie May – that's who I am, and that's who I'm going to stay.'

'Of course. Forgive me, darling.'

'Perhaps you'd like to rename the kids – Elizabeth and Margaret should be good enough for your parents if it's good enough for the daughters of the King and Queen.'

They had ended up laughing about it, but it still rankled. If they don't like me, that's their bleeding bad luck, she told herself on the journey – but was a bundle of nerves by the time they reached the long drive of Becket House in Faversham. She had never before been anywhere so grand, apart from her honeymoon night in the Queen's Hotel.

They had been forced to pull-up several times on the journey for Hannah to be sick, Queenie fortunately anticipating this problem and asking Paul to stop as they neared the house so that she could change the miserable child's clothes and wash her with a damp flannel. By this time Emma was threatening to succumb to the same ailment.

They were admitted by the maid but Olivia Knight appeared immediately, a welcoming smile on her face that embraced them all swiftly before she held out her arms to her son. 'Darling boy!'

'Mother, dear.'

Queenie watched their fond embrace with misgivings. Was she going to have to fight this one too for a share of her son? What was it about posh mothers? Didn't have enough to do, or to worry about, so they tried to smother their kids? Mind you, she hadn't met many.

Olivia released Paul reluctantly and turned to his family. 'So this is . . .?'

'This is Queenie, mother,' said Paul with clenched jaw.

There was a noticeable pause before his mother said, 'Welcome, dear,' but she smiled kindly.

She had a sweet face, Queenie thought, like the Virgin Mary on a Christmas card. 'Mrs Knight,' she muttered, only just stopping herself from bending a knee to this regal lady who wore her silver hair like a coronet above her aristocratic brow.

'You must call me Mother like Paul does.' Her clear-grey eyes swept a quick appraisal over her new daughter-in-law, carefully concealing an opinion. 'And here are the little girls.' She bent towards them with a gentle smile.

'Hannah and Emma,' introduced Queenie, pushing them forward. 'Remember your manners,' she prompted the awed children and they both bobbed the curtsy she had been teaching them for days. Paul gave her a quick frown, indicating that this had been unnecessary.

'What pretty girls,' observed Ovivia, tactfully ignoring this over-exuberance of respect. 'I expect you're tired and thirsty after your long drive. Come through to the conservatory and have some lemondade.' Taking Paul's arm, she led the way. 'You look tired, my darling. Is your poor arm completely healed? Your father will join us for lunch – '

'He's in his study? I would have thought that he could have put himself out to come down to meet us. Just for once.'

'He's very busy, Paul. So many documents – '

'Even he has to take time off occasionally.'

'You know your father, darling. Always been the same. Doesn't know how to relax.' They entered the high-domed conservatory off the dining-room, with its views over the garden.

'What a lovely room,' Queenie commented, 'and all these plants. I don't know a thing about plants.' She giggled nervously. 'Just about know the difference between a rose and a daffodil.'

'Indeed? Here we are, girls, I found some of Paul's – Daddy Paul's – jigsaw puzzles and books from when he was a little boy.' Olivia turned to him, shaking her head, 'So young to be a father.'

Paul encircled Queenie with his arm. 'To be one in my own right in less than seven months' time, Mama.'

His mother gave the faintest of shrieks. 'So soon!'

'Paul wants a boy – a grandson for you,' said Queenie defensively.

Olivia gave no answer as she poured home-made

lemonade from a crystal jug, then subjected Queenie to a tour of her plants and their Latin names while Paul, throwing his wife an encouraging glance every so often, helped the children to start a puzzle.

Paul's father found them in the conservatory an hour later.

Looking up at the figure who suddenly appeared in the doorway, emanating vigour and piercing them all with his razor-sharp glance, Queenie felt a twinge of fear. She jumped up from her chair to be introduced and Paul rose also. Frederick came forward, looked deep into her eyes and clasped her hand between both of his. Queenie gave a silent sigh of relief. From the approval in his golden eyes, she knew she wouldn't have any trouble from him. They exchanged a conspiratorial smile.

Luncheon, as they called the midday meal at Becket House, was a bit of an ordeal, however. Emma ate too much of the fish starter and then picked at the main course. 'Don't want it,' she said, starting to wriggle off the seat. 'I want to go and play.'

'No. Eat your dinner, Emma,' Queenie grabbed her. 'Look how nicely Hannah is eating hers.' And Hannah was behaving beautifully – thanks to Violet Jackson's tutelage.

'Come on, Emma – try.' Paul's tone was impatient.

'Little girls who don't eat their lunch can't have a nice pudding,' added Olivia hopefully.

The little girl scowled and pushed it around her plate. 'Don't look like that, Emma,' said her mother desperately. 'Don't you want the nice lady to see what a pretty girl you are?' Queenie reached over and thrust a spoonful into Emma's mouth. The child chewed on it with an expression of disgust on her face, then pointed to a silver-framed photograph of a Labrador on top of a cabinet. 'Where's that bow-wow?'

'How many times have I told you not to speak with

your mouth full, Emma?' Paul was embarrassed. 'And stop that baby talk. It's a dog.'

'That's poor old Duke,' said Frederick easily. 'Remember what a good gun-dog he was, Paul? Yes, well Emma, he got in the way one day when we were on a pheasant shoot, and was accidentally shot dead – Bang!'

Emma swallowed the food down. 'Dead?' she asked, wide-eyed.

''Fraid so.'

Emma's brows drew together. 'Poor little sod!'

There was a moment of startled silence. Paul's expression was furious. With heightened colour, Queenie smacked her daughter's leg under the table. 'I've told you not to say that.'

'You say it! And so does Gran,' cried Emma with childish logic, and began to bawl. Hannah's face crumpled in sympathy.

'Oh, for God's sake!' Paul stood up and swept the child off the chair. 'Go next door and look at the books while we finish lunch. You too, Hannah.' The children ran out crying, leaving everyone looking embarrassed, including the maid who was hovering at the sideboard. Queenie started to rise to go after them, but Paul grabbed her arm and forced her to sit. 'You must understand, Mother and Father, that it will take a little time for Queenie's daughters to . . . to get used to – '

'I'm sorry, I'm sure,' interrupted Queenie bitterly, 'if my kids don't come up to scratch,' and Paul responded, 'That sort of remark doesn't help.'

'What a lot of fuss over nothing,' bellowed Frederick. 'Dish up two bowls of that blancmange, Mary,' he instructed the maid, 'and I'll take it into the little girls.'

Paul and his mother exchanged a surprised look. Frederick came back a few minutes later. 'Right as rain, now. Nice little things. They'll soon learn.'

'We are going to have a grandchild, Frederick.'

'What!' With a wink at Queenie. 'Not wasting any time, you two.'

During the afternoon, the children were urged to put on their coats and go into the garden, while Frederick took Paul to his study for a man-to-man chat about the progress of the war, and Olivia gently quizzed her daughter-in-law on her past.

The peace was interrupted by screams from down the garden. The two women ran down the lawn to discover Emma floundering in the fish pond. 'Oh, my God',' shrieked Queenie. The hysterical child was rescued and scolded and shaken by her mother. 'Can't trust you for a moment, you bleedin' little nuisance.'

'Hannah pushed me,' she shrieked.

'She never!' But seeing Hannah's coolly defiant look, Queenie realised she had. The little bugger. Instinctively, she reached out and slapped her face. Hannah's eyes expressed outraged dislike.

Emma, dripping and squealing, was taken back to the house to be put in a warm bath and the maid was dispatched to the village to borrow some of her granddaughter's clothes.

'A disaster from beginning to end,' complained Paul as they drove away after tea.

'Sorry, I'm sure! But I can see how you, being brought up in that morgue, turned out so bleedin' stuffy.'

'How can we expect Emma to speak well when you swear like you do?'

'It's not swearing where I come from – it's just a way of talking. Suppose you'd say "*awfully*" or "*jolly*".'

There's no need to be sarcastic.'

'There's no need to be . . . stuck up neither.'

'Oh, for heaven's sake.'

Paul lapsed into moody silence and Queenie studied his stiff profile. Will we ever get it right? she wondered. Me and the kids will never come up to expectation and Paul and I will go on bickering like this for the rest of our lives. Oh no, I couldn't bear that.

And will I ever get it right? Behaving just like Ma, slapping and shouting at my kids, when I want to do so much better. But we can't help it, can we, copying our parents? Paul can't help being stuck-up and snooty, any more than I can help being rough and swearing. But I did think I was getting better. She sighed. Well, *I'm* not going to sulk all the way back to Pompey.

Queenie turned and giggled at Emma, wrapped in a blanket in the back seat. 'It was funny really, you falling in the pond, wasn't it, pet?'

'Hannah pushed me.'

Hannah stared at her mother. 'Why did you do it, darling? You knew it was naughty.' Hannah shrugged.

'It was a joke, wasn't it, Hanny?' laughed Emma, peering up into her sister's face.

'Shut up,' snarled Hannah.

'I'll kill you both when I get you home.' The threat was enough to keep Hannah's mind off being sick at least.

'Did you like my mother?' Paul asked with a placatory sideways look.

'She's lovely. But Paul, you got to realise, I'll never be a lady like her, no matter how hard I try.'

'She's been bred to it.' He reached out and patted her hand. 'But don't worry, my darling, you'll be fine. I got the impression that the old boy liked you.'

'So did I.' Queenie grinned, remembering how Sir Frederick's hand had lingered on her bottom as he kissed her goodbye.

'Paul would never have married that girl if it hadn't been for the war. He knows she will never do, that's why he didn't bring her to see us before they wed. He knew we'd persuade him against it.' Olivia walked up and down her elegant lounge with nervous haste after her son and his family had left.

Frederick dragged his eyes up from the *Sunday Times* and the article about the Russians crossing the Rumanian border and looked at her over the top of his glasses with ill-concealed impatience. 'What's that, dear?'

'Breeding will out – and the lack of it. Oh, she tried hard, but some of the words that slipped from that girl's lips!'

'There's nothing wrong with Queenie. The rough corners will rub off, just as mine did. I wasn't out of the top drawer. Remember? She'll be all right. I like a girl with spirit. Damned pretty, too.'

'Damned pretty!' his wife said with unusual scorn. 'There are plenty of pretty girls around from good families. I just can't understand what Paul sees in her.'

Her husband's mouth twisted wryly. 'I know you can't, dear. But, being a man, I think I can.'

'I suppose it's *sex*!' Olivia flung the word at him and swept from the room, leaving her husband looking after her in astonishment. He did not remember ever hearing that word from her. He had always assumed that Olivia never sullied her mind or her imagination with such words, let alone carnal thoughts. Marital intercourse between them, verbal or physical, was kept to a minimum, the latter certainly not requiring discussion.

An incident came into his mind. An occasion, many years ago, when Olivia, flaunting the unwritten rules in a shocking manner, had almost upset the apple cart.

'You wish I was *her*, don't you?' she had asked with a hint of passion after a passionless coupling that had left him sighing with frustration. 'You wish I was Alice.'

After a moment of amazed silence, he was able to answer, quite truthfully, that he did not. After all, he was a realist who knew there was no such thing as a perfect woman. No woman could satisfy all a man's requirements, so the best any man could do was to decide if a certain woman, at any given time, could provide what he needed most at that time.

He had met Olivia at a most opportune stage of his life. Having proved his abilities as a ministerial assistant, he was at that time striving for social advancement and in Hugh Latimer's daughter he recognised a satisfactory adjunct to his public life. Beautiful enough to elicit a pleasing envy from his peers, she would be a model mother, an efficient if not sparkling hostess, and would give him absolutely no trouble.

But, while acknowledging her suitability for the above posts, he accepted that this timid, shy and pure girl would not satisfy all his needs. How fortunate he was – and wasn't it amusing – that Alice, possessing a more vital version of the beauty that had attracted him to her sister, was the other side of the coin.

In Olivia's twin he found the passion he craved, made all the more poignant by the infrequency of their trysts. The fact that they met so seldom in his London apartment made their relationship bearable, because he knew that the very things that attracted him to Alice – her unreliability, her dangerous decadence, her extravagance and the hint of mental instability – would have driven him away from a closer relationship. Alice was not fashioned for permanence.

Frederick's heavy face creased in a self-satisfied smile. What a fortunate man he was – he had it all. The two sides of a coin that combined to give him all he needed from the lesser sex.

And he was quite sure that, in spite of her flash of insight about Alice all those years ago, Olivia suspected nothing.

'I shouldn't have married him, Ma.'

'Well, you've made yer bed, our Queen, and now you've got to lie on it.'

'That's a great help, I must say. You encouraged me, didn't you?'

'Nobody ever told *you* what to do! Anyway, what's wrong with him, I'd like to know? He don't beat you or go out drinking every night. He's a decent young chap with good prospects, ain't he? What more do you want?'

'Don't know.' Queenie stirred her tea thoughtfully. 'I know what I don't want, though. I don't want this baby, I don't want to be stuck at home all day, and I don't want to have to watch me mouth all the time. I just want to be myself and have a bit of fun.'

'Me, me, me!'

'I know, I'm an ungrateful bitch. I mean . . . it's all right most of the time. We're good in bed together – '

'Queen! You know I don't like that sort of talk.'

' "Working class prudery", Paul calls that.'

'I don't care what Paul Knight calls it, I'm not having that sort of thing talked about in my house.'

Queenie giggled. 'Just listen to you and Lil sometimes.'

'That's different.'

'It's time you realised I'm a woman too. Anyway "that sort of thing" goes on all the time, don't it? *You* should know, Ma, and how do you think I got pregnant? Let's be glad something is all right.

'But we're so different in other ways. You should have met his Mum and Dad. Talk about posh! And what a house. All this silver on the table, and a maid, and Mrs Knight looking like someone in a film. Old Freddie had a gleam in his eye though – pity Paul isn't a bit more like him.'

'Well, you've always got a bit of both parents in you, haven't you? You think you're just like your Dad, but I can see me in you, too.'

Queenie nodded. And how I hated the bit of you that I saw at Paul's house, she thought to herself. Slapping Hannah's little face for a bit of mischief. When I think what I used to get up to! But I was embarrassed in front of Paul's ladylike mother.

Beatie was cackling. 'I'd like to have been a fly on the wall, specially when our Emma started playing up. And then falling in the fish pond. Oh, my word.'

'It's no good – I'll never be a lady. And it's all your fault, Ma.' She gave Beatie a playful push.

# · *Forty* ·

Both unbearably tense for different reasons, Queenie and Paul's relationship continued to see-saw through April, May and the first days of June, even though they saw little of one another.

Paul was on edge, his mood veering between exhaustion and euphoria. With increased E-boat action in the Channel – the Germans reconnoitring the huge build up of vessels along the south coast and particularly in the Portsmouth and Isle of Wight waters – the 'little ships' patrolled continuously and were often in action.

In the middle of May there was a large scale exercise off Worthing, to try out the defence measures that were planned for use off the coast of France after the invasion. *Grey Ghost* and two others of the flotilla were successful in chasing off and damaging some E-boats that managed to break through the line of defence. But one of Paul's friends was killed, depressing him deeply.

Queenie tried to make allowances for Paul's moods, aware that Operation Overlord was looming, but she couldn't put her own misery aside, guilty as it made her feel, and she could not forgive him for his irascibility towards the children. He was jealous of the time and attention she gave them, wanting her to put everything aside for him when he was at home.

'I don't know what you're going to be like when Christopher is born,' she accused. 'How're you going to cope with disturbed nights and teething and dirty nappies?'

Paul groaned. 'We'll get a nanny.'

'On your pay? In this tiny flat? Don't make me laugh.'

'I can't be concerned about that sort of thing at the moment,' he said wearily. 'Too much on my mind.'

Overhanging the everyday strain for Queenie was the fear that her husband would be killed, leaving her in a worse position than before she married him.

She used to make herself look nice if she was expecting Paul, but occasionally, not knowing when he was going to get a few hours off, he found her slopping around the flat in slippers, her hair in Dinky curlers under a scarf and no make-up on her face. 'God, you look like a charwoman,' he said with a disgusted look on his face on the last occasion.

'What d'you expect when I'm doing the housework? Anyway,' she flung at him bitterly, 'charwoman's just about my level, isn't it? You knew that when you *begged* me to marry you.'

They were both spoiling for a fight. His mouth tightened ominously and she watched him struggling for control. 'Look, darling,' he said at last. 'We're both under an enormous strain. Let's not quarrel, for God's sake. Tell you what, get your glad rags on, and I'll pop down and see if Joan can sit in with the kids this evening. We'll have a couple of hours out on the town.'

She hesitated, reluctant to compromise, to be deprived of a chance to vent her grievances. Oh, grow up, she told herself, noticing the shadows under his eyes. She agreed, and they enjoyed themselves at Kimbells and aired a few differences amicably.

'What's happened to that lovely girl I married, darling? She was so full of life, so spirited, so determined not to let things get the better of her. I shan't forgive myself if . . . I've spoiled all that.' He took her hand, massaging it with a desperate need for her understanding.

She wept. Paul raised her chin and cradling her face between his hands, thumbed away her tears. 'I love you.'

'I'm so sorry, Paul. I'm a mean cow and I'm just tired.

But you, you're worn out with all that's going on, and the worry of it, and I just think of myself. And what have I got to moan about, after all? A good husband, enough housekeeping, two nice kids and a third on the way. And we'll love our little Christopher when he arrives, won't we? Poor little sod isn't getting much of a welcome is he?'

'Of course we'll love him. My son! I shall be so proud. And our little girls – we'll be a happy family when all this is over.'

'Just promise me it will all be over soon – this bloody war. Then perhaps we can get sorted out and start living.'

'I promise, darling.'

Queenie smiled through her tears. 'It will all come right, won't it? I keep telling myself there's thousands worse off, and I do want to be a good wife to you, Paul.'

His fine eyes beguiled her. 'Let's go home,' he whispered. 'And you can prove that last statement to me.' They leant towards each other and kissed – just as the air-raid siren wailed. Cursing and laughing, they rushed to the nearest shelter, where they spent the next two hours worried sick about Joan and the children who would have gone to the shelter on the north side of Southsea Common. Holding hands in the earthy-smelling gloom with a crowd of grumbling strangers, they longed to be in bed together. Before the All Clear went, Paul, consulting his watch frequently, announced that, air-raid or no air-raid, he had to get back to base.

'Oh no!' wailed Queenie.

'Sorry darling – I'll be shot at dawn if I'm late. Take care of yourself.' He kissed her. 'Give my love to the children.'

'When will I see you again? Tomorrow?'

He hesitated. 'I can't promise anything.'

The next day Queenie washed her hair, took out the curlers after lunch and brushed her dark locks into a shiny page-boy. She plucked a few stray hairs from between her brows and applied some make-up. 'You should be ashamed of yourself,' she told her reflection. 'The way you let yourself go. It's a wonder Paul didn't pack his bags and leave for good.' Come to think of it, there wasn't much of his left at home to pack anyway. He'd been stowing it on board *Grey Ghost* over the last couple of weeks, ready for . . .

Queenie's stomach contracted with fear. From all the signs it would be happening soon. The invasion of France. These days there were always ships passing on the width-of-the-road view she had from her front window. Ships of all shapes and sizes, full of men, preparing themselves . . . for what exactly?

It was a wonder, Queenie thought now, that she had stayed as sane as she had with all the worrying she had done over her men since September 1939. But, with a bit of luck, they were really going to teach old Hitler a lesson this time. When the doorbell rang, she hurried to answer it, assuming that Paul had forgotten to take his key.

A soldier stood on the doormat that had the word WELCOME set into it in darker fibre.

'Yes?' she asked.

'Don't recognise me, Queenie?'

Her eyes travelled over the young corporal. Attractive. Dark hair slicked down with Brylcreem, broad khaki-clad shoulders, brown eyes, pock-marked skin – 'For Gawd's sake! Spot – Dicky! Lil didn't say you were back in Pompey.'

'Hello, Queen of my heart,' smiled her childhood neighbour – the boy who used to spy on her when she was in the back yard. Amazing how such a lanky, spotty lad could turn into quite a fanciable and confident man.

'I had to come up to Southsea, so I thought I'd look you up for half an hour. And you're looking lovelier than ever. I always did fancy you, you know.'

'I do know,' she laughed. 'Come in, Dicky. Come on

through. Gawd, how many years is it since I saw you going off in your uniform?'

'Must be getting on for five, I joined up at the beginning.' He followed her into the front room. 'A lot has happened to you over the years I hear, Queenie.' He stood appraising her with his eyes. 'Quite the lady now, I believe, married to a naval hofficer and all that.'

'You know me though, Dicky. I'm a Portsea "Irk" at heart.' Queenie found herself thinking that 'Spotty Dick' had turned out quite well after all. Even the scars from the acne of his teens added a rough masculinity. He and she were out of the same mould. If she hadn't been so anxious to escape and if she'd never met Keith . . . who knows? 'I'm ever so pleased to see you. Make yourself at home. I'll just pop and make a cuppa tea.'

But he followed her out to the kitchen and chatted while she put the kettle on and got the cups out, and she was pleased to be able to laugh at their childhood pranks, sit at the kitchen table with him and just be herself for a change.

'You was such a tease,' he chuckled. 'Here, remember that time you was goin' down the yard in your underwear and found the old tramp asleep on the bog – '

'And ran back and fell in the bleedin' bath of cold water. Never screamed so loud in me life. I *knew* you was peeking from your window, you dirty devil.'

Paul heard gales of laughter coming from the kitchen as he came through the front door. Oh, Christ. One of Queenie's damned relatives. He'd only got an hour, and he wanted his wife to himself before the children came home from school. Still, if it was Eddy, he'd understand and clear off.

He opened the door and saw Queenie, done up to the nines, lolling at the table and holding hands with a soldier. A stranger. Her brother Billy? No, this chap was only a corporal.

Queenie, her face going bright red, pulled her hand from the man's grasp. 'Oh, Paul, I wasn't expecting you – '

'So I see,' he managed in a strangled voice, the rage of suspicion threatening to choke him.

'I mean, not till later. This is . . . this is Lil's son, Dicky, from number ten Baker Street. We grew up together. He was up this way so he just popped in to see me.'

Paul spun his cap onto the table in a vicious gesture. 'Then he'd better pop out again – before I bloody well throw him out.'

Looking belligerent, the soldier stood up. 'There's no need to take that attitude, Guv – '

'Out!'

'All right, all right, I'm going.' The man walked towards him and sidled past with his hands raised defensively, 'I'm going, all right?' He backed up the hall as if expecting to be attacked. Paul, with clenched fists, was sorely tempted. At the front door, the soldier called out, 'Sorry, Queen', before letting himself out.

Paul turned to see his wife staring at him with blazing eyes. She stamped her foot. 'You've no right to embarrass me like that in front of my friends. What could he have thought?'

'What about what *I* think, for Christ's sake – *Queen!*' Paul shouted, taking a threatening step towards her. 'How long has it been going on?'

'Going on? Going on?' screamed Queenie, her bosom heaving beneath her blue cotton bodice. 'Just what do you mean? A friend calls in to see me out of the blue, all friendly like, and you accuse me – *what* are you accusing me of?'

'It doesn't take much imagination, does it? I come home to find you all tarted up, holding hands with a fu- with a bloody soldier. God knows what I'd have found half an hour later. Or what the kids would have witnessed when they came in from school.'

'You're letting your nasty imagination run away with you, then, aren't you?' she shrieked, hands on hips.

'Just listen to you – ' face twisted and ugly with scorn ' – you sound like a bloody Portsea *fishwife*.'

'Well, that's what I am, ain't it?' she shouted with bitter satisfaction. 'Common as muck. Your mother thinks so. I'll never be good enough for you, Mr Bloody Perfect. And whatever I say, you're goin' to believe the worst of me. So there!'

He leaned over the table till they were eyeball to furious eyeball. 'And you've just confirmed my suspicions. You always shout when you know you're in the wrong.'

'Oh!' she gnashed her teeth. 'You rotten swine – I hate you!'

'The sentiment is reciprocated.'

'The sentiment is reciprocated,' she mimicked savagely, shaking her hair at him. 'Can't you just speak normal? Oh!' She grabbed a teacup and flung it at the wall narrowly missing his head.

Paul grabbed Queenie's wrist and twisted it, making her scream. Wrenching from his grasp, she ran to the door. To find Hannah and Emma outside it, goggle-eyed with fright.

'Get to your bedroom,' Queenie screamed, giving them a push, 'and shut the door.' They ran off howling and she turned back to Paul. 'Now look what you've done,' she accused shrilly. 'Scared the kids to death. They probably thought you were murdering me.'

Appalled, Paul's shoulder's drooped. 'I've done nothing except interrupt one of my wife's little . . . peccadillos.'

'Pecca what? Well, whatever that means, I have *never* yet deceived you with another man.' Two bright spots of colour stained her cheeks.

'It was going to be the first time, was it – since our marriage?' His voice had dropped but he still wanted to wound her. 'It was bound to happen sooner or later, though, wasn't it? I had my suspicions after that rating and the Totterdell's Hotel business.'

'That was just . . . a one-off mistake – '

'So now you admit it. You lied to me.' *I can't bear it. I just can't bear it.*

'I did not. I told you that what happened before I met you was none of your business. I still say it. You *begged* me to marry you, remember?'

'More fool me. And if you're admitting to that – why not tell me now, how many others there have been. I might as well know the worst. You told me that Keith Jackson had seduced you but I don't suppose it took much effort on his part.' His mouth twisted cruelly as he fired his final salvo at her. 'No doubt by the time he came along you'd had lots of practise in the back alley with young Dicky from next door.'

He had gone too far. He knew it before she stepped forward with blazing eyes and dealt him a stinging blow across the cheek. He deserved it. He welcomed the pain.

'You're so twisted with jealousy you'd believe anything,' she hissed. 'Try this for a start. There were several before Keith of course – I started early! Then I had a little fling with his brother, Michael. Well there wasn't anything else to do, stuck down in Cornwall.'

She clenched her fists in an effort to stop shaking as she continued. 'After Keith was killed there was a young airman, a petty officer, that ginger-haired sailor, and several more that I can't remember. Oh, yes, and a few Yanks – couldn't leave out our brave allies, could I? Just one night stands of course.'

They stared into each other's eyes: hers defiant, his appalled. Paul had got what he asked for and he didn't know how much of it to believe. He felt sick. 'I'll get the rest of my gear and be off,' he muttered.

'Do that. And don't bother to come back.'

'I won't.' *That choice might not even be open to me.*

'I won't be here anyway. I'm going home to Ma and I'm going to get a divorce!'

He picked up his cap and left the kitchen. Going into

the bedroom, he put his last two shirts and some underwear in a bag – and a photograph of Queenie and the children. He always carried a rather sultry one in his wallet, but this one showed her laughing like the young, uncomplicated girl he had taken her to be when they first met. How mistaken could one be? Taking a last look around the bedroom in which they had shared their happiest moments, he walked to the front door. He was about to go through it when he remembered the children. Poor little morsels.

He poked his head round their door to find them huddled on one of the beds. 'Can I come in?' he asked with a strained smile. They flinched away as he reached the bed and sat on the edge.

'It's all right now, don't be frightened. You know – grown-ups can be awfully stupid sometimes. They have quarrels over silly little things, just like you do, but it doesn't mean they don't love each other.' His voice cracked and he finished painfully, 'When you two have a quarrel you always know you love each other, don't you? And that it will be all right again.' He took out his handkerchief and blew his nose. Could it ever be all right again after the things he had said? He didn't mean half of them – not really.

The little girls still looked at him with huge, mistrustful eyes. 'I've got to get back to my ship, so I want you to go and give Mummy a big hug to make her feel better. And I want you to remember that I love you both very much.' He bent forward to kiss them and Emma wound her soft arms around his neck, but Hannah turned her face away.

Shutting the front door, Paul hesitated for a moment, tempted to go back, hoping Queenie would run after him. He understood now what it meant – the saying that someone's heart felt like a lump of lead – because that's exactly how his felt.

If he went back to her now, could he make it right? And if he did, could he cope with the emotional release at the moment, when he had to keep strong and level-headed for the task ahead? He looked at his watch – Christ! He'd be late as it was if he had just missed a bus to the harbour. Taking the stairs two at a time he reached street level and ran up Castle Road to the bus stop.

Queenie sat tense in the kitchen, hoping that Paul would come back and tell her he didn't believe the awful things she had said and that he hadn't meant the foul things he had shouted at her. This was the worst row they'd ever had. He'd take her in his arms like he usually did after a quarrel, and everything would be all right again – until the next time. It seemed that tensions built up between them and eventually exploded. Then they'd get their grievances off their chests, and he'd be really sweet and spoil her rotten, and it would be lovely for a while.

Everyone did it, didn't they? Her family were always rowing about something, but they soon got over it. She remembered the slanging matches Ma and Dad had – coo, they really were something. Then the kids would be given a penny or two to spend, to get them out of the house while her parents made up, and everything would be smelling of roses for a day or two. She bet even Paul's parents had their ups and downs, though she couldn't imagine old Olivia really letting go.

But this row had been really serious – perhaps she should go to him? No, she bloody well wouldn't. He had said unforgiveable things to her and he could jolly well suffer for a bit. When she heard the front door close and knew he wasn't going to come and apologise, she gave way to a storm of tears. Tears of sorrow, anger, guilt and bitterness. The bastard! But afterwards she felt a bit better. Then Emma came and cuddled her and Hannah leant against her, and she felt a lot better.

'Your eyes is all red, Mummy.'

'I'm sorry if Daddy and I upset you, darlings,' she

sniffed. 'Grown-ups are worse than kids sometimes, you know. They have silly quarrels but – '

'But they still love each other,' said Emma.

Queenie looked at her in amazement. 'You *are* a clever girl.'

'That's what . . . Daddy said,' added Hannah, hesitating as she always did before calling him by that name.

'Daddy said? You mean – just now?' The children nodded. 'Fancy that now. He drives me mad at times, you know, but he can be . . . very sweet. Oh, well, kids, let's get your tea. Like Scarlett O'Hara said, "I'll think about it tomorrow." Coo, who wouldn't? if it was dishy old Clarke Gable.'

# · Forty-one ·

The weather was foul for June – strong winds and a rough sea. At just after four in the morning, in spite of the poor conditions, the Order had come through from the top. *Operation Overlord* was about to commence again after the aborted attempt of the previous night.

'Think the "gremlins" will be against us again, Paul?' Lieutenant Wilkes asked with all seriousness on the bridge of *Grey Ghost* as she prepared to leave port.

'Not at all, at all, sir,' Paul assured Wilkie with an atrocious attempt at an Irish accent. 'Didn't I put a saucer of gin on the wardroom table, begorrah? The others swear they didn't drink it, so 'twill be the "Whimsical Macgoffleys" are with us this time, to be sure.' The bad and good fairies that accompanied the Coastal Forces.

'Mmm. It's going to be a dirty trip again but at least this weather will give us the element of surprise, eh? The Hun won't expect even the mad British to put to sea on a night like this.'

'No, they'll all be safely tucked up in their beds.'

'We hope.' The two young men exchanged a long look. 'Better get going then,' Wilkie said.

'The best of British,' Paul replied as they shook hands.

*Grey Ghost* and the rest of her flotilla slipped through the inner boom between Portsmouth and the Nab Tower and out into the English Channel. This was it! D-Day. The Allied invasion of France was underway.

*

Paul and his crew, having witnessed the build-up of invasion craft over the previous months, could nevertheless hardly believe their eyes. They were agog with excitement as, in the dim light, they surveyed line after line of landing craft ploughing through the waves, stretching as far as the eye could see in either direction. An awesome sight, and one which would bring the bile of fear into the throats of the enemy when they witnessed the approach of this armada.

The little ships of the Coastal Forces took up their defensive positions on the flanks of the 'spearhead' convoy, some acting as navigators.

In spite of the euphoria of excitement, before long the rough sea began to take its toll of the crews, and Paul, feeling uncomfortably queasy, felt very sorry for the soldiers, unused to the motion of the sea, cooped up in those troop carriers. All except for Queenie's friend, Dicky, who was probably among their number – it served him right! But those poor blokes – to have to swarm ashore and fight a bloody battle on the beach after they'd been retching their guts up for hours – it didn't bear thinking about.

Paul had spent a few minutes looking at his wife's photographs before they prepared to slip moorings.

'Spare me, God, I beseech you,' he had prayed, 'to come back to Queenie and ask her forgiveness.' I don't think I really believed the things I said – or that she was up to anything with that soldier.

'Help me to overcome this curse of jealousy. I love my wife and I must learn to accept that she had a life and other loves before me.' But please . . . make the things she told me not be true. Surely the words were spoken in spite and anger, just as mine were.

'Help me to overcome my weaknesses. Fight the good

fight with us tomorrow against the enemy. Let good prevail over evil.'

Praying had calmed his troubled spirit and fortified him for the crucial task ahead. But now, on the heaving bridge, showered with blinding spray that mingled with his tears, he asked himself again – Why, oh why, do we hurt the ones we love? The cruel wounds inflicted by thoughtless words could never heal completely.

As the spearhead of the invasion forces neared the enemy coast at dawn, minesweepers went ahead through the morning mist, sweeping clear the approaches to the wide Bay of the Seine.

The flotillas of the Coastal Forces under the Portsmouth Command bore away to the west towards Cherbourg, while the others went east towards Le Havre. Their objective: to confuse the enemy by carrying on activities close to the shore behind heavy smoke screens, in order to divert attention from the area of the intended landings.

In poor visibility, early on the morning 6 June, 1944, combined British, American and Canadian forces under the command of Eisenhower and Montgomery began their assault on the beaches of Normandy. The Germans were indeed surprised, their leaders having swallowed the 'disinformation' put out by the British, and believing that the expected invasion would be at Calais, the shortest sea-distance. Most of their superior Panzer Divisions were concentrated there.

When Paul didn't come home the day after their row, Queenie was depressed and angry all day. She had no way of knowing if he was staying away to punish her or if he genuinely could not get away from base. Her mood swung between forgiving him and wanting to divorce him. It just wasn't fair.

The following morning a hammering on the front door woke her up with a start. Queenie jumped out of bed, immediately feeling sick. She had discovered that if she took her time over rising – and if Paul was around to bring her a cup of tea in bed – she could beat the morning sickness of pregnancy.

Pulling on her dressing-gown, she glanced at the clock. Almost eight. The alarm was due to go off any moment now. 'All right, I'm coming,' she cried crossly as the banging came again. 'Probably only the postman,' she told herself going up the hall, one hand each side of her stomach. It must be a boy – she hadn't been as sick as this with her other pregnancies.

'Queenie! Are you there?' came a familiar voice through the door.

'Phyllis. I was still in bed. What you doing here so early?' she asked as she opened it, feeling a twinge of alarm. Phyllis, carrying a mac over her arm, was beginning to bulge with her five month pregnancy. On her face she wore a worried expression.

'My Gawd. What's happened? Is it Eddy, or Ma?'

'Came to see if you was all right – if you've heard.'

'Heard what?' Wide-eyed with fright.

'The invasion – it's started. Haven't you heard the news?'

Queenie's jaw dropped, along with the downward swoop of her stomach. 'You mean . . . they've gone?'

'They're *there*, girl!' Phyllis bundled Queenie into the hall and shut the door saying, 'Come and look out of your front window,' and pulling her by the hand to the front room.

Ship after ship passed by on the little glimpse of sea between the buildings at the end of the road. 'They've just been *streaming* out, but on the news flash first thing, it said that the "spearhead of the invasion" had reached the beaches of Normandy and started the landings. Eddy says he reckons the "Little Ships" would have escorted the spearhead.'

Queenie stumbled to a chair, faint and nauseous. 'Oh, my God, Phyll. I wonder if Paul's all right.'

'You look awful, Queen. Can I do anything to help?'

She shook her head. 'There's nothing anyone can do. But you could tell the kids to get up and wash and dress. They can get clean knickers out of the drawer. I . . . I've got to go to the bathroom.'

Ten minutes later, Phyllis was making toast for Hannah and Emma as their mother sat ashen-faced and silent at the kitchen table. 'Mummy's not feeling very well, today, girls,' said their aunt, pouring out tea for them all. 'Still, you get off to school and she'll be all right by the time you get back. I'll look after her.'

The sound of their voices washed over Queenie as she sat, numbed with fear and remorse. When the children had gone, Phyllis sat down and held her hand. 'It won't do no good you worrying yourself sick – '

'You can talk – your Eddy's safe and sound in the dockyard.'

'I been through it with John – remember?'

'Oh, I'm sorry, Phyll. It's just that I . . . I've been so wicked. We had an awful row and I let him go without saying I was sorry. You know how it is. I told him some horrible things which weren't true. He must have been very upset, and now he's had to go off on this bloody rotten invasion. Oh, I wish I was there to kill a few Germans.' And she burst into tears.

Phyllis put her arm around Queenie's shoulders. 'Don't take it so hard. It takes two to make a quareel, don't it? Did he say *he* was sorry?'

Shaking her head, Queenie told her the story, embellished with tears, of her unexpected visitor and the row that he caused between her and Paul. 'It's a funny thing, Phyll – Keith and I had a row just before he went off and got himself killed, but at least we had the chance to kiss and make up. I'll always be glad of that. But if . . . anything happens to Paul, I'll have it on me conscience for the rest of me life.' She cried again.

'I've been rotten to him, you know, Phyll. He persuaded me to marry him, and in the end I did. Not because I loved him, but because I thought he could give me and the kids the sort of life we wanted. Like I told you, it was a sort of bargain. This is my punishment.'

'Don't talk such rubbish. He got what he wanted, didn't he? and you've done your best. He'll come back, you'll see, and you'll fall into each other's arms and live happily ever after.'

Queenie gave a shuddering sigh. 'He'd never have married me if it wasn't for the war, Phyll. We just aren't suited. He's so *jealous*, and he expects everything to be just so, and the kids and me to be perfect. He's got a temper. I have too, I know. And of course, I'll never be right as far as his bleedin' parents are concerned.'

'Bugger them! But he must have some good points, Queen?'

''Course he has. He's generous and he can be really sweet – but then sometimes I think he's a bit soppy with it. Never satisfied, am I? He tries ever so hard with the kids. Oh, he gets a bit cross with Emma sometimes but they love each other. Hannah's a bit difficult – you know, moody. Won't tell you what's wrong. Sometimes he's taken her out for a walk on the Common, just the two of them, to see if he can get her to talk.

'I know he loves me, Phyll. And . . . he's ever so good in bed!'

'Well, then . . . what more can you ask?' They laughed. 'You're looking better.'

'I feel better for talking about it. It's just that we fall out so often and – '

'He must be under a lot of strain – all this patrolling and fighting in the Channel and the build up to this invasion.'

'That's why I feel so guilty. And then, we've only been married five minutes and I go and get pregnant.'

'Takes two for that an' all.'

'I know. But he wasn't keen at first, any more than me, but then he got to thinking it would be all right if it's a boy. He's going to be bloody disappointed if it's another girl.'

'He'll love it whatever it is. Eddy can't wait for ours.'

Queenie smiled. 'It's one of the happiest things that's happened for years – you and Eddy. He used to think no girl would have him, you know, and that he'd never be a father.'

'I'm glad he thought that – he sort of saved himself for me. We're so happy. And you will be, Queenie. Give it time. And when the war's over – '

'Will it be any better? I been thinking lately, and I've realised something, Phyll. Part of the trouble is that he wants to change me. He thinks he's doing me a favour by trying to get me to be more like him and his family.'

'You always wanted to get on, didn't you?'

'I wanted a better life, it's true. But now I know that the only way I can have it, is by being someone else. It's not good enough to be Queenie Ellis any more – Joshua Ellis' daughter. Or even Queenie Jackson. No, to be Mrs Paul Knight means I got to grow away from my family, Phyll.'

'You don't get anything for nothing in this life, do you?' asked Phyllis thoughtfully. 'I wonder what price I'll have to pay for me and Eddy being so happy.'

Queenie nodded. 'And I've got to make a decision. Do I love Paul Knight enough to turn my back on my past. I just don't know . . .'

Frederick Knight was reading the London *Evening News*. '"WE WIN BEACHHEADS",' he read out to his wife. 'Bloody marvellous! "Montgomery Leads British, US, Canadian Force. Four thousand ships, eleven thousand planes in assault on France. All going to plan – Premier." God, Olivia – you know what this means?'

His wife turned towards him, immaculate and dignified as ever, apart from eyes red-rimmed from crying, on and off, all day. 'It means our son will probably be killed off the shores of France,' she said bitterly.

'Trust you to take the narrow view – '

'Narrow view! I've only got one son, and he is the dearest thing on earth to me.'

Frederick raised an eyebrow at his wife's unusual vehemence. 'He'll be all right, my dear. I love him too, you know, but this – '

'I sometimes wonder,' Olivia interrupted – something she did not normally do. 'Indeed, I have come to the conclusion, Frederick, that there are only two people you love. The first, by far, is yourself – and the second is Alice.'

Frederick could not have been more surprised if she had plunged a knife into his chest.

Olivia scorched him with her scorn. 'You've always taken me for a subservient fool, Frederick Knight. But I've always been perfectly well aware why you married me, and I've always known about you and my sister. But I tell you now – if Paul does not come back from France, I shall leave you.' She turned, leaving the room echoing, and her husband stunned.

Encouraging bulletins continued to be issued about the Normandy invasion – apart from sad news of heavy losses of American troops on the stretch of coast code-named 'Omaha'.

Frederick was elated but at the same time worried about Paul's safety. And Olivia! He always thought he had his wife well-trained. He could not get over the way she had turned on him. Accusing him of not loving his son! Of course he loved the boy – just wished in the past that he had shown a bit more backbone, that was all. But he was all right now. He had grown into a fine young man. Perhaps he should make an effort to let the boy know that he thought so. Damned difficult, these emotional things.

As for Olivia's relevation that she knew about Alice – that had really shaken him. If she were to leave him, it would not do his career any good. And, he realised with surprise, he would miss her.

# · Forty-Two ·

Paul surveyed the aftermath of the invasion – it resembled one of those nightmarish paintings of Hieronymous Bosch. A scene from hell – with sounds to match.

Under a lowering sky, miles of sandy shore was littered with tiny soldiers, tanks, barbed wire, equipment and all the debris of war. Landing craft and transport vehicles were beached in the shallows like stranded whales, disgorging more men and equipment. Several barrage-balloons glinted silver as they swung round on their moorings. In the partly constructed harbour – being created from the concrete 'Mulberry' caissons that had been towed across the Channel and sunk – every conceivable type of vessel was pitching and tossing on a stormy sea.

The guns of British battleships pounded the German positions beyond the beaches. Planes roared overhead to add their destruction. Plumes of smoke and flashes of fire rose from the explosions.

Chaos. Yet, incredibly, beyond the German positions which were falling rapidly into British hands, lay vast tracts of serene, flat Normandy countryside. And the rest of France – waiting to be liberated.

In spite of snatching a few hours' sleep amidst the noise and bustle, Paul was utterly weary. Night after gruelling night the flotillas of the Coastal Forces, supported by frigates and destroyers, had patrolled the waters north-east of Cherbourg. They protected the western flank of 'the spout' – the sea channel of supply and communication between the Isle of Wight and Normandy.

Many fierce battles had been engaged with similar German vessels coming out of Cherbourg harbour and attempting, without success, to break through the British lines to the American area. Comrades had been killed.

In battle, the adrenalin of excitement took over and swept away the horror, the noise, the stench of warfare. Seeing enemy craft blown sky-high by mines, or sinking or burning through British action, one rejoiced. War brutalised humanity – sullied the human soul.

Paul sighed. He was so weary of it all. He just wanted to go home to his wife and children. He wanted to go home and cry in Queenie's arms. But would she be there for him? Could she forgive him?

Queenie had tried hard, he knew. She had always been honest in that she had never attempted to hide who she was and where she came from, but it hadn't been good enough for him, had it? He wanted her to become someone else. But only for her own good, surely? so that she could fit comfortably into the life he was going to make for them. It was obvious that, if he was spared, he was going to need to be more tolerant, more understanding. With compromise, surely they would work it out.

Paul's thoughts winged upwards like a prayer. Please be there, darling. You must be. I need you so much – and you need me, don't you? It has been difficult for us: the war, the children, the coming baby, our different backgrounds. But I'm sure it will all come right if we have love between us – and I love you so much.

On one of Queenie's visits to her mother, she was persuaded by Beatie to go with her to see Lil. 'Poor old gal's veins are playing her up something awful and she can't git around like she used to.'

'Whose veins wouldn't play them up, carrying that weight around all these years?'

Beatie cackled with laughter. 'You are rotten. Wait till

you get old. Anyway, it'll cheer you up, we always have a good laugh with Lil.'

'How would you like to be at sea in this?' yelled Queenie as they struggled, arm-in-arm, against the wind that funnelled through St George's Square. Drawing abreast of the church, Queenie had an overwhelming urge to go in, but she felt that Ma needed her support. She was looking very frail these days.

Butcher Street and Baker Street were shabbier than ever, one or two more bomb craters having appeared since Queenie's last visit. Several of the shops had closed down because of death, evacuation, or the lack of anything to sell.

Lil was pleased to see them. 'But you don't look well, Queen. Pregnancy playin' you up?'

Queenie shook her head. 'Just worried about Paul, Lil.'

''Course. Our Dicky's over there too. Hallelujah! God save the pair of them. Sit down and I'll brew some tea.'

Queenie had not thought of poor Dicky going off in a troop carrier and being put ashore. She imagined him fighting bayonet to bayonet with German soldiers, and felt sick. 'Did he tell you he called in to see me, Lil?' she asked in a small voice.

'He did, love, and said he was chucked out wiv a flea in his ear by your Paul. You was only sitting in the kitchen all innercent, he said. Was that true?'

Queenie nodded. 'We were just having a laugh over old times when Paul come in. Can't blame him for being fed-up, I suppose. He'd just rushed home for a bit of . . . "how's yer father" before going off on this rotten invasion and he finds his wife laughing and holding hands with a strange bloke in the kitchen. He's jealous at the best of times.'

Lil tutted as she brought her battered aluminium teapot to the table. 'Oh, me poor old legs,' she moaned as she sank onto a chair. 'It's me veins, you know, Queen.'

'You can have an operation, you know, Lil. They sort of pull the veins up and tie them off or something.'

Lil shuddered. 'I'd rather suffer, thank you. If you ask me, women were put on this earth to suffer. It's the cross we have to bear. If it isn't belly-ache and birthing children, it's watching over them with fear till they're big enough to go their own way.'

'And it don't end there,' added Beatie. 'When they're grown, the boys get sent off to war . . . and some of them don't come back.' She wiped a tear from her eye. 'And you worry jest as much about the girls. Terrified that they'll die in childbirth, or make an unhappy marriage . . .'

Queenie looked at her mother, surprised, 'I never thought you worried about *me*, Ma. I thought I just got on your nerves.'

Beatie flushed and fiddled with her teaspoon. ''Course I worry about you, you daft hap'orth. Oh, I know I've got a funny way of showing it, but it's easier with boys. With a daughter – you're afraid to get too close. I suppose it's like Lil says, you know the suffering they've got to do and you can't afford to be soft – 'cos you want them to be able to stand on their own feet when it comes to it.' She flapped her hand at her daughter. 'Now you've got me talking rubbish.'

But it wasn't rubbish. Queenie had never before heard her mother make such a personal statement, and she digested it slowly as she sipped her tea. It could explain so many things. It could explain why she always felt her brothers were better treated than she was, why her mother was always so harsh with her.

'Remember how you thumped me when we lived at number twelve and I let on I was pregnant, Ma?'

'I thought you'd ruined your life, silly little cow.'

'Didn't we all?' added Lil.

'But you were pleased when I married Keith.'

'He was lovely. Would have given you a decent life if he . . . if he'd lived.'

'We all liked Keith,' said Lil.

Queenie didn't tell them that, if he'd gone on womanising, she probably wouldn't have stayed with Keith after the war. She wasn't going to share a man with anyone! She would not have shared Ray with his wife. 'You didn't like me going with that petty officer though, even though we were in love.'

Beatie's black eyes flashed. 'I've seen enough grief over that sort of thing, my girl. They *never* leave their wives.'

'They never do,' agreed Lil, shaking her head, and going on to recount the misfortunes of a previous neighbour who got mixed up with a married man, but Queenie didn't listen – she was thinking.

Perhaps her mother's logic was rather twisted, and she wouldn't want to follow it with her own kids, but she thought she understood at last. Beatie had, to the best of her ability and with a great deal of heavy-handedness, tried to guide her daughter through the minefields of life.

'. . . My brother-in-law, Bert, had that poor woman on the side for years, but would he leave our Ethel?' Beatie was saying.

'She had to wait till your sister died, poor cow.'

'That's men for you.'

'Oh – I know.'

Queenie smiled as she watched them – friends for most of their lives, sticking together through thick and thin. They'd had their rows and misunderstandings, but they always made up pretty quickly because they needed each other. Rather like a marriage. They were growing old together.

She looked around the shabby but clean kitchen and remembered the years her family had spent in a similar one next door. 'We had some happy times in number twelve, didn't we, Ma?'

'And some tragic ones,' sighed Beatie, remembering the death of her babies and her husband. 'But we had some laughs all the same, din't we?'

'Hannah and Emma were born next door.' She remembered how kind her mother had been at their births and how tenderly she had looked after the babies. They had pulled together through the bad times and enjoyed the good.

Her mother nodded. 'But there were times when you was kids, Queen, when I din't know where the next meal was coming from. Hard times.'

'I remember, Ma.'

'Well, I don't want that for you, my girl. You've got a good man in Paul, who can give you a decent life. I know you've got your difficulties – what couple hasn't – ?'

'Hallelujah!' agreed Lil with feeling.

'I hope you're goin' to have a real go at this marriage.'

Queenie sighed. 'I've got some . . . weighing up to do, Ma. You know, the good against the bad. If you think you can get home safely in this wind, I better be off for the kids coming home from school.'

Beatie cackled. 'With the wind up me jacksie I'll be home in a jiffy. Take care now.'

Queenie bent and hugged and kissed her mother. 'You take care an' all.'

'Get off, you daft beggar.' Beatie gave her a playful shove.

Pushing the heavy church door shut against the wind, Queenie leant against it and, eyes closed, let the almost suffocating quiet of the building penetrate her being. She opened her eyes to look the length of the church to the altar and smiled fondly. She'd walked up that aisle so many times during her life it was a wonder there wasn't a Queenie Ellis-sized groove in the floor. Walking a few paces forward in the imagined groove, she slipped into a pew.

Yes. The happiest trip up the aisle had been on her first wedding day, in her turquoise dress. No white for her –

already a sinner. But no thunderbolt from Heaven had struck her down. It had seemed that day, with the sun shining, that she was all set for a wonderful life. Who would believe the things that had happened since?

Then there were the Christenings – Hannah's, Emma's and all the cousins'. Her Dad's funeral – what a black day that had been. Billy and Vera's wedding. All the childhood Sundays she had attended morning service out of habit or force.

She'd never really questioned the existence of God, just prayed to Him out of habit or when she was unhappy, or wanted something very badly, like when she wanted Keith Jackson after meeting him in the fish and chip shop.

It was Keith who sowed the seeds of doubt in her mind with his atheism and then, when he was killed, she had hated God for a while. He let people make war, let husbands and fathers be killed.

But now, in the peace of the church of her childhood, Queenie came to an understanding. It was *people* who did these things to each other. From wholesale deliberate slaughter, nation against nation, to the tiny individual battles that hurt only the couple involved. Why did you hurt most the people you loved the most?

Repentant, Queenie sank to her knees and clasped her hands under her chin. Tears welled from beneath her eyelids as she mouthed her prayer.

'If You are there, God, and I hope You are, I'm asking you to forgive me.' The Lord's Prayer, recited without thought in childhood came to her with new meaning. '"Forgive me my trespasses and those that trespass against me . . ."'

At the end of it, she felt a lot calmer. 'Please, God, make me a better mother, look after Ma, and please, please, bring Paul back safe.'

She had married Paul for the wrong reasons, for what he could give her and her children. But instead of being grateful to him, she often felt resentful at his criticisms, and at the fact that she knew his parents couldn't possibly approve of her. Also, in her stubbornness, she resented his attempts to 'improve' her, knowing that it meant she must change. But she had to admit that might not be a bad thing after all.

They had their problems, they were both far from perfect. But she was desolate that she had sent him away unhappy, because no one deserved that sort of treatment from someone they loved. She knew Paul loved her – he had told her often enough. But she never had said those words to him. He used to ask her sometimes, looking at her so hopefully, 'You do you love me, don't you?' And she used to answer, ''Course I do, you daft bugger' or, 'What d'you think, you soppy date?' or 'You're not a bad old stick'. Partly because she was a bit shy with him, but mostly because she wasn't sure.

'But if you send him back to me, God,' she prayed in her head, 'I promise I will be a better wife. If I try a bit harder I'm sure I can make him happy. I've always been attracted to men who can offer me a better future, and for the second time I've got that chance for myself and my kids. Send Paul back to me and I'll do all I can to make a good life for us all.'

# · *Forty-three* ·

Queenie stood at her window, day after day, watching the slice of sea at the end of the road. Ships continually passed by on the sunlit water. The weather had settled down to be more like June these last few days, having 'roared in like a lion'.

Hard to believe that across the Channel battles were raging and that here, at any moment, sirens were likely to wail, calling them to the shelters. Yesterday, she had seen her first V1 rocket, droning over the rooftops of Western Parade. They weren't always spotted in time. Suddenly the drone stopped and the silence as the bomb stood poised to drop was deafening. She had dived into the shelter just before the explosion. How could Hitler be sending these horrible things over now, when we were supposed to be winning the war at last? But we only had the beaches of Normandy, didn't we? There was the whole of France to liberate, and then the rest of occupied Europe. When would this bloody, rotten war be over?

Where was Paul? What hell was he going through? Difficult to imagine back here in the peaceful sunshine. Oh, it was so cruel what those poor men had to suffer and she felt so guilty that she was safe. But that was silly because the children and the unborn baby needed her. Life had to go on.

Please come back to me, Paul, even though I don't deserve you. Queenie felt sick with dread. Those promises she had made in the church seemed pointless now – he might never return.

*

The flotilla engaged E-boats several times a night for many nights. After being caught napping on the 6 June, the German crews were now making a valiant effort to wreak some vengeance on British shipping, but were hopelessly outnumbered and often confined to the safe harbour of Cherbourg by the actions of the Coastal Forces flotillas.

One dark night, on the third successive encounter with enemy boats, Paul's flotilla scattered a mixed group of enemy gunboats and corvettes and split up to pursue individual targets.

Having chased a corvette into Cherbourg and done some damage to her superstructure on the way, *Grey Ghost* turned back, with a thankful crew, to re-group with her sister ships. Approaching the Mulberry harbour off Arromanches they made out the dark shapes of three immobile gunboats.

'That's four of us,' shouted Wilkie, scanning the surrounding area of sea through his binoculars. 'Hope the fifth one is all right.'

'Haven't lost one yet,' responded Paul. 'Pretty good record, that.'

They dropped speed and motored towards the group, signalling their approach. 'No response,' Paul called uneasily as they closed on them.

'Illuminate! Illuminate!' yelled Wilkie, in sudden panic – just as the guns of the three German boats opened fire on them . . .

## · *Forty-four* ·

Queenie's heart stopped as, from her window she saw a naval officer coming down Castle Road.

The man's gaze seemed to lock with hers from way up the street and, with hands clasped tightly at her breast, she watched. Her heart raced crazily. Was it Paul – or was it one of his shipmates come to tell her Paul had been killed?

As the man came closer, she realised that without doubt it was him. Biting her lip to hold back the tears, she raised her hand. He halted for a moment below the window, looking up, but made no gesture. Slowly, apprehensively, not knowing how she was going to greet him, Queenie went to open the front door.

As Paul came into view on the landing below the final flight of stairs, she cleared her throat and said, 'The conquering hero returns, I see', hating herself for being flippant at a time like this. After all he must have been through. But she was so nervous.

His mouth twisted into the suggestion of a smile as he looked up at her. 'There were times when I didn't think I would.' Coming level with her, he stopped a few paces away. 'I'm glad you're still here.'

He seemed so detached that the appalling thought entered her mind that he had only come back to collect the rest of his things – that, because of their quarrel, he wasn't coming back to her at all. She nervously pressed her hands together in front of her chest. 'How . . . how long are you back for?'

'As long as it takes to repair *Grey Ghost*. Got badly shot

up – lucky to have escaped at all. Had to bring the old girl back to Pompey for extensive repairs.'

'Oh!' she said faintly. He could so easily have been killed.

'Poor old Wilkie was badly wounded, but he'll probably pull through. I'm acting officer-in-charge.'

'Congratulations.' Yes. There *was* a new authority in his bearing, a new firmness in his thin face. He had been an enthusiastic boy with shining eyes and a hesitant manner when she first met him – was it only a few months ago? Now she saw that, though obviously exhausted, in need of a shave, and with eyes shadowed by his recent experiences, he was a man.

Silence stretched between them – a yawning chasm, until he asked quietly. 'Do you love me, Queenie?' And even knowing how much depended on her answer, she could only bite her lip, the lump in her throat making her unable to say anything.

She saw the glint of tears in his eyes, a slight trembling of his lips. She saw his desperate need.

Queenie stepped forward into the circle of Paul's arms and laid her face against his chest. She could hear his heart thudding. Looking up into his eyes, she whispered through her tears, 'I was so afraid that you would not come back and that you would never know – just how much I love you, my darling.'